Relations Such As These

Relations Such As These

A Pride and Prejudice What If Story

Sara O'Brien

Relations Such As These

Copyright © 2009 by Sara O'Brien

All rights reserved including the right to reproduce this book,
or portions thereof, in any form whatsoever.

ISBN 978-0-557-13646-9

Book and cover design by Sara O'Brien, back photograph by Laura O'Brien

sobrien1971@yahoo.com

****

For my friends at The Meryton Literary Society, and especially Nina, Meg, Mary Anne (MAB), Mira, and last but certainly not least my mother, all of whom helped to set me on the right track, and encouraged me.

****

Prologue

"Darcy! I found you at last! I have searched all over town for you."

Darcy took off his heavy fencing mask at the muffled yet intelligible sound of his cousin shouting his name.

"That is odd, Fitzwilliam, you should know that I fence here every Tuesday morning. Now what can I do for you?" Darcy, hot and sweaty from the brimming London heat, grimaced after nearly being bested by his friend Sir Robert Stone.

"Whoa there, do not look at me like that; I am not the one who bested you out on the floor!" His cousin retorted.

"What do you *want* Richard?" Darcy said with a sigh, after removing his well-worn gloves.

"I wanted to tell you the good news, but now I am uncertain if I should or not. In fact, now that I think on it, it may not be very good news at all." Fitzwilliam laughed.

"Tell me *what you want, already*!" Darcy loomed before Fitzwilliam.

Realizing this would be an inappropriate time to tease his younger cousin as Darcy had just taken off his shirt, Colonel Fitzwilliam relented, I spoke with Bingley, the other night at the opera, and he said that you intended to accompany him into the country... I believe it was Hertfordshire, was it not...to look at an estate there?"

"Yes, and what concern is that to you?"

"The war office has given me a request from Colonel Forster to visit the town of Meryton to determine if there are sufficient quarters there for the militia to stay there during the winter... I figured since you and Bingley will be going there soon, I may just as well go with you."

Darcy frowned at his cousin, "And, why would you want to leave the delights of town? I rather thought you had found your..." He raised an eyebrow, "'Entertainments' here. Why would you want to leave your friend… friends?"

Fitzwilliam shrugged, "No reason, other than my 'friend' has been quite out of humour of late, and seems to be rather under the weather, or should I say, under the influence of the weather…it has been so hot here, escaping to the country may be the ideal solution for us. Perhaps we could even find a swimming hole and cool off like we did as boys, ay Darce?"

Darcy glared at him, "Fitzwilliam, we are grown men! It is time 'we' grew up and became more serious about our lives. And as far as going to Hertfordshire, or Meryton, I care not if you go, as I have told Bingley that I would help him appraise the estate there before he makes any hasty decisions."

"Ah, that is probably a good idea. You never know when he will spot another pretty face, and lose himself in her charms…ha, we are not likely to find anyone special there in that part of the country, ay, Darce?"

"No, not likely, but still, I should go to help keep him out of trouble, and if you would like to help me with that, I will not object." Darcy finished changing into dry clothes and he and his cousin left their club. To Hertfordshire they were to go…and with them the best laid plans to stay out of trouble would follow.

Chapter 1

Late August 1811

Elizabeth Bennet sat in the farthest sitting room at Longbourn, trying to concentrate on the 'Tempest', and wrap her mind around the Ariel character when the heat became too unbearable for her. *This is an excellent time to go to Brooks Pond; it should be cool enough there.* She decided. Elizabeth rose with the intention of walking to the watering hole. Located on the adjoining estate of Netherfield, near her father's estate Longbourn. *I shall be safe from any witnesses there, as nobody has gone there since the place was vacated six months ago.*

Taking her usual route, Elizabeth slipped into the timber between the properties, enjoying the coolness the shade under the treetops afforded her. During this time of year, she did not wear anything heavy, only a slight petticoat under her light muslin dress. In response to the heat of the past few days, she left her stays off, even though she usually regretted it by the middle of the day due to her generous upper measurements. *I shall find some relief when I dive into the water...oh, it will feel most excellent! While she thought about the misery of the heat and the relief of the watering hole*, she almost missed the faint noise coming from that same direction.

As she approached, she heard muffled sounds of male voices and splashing water. *Someone is at the pond! But who could it be? No one else has ever come here, except for the previous tenants, and even they did not swim in the pond except maybe once or twice in all of the last ten years!* Elizabeth crept through the brush separating the timber from the banks of the pond, and gasped in amazement at what she saw through the clearing.

There, in the pond, were three grown men, as nature made them. In the deeper part of the pond, swam a blonde haired slight gentleman who had a mop of wet curls plastered to his scalp. He had fair skin, and Elizabeth could just make out his derrière as he glided through the water towards the bank. There were two other gentlemen at the banks, soaking up the mid day sun, and the sight of them made Elizabeth feel as if she was standing on the surface of the sun.

She flushed all over as the two gentlemen stood in full sight, naked from head to toe. She had seen statues of men in museums, but nothing had ever prepared her for the real specimen. The man of medium height with sandy hair had fair features with a moderate patch of sandy hair covering his chest and below, but he had a bit more musculature than the man that she first saw swimming in the middle of the pond.

Her attention, however, finally rested on the gentleman with a thick head of dark curls and a patch of dark hair over his chest and below. Elizabeth froze at the exhibit in front of her, as the man was quite tall and had even more musculature than his two companions, including the thighs of an expert horseman. She held her breath as her eyes lingered on his chest and thighs, which simultaneously mesmerized and discomposed her. He did not resemble any of the statues she had ever seen in a museum. No words could define how she felt at the picture before her, and she knew that propriety and decency dictated that a maiden should never see such a display, but her natural curiosity overwhelmed her and she fixed a stare onto the man's body, unable to tear herself away.

The two men began talking and laughing, pointing to where she stood on the bank opposite them. Thinking she would be spotted if she had not already, she turned as quietly as possible and darted back towards Longbourn. She felt much warmer than when she sat in the back parlour facing full south. It became impossible to remove the images of the nude gentlemen from her mind, and that is the last vision she had that night, before she drifted off to sleep.

~*~*~*~

The next morning during an unseasonably warm spell, three gentlemen galloped thru a meadow towards the Netherfield Estate in

Hertfordshire. Mr. Charles Bingley intended to carry out his late father's wish for him to own an estate, thus becoming the first of his family line to do so. Mr. Bingley, lacking experience in estate management, decided to bring along a longtime friend from Cambridge, Mr. Fitzwilliam Darcy, to aid in selecting a property to lease.

Darcy exhibited an expertise in estate management, and Bingley knew he had much to learn from his friend. The income they gained from the Pemberley Estate in Derbyshire had helped the Darcy family become one of the largest and richest land owners in the kingdom. Darcy provided ample care to his tenants, and they held a deep respect for the young master in return. The servants working in Pemberley remained loyal to the Darcy family through many generations. *What more could recommend a master of a great estate than loyalty, devotion, and last but not least a healthy fortune?*

Bingley knew his friendship with Darcy was a subject of discussion in town as there could not possibly be two more different characters that could be friends. Darcy comported himself with a severe countenance while Bingley displayed a light hearted and jovial one. They were a balanced complement which made their friendship strong. Whenever they gathered, one gentleman would skirt the outer room while the other would dance every dance. They had an odd friendship, but each held the other in the highest respect.

They would spend time visiting in each other's homes, which gave Bingley some insight to how an efficient household should be run. Therefore, when an estate had come up for lease, he requested that Darcy come along with him to inspect the property. Since it happened to be near enough to town, the gentlemen decided to ride to Hertfordshire to take a look at the property. *After all, what could be the harm?*

As it happened, the three gentlemen had set out in the mid afternoon, the day before from town and stayed at The Red Lion Inn in Meryton. They decided to make an early day of it to check upon the grounds of Netherfield and assess the town for possible lodgings for Colonel Forster's troops.

Being good horsemen, they galloped along a meadow, each man lost to their own musings and without much awareness of their surroundings. Truth be told, Bingley seemed to be simply enjoying the ride and said, "This does seem like a pleasant place does it not, Darcy, Fitzwilliam?"

Fitzwilliam replied, "It does indeed, Bingley, such large meadows for the horses and the timbers for shade…yes this could be a decent prospect."

Darcy said, "Let us not make any hasty decisions based upon some 'pleasantness' of the prospect or the size of the meadow." He pointedly looked at his companions, "We must ensure that there are no major issues with drainage or major repairs…you realize that could cost you much more than the lease if you are not careful, Bingley."

His two companions scoffed at his sober remarks but did not comment further after studying his serious mien.

For some time, Darcy had been quite cross. Since leaving Ramsgate he grew even more irritable, lodging a complaint about every little issue. *It is difficult even for me to believe the profligacy and total want of propriety that had been demonstrated so cruelly by my old childhood acquaintance!* The man, George Wickham, had almost seduced his sister, Georgiana, and convinced her to elope with him. This excursion was the first since that fateful trip to the resort town, and he found himself still uneasy.

As the gentlemen rode on, they all failed to notice a young gentlewoman walking along the property line near the meadow at the timberline. Within seconds, Darcy noted her presence and quickly pulled back hard on the reigns. He could feel his heart racing violently at the fright of nearly trampling this inattentive young woman.

He saw that she had jumped back and landed on her posterior to avoid the collision. Jumping down from his horse, he rushed to her aid. "Are you alright Miss? Are you injured?" He asked as he leaned down to assist her from her rather ungraceful decent.

To his utter shock, the woman actually had the audacity to frown at him. "Yes, I believe that I am uninjured," she retorted. "You know you should pay far greater attention to the road before you, as you ride. I could have been killed!"

She straightened and began dusting off her dress. At that moment she looked fully at him and, startled as if she recognized them. Then she glanced at Bingley and Fitzwilliam. Her eyes widened momentarily as she blushed and avoided his stare. "What could you mean coming forth on this trail without as much as a consideration for others who may be traveling on it?"

Her obvious assertion that he was the one in the wrong, had Darcy taken aback. He addressed her in a haughty manner. I beg your pardon, madam, but I do believe that it is unreasonable to assume anyone would be traveling along this trail at such an early hour, much less a lone woman. What could you mean by walking alone here, and at this time of day?"

The woman flushed rather prettily, he thought, and then replied with apparent frustration, I happen to be walking along the boundaries of my father's estate, as I usually do of a morning! Besides, what difference does it make whether or not I am accompanied for a walk? I am quite able to handle myself, thank you very much!"

Darcy looked up quickly towards his companions who had dismounted and approached where he and this unidentified country chit now stood. He noted Fitzwilliam caressed the woman with his eyes as he was want to do with most any female. Darcy shook his head and rolled his eyes at his cousin's never ending pursuit of another conquest. Bingley was little better as he did a slightly more circumspect look at the woman which caused Darcy to look at her again to see what entranced them so much.

It did not take him much time to determine that, though this woman was small in size, she had womanly curves and a nice bosom. She also had a fierce and passionate look about her large dark eyes that one might find it challenging.

Surprised at how quickly his thoughts turned towards those more carnal in nature, he refocused upon her misstep and opened his mouth to speak, but before any words left his lips, Fitzwilliam addressed her, "Are you alright miss? You have not been injured have you?" He smiled his wide easy disarming smile which further irritated Darcy.

She suddenly looked up and gave Fitzwilliam a beautiful slow smile accompanied by a blush and a glint in her eye, I reassured your friend that I am fine sir, no harm done, just a little dirt is all...thank you."

Fitzwilliam gave his cousin a smirk then turned his attention back to the woman, I must apologise for my cousin, Fitzwilliam avoided

Darcy's glare, "We were distracted while riding out early to the Netherfield Estate in order to check the property out and were quite inattentive to our path; do you often walk this way?"

Darcy became more aggravated but he could not determine who irritated him more... the impertinent little piece who dared to accuse him of not paying attention, and who had by now, fallen for the charms of his flirtatious cousin. That same cousin was dressed in his red uniform and was being...himself. He noticed her avoiding eye contact with any of them, and felt it due to some subversion of some sort. He could not quite figure her out.

The impertinent piece answered Fitzwilliam's query. I walk this way frequently as my father's estate is just through the clearing on the other side of the timbers." She glanced at Darcy. I was walking at this hour as the warm weather is likely to increase and felt it prudent to walk out earlier rather than later." She hesitated a moment and then asked Fitzwilliam, "Do you mean to imply sir, that you may soon be joining the neighbourhood?"

Ah, there you go again little miss, avoiding eye contact, for you certainly know that you were in the wrong! Darcy mused as his gaze locked on her features.

By that time Bingley joined their group. "We had thought we may look upon the estate," he snuck a glance at Darcy, "and may possibly be joining the neighborhood sometime soon. Am I to understand that you are to be my closest neighbors then?"

Darcy chuckled to himself ...*Bingley also has an annoyingly easy manner especially when there are pretty women around.*

"Yes, our home is about three miles hence through the timbers and the other pasture. I do believe we would be the closest of the whole neighborhood sir."

Bingley smiled back at her in his annoyingly pleasing manner. "Ah that is good to know. Tell me do you have other family? Do you have brothers or sisters?" he asked.

Darcy rolled his eyes again. ...*There he goes again fishing for another romance. Bingley, will you never learn there is nothing to be had in such places as these? She cannot be more than a mere country squire's daughter with a paltry dowry and if she has any sisters what would the likelihood be that they would be nearly this tolerable?*

He heard her respond to Bingley, "Yes, I have four sisters, and no brothers sir. They are all at home right now." Again she looked over to Darcy, I am afraid they do not join me this early. Only my eldest sister is up at this hour, but she does not, as a habit, walk out at such an early hour."

"I see," said Bingley, "and do your sisters usually join you at times when you go out walking later in the day?"

Darcy could not believe his ears. Here was this woman who nearly got herself trampled when she darted out into *his* path and she was flirting with Bingley and Fitzwilliam. *No doubt she is searching for a husband.*

"At times," she replied. I am the true walker in the family, however, I cannot think of a better way to start the day than to be outside, enjoying nature and gathering one's thoughts without disturbances."

What is all this flushing about? Surely you could not have been exerting yourself that much! No doubt you were thinking about catching a husband instead of paying attention to where you were walking miss! Darcy mused.

Fitzwilliam, never one to miss his part of a conversation with a pretty face asked, "Might we enquire who may be the lovely neighbours nearest to our friend, madam?"

Darcy noted her rosy cheeks and enticing smiles as she answered his cousin rather coyly, "It is my father, Thomas Bennet's estate of Longbourn, though it is not for me to say how lovely we are, I do thank you for the compliment, sir."

Fitzwilliam, ever the sly and easy mannered one, asked in his teasing tone, "And which of Mr. Bennet's daughters might we have the pleasure of addressing madam?."

Though he rolled his eyes at his cousin's banter, Darcy could not help but listen attentively, although he did not decipher the reason for his attentiveness at present, when the woman introduced herself.

"I am Elizabeth Bennet, sir, the second daughter to Mr. Bennet, and may I enquire whom I may be addressing as well?"

Darcy heard her bemused tone of voice and could not help but be drawn to the brightness of her eyes.

Fitzwilliam grinned as wide as ever and replied to her teasing with his own good humor. "It would be a pleasure. I am Colonel Richard Fitzwilliam of Matlock in Derbyshire. I am delighted to meet you, Miss Bennet, and now may I also introduce you to my rather thoughtless cousin?" He smirked at Darcy with an amused glint in his eyes, "Fitzwilliam Darcy of Pemberley in Derbyshire and our friend, Charles Bingley."

As Fitzwilliam completed his introductions he bowed to Miss Bennet and she in turn curtseyed to each of them.

"I am pleased to meet you gentlemen," she said with a smile. "We should hope for you to join us for tea in the near future. I am sure you can find many pleasant families in this neighborhood of which we are but one." She glanced at Darcy as if studying him before her eyes returned to Fitzwilliam and Bingley, "And we are very delighted to have new acquaintances as pleasant as you." She smiled towards Fitzwilliam and Bingley.

Bingley replied, "We look forward to making your further acquaintance, Miss Bennet, and that of the neighbourhood. I sincerely hope that our first meeting did not reflect poorly upon our party... since we nearly trampled you. We are truly sorry to have come upon you such as that...as our first impressions have been very favorable."

Miss Bennet observed both Fitzwilliam and Bingley, from the corner of her eye, before she looked up making eye contact with Darcy. She quickly looked away from him and addressed Bingley, I assure you, Mr. Bingley, that we could not think poorly of such agreeable and pleasant acquaintances. I assure you that I am fine and there was truly no harm done. Besides, I have made the acquaintances of such fine gentlemen, and who, after all, could complain about such a thing?"

Darcy watched her eyes sparkle with mirth.

"I hope you do indeed become our closest neighbour, sir, as this estate has been empty for some time, and such a pity too as it is well kept and has good grounds." Both Fitzwilliam and Bingley smiled at her and smirked at Darcy. Miss Bennet continued, "It would be good and well to have a family settled here to care for it."

Darcy thought he could see some actual concern for the disposal of the estate and thought it unusual to see such behavior in such a young woman in regards to such matters.

Darcy frowned momentarily and at that moment he found himself being observed by this Miss Bennet. She frowned also and suddenly he felt self conscious.

She addressed them with her chin raised. "Well, gentlemen, it has been a pleasure to make your acquaintance. I hope to see you joining us for tea. I will leave you now as I believe I have taken up too much of your time. I should bid you a good day and a safe journey." She looked back at Darcy pointedly and curtseyed to him and then Fitzwilliam and Bingley.

Darcy thought he could detect a small smile upon her face when she turned which only caused him to frown again, and then he recalled her last address. He bowed and spoke in his commanding voice, "We hope you have a good day as well, Miss Bennet, and hope that you have a safe journey back home." He nodded to her curtly, and noted her eyes glinting again as if she were still angry about their earlier encounter.

Again she flushed, but recovered quickly as one eyebrow shot up. She smiled tightly, but before she could say anything else, Bingley responded, .Yes, Miss Bennet, it has been a great pleasure to make your acquaintance as well. We also look forward to meeting more of the neighbourhood soon. Please take care until we meet again."

Bingley made his bow then Miss Bennet looked towards Fitzwilliam who addressed her last. "Miss Bennet, I too look forward to meeting you again, hopefully under more pleasant conditions," he said with an amused glint in his eyes and a smirk. I shall look forward to continuing our pleasant new acquaintance. I bid you farewell and safe journey madam." He bowed and looked straight into her eyes.

Miss Bennet blushed from her neckline …not that he necessarily looked at her neckline…or anything else for that matter. She curtseyed one last time and turned back to the timber towards Longbourn. Bingley and Fitzwilliam smiled as they watched Miss Bennet retreating back, then they glanced at each other and finally at Darcy. Both of those gentlemen were looking at Darcy who also watched her, and raised an eyebrow giving them a rather puzzling look. He snapped out of his trance and frowned at them straightening his face. He pulled back his shoulders, threw a glance in the direction of the timbers and walked towards his horse as his companions smiled at each other and glanced towards the timbers as well before mounting their horses.

This may prove to be an interesting venture yet. It looks as though Bingley may have already made up his mind on this neighbourhood! Darcy mused.

Chapter 2

As she watched the gentlemen gallop towards Netherfield after their accidental meeting, Elizabeth could not help but notice how upright the gentlemen sat astride their horses. She recognized them, as she felt certain that these were the gentlemen she saw in the watering hole the day before. When she saw Mr. Darcy, she did feel a rush of heat at seeing him now fully clothed, and found him haughty, and …well, overbearing. After her initial shock, she found Colonel Fitzwilliam and Mr. Bingley to be charming though.

It had been a while since she had met any new men of quality. I *hope Mr. Bingley does take the lease to Netherfield. He seems so nice and would present a good match for Jane. The colonel seems like a man with such easy manners as well…so unlike his cousin who was so …rude! Mr. Darcy missed the fact that he had not seen me until I jumped out of the way! And instead of apologizing for his inattention, he was so…presumptuous! I shall not dwell on them, though, as it is unlikely to come to anything serious.*

Though Elizabeth thought this, she still had an uneasy feeling… she could not dismiss Mr. Darcy outright with his staring, piercing eyes.

With those thoughts plaguing her, Elizabeth made her way back to Longbourn without any further mishaps. She found her father and sister at the breakfast table. They both smiled as she approached.

"How was your walk, Lizzy? Did you find anything interesting while you were out?" Mr. Bennet asked, eyeing her dirty dress when she came into the dining room and approached the sideboard.

Smiling while she took her seat at the table, Elizabeth responded, "Indeed, I did, papa. There were three gentlemen looking at Netherfield Park for a possible lease, and they seemed to be amiable as well." *And quite handsome and such happy manner's too...well at least two of them any way!* Elizabeth thought to herself.

"Gentlemen! Do tell, Lizzy. Did you enquire if they were single gentlemen with a fortune? Surely your mother would be in raptures with such news!" Mr. Bennet said with a raised eyebrow and an amused smile.

Elizabeth laughed. I cannot attest to their fortune, but they wore well tailored clothing. As far as their status, you know I could not ask such a question. I am, however, tempted to believe they were single, at least two of them anyway."

"Well then, I see we have at least two well situated gentlemen possibly coming into the neighbourhood. What entertainment could be had should they decide to let Netherfield Park? Your mother will have you all married off by Easter." Mr. Bennet happily replied.

"Do you think they will indeed be leasing Netherfield Park, Lizzy?" Jane interrupted.

"I cannot say for certain," Elizabeth said, "but they seemed promising though." She smiled as she poured a cup of coffee. "They were inspecting the park and seemed to be impressed with our neighbourhood."

"Well, well, well... better and better," Mr. Bennet said, "Your mother will have at least one of you married off come Easter if not sooner, and in the meantime, I will be in my study with the door soundly shut." Still smiling, he wiped his mouth, rose from the table, and headed in the direction of his study before his daughters could respond.

"Lizzy, how did you come to meet these gentlemen?" Jane asked. "Did you meet them on the horse trail while you were on your walk?"

Elizabeth flushed at the memory of her not so graceful tumble earlier, then glanced down into her lap as she answered, "You could say that Jane. Actually, I was almost trampled on by one of them." Jane looked alarmed and Elizabeth sought to reassure her, I managed to jump out of the way before I was seriously injured." Observing her sister's shocked stare, she added, "However, I managed to end on my backside with a rather ungraceful fall. I dirtied my dress."

"What happened when you fell? Did they stop to assist you?" Jane frowned.

"Yes, the first gentleman, the one who almost ran me over, did stop, and then his other two companions joined him. That is how I met them. I am afraid that neither Mr. Darcy, the first gentleman, nor I attained a good first impression of each other." Laughed Elizabeth.

"We exchanged some rather heated words at first, and I do not believe he thought well of young country misses walking out all alone without an escort," I *wonder what he would think, should he discover that he was observed swimming in the watering hole by that same country miss?* She pondered with a smile, "however, his companions seemed quite pleasant and friendly, and they told me that they might lease Netherfield Park, my dear Jane."

"What do you mean by 'heated word's'? Lizzy, surely you could not have argued with a complete stranger. I cannot believe that anyone could have anything bad to say to you directly upon first meeting, especially when you were out on one of your walks. What did this Mr. Darcy say to you to make you think this?"

"Well, after I scolded him for not paying attention to the path, he said to me, 'I do not believe it is reasonable to assume anyone would be traveling along this trail at such an early hour, much less a lone woman." Elizabeth imitated a deep voice, and then laughed.

"I could scarcely believe anyone could still hold such antiquated beliefs and have such ill manners, and I was quite put out to be addressed in such a way... as if I were an errant child! His friends, however, seemed very nice and contrite. They came to my aid and introduced themselves," she said. "One of them, a Mr. Bingley, had even enquired if I had any siblings." She smiled at Jane, a teasing twinkle in her eyes.

Jane smiled back, I am sure Mr. Darcy did not mean to sound so foreboding, Lizzy. After all, he almost trampled you; it had to have been frightening to him. Besides, if he were from town and from a certain circle, it would be unusual to see an unescorted gentlewoman traipsing around, that is all. But what of the other two gentlemen? What were they like?"

"There was a Colonel Fitzwilliam," Elizabeth blushed, remembering yesterday, "who is a cousin to Mr. Darcy and unlike his cousin, the colonel, seemed to be quite nice and friendly, though not quite as handsome. However, what he did not have in looks, he made up in his amiable manners. Lastly there was a Mr. Bingley, the gentleman looking for an estate to let. He was also the gentleman who enquired as to my siblings." She raised an eyebrow again, looking at Jane with a smile. "He had happy manners, pleasing friendly personality, and not to mention good looks. Just what a gentleman ought to be!" She laughed.

Shaking her head, Jane responded, I do hope our mother does not go into her 'fit of nerves' should they decide to let Netherfield Park, else there will be no end to talk of throwing us 'in the way of rich gentlemen'. But it would be nice to meet new people just the same." Jane glanced at her sister, "If you found them quite amiable, I am sure I will also find them to be wonderful also."

"You would like many a stupider person, Jane, but I give you leave to do so, as I agree with you about Mr. Bingley and Colonel Fitzwilliam. I am not, however, so convinced about Mr. Darcy." Elizabeth added with a frown, she could not help but dwell on him. Even after such a brief encounter, he penetrated her consciousness too much for her liking. The image of his nude body still flooded her memory.

"You did not find Mr. Darcy agreeable…but what of the other gentleman, the Colonel, Lizzy, or were you still too angry about almost being run over to think about him?" Jane teased.

Elizabeth quirked an eyebrow, "Perhaps, I did notice a rather flattering colonel who seemed to not mind my rather hoyden like behaviour, and I would not mind becoming better acquainted with him and his friend."

"Indeed, Lizzy? I shall keep that in mind if we find ourselves in their company in the future, for I will be sure and not fall in love with him then!"

Elizabeth laughed and shook her head at Jane, I shall endeavor to remember *not* to mention the existence of any single gentleman I meet, as I am likely to be matched with them too, but honestly, I doubt that when these gentlemen hear that we have little fortune, or even connections that they would be interested in pursuing us, or rather me and our sisters, but then there is you. If anyone of us is likely to find any such suitor, it would be you, dear Jane, as you have quite ten times the beauty of any of us, and all the goodness. No, it will be up to you to secure a man of good fortune and raise our prospects." Elizabeth finished with a warm smile.

They finished their breakfast in companionable silence in time to avoid the loud and senseless chatter of their mother and youngest sisters Kitty and Lydia.

~*~*~*~

Later that evening, as Elizabeth prepared for bed, she reflected on the morning's discussion whilst sitting in front of the looking glass and brushing her hair. She had always been less secure about her looks than her wits, and grew even more sensible of the conversation with Jane about their prospects.

With five unmarried girls in the family and little dowry, Elizabeth knew she and her sisters had little to recommend them but their looks and their personalities.

She understood that at least one of them must marry very well in order to secure the future for the rest of them, and in this neighbourhood, that prospect did not seem very likely. *With this new development, life could get very interesting, and what is better than being well situated with a kindly gentleman?* Elizabeth laughed at herself, recognizing she sounded like her mother. *The colonel seems to be a nice sort of gentleman, so pleasant and kind, even a bit of a flirt, and not unpleasing in appearance either. I would not mind meeting him again. Indeed not!* She blushed at the remembrance of the gentlemen at Brooks Pond.

Other thoughts intruded, however, sobering Elizabeth's mood. Though Jane was a gentle, well mannered woman, in no way could she say the same of her other sister's. *Mary is perhaps, not as bad as the two youngest, though she is always sermonizing; however, Lydia and Kitty are simply wild. Most of the time at home and in company, they are loud and unrefined, speaking without so much as a forethought to what they would say or should they even say it. They think nothing of running around, arguing and talking loudly, out of turn.*

Our mother is no better, with her 'fit of nerves', and loud boasting of inconsequential matters. She incessantly gossips, and never bothers to check the behaviuor of Lydia or Kitty. If only papa would exert himself to control them. What is worse, we have no fortune, or even connections to shield us from censure. How could I even think to have them introduced to the likes of the men I met earlier today? My younger sisters and my mother's behavior would do us no credit at all; we would be looked upon derisively, especially by the likes of Mr. Darcy and his ilk.

Elizabeth stood up from her dressing table to open the window then blew out the candles and hopped into bed, covering herself with a light sheet. Lost to her thoughts she relived yesterday's discoveries and this morning's walk. Her uneasiness, at last she realized, seemed to revolve around her concern for what men like Mr. Darcy or others of his ilk would think of them.

More than likely, Elizabeth admitted to herself, *men like Mr. Darcy would not consider young women such as myself—women with no dowry, connection nor fortune to recommend them as worthy enough to be among their acquaintances.*

It hurt to think that her sisters'and her future would be at the mercy of their as yet faceless husbands, and as women they were powerless to do much about their current circumstances. *If we do not make good matches we will indeed be in desperate straits when papa is no longer.* It was a sad thought for Elizabeth, as she was closest to her father and did not want to think on his demise or his shortcomings.

Mr. Darcy! Elizabeth could not understand why she still bothered to think about the man. She did not understand why the man had caused her such inner turmoil. She usually laughed at such follies and dismissed them easily, but Mr. Darcy had caused her to do some self-examination and she did not like it. She had always been thought of as discerning, witty, and intelligent and confident of herself, but here was this man who was so…intriguing and unsettling to her peace of mind.

Chapter 3

A fortnight after Elizabeth's first encounter with the Bingley party, she and her family made their way back to Longbourn after church services. Mrs. Bennet glanced at her husband and said, "My dear Mr. Bennet, have you heard the news?" Not waiting for a response, the excited matron declared, "Netherfield Park is let at last!" When her sober spouse did not reply, she pressed further, "It is true, for I just had it from Mrs. Long."

"Is that so, Mrs. Bennet?" Her spouse replied in a disinterested tone.

"Yes, yes it is."

Elizabeth looked to Jane with an inquisitive raised eyebrow. Her mother's comment piqued her interest. *Could it be that those gentlemen I met are going to return after all?* Elizabeth started to feel a sense of … she knew not what… perhaps excitement at the possibility of seeing those two gentlemen who had been so kind and friendly to her in August, or perhaps a feeling of apprehension in regards to *that* third gentleman who had unsettled her.

Mrs. Bennet answered Elizabeth's voiceless query, I have heard from Mrs. Long *and* my sister Philips that a young man of large fortune would lease Netherfield Park before Michaelmas."

It must be them, for whom else could it be? There has been no one else to view Netherfield Park for some time. I must endeavor to find out for certain if it is them. Elizabeth did the unthinkable and started to question Mrs. Bennet about the subject.

"Did Mrs. Long happen to mention who the gentleman was? Did she give a name?"

"Bingley, and he is single, with a large fortune of four or five thousand a year." Mrs. Bennet gleefully proclaimed, and then launched into raptures about her 'girl's good fortune', which Mr. Bennet encouraged for the purpose of his own amusement, as he looked back to Jane and Elizabeth with a smile.

Elizabeth and Jane were greatly entertained by their mother's predictable overwhelming happiness about a young gentleman of fortune moving into the neighbourhood. *Mama will be hard to countenance until we have all made the gentleman's acquaintance. There will be no peace until then, but I cannot wait to renew my acquaintance with the gentleman's party.*

Jane interrupted Elizabeth's thoughts with a quiet address, "Well, Lizzy, it looks as if we will get to meet the mysterious Mr. Bingley after all. When do you suppose *we will* meet him?"

"I do not know Jane, maybe they will join us at one of the assemblies in Meryton, but if not, maybe we can journey through the timbers or the meadows and jump out of the way of their charging steeds!" Elizabeth laughed.

"Oh, Lizzy!" Jane shook her head at her sister as they made their way through the front door and into the back parlour.

~*~*~*~

Two weeks later, sans Mr. Bennet, the Bennet ladies arrived at the Meryton assembly for the Harvest Moon neighbourhood dance. The entire town looked forward to this dance as they hoped to catch a glimpse, or more likely an introduction, to the newest addition to the neighbourhood. Many believed that Mr. Bingley and his party would come tonight. Some of the heads of the predominant families had already been introduced to Mr. Bingley and his party. Others were anxious to become acquainted as they still had unmarried daughters.

Although Mr. Bennet had made the gentleman's acquaintance, he did not wish to attend the assembly, and therefore would not be able to introduce them. Mrs. Bennet was very displeased, to say the least, with her spouse.

Elizabeth felt it may be best for her father to avoid all of the Meryton busybodies, as her father would be cross if he were forced to join them at the assembly. *I am glad that I was sensible enough not to mention to mamma my earlier meeting with the gentleman and his friends that day at Netherfield!*

Elizabeth rationalized that her mother would be insistent in her demands that she introduce them all to the gentlemen as soon as he took up his lease at the house, making her look as if she were pining for a husband. Or worse, her mother would expose them all to censure in some way and give Mr. Bingley's party a very good reason to look upon their family with derision. She also did not want Mr. Darcy to be able to hold anything else against her.

No, it is best to be silent on these matters and if they wish to renew their acquaintance with me, they will act. Elizabeth did not wish to appear too eager and forward. Mrs. Bennet was a true proficient in exposing herself, but Elizabeth hoped that her mother would temper herself upon meeting the gentlemen.

Mr. Bennet received the gentlemen at Longbourn shortly after Mr. Bingley's taking possession of Netherfield Park, but they were not introduced to the ladies of the house as they spent the entire visit in Mr. Bennet's study. That vexed Mrs. Bennet to no end, and she made her displeasure known to Mr. Bennet when she discovered the gentlemen left without her having made their acquaintance. The spectacle would have been amusing to Elizabeth as well, had she not been so curious as to the results of their visit so soon after arriving at Netherfield. Her father hinted that they had acknowledged some prior acquaintance with Elizabeth, and that they were considering attending the assembly dance.

Finding herself frequently looking towards the direction of the entry way, Elizabeth castigated herself for being so…*so…like Lydia*. When Mr. Bingley's party finally arrived at the Meryton Assembly rooms, the dance had already begun, but with such an anticipated party, people stopped dancing and everyone's attention was brought to the new arrivals. In the uncomfortable first few moments, everyone froze in place until Sir William Lucas made his way to Mr. Bingley to welcome him and his guests to the assembly. With a bow and cordial smiles, Mr. Bingley and Colonel Fitzwilliam greeted Sir William, and with a curt bow Mr. Darcy and Mr. Hurst perfunctorily addressed him as well.

The Bingley party also consisted of two elegantly attired, and decidedly standoffish ladies, who exuded superior airs. The ladies of Meryton were impressed with the gentlemen's good looks and good comportment, but they were envious of the ladies' fashionable attire. *This is quite a spectacle with most of Meryton pining to see the newly arrived neighbours from town. How entertaining to see their reactions to Mr. Bingley, the colonel, and Mr. Darcy. It shall be interesting to see how that man reacts to our society!*

As she watched the Netherfield party, she noted Mr. Bingley and Colonel Fitzwilliam scanning the assembly room for someone. When their eyes rested upon Elizabeth and Jane, they smiled and nodded, then made their way towards her. When Elizabeth saw their reaction upon spotting her, she nodded in response, which to her consternation did not go unnoticed by Mrs. Bennet...nor to most of the assembly room.

Mrs. Bennet said urgently to Elizabeth and Jane, "Look! Here they come, smile girls, smile!"

Elizabeth ignored her mother and eyed the approaching gentlemen... Soon, Mr. Bingley, Mr. Darcy, and Colonel Fitzwilliam stood in front of Elizabeth's party. They bowed and Elizabeth her curtsey in greeting.

Colonel Fitzwilliam addressed Elizabeth, "How do you do Miss Bennet? It has been a few weeks since we met last. Tell me, have you recovered from our first meeting enough to dance?"

Elizabeth noted Mr. Darcy rolled his eyes then turned his head to avoid anyone's gaze. His demeanor was haughty. She felt a sense of indignation towards him. *How dare he come into our society and act as if he or his cousins or friend are too good for us?*

For spite and for the pleasure of dancing, Elizabeth answered, "Yes, Colonel Fitzwilliam, I am recovered, though our first meeting was hardly enough to keep *me* from dancing. You see, I quite like to dance." Elizabeth said with a teasing look at both the colonel and Mr. Darcy.

"Well then, may I claim the next dance if you are not otherwise engaged? That is, of course, after you have introduced us to these lovely ladies." the colonel finished after a glance to Mr. Bingley.

Happy to comply, Elizabeth said, "Of course, Colonel Fitzwilliam, Mr. Bingley, Mr. Darcy, may I introduce my mother, Mrs. Thomas Bennet, and my sister, Jane Bennet? Mama, Jane, this is Colonel Richard Fitzwilliam, Mr. Charles Bingley, and Mr. Fitzwilliam Darcy."

The gentlemen acknowledged Mrs. Bennet and Jane, and the ladies, in turn, made their curtsies to the gentlemen.

"We are delighted to make your acquaintance, ladies. May I take this opportunity, Miss Bennet and request this next dance if you are not otherwise engaged?" Mr. Bingley asked.

Jane blushed and gazed downward, through soft lashes, she replied, "No, sir, I am not engaged, and would be delighted to dance the next with you."

While the two pairs approached the dance floor, Elizabeth saw Mr. Darcy make his way back to his party's guests. She noticed her mother fuming over his lack of manners at not staying to talk to her, or at least dance with one of her other daughters.

He then requested the hand of the woman Colonel Fitzwilliam indicated as a Miss Caroline Bingley. This Miss Bingley accepted his application for her hand and they also made their way to the dance floor, near where the colonel and Elizabeth stood.

Elizabeth saw Miss Bingley glance toward Mr. Darcy and roll her eyes as she looked around the assembly. She felt affronted by that woman's apparent slight. The lady looked upon the assembly with an air of superiority, and seemed unable to concentrate on the dance rather than the *disagreeable company* that came with the congenial colonel and Mr. Bingley.

Locking eyes with Mr. Darcy, she raised her eyebrow, made a slight smile, and then turned to face Colonel Fitzwilliam with an even greater smile. The dancers began the set and Elizabeth drew her attention back to the dance and her partner.

"I am pleased, Colonel Fitzwilliam, that you and your friends decided to join us here in Hertfordshire."

The colonel smiled in response, I am glad to hear it after the last time we met. I feared that you may dread our return after we nearly trampled you."

"No, I must say it does provide me with an amusing story to tell, though I remain unsure of what credit it does me." Elizabeth laughed.

"Well, we were not paying that much attention to our path after all...just enjoying the scenery."

They weaved through the line and met again, and Elizabeth enquired with some amusement, "May I take it then, that you approve of our humble county, sir?"

"Yes, I do indeed. It has proved to be a more pleasant place than I imagined at first." He glanced towards Mr. Darcy, then back to her and smiled, I believe there is much more to amuse us here than country dances, and books, as my cousin allowed it would be." He replied with a note of humour.

Elizabeth felt her ire rise towards Mr. Darcy. She still felt as if that man intended to slight her due to their earlier encounter in the meadow at Netherfield, by insinuating her society was less entertaining and refined. The vision of the colonel and his cousin at Brook's Pond played through her head, and she blushed at the memory, reminding her that no one was above acting frivolous at times.

She hid her irritation, though, with a lighthearted question, "And you do not find those pursuits to your liking, colonel?" She smiled at him, removing the sting behind her statement.

He looked at her, "Well, Miss Bennet, that is hard to determine. I suppose I find them plenty entertaining, if there are such delightful partners as there are here. As far as the other... well I do not read as much as perhaps... my cousin, but when I do, it is usually military related or subjects about world history." Then laughing, I have no patience for poetry or philosophy."

Laughing together, they found easy conversation while dancing. They talked about the countryside and town, and about music, but Elizabeth found it difficult to enjoy her dance when she saw the look of censure from Mr. Darcy and Miss Bingley. To make matters worse, her two youngest sisters, Lydia and Kitty grew louder and more obnoxious as the dance went on. They provided a constant source of embarrassment to Elizabeth in that regard, but it rather unnerved her when she saw Mr. Darcy and Miss Bingley give a derisive look towards her sisters.

This dance has not turned out as I hoped! It is bad enough that Lydia and Kitty act as they do, but it is even worse that they must exhibit such poor manners in front of Mr. Darcy and that sour Miss Bingley. I can imagine how low an opinion they must hold of our family now! When the dance ended, she was more than glad to leave the dance floor.

As the colonel escorted her to her mother's side, he offered her his compliments. I must say how well you dance, Miss Elizabeth. I believe I have had more than a bit of exercise while dancing, and find I am quite parched. May I get you something to drink?"

Mrs. Bennet responded enthusiastically, "Oh yes, colonel, it is most generous of you to offer, we thank you." The elder woman smiled coquettishly in the colonel's direction. Jane and Mr. Bingley joined them, and Mr. Bingley also offered to get some refreshments.

The colonel said, "It would be a pleasure, we shall return directly, ladies."

They bowed and made their way to the table with glasses of punch. Mr. Darcy stood near the table, sipping a glass of something, when the colonel approached. Elizabeth eyed Mr. Darcy and saw him give the colonel a stern look before the gentlemen exchanged words. Mr. Bingley was diligent in tending to his duties of pouring punch for the ladies and seemed oblivious to their conversation. He said something to Mr. Darcy and both the colonel and Mr. Bingley smiled at each other as Mr. Darcy scowled at them.

The gentlemen looked over towards where Elizabeth stood with Jane and Mrs. Bennet, and before she knew what she was about, Elizabeth wound her way towards the gentlemen. She managed to hear the last of Mr. Darcy's comment, "You had better go back to your partner's smiles and fine eyes. I am not inclined to dance with those whom I am not particularly acquainted, nor those who appear to lack good breeding."

She felt herself flush and glared at him, feeling her ire rise again. As the gentlemen turned to where she stood, Colonel Fitzwilliam asked, I hope you are well, Miss Elizabeth, may I escort you back to your mother?"

He had the good grace to flush at his cousin's rude remark.

Taking a deep breath and trying to hide her consternation, she responded, I believe so, colonel, as I would not want to put anyone out at having to entertain such tedious company."

As she walked away, she looked back at Mr. Darcy, and catching his eye, she shot him an angry, defiant look. Turning back to address the colonel as they made their way towards their destination, she sweetly said, I did enjoy the dance. It is most pleasant to find *agreeable* partners." She turned and looked pointedly at Mr. Darcy.

The colonel sighed, "Ah, that...I was afraid you may have overheard my fastidious cousin... Miss Bennet, please do not take what you may heard to heart," he glanced away for a moment. "You see, he is not comfortable in large assemblies, even in town, and can be quite severe in these settings, giving offence, and hiding behind his superiority, and... well putting his foot in his mouth. Please understand he is really not like that when you get to know him."

I cannot imagine how he manages to obtain many friends with such an attitude. Tell me, does he reserve this for country dances or is this his status quo for all the dances that he attends?" She did not wish to dwell on his pointed looks towards her rather inappropriate younger sisters, as she could consider the implications of that later.

"No, I assure you he does have many good friends, and he is well respected among the ton at any dance or around large crowds for that matter." Colonel Fitzwilliam sniggered, and then smiled down into her eyes.

She smiled back at him with a genuine wry smile. "T'is a shame to find no enjoyment with ones surroundings. I could not imagine taking myself so seriously, because I do like to find amusements in all things ridiculous, for I dearly love to laugh." She gazed at him through her eyelashes and did just that.

Both parties endured the rest of the evening with little more than lighthearted conversation, and Elizabeth found many enjoyable dance partners, including Mr. Bingley. She could not help but notice, however, that Mr. Darcy's eyes were frequently upon her, and she again felt unsettled at this man's perusal of her. *What does he mean staring at me so?* Elizabeth could not forget how he stared at her. It evoked chills down her spine as she dwelt upon it that night, and she found it hard to sleep.

Chapter 4

After the Meryton assembly, the Bingley party made the journey to Netherfield Park in relative silence. Bingley made occasional comments about the 'angel', Miss Jane Bennet. *Great,* Darcy thought, *it seems Bingley is setting his sights on a new 'angel' already, and likely, will make a fool of himself.* His friend had a poor habit of falling in and out of love. Darcy felt her family, with the exception of perhaps Mr. Bennet and Miss Elizabeth, was unrefined and lacking... good breeding was not a strong point in the education of the mother and younger girls.

As Darcy made his way to his suite of rooms, he pondered the events of the dance. He could not forget the looks Miss Elizabeth bestowed upon him... *so ... so sharp and fiery.* Though he was not sure, he sensed that she may have overheard his comments to Richard, and perhaps even have taken personal offense to his slight of her family. He stopped before he opened the door to his room with a horrifying idea - that she may have even thought he meant *her* as being ill bred.

She could not have thought that I meant those comments in regard to her? He said to himself as he entered the dressing room.

"Sir?" Responded Baxter, his valet, who had come to assist him to ready for bed.

Startled at his valet's appearance, Darcy responded, "Oh, it is nothing Baxter, I was just ruminating on a previous conversation."

"Very good, sir." Darcy's man helped him to undress, "Will you be needing anything else tonight, sir?"

"Ah, no…no thank you Baxter, that will be all for this evening. You are free to retire for the evening. If I need anything further, I will call for a footman."

"Thank you sir, good night." The man bowed and left his master.

Darcy was finally left in peace. He tried to get some sleep, but his thoughts lingered upon the assembly. His cousin, Richard, had bent over backwards to impress Miss Elizabeth, not bothering to hide his admiration of the lady in front of Darcy or the rest of the guests there. *What is it to me?* Darcy asked himself.

He could not understand why it should bother him so much. He found his cousin's display's distasteful, and tried to warn him about exciting false hopes. Though he found Miss Elizabeth impertinent, he had to admit to being intrigued by her grace and liveliness, and could easily understand the attraction to such a woman. His thoughts drifted back to what happened at the assembly earlier.

He stood at the refreshment table when Richard joined him, then commented in a low voice to his cousin, "Take care to guard your behaviour, Richard. You are making a spectacle out of yourself and if you do not take care, you will excite expectations in that lady… if you have not already in her mother, judging from that lady's raptures at noticing your marked attentions to her daughter!"

In a relaxed and unconcerned manner, Richard looked at him, "Darcy, I see no harm in enjoying myself with such fine company. Does she not have to most beautiful expressive, fine eyes? Just look at her man! I think that perhaps you may be jealous of my partner, and wish that you were with her instead of Caroline earlier?" He teased.

"I am only obliging Bingley's sister; it would be rude to not ask her for a dance. Besides, I know no others here, and you know that I do not dance with someone unless I am particularly acquainted with them!"

"Well then you should be also obliged to dance a set with Miss Elizabeth, seeing how you are 'particularly acquainted' with her as well."

Bingley joined them, I must say, the Bennet ladies are quite lovely, Darcy. Did you not see the angel that is Miss Jane? I could dance the whole evening with such loveliness before me - especially when she bestows such pretty smiles."

As the other two looked towards the Bennet ladies, Darcy scowled. *I shall have to observe these two, for they will do something foolhardy and connect themselves with a family with little fortune and even less breeding.* He then noted Miss Elizabeth looking in their direction and looked away.

Bingley asked him, "Are you enjoying yourself Darcy? I say, you should dance with Miss Elizabeth, though she is not as beautiful as her sister, she is still very lovely. I would even go so far as to say lovelier than most of the ladies in the ton."

Richard nodded his agreement with an appreciative smile.

"I am only here as a favor to *you*, Bingley. As to the loveliness of the lady, that is hardly the material point; they are a gentleman's family to be sure; *but*, they have little fortune, and from what I have ascertained little breeding as well... aside from the two eldest Miss Bennet's, that is."

At Bingley and Richard's scoffs he said, "You had better go back to your partner's smiles and fine eyes." He pointedly looked at his cousin and Bingley, *I am not inclined to dance with those whom I am not particularly acquainted, nor those who in general lack good breeding.*"

Just then, he happened to turn and saw none other than Miss Elizabeth, who had made her way to their party without him hearing her approach. He could see her pretty blush and the fiery look in her eyes, the same look she bestowed upon him while he danced with Caroline. He could not deny the fiery sparkle of her eyes was almost... *enchanting*.

She started to talk with Richard, however, and Darcy could see her occasional glances at him, which caused him to flush. He grew apprehensive and self-conscious. *Surely she did not hear that last comment. She would resent that, and would have made some comment in response, would if she had...will she not?*

The rest of the evening, he felt himself drawn to look upon her, as a moth to a flame; he studied her character and mannerisms. She easily interacted with everyone there; she had no appearance of artifice, or malice, and everyone there seemed to enjoy her company. *She was such an unusual young woman, so self assured and graceful.*

As he lay back in the bed in his room at Netherfield, with his arms folded behind his head, he thought of her situation. *She is the second among five daughters of a simple country squire. All five of her sister's are out at once, and the two youngest are so wild and unrestrained! Their mother does not even bother to check them! What is she thinking? Indeed the daughters, minus the two eldest, are unacceptable. No, it will not do for either Bingley or Richard to get involved with the two eldest. I must keep an eye on them both. They need to check their attentions, as they are both so charming to the ladies, especially the pretty ones, and may raise false hopes and expectations. They have had entanglements in town;*

Richard is worse than Bingley in that respect. It would not do for Richard to harm Miss Elizabeth.

He started at that last thought. *Why should I care if she was harmed by some flirtation?* He realized then that he was starting to feel…something for Miss Elizabeth… For some unexplainable reason, he was drawn to Miss Elizabeth Bennet and resented Richard's attention towards her. There was, however, little he could do to stop him from behaving in such a way, other than withdraw his support of Richard.

Though Darcy was privy to his cousin's predispositions to seeking entertainments with those of the fairer sex, he never let his cousin's dalliances bother him to this extent. He could not reconcile himself to be casual in regards to Richard's marked attention towards Miss Bennet. *Why should I care what he does in this little shire? It is of no consequence to me! Let him make a fool out of himself with all of his pretty words! I care not, but for our family's reputation.*

He resolved to discuss Richard's behaviour at the assembly with the man in the morning. Darcy, however, still did not find sleep any easier after making that resolution. Envisioning Miss Elizabeth's lively discussions with the people at the assembly, as he tried to find slumber, he tossed and turned, unable to find peaceful rest as he recalled the way she had looked at his cousin during the evening. *Could she look at me thus also?*

When he first recognized her across the assembly room and their eyes met, his heart started beating rapidly. It was the first time ever in his life that that happened to him. He was discomforted at the newness of his heart racing from just a look and immediately put on a mask of indifference, which was his usual defense against any new or uncomfortable situation. He felt his ire rise when Richard and Bingley made directly for her party. He knew that those two were always attracted to a pretty face, and with such an inducement, he could hardly blame them, but it irritated him to see how easily they could fall into conversation…about anything… while he stood by.

"This is going to be a long visit to the countryside." He moaned as he beat his pillow yet again, before he found a fitful rest.

Early the next morning, upon awakening, Darcy made his way down to the breakfast parlour. Darcy went to the sidebar, scooped up some scrambled eggs, and toast, and balancing his cup of coffee in his other hand on its saucer, easily made his way to the table. After starting on his eggs, he heard his cousin walking through the hall towards the parlour.

Richard arrived with a cheerful smile on his face.

"I see you are up early as usual, Darcy." Scooping up a heaping pile of eggs on his plate, he half turned and looked sideways at Darcy. "So what is on your schedule this morning?"

Taking a sip of his coffee and replacing it back on its

saucer, Darcy replied, I believe Bingley plans to go hunting for duck with Hurst, and asked if we would be joining them."

"Ah, well then I suppose we should join them. If Hurst is still recovering from last night's entertainment, he may not be as steady a shot, and it would be unconscionable to let poor Bingley pay for our lack of supervision."

Darcy tried to think his way through to addressing his cousin about the latter's behaviour with Elizabeth Bennet last night at the dance. They sat in quietude for some time until Darcy finished his breakfast. He kept looking up from his plate towards his cousin, pondering how to proceed, when his cousin noticed that he was being studied.

"What is on your mind?" sighed Richard.

"I have been thinking about last night."

"Ah, yes, it was quite amusing was it not? I enjoyed myself immensely." His cousin sipped the last of his coffee.

"I had not noticed." Darcy replied sarcastically.

"I know how much you enjoy this sort of things, Darce, but you should be accustomed to them by now. I cannot, for the world, understand why you seem to delight in making yourself so disagreeable at these functions. There is usually pleasant enough company, and last night was simply divine." Richard finished with a rakish grin.

This annoyed Darcy even more. "Yes, I noticed that you seemed to attach yourself to Miss Elizabeth Bennet rather more than decorum tolerates!" Darcy glared at his cousin.

"What?" Richard looked puzzled. I was only being polite. Besides, I did not notice you taking any pains whatsoever to address anyone at the assembly other than our party. Do not tell me that you are not comfortable talking to people whom you are not already acquainted with, as that is a very poor excuse. You had already met Miss Elizabeth, and you could have danced with her. Hell, Darcy, you could have also been civil and talked to her."

At Darcy's frown, he added, "Do not look at me like that. I am not as fastidious as you are, Darcy, and there is nothing wrong with her. As a matter of fact, I found her quite delightful. She has such grace and beauty, and she is so lively…and those eyes! Did you not notice the sparkle in them? One can almost see her emitting sparks when she looks at one!" He smiled.

Richard sat back in his chair while he expounded on Elizabeth Bennet's many fine attributes, which did little to allay Darcy's concern for his cousin becoming attached to this country miss. Darcy came out of his chair with extreme irritation by the end of his cousin's dissertation.

"Richard! Think about what you are doing! For G-d's sake! Did you not happen to notice that she has four sisters who are out already? The youngest two are hardly ready to be out in society, or did you happen to miss their flagrant flirtations or their running and hopping around on the dance floor? Why, the youngest cannot be any older than fifteen. Their mother was no better, with her loud tittering about the eldest Miss Bennet dancing with Bingley, and how she would likely be favoured by him to make a match, and how that would throw the other girls in the way of other rich men!" Darcy ran his hands through his hair, "And she made no effort to check the younger ones' behaviour last night."

"Darcy, what is the harm in enjoying one's self at a dance?" Richard shrugged his shoulders, "Besides, Miss Bennet and Miss Elizabeth acted commendably. How could you protest that? Look, I know you do not like to go to balls or dances, because of the plotting of match making mamas. I am all too familiar with them to be insensible of their ways, but I do not see anything in Miss Elizabeth's or Miss Bennet's manners to make me think anything but well of them. If you do not wish to be in their company, I can make your excuses, but I will not deny myself the pleasure of their company due to you uneasiness."

"Richard, it is not fair to either Miss Elizabeth or Miss Bennet for you or Bingley to trifle with them and raise their hopes up, or have you not considered that?"

At his cousin's scowl, Darcy continued, "You know that you, as a second son, even an earl's second son, need to marry well. I will not even go into your exploits with a certain Mrs. Heartherton, as it hardly signifies that an honourable gentleman would have such entertainments. But these are young maidens unaccustomed to the ways of the world. I should not have to remind you, Richard, that it would not do to raise up hopes that either of you have any intentions to fulfill."

"I do not think that it should be…. Before Richard could finish his response, their private conversation was interrupted by the early appearance of Caroline Bingley.

"Gentlemen, how are you this morning?" she cooed, more to Darcy than his cousin.

"Good morning, Miss Bingley." They said in uncomfortable unison as they stood and bowed to her. Darcy wondered how much of their conversation she overheard. He and Richard eyed each other uneasily.

Richard was the first to gain his equanimity and address the lady, "We are well, Miss Bingley. We were just discussing last night's dance."

Caroline snorted and rolled her eyes, "Yes, it was quite tedious, was it not colonel?" She then smiled smugly at Darcy, I could hardly keep my countenance last night! Such people, so simple and unrefined! Why, did you notice those youngest Bennet girls? They were wild! And their mother! It is no wonder the younger ones run about in such a wild manner! But, it is a shame that Miss Jane Bennet hails from that same family, and I suppose Miss Eliza is tolerable as well. Perhaps Louisa and I shall amuse ourselves and invite them to come dine with us sometime during our visit and show them some superior company. At least we can have some amusement in this…this…place."

She looked at Darcy, and smiled, "Do not concern yourselves, gentlemen, we will invite them when you have another engagement elsewhere."

Richard shook his head and rolled his eyes at Darcy when Caroline had looked away. Everyone was well aware of the fact that Caroline Bingley, or as she has been known to be called 'pinning Caroline' behind her back, had aspirations of becoming Mrs. Fitzwilliam Darcy.

Darcy tried to avoid her whenever possible and only tolerated her for her brother's sake. Though he doubted she was that cunning, he always made certain that, whenever he was staying under the same roof with her, all the doors to his suite were locked at night to ensure that she could not get to him in his rooms. *Nothing could be worse than being bound to that mercenary shrew for eternity.*

As soon as could be deemed civil, Darcy made his excuses to the other two and exited the room. He avoided the hall and headed down the servant's hallway, towards the stables, to avoid being followed by Miss Bingley. He hoped that she had not heard the last part of his conversation with Fitzwilliam. It would not do for her to be privy to anything so private, even if it was about his cousin. Darcy guarded his and his family's privacy stringently. No one enjoyed being fodder for gossips of the *ton*, least of all him.

What he needed now was a good hard gallop through the country side to work off his uneasiness. That last talk with his cousin proved to be a dismal disappointment. *I should have known that Richard would do as he pleased when it came to women; it was always a hard fought battle to dissuade him from pursuing his course when he saw fit. Why is he so determined to trifle with Elizabeth? And why do I care so much...it is none of my concern.* He tried to determine what his next move should be to ensure no one was hurt in their foray into this little shire.

When he reached the farthest edges of Netherfield Park, the dew was starting to dry on the grass, and as he surveyed the land, he thought he saw a flash of colour in the timbers. Before he could make out what it was, it vanished. Shaking his head, he determined it was past time for him and his mount to head back to the manor house. Perhaps not, as involuntarily, Darcy found himself galloping toward the flash of colour.

Chapter 5

Elizabeth heard the sound of a horse galloping. Startled, she looked through the meadow and saw a man riding past the timber at Netherfield Park. She stood still and observed Mr. Darcy for a few minutes, trying to remain hidden. She did not understand, for the life of her, why she felt ... drawn toward him, as if there was a mystery under that stern exterior of his that she wished to solve. When he looked towards the direction of the timber, she needed to move out of his range of vision, and hid herself behind a large tree trunk.

She did not see a severe mask upon his face. Instead he appeared as though he were thinking his way through a maze. He had a soft look about him. She thought him most handsome atop his horse. She had noticed before that he was an attractive specimen of a man, but at that moment he was almost Adonis-like in his youth and beauty. She felt as if he were staring right through her, as his gaze rested in the general direction of where she stood. Feeling a tingling sensation when his eyes rested in her direction, she thought she was becoming cold or... something.

Disconcerted, she turned and quickened her pace towards home. For the life of her, she could not reconcile the man's behaviour with whom she had observed riding this morning. It was as if he were two different people. *Why am I concerning myself about Mr. Darcy.s behaviour? He is nothing to me. It is not as if he has concerned himself with me or my affairs.* She resolved to forget about this morning's ramble towards Netherfield. Try as she did, however, she still had an unexplainable and unsettling feeling in the pit of her stomach.

Struggling to make sense of Mr. Darcy and her reactions to him versus her reactions to his cousin, she reflected on their individual interactions with her. The colonel, she felt, was such an easygoing man, who had no airs. She found him to be amusing, light hearted, and kind.

As far as she knew, Mr. Darcy was haughty, felt above most of Meryton society, and disapproved of the colonel's attentions towards her. *Why? Why is that any of his concern? And what was he thinking about in the meadow? Was he, perhaps, thinking about last evening when he was at the dance, that his cousin should not consider encouraging some country miss?*

She saw the cousins' interactions at the assembly and the day they met, which intrigued her. The colonel defended Mr. Darcy, that she could easily tell, even when the latter insulted her at the dance. *He defended Mr. Darcy's character. He even went so far as to offer excuses for Mr. Darcy's behaviour, and described with some affection, Mr. Darcy's manners in familiar company. How is it that one cousin is so easygoing and relaxed, while another is so tense and haughty... even to the point of rudeness?*

Lost in thought, she walked back toward the direction of home. When she returned to Longbourn, she found Jane outside cutting flowers.

Upon seeing Elizabeth, Jane said, "How was your walk, Lizzy? Did you go through the timber?"

"Yes, I did." She said, staring off to the distance.

"And did you see anything interesting, or were you woolgathering all this time and did not pay any attention?" Jane teased.

Elizabeth looked at her sister, I went out to enjoy the day, and at the edge of the timber, I saw Mr. Darcy sitting on his horse in the meadow. He had this... this look about him...I cannot make sense of it."

Jane smiled, "And why would you desire to do that? I thought you did not care about him. Have you changed your mind? I had rather thought you preferred Colonel Fitzwilliam."

Elizabeth smiled, "As far as Mr. Darcy is concerned, I cannot put my finger upon it as to why, but when I espied him he had a ... well... youthful, soft, and kind look about him. It caught me off guard to observe that while he was deep in thought, some tenderness had seeped to the surface, in contrast to his usual hauteur." She laughed, "As far as the colonel... well, he is nice, and friendly, but I cannot reconcile the two of them. I had been contemplating their relationship with each other, and I know that the colonel does think highly of his cousin, but I think they do not always agree with the other on... certain subjects. There seemed to be a minor disagreement between them last night at the ball."

Jane looked at Elizabeth with her kind eyes, "Lizzy, you and I are close to our own family, is it not reasonable that, they to, are that close… almost as brothers, I think, from what Mr. Bingley said. According to him, the colonel relies on his cousin, but for what, I am not sure… he did not say. I do know that Mr. Bingley also thinks highly of Mr. Darcy. He said that his servants are the most loyal servants he has ever seen, and that there are several families who have served him for many generations, so he cannot be a bad man."

Elizabeth felt inclined to rely on her own views, as opposed to Jane and Mr. Bingley's. She knew Jane saw the best sides of people, and ignored their faults, for which she was grateful for her own benefit, but when it came to others, she believed Jane was too undiscerning. She felt Mr. Bingley shared this characteristic and would, thus, be unlikely to think poorly of either of them. *I wonder though, at how much influence one has on the other?*

Jane continued cutting flowers, "Perhaps, you should not be so hasty to judge either man. There are many things we do not know about them. They have only just recently joined the neighbourhood."

"I suppose you have not made any judgments on a particular gentleman yet?"

Jane looked at her with a smile and flushed. They finished cutting the rest of the flowers in light conversation.

~*~*~*~

Within a fortnight Meryton was abuzz with news of the impending arrival of an encampment of the militia for the winter. Darcy assumed Richard had informed Miss Elizabeth about the militia being in Meryton. He noted how his cousin often seemed drawn to her. Their parties were frequently in each other's company. One evening, shortly after the arrival of said troops, they all met Colonel Fitzwilliam's friend, Colonel Forster, at a party given by Sir William Lucas.

As Elizabeth conversed with her neighbours and Colonel Forster, Darcy stood nearby, observing and listening to her interactions. Miss

Elizabeth looked at him and, in her usual teasing manner, said to Colonel Forster. I hope when you are settled, Colonel, you will give a ball."

Darcy fought to keep his lips from twitching at her teasing. He had become accustomed to her mannerisms by now.

After she drew away from Colonel Forster's grouping and entered into Mr. Darcy's direct company, she addressed him. "Did you not think, Mr. Darcy, that I expressed myself uncommonly well just now, when I was teasing Colonel Forster to give us a ball at Meryton?"

Darcy, surprised but not disappointed at her address, replied lightly, "With great energy; but it is a subject which always makes a lady energetic."

"You are severe on us."

Charlotte Lucas rescued him from her teasing by encouraging Elizabeth to play and sing at the pianoforte.

Though Elizabeth acted as if she were loath to do so, she acquiesced to Miss Lucas' demands. Many of their neighbours looked delighted at the prospect of Elizabeth's singing and playing, and when she was done, he could understand why. *She has such great feeling and ease while performing*, Darcy observed. He was impressed by her musical ability, but noticed that he was not the only one enjoying her talents.

His cousin, Richard, also watched Miss Elizabeth perform with a passionate look, which unsettled Darcy. He shifted in his seat, not knowing why. He moved closer to her and observed. Richard watched Miss Elizabeth intently as she sang, and suddenly, Darcy noticed the direction of his cousin's gaze.

As she sang, her countenance radiated with beauty and grace. The way her breasts swelled when she took a breath caused Darcy to grab hold of his. Startled, he realized the direction of his thoughts. *This will not do!*

His current preoccupation mortified him, but try as he did, it would not go away. In addition to his admiration of her talents and her impertinence, he started to feel drawn to her physical attributes as well. He grew uncomfortable with such images. *She is beautiful to be sure... her figure is light and pleasing, and her eyes...so expressive.*

He forced his thoughts of her person to turn toward thoughts of her family and their lack of good breeding.

After Elizabeth vacated her seat, Mary Bennet moved to the instrument and began her exhibition. Soon after *she* started, Darcy sensed that she had practiced the execution of the song on the instrument, but had not done much else for her performance. The younger Bennet girls, along with Charlotte's siblings and a few militia officers, required music suitable for dancing instead of the concertos Mary preferred, and requested a livelier tune. When she protested, Mrs. Bennet chastised her.

"Oh, Mary! No one wants your concertos! Play a jig!"

Sir William stepped in and managed to persuade her to play a different offering. I am afraid our tastes are different Miss Mary, but I see no harm in a livelier tune for entertainment."

This scene played out in front of those gathered in the parlour. Darcy disapproved of Mrs. Bennet's ill manners. He felt she should not have chastised her own daughter in front of the assemblage. He looked over to where Elizabeth stood and saw her watching him, which surprised and pleased him. He noticed her lovely flush and appreciated what it did to her complexion, but then remembered the cause of her flushing. He saw Elizabeth glance from him to where her sisters danced with some officers.

Her younger sisters, Lydia and Kitty, danced exuberantly, laughed loudly, and hopped wildly on the dance floor. Darcy noticed Sir William Lucas come over to him and make light of the dancing in one quarter of the room. He lost his patience with the gentleman as he droned on about the refinement of dancing, talked about houses in town, and mentioned his presentation in town, until Darcy was at his wits end. Darcy felt a sudden flood of relief upon spotting Richard making his way from the officer's corner towards them.

Sir William caught his attention, however. "My dear Miss Eliza, why are you not dancing?" He turned toward Darcy, "Mr. Darcy, you must allow me to present this young lady to you as a very desirable partner. You cannot refuse to dance, I am sure, when so much beauty is before you."

Sir William attempted to offer her hand to Darcy, which she resisted. *Why would she decline me?*

Darcy noted that Miss Elizabeth blushed from her bosom to the roots of her hair, but she politely declined.

"Indeed, sir, I have not the least intention of dancing. I entreat you not to suppose that I moved this way in order to beg for a partner."

Darcy did not oppose the notion of accepting her hand in the dance. "Indeed, Ms. Bennet, I would be honoured, if you would dance a set with me." *Please say yes.* He hoped for a chance to hold her… hand.

Sir William chimed in, "You excel so much in the dance, Miss Eliza, that it is cruel to deny me the happiness of seeing you; and though this gentleman dislikes the amusement in general, he can have no objection, I am sure, to oblige us for one half hour."

No, no objection at all. Darcy did not wish to examine his reasoning at that moment. He disliked Richard's attempts to make inroads with her, as he supposed that she would be disappointed in the end. *There is no way, Miss Elizabeth, that Richard could ever have you. You could not afford him, nor would I have it.*

Richard then joined the group, and Darcy saw disappointment written in his expression. It pleased him that Elizabeth declined to dance with him, as it meant she could not accept Richard. Darcy gave his cousin a stern look, and Fitzwilliam frowned back at him. *You will not be able to treat her in an ungentlemanly manner cousin. She is not one of those women from town who will tolerate your inane speeches as you are accustomed to. No, she is finer than that!*

Ignoring his cousin, Darcy turned to observe Miss Elizabeth walking towards her youngest two sisters, as though determined to have a word with them. He watched as they paid no heed to her. *It does not appear as if your words of reprimand will work, Elizabeth. Your mother does not even register that their behaviour is untoward.* Seeing the unruly actions of the youngest Bennet daughters made Darcy more grateful for his relationship with Georgiana, who listened to him with adulation.

Darcy saw Richard approach Elizabeth in an obvious attempt to monopolize her attention, but all he could do was to stand back and watch. They each seemed to be enjoying the company of the other. It was more than he could tolerate. He noticed them glance his way occasionally, and Richard had a glint in his eyes when he did so, which piqued Darcy's curiosity. When he heard Elizabeth's melodic laughter, he moved to where they stood, but they ceased talking and he could not hear their conversation. After a few moments of silence, he joined their discussion.

"How are you enjoying this evening, Miss Elizabeth?" Darcy asked in a soft voice.

"Very well, Sir." She glanced at Richard with a slight smile, then turned back to Darcy with an arched eyebrow.

Richard watched him interact with Elizabeth, never taking his eyes off of her, and Darcy did not like this one bit. Darcy saw the slight frown on his cousin's face when he joined them, but felt; it serves him right trying to play with her in such an infamous way. "If you do not mind, could I have a few words with you, Colonel Fitzwilliam? I will return him back to you shortly, Miss Elizabeth."

She frowned at him, but allowed them some privacy. She then moved to talk to her father, but kept glancing towards them while conversing with Mr. Bennet. Darcy did not know what to make of her looks, but decided to focus his attention on Richard.

"So what is so important to tear me away from such delightful company, Darcy? Is there some urgent business that cannot wait until we at least get back to Netherfield?"

Darcy frowned, "Richard, do you not realize that with all of your attention towards Miss Elizabeth, you could be exciting her expectations? I should also warn you that I did catch you staring in... inappropriate places!" He hissed under his breath.

"I thought I had warned you of such things before! Have you not learned anything? You are already involved with another. To trifle with a gentleman's daughter is unconscionable! I do not wish to make a scene in this environment, but I must warn you that I will insist we leave, if you continue this behaviour!"

"Do not be ridiculous, Darcy! I am not trifling with Eli...Miss Elizabeth, and I am my own person. I can make my own decisions!" Fitzwilliam had the good grace to blush with his slip of the tongue, Darcy noted, but it did not make him feel any better about his cousin's intentions towards the woman he knew in his heart as 'Elizabeth'. I *must see to it that this does not develop into anything else!*

"Need I remind you that you are not free to do as you please? You rely upon me as one source of support, and if you continue to play these games with innocent gentlemen's daughters, then I will do as I see fit."

Richard scowled at him, and looked around to see if they were being observed. The only one that watched them, Darcy noted, was Elizabeth. They both looked back at each other and stared each other down until Richard turned away and walked toward their audience. Darcy watched Richard and Elizabeth converse with each other as they each stole glances in his direction. He was infuriated.

Chapter 6

The next week Miss Bingley and Mrs. Hurst invited Jane to dine with them at Netherfield. When Jane and Mrs. Bennet read the invitation aloud, Elizabeth could not be more surprised to hear that the superior sisters would deign to invite one of the lowly Bennet's to entertain them. *It must be that they could not find enough sport in examining Charlotte or Maria Lucas, but the more likely reason is so that they may find fault with our family, although it is impossible to find fault with dear Jane.* Elizabeth felt disappointed that the gentlemen would not be dining with them, but Jane remained anxious to accept the invitation none the less.

"May I take the carriage?" Jane asked her parents.

"No, my dear, you had better go on horseback, because it seems likely to rain, and then you must stay the night." Mrs. Bennet responded.

"That would be a good scheme, if you were sure that they would not offer to send her home." Elizabeth said.

Elizabeth could not help but roll her eyes at her mother's plotting. She thought it a transparent plan to throw Jane in the way of Mr. Bingley, and felt sorry for Jane's status as a pawn for those schemes. *I cannot believe that the Bingley's and their party will not see what her intent is! When they learn of her part in sending Jane in such condition they will never want to associate with us!*

"The gentlemen will have Mr. Bingley's chaise to go to Meryton, and the Hurst's have no horses of their own."

"I had much rather go in the coach," Jane said.

As much as both Elizabeth and Jane tried to make Mrs. Bennet see reason, and implored Mr. Bennet to exert himself to heed the request for the carriage, neither Elizabeth nor Jane succeeded in securing the conveyance for Jane. Jane, therefore, was obliged to take the old hag, Nellie, to Netherfield. *Oh, heavens! This will not do to impress anyone at Netherfield! I can just imagine what Mr. Darcy will think!* Elizabeth stopped herself from dwelling upon that matter.

He does not approve of his cousin paying any regards to me... What difference does it make to him? Why should I concern myself with that man's approval? For the rest of the morning, Elizabeth endeavored to busy herself to avoid thinking about how the Netherfield party, but the thought of one man's stern countenance kept interfering.

Later that day, Elizabeth watched as Jane rode Nellie toward Netherfield and her figure became smaller and smaller in the distance until she could not be seen anymore. The temperature turned cooler, and Elizabeth became concerned for her sister, as three miles was no easy distance in the pouring rain when one sat atop an old nag. *This is not going to be a quick ride... poor Jane. Miss Bingley and Mrs. Hurst will make derisive remarks at our expense! Mama should think more clearly about how her scheming will appear... no, she will never change!*

As Mrs. Bennet predicted, Jane had to stay the night at Netherfield. The next morning, Elizabeth learned that her sister felt unwell, and the local apothecary, Mr. Jones, had been summoned to see her at Netherfield. Elizabeth was furious with her mother. *Why can she not see sense? Does she not realize how ridiculous she makes us seem with her silliness and maneuverings?* Jane sent a note to Elizabeth explaining her circumstances, and Elizabeth felt the need to go to Netherfield to see to Jane, out of concern for her sister. She also wanted to see the interactions of the two gentlemen staying there.

"I shall walk to Netherfield this morning to see Jane, and ensure that she is not any worse than she has led us to believe."

"You shall not, you silly child! What would the colonel think of you, should you arrive upon their doorstep all covered in mud? No Lizzy, I will not have you do such a thing! You shall go in the carriage! I shall talk to Mr. Bennet, and we shall see you off in the carriage."

Elizabeth knew of her father's reluctance to part with the carriage, as today the horses that pulled it were more useful to the wagons for harvest.

"I would rather walk, as it is such a nice day, mama, and besides I do think that the horses would be more useful elsewhere." She looked to her father for confirmation, and he acknowledged the fact with a nod. Mrs. Bennet huffed at them, and frowned.

Elizabeth readied herself for her walk to Netherfield after breakfast, dressing warmly, and wearing the appropriate shoes for the terrain. She never had much use for fashion, when it did not have a function.

"Now Lizzy, do not behave as you are wont to do… that is do not be disagreeable and headstrong. The gentlemen do not like ladies that disagree with them." Mrs. Bennet said as she nodded her head, "Show them that you are deferential to their opinions, and perhaps you may end up the next Mrs. Fitzwilliam. Oh, how well that sounds! Now off with you, and remember to behave like a lady… no running about like some hoyden!"

Elizabeth looked back before her father closed the door, and she could see his wry smile as he shook his head. *He takes such pleasure in watching mother's ridiculous antics. T'is too bad that he does not take pains to check her or Lydia or Kitty's behaviour. Though I love you dearly, papa, I cannot but disagree with your methods of dealing with your family.*

Elizabeth managed to trek through the timber adjoining Longbourn to Netherfield Park without getting too dirty or too wet. When she reached the meadow, she came upon Mr. Darcy riding his horse. He started at her sudden appearance as she came out from under a low hanging bough, though he managed to regain his composure enough to greet her.

"Good morning Miss Bennet."

"Mr. Darcy, good morning." She curtseyed to him.

Elizabeth caught his questioning look and explained her sudden appearance, I am come to see my sister." She felt like a child explaining herself, then became annoyed as he stared at her.

Mr. Darcy blinked several times before responding, "On foot?"

"As you see."

At Mr. Darcy's lack of response, Elizabeth became frustrated and looked towards the manor house then back at him, at which time he dismounted his horse.

"Shall I escort you then, Miss Bennet?"

"I do not wish to trouble you sir, as it appears that you were enjoying your ride. I can manage, I thank you."

"It is no trouble at all, Miss Bennet. I can ride anytime, besides I need to finish writing letters to my steward, in order to post them today."

She nodded her head, and they walked back to the house. *Why does he bother to put himself out at times, only to withdraw at others? And why is he so quiet and yet pleasant at other times? I cannot make him out at all.* She almost shook her head at that thought but caught herself just in time.

When they arrived at the house, they were greeted by a very perturbed Miss Bingley. "Why …Miss…Eliza, what a…surprise to see you here on such a morning."

Ignoring her hostess's narrowed eyes, Elizabeth greeted her, "Yes, it is a lovely morning after such storms, is it not? I dare say that even Mr. Darcy seemed to enjoy the grounds on a bright morning, but I shall not take much of your time, Miss Bingley, for I came to see my sister." She shot a glance at Mr. Darcy.

Miss Bingley, looking quite put out, acquiesced to her request, "Well then…I suppose I should show you to her rooms." Glancing towards Mr. Darcy, I will direct Miss Eliza to Miss Bennet's rooms, and if you should need anything, please do not hesitate to ask." Curtseying to Mr. Darcy, she had a simpering smile, and gestured for Elizabeth to follow her.

"I thank you Mr. Darcy, have a nice day." Elizabeth curtseyed to him and half turned towards the doorway.

Mr. Darcy flushed and looked at Elizabeth intently for a moment before looking back at Miss Bingley, "Indeed…it does look to be a much improved day, Miss Bennet." He then glanced over at her and bowed before taking his leave, his eyes never leaving hers as he did so.

Elizabeth eyed him back, but stayed silent, wondering at his intent stare.

Miss Bingley interrupted their staring, "Well then, shall we ...Miss Eliza?" Before they left the room however, Miss Bingley suddenly turned back into the room, "Oh, Mr. Darcy, I shall only be gone momentarily...to give the Misses Bennet's their privacy...I shall come back, should you have need of anything."

"That should not be necessary, Miss Bingley, I am going up to my rooms to write to my steward, and that may take quite some time."

Elizabeth tried to suppress her smile at Miss Bingley's disappointed look as they ascended the stairs. Before entering Jane's room, she saw Mr. Bingley come out of a nearby doorway.

".Miss Elizabeth, how do you do today?" He seemed rather nervous, which Elizabeth attributed to concern for Jane. She became more anxious about Jane's condition. *It is pleasing to know that he seems to care for dear Jane. I hope he does not use her ill, or disappoint her.*

"I am well, sir, I hope all is well today?" Elizabeth searched his face for a reason for his nervousness.

"Ah...yes...yes, I am well, I ... wanted to make certain that Miss Bennet was well tended...the staff...I needed to ensure that they were seeing to her every need."

Elizabeth raised an eyebrow. *My, he has such an obvious mooncalf look to him... He does seem to be in a fair way of falling in love with Jane, if he has not already.* I am sure she is being better tended here, sir, than at Longbourn, for we do not allow anyone to rest in silence there." She laughed.

He gave a nervous laugh and bowed, I shall not interfere with your visit then, Miss Elizabeth. If there is anything that we can do for you or MissBennet...anything at all, please do not hesitate to ask."

"I thank you, sir, for allowing us to trespass upon your hospitality."

He smiled, "Not at all, it is a pleasure to have you here, Miss Elizabeth."

The butler showed Elizabeth to the room where Jane was convalescing, and she spent the remainder of the morning and afternoon in her rooms. When the afternoon neared three o'clock, Jane was so loath to see Elizabeth go that the invitation for her to stay for the day was exchanged for an invitation to stay with Jane until Jane improved enough to go home.

~*~*~*~

Darcy paced his room like a caged tiger ready to spring at its prey. He had left Elizabeth's company to write his letters to his steward only to find that he was too distracted to do that. He had walked behind her and had watched the way she glided forward with her hips swaying, and he could not have helped but notice how well she looked when she came upon him from the timber…such bright eyes and a brilliant complexion, not to mention her heaving bosom when she seemed out of breath. He had felt as if he were going to melt by the time they arrived at the manor house together. Struggling to release himself from such memories, he ordered a bath… a lukewarm one.

The memory of her presence set his senses reeling as he recalled the whiffs of her lavender water. Watching her locks bounced, having escaped from their pins had enchanted him. There was no denying his arousal, and thus he had needed to stay behind her- least she saw such an unbecoming thing. It was most fortunate his arousal had been squelched when they had spotted Miss Bingley coming toward them, no doubt to plague him. In truth, he had been imagining Caroline in an effort to relieve his thoughts of his very uncomfortable arousal.

Basking in the lukewarm water, Darcy realized that his initial fascination with this little impertinent country miss had evolved into an obsession. *Elizabeth Bennet is unlike any woman I have ever met. She does not cower or defer to anyone for their opinions, and she is such a lively adversary, using wit instead of airs and veiled insults.* He laughed, *If she were a man, she would have done well in the debates at Cambridge.*

Thoughts of Cambridge reminded him that Richard stayed at Netherfield as well, and in the same wing, which did nothing to ease his restlessness. *Why did she have to come now? Most likely, her mother wished her to come and throw herself in the path of 'rich men'.*

But what of her intentions? What is it she is here for? Darcy hoped she came to see to her sister's well being and nothing else- such as becoming better acquainted with his cousin. *And Richard had best behave in a gentlemanly fashion towards her, for he has an entanglement he can ill afford! I shall watch to see how they interact, and, if necessary, I shall know how to act!*

Nothing grated on Darcy's nerves more than Richard's propensity to 'charm' the ladies. While there could be no better friend or ally than his cousin, there could be no such man who used his charming personality and his background as the second son of an Earl and an officer to indulge in flirtations-save perhaps Richard's older brother. Darcy took issue with his dishonourable behaviour several times, but he disregarded Darcy's advice and was now working his charms on Elizabeth.

That is intolerable! It shall not be borne, Richard... I will not sit idly by and watch you break her heart! You may have your Harriett's, but she will be my Elizabeth. Darcy stopped the train of his thoughts, realizing what his mind had just told him. *I must take care, for there is too much riding on whom I choose to make the mistress of my heart.*

He paced for a while longer, however, finally acknowledging the time; he sat down to write to his steward. Later that day he and Bingley, along with Richard and Hurst went shooting, which diverted his attention from …from impertinent country misses and their bouncy curls… for a while.

After dinner, the group, sans Miss Bennet, gathered in the parlour. Richard immediately addressed Elizabeth, "How does your sister this evening, Miss Elizabeth?"

Darcy frowned at the sight of beautiful smile in response to his cousin, I am afraid not any better, Colonel Fitzwilliam. My sister still complains of a sore throat and is feverish."

"I am sorry to hear it. I wish there was more I could do for her to make her comfortable."

"I thank you Colonel. I believe she is comfortable here. I am so thankful that Mr. and Miss Bingley have been kind enough to allow me to stay here to look after her."

Bingley joined the conversation, I would not have it any other way, Miss Elizabeth. You and Miss Bennet are welcome here as long as you need. We are neighbours, after all."

"I must agree with Mr. Bingley's offer, Miss Elizabeth. It is a pleasure to have such lovely company." Richard chimed in.

Darcy became alarmed at the amount of flattery and attention that Richard displayed towards Elizabeth, and grew even more so when he saw her bestow that beautiful smile and her bright eyes upon him as she responded, "We thank you for your generosity and kind words, sirs, you are both very kind."

"Anytime, Miss Elizabeth, it is our pleasure." Richard repliedwith a soft look.

Darcy glared at Richard, who ignored him and continued to admire Elizabeth, which infuriated him all the more.

Miss Bingley frowned at Richard's comment and asked Elizabeth, "Would you care to join us for a game of whist, Miss Eliza?"

"I thank you, no. I do not think I shall stay downstairs for much longer, before I go back to join Jane. I shall read instead."

"Rather singular. You prefer reading to cards?" Mr. Hurst scoffed.

Miss Bingley sneered, "Miss Eliza is an accomplished reader, and enjoys nothing else."

Darcy noticed Elizabeth grimace at Miss Bingley, I am not an accomplished reader, and I enjoy many things."

"I can attest to some of Miss Elizabeth's other accomplishments, as I know she is an excellent walker, and a delightful dancer." Richard smiled at her then held his chin high and raised an eyebrow as though issuing a challenge at Darcy.

Darcy shot Richard a withering glare, which he thought could have frightened the worst ruffian in the kingdom. He could not determine his cousin's intentions, but he knew that Richard had often displayed his admiration in a blatant manner, and… to Darcy, it appeared that Elizabeth did not show an aversion to his attentions.

That Richard was attracted to Elizabeth, Darcy was certain. He had known his cousin all of his life, and he knew his mannerisms. What concerned Darcy was his cousin's open demonstration of his admiration of her. *Fitzwilliam is in no position to disregard the subject of a potential wife's lack of fortune. This is unbearable to watch. He is too attentive to her, and if he does not cease, they will both end up hurt...though I will ensure he does so to the greater quarter. I must find a way to get him away from here...but how?*

Chapter 7

The second day of Elizabeth's stay at Netherfield found Jane much improved from the night before. Elizabeth relaxed more and decided to spend time away from her sister's room while Jane rested. Entering the breakfast parlour, she found it was occupied by Mr. Darcy. Upon seeing that they were the only ones there, she momentarily froze before finding her voice.

"Mr. Darcy, good morning. I had rather thought I might be the first person downstairs this morning."

"No, Miss Bennet, my cousin and Mr. Bingley rise around half past seven, and the Hurst's and Miss Bingley arise *much* later."

She could detect a half smile on his face as he responded to her. *How handsome he appears when he smiles, she mused.*

Feeling a fluttering in the pit of her stomach, she discovered she had not much of an appetite, but took some toast and coffee, and sat down opposite to the gentleman. He started conversing with her as she stirred her coffee.

"Hertfordshire seems a rather quiet county, Miss Bennet. I have enjoyed the comforting calm here, but then I prefer the country to town."

She glanced up and saw him looking intently at her.

Amazed at his easy manner of address, she eyed him hesitantly, and replied, "Yes, I too, find it comforting with all the quietude here, but then I have always lived in

Hertfordshire. That is, except when I visited my aunt and uncle in town on occasion. I would have to agree with you, however. I find town quite noisy and it is difficult to find peace in a houseful of lively children when I visit."

Mr. Darcy smiled, "Do you visit town often, Miss Bennet?"

"As often as I am able. My aunt and uncle send for Jane and me three or four times a year. It is a nice change of scenery, though, so I do not mind the noise." She smiled. *And that noise is so much more preferable to that of mamma and Lydia and Kitty.*

"And how many cousins do you have, Miss Bennet? Are they very young?"

"Four cousins, sir, and the eldest is nine. The youngest is three. We very much enjoy them, as they are a great source of amusement." Elizabeth laughed at her recollections. "Forgive me, Mr. Darcy, I should enquire about your family. Do you have any other cousins aside from Colonel Fitzwilliam?"

His face dropped, "Yes, the colonel has another brother, my cousin James, the Viscount Matlock, and we have another cousin in Kent, Anne de Bourgh. I am much closer to the Colonel, however, we grew up together, and spent much time at each other's homes." He took a deep breath, and continued, "As a matter of fact, he is co-guardian with myself, of my sister, Georgiana."

Elizabeth noted the slight change in tone when Mr. Darcy mentioned his cousin, the viscount, and also when he mentioned the Colonel, and it made her wonder at the difference. *It seems as though he does not have the same relationship with this 'James' that as he does with Colonel Fitzwilliam.*

"I see, and do you and the colonel ever have problems raising a young lady?" She saw Mr. Darcy's startled look upon his face, but was saved from making a response by that very same person.

"I say, what a delightful sight! How are you this morning, Miss Bennet? Darcy? Well…I hope." He smiled and bowed to her, then nodded his head towards Darcy. He then enquired of Elizabeth, "And is Miss Jane much improved this morning?"

Elizabeth and Mr. Darcy both acknowledged Colonel Fitzwilliam's greeting, and made their positive responses. They finished their breakfast with light conversation. Mr. Bingley joined the group before long, and upon seeing Elizabeth, immediately asked after Jane, "Miss Elizabeth, I am anxious to hear if Miss Bennet is showing any signs of improvement."

"She is, thank you Mr. Bingley, it would seem that her fever has broken and she has been resting since." Elizabeth noted a look of relief upon his anxious face. *He seems to have an honest concern, this bodes well for Jane.* A brief conversation amongst the whole group about the trials of having illness then transpired, and then Elizabeth excused herself to look in on Jane.

~*~*~*~

Later that day, Darcy sequestered himself in Netherfield's library. He attempted to avoid Miss Bingley and Miss Elizabeth, but for different reasons. Miss Bingley, no doubt, noticed his attraction to the newest addition to their party and, in response, became more insufferable with her sharp tongue and barbs aimed at Miss Elizabeth. He tried to avoid the latter due to that very same reason, feeling the risk of further attachment and exposing his further preference for her, should Miss Elizabeth be much more in his company. His physical response to her was undeniable, however.

This mornings tete-a-tete had been pleasant, perhaps a little too pleasant for his comfort. *Miss Elizabeth is becoming quite a danger to my peace of mind. How can she be so perceptive, yet sound so innocent? She may start to feel an attachment, if I do not check my attentions towards her. This is a dilemma…do I want to dissuade her from forming an attachment?*

The door to the library opened as Miss Elizabeth walked inside the room. At first, she did not seem to notice him as she proceeded to the shelves to peruse the sparse selection in Bingley's collection. She settled on a rather thick book; Darcy noted it to be a translation by Pope. *This is a pleasant surprise that I am not the only person within these walls to appreciate such works.*

When Miss Elizabeth approached the desk and chairs, she started as she looked up and saw Darcy sitting in a chair in the corner. Noting a pretty blush travel from her bosom up her face, Darcy felt tightness around his collar and heat traveling through him, unrelated to the fire nearby. He stood up and they awkwardly acknowledged each other, with Darcy finding his voice first. He gestured towards a chair across from him.

"Miss Bennet, please make yourself comfortable. I trust you found something in this sparse library to please your tastes?"

She looked at the offered chair with a raised eyebrow and replied, .Um...yes...Mr. Darcy, I thank you. This same volume is in my father's library, and although I have read it before, it has been some time ago." She moved to the chair and sat down. I always feel that where there are books, there is always something of interest that can be found, as one may see things in a different light when re-reading the same book, do you not think so?"

Sitting down across from her, he nodded, I could not agree with you more, Miss Bennet. I always refer to my books when I need to research estate management issues. Though I listened to my father and his stewards and read diligently, there always seemed to be things that I had forgotten, or missed with the first perusal. I suppose that is why my library is full of various books, but then I will not excuse the neglect of any library." He smiled at her, happy to be talking of books and finding that they seemed to share the same views.

Darcy saw her shiver and shift in her chair, then noted her eyes widening and a flush appearing on her face again. He asked with concern, "Are you cold, Miss Bennet? You may sit over here. This chair is closer to the fire." He gestured to the chair next to him.

She shook her head, "No, I am fine, Mr. Darcy. I shall be all right." She looked at him with what appeared to be an earnest interest, "Might I enquire, sir, how many volumes you have in your library? I assume it is quite vast."

"It is indeed, as it has been the work of many generations. I believe I can safely say that there are at least fifteen or twenty thousand volumes of a wide range of subjects there, quite possibly more."

He saw her eyes widen at his declaration, and her response was barely audible. I see, it must be quite a sight to behold."

"Yes, I suppose it is."

He smiled to himself, envisioning an image of her entering Pemberley's library, as he guided her through his home, but then he checked himself. *What am I thinking? Why does it seem such a confusing image? Much better her, than Anne or Caroline Bingley.*

Conversation dwindled as they both seemed to be lost in thought, and they spent another half hour in companionable silence.

Dinner proved to be a strained affair, after Miss Bingley found Darcy and Miss Elizabeth alone together in the library. Her behaviour towards Miss Elizabeth bordered on outright hostility. She did not appear to be able to stop herself when Miss Elizabeth addressed the colonel about his duties thus far with the army after they had finished their meal.

"I suppose the militias are quite a fascinating subject for *you*, Miss Eliza. Your relations seemed to be quite attentive to the officers last week at Sir William Lucas's." A sharp look accompanied the forced smile she gave to Miss Elizabeth.

Miss Elizabeth seemed to have understood her pointed remarks, for Darcy noted she responded in equal measure.

"Like my interests, my fascinations are just as varied. Our 'attentions' are meant to make to make all newcomers and guests to our neighbourhood feel welcome, Miss Bingley." Miss Elizabeth gave Miss Bingley a challenging look.

Miss Bingley ceased her attack on Miss Elizabeth. Darcy felt a sense of triumph for Elizabeth as he witnessed their sparring. Unfortunately, however, Miss Bingley continued her simpering attentions towards him, as he watched Miss Elizabeth with his cousin. He turned his attention back to his plate when Miss Bingley directed her attentions to him again.

"Really Mr. Darcy, what we have to tolerate! Such countrified manners and impertinence! Miss Eliza seems to delight in the attentions of Colonel Fitzwilliam, have you not noticed? She is just like her younger sisters, seeking the attentions of any man in a red coat." When Darcy refused to respond to her vitriol, she continued, I for one hope that *poor*, dear Jane recovers quickly. Not that I mind *her* company, but the impertinent behaviour of her sister is quite intolerable, do you not think?"

Darcy could not disagree with Miss Bingley more. He very much wanted her to leave him alone and quit her snipping comments about Miss Elizabeth. He did, however, note the attention Fitzwilliam was paying to Miss Elizabeth though, and just observing that made him squirm in his chair.

I have got to get Richard away from Miss Elizabeth. No good can come of his attentions towards her, and I could not bear to see her hurt by his perfidy. She deserves so much better than to be treated so infamously, yet she does not seem to mind his attentions towards her... in fact if I am not mistaken, she rather seems to enjoy his company. If only she knew his real habits and tendencies... yet I could not betray him... could I? Richard cannot afford to marry such a woman, yet he cannot or will not, it seems, stay away from Miss Elizabeth. Thinking about his cousin's numerous flirtatious looks directed at Miss Elizabeth that moment, Darcy asked silently, *what is it you are after Richard? Leave her to someone who will see the true worth in her!*

His reverie was broken when he heard laughter from the other end of the table, where Richard sat across from Elizabeth. Darcy burned with curiosity as to what had so amused them. They engaged in their own conversation, away from the others. *I know Richard too well to think this is just a passing fancy. He has never behaved in such a way with any other woman, and he is paying no heed to what I have told him. It is his usual flirtation, yet there is something more in his manner. That look in his eyes shows how much he desires her, but what to do about it other than confront him or threaten him with withholding financial support? He cannot afford to marry someone of her circumstances... and I will not allow him to offer anything else!*

The group separated after Bingley offered port to the gentlemen and Hurst accepted, leaving the ladies to go to the music room. When the gentlemen went to Bingley's study, Darcy's cousin avoided him, and Richard introduced lighter subjects that Bingley found interesting: hunting, fishing, and the Bennet ladies.

"I say Bingley, Netherfield is so much more... entertaining since we have the Bennet ladies to keep us company, albeit one of them is rather infirm, but I am sure she will be much improved from what Eliz... uh... Miss Elizabeth has said."

"Here! Here!" Bingley began, but Darcy stopped listening to them as he contemplated the meaning of his slip of the tongue.

Darcy gave his cousin a sharp look and wondered, *What is this with his using her given name... surely she has not granted him such liberties? No she would know better than that. None-the-less, I shall have to be diligent in keeping an eye on them both, when they are together or apart.* When Richard glanced at Darcy, he looked away and the subject was not discussed further.

The gentlemen joined the ladies and Richard requested that Miss Elizabeth play for them. She acquiesced and Darcy watched in dismay as his cousin volunteered to turn the pages for her. After several moments of surreptitiously observing them laughing and conversing, Darcy decided to approach them at the pianoforte.

As he came closer to the instrument, Elizabeth teased, "What brings you to our corner, Mr. Darcy? Do we disturb your peace, or did you come to request something more to your tastes?"

He smiled, and gazed directly at her, I am sure that you, Miss Bennet, are quite capable of choosing a piece of music that would easily suit my tastes."

Her smile faltered as she flushed and squirmed in her seat. Richard directed a questioning look at him, and then turned his attentions back to Elizabeth. "Perhaps, Miss Bennet, if we can get Miss Bingley or Mrs. Hurst to play for us, then I might have the pleasure to reclaim at least one dance, as you are still in my debt from last week. What say you to that?"

Elizabeth seemed rather nervous and looked up to Darcy, and then smiled towards Richard, declining politely, and using the excuse that she would be needed by Jane soon. Shortly thereafter, she left the gathering to ascend the stairs to her sister's chambers. *Thankfully she declined Richard's request to dance. Could it be that she realizes he is trifling with her?*

Darcy felt her absence keenly, when she left the room. He settled into a chair in the corner by the fireplace to read a book. Try as he may, he could not concentrate on the words. He contemplated the expression of the eyes on the face of a pretty woman instead.

~*~*~*~

The second full day that the eldest Bennet ladies were at Netherfield brought their mother to the house. Worse, the younger sisters came with her. The whole party could not stop gaping at the furnishings, and paintings, and all the fineries of the house. Mrs. Bennet sat in the main parlour after looking in on Miss Bennet, and commented on how well her 'dear Jane' was being taken care of at Netherfield, and how she would not likely get that much attention at Longbourn, if she had been at home.

Turning his attention away from the vulgarity of the mother, Richard glanced towards Elizabeth. He could identify a pretty flush upon her face that went all the way down to her neckline, which in turn caused him to flush, but for a different reason. Standing behind a tall chair, he watched her, barely paying attention to what was being said in general, and thought about her lovely white skin, and her beautiful eyes. It was a sight he went to sleep with and what he dreamed of in great detail each night since arriving at Netherfield. Just thinking about that made him more uncomfortable physically, and he was struck with the realization that perhaps that was why Darcy would be seen so frequently with his back to the window while in the company of that same lady.

He knew that his cousin disapproved of his becoming attached to her, but for some reason, he just could not resist her charms. *She is so unique...so very unlike the women of our society... the Miss Bingleys and Mrs. Hurst's. She is so innocent as well... oooohhhh, what it would be like to have her... if only I could be in James situation. He has nothing to worry over, other than overspending his weekly stipend on the gaming tables at places like Blake's. If I only had such an income, I would offer for her, and say to hell with whatever anyone else would have to say. I doubt that she would mind if we did not go into town. I think that perhaps even Darcy appreciates her...he does seem very attentive to her.*

As he thought about this, he could see Darcy watching him, but then he turned away. There was a commotion in the front foyer as an express rider came to the front entrance of Netherfield. Nichols came in shortly afterwards and said, "Here is an express for Colonel Fitzwilliam."

When he saw who it was from, he paled.

Chapter 8

As soon as Colonel Fitzwilliam saw Harriet Heatherton's writing on the missive, he knew it could not be good news. She would never dare to write to him unless there was a significant problem. The imperturbable Colonel found himself anxious to read the letter, but did not want to attract any more attention to himself than he had by receiving this missive. Smiling to the parlour full of people, he excused himself as politely and quickly as possible. I am sorry to have to leave this gathering, but it appears I have some business to attend to… so if you will excuse me, I shall see to it and return momentarily." He glanced towards Darcy.

Schooling his face to mask his concern, he bowed to the ladies, and with one last parting look towards Miss Elizabeth, he quit the room.

Once he reached his room, he tore open the letter, and his heart sank.

15th October 1811

My dear Richard,

I am forced to send this letter to you to inform you that the consequences of our liaisons have resulted in the conception of a child. I am quite certain, as I have felt the babe quicken. This was the most delightful sensation that I have ever felt, but it is sad when one reflects upon our present understanding, and the life our child will face. I cannot stay much longer within these living arrangements, at least not here in town. Dear Richard, do not be angry with me, I did not tell you any untruths about my being unable to conceive. My Albert and I were never able to conceive in our twelve years of marriage.

I write to you now to request your assistance in arranging these matters. Although I do not foresee you making an honest woman of me, I do require your support with the necessary arrangements for the remainder of my confinement, and support for this child as well. If I do not hear from you soon, I will be forced to bring this matter to the attention of the Earl.

Ever Yours,

Harriet

Richard paled and went into a cold sweat after reading the letter. He knew his father would be furious if he found out about his mistress having conceived his child. He feared disownment should it become common knowledge, as his father had a low tolerance for blemishes upon the family name.

Colonel Richard Fitzwilliam had always been dependent on financial support from his family. His father and Darcy were his biggest sources of financing, and though he made decent earnings as a colonel in his majesty's army, it did not provide for him in the manner that he had grown accustomed to throughout his life. He had been raised as the second son of the Earl of Matlock, and had never known what hardship was... nor did he intend to find out, either.

With a soldier's quick plotting, he formulated his plans to be away to town, and rang for his valet, Carsons, who could pack his things for the trip with great efficiency. *This whole affair could not have turned out worse! I must think about what to do! And, oh...Miss Elizabeth Bennet... how it will pain me to leave you behind, my lovely rose. No other woman could compare to you. If only I were not the second son, or had much fortune, things may have turned out differently!* His thoughts were interrupted when his man arrived in his dressing room.

"Carsons, I must away immediately. I have urgent business in town, and I need only bring the essentials, and the cache of my papers." He said distractedly. "Oh, and have the stables ready my horse, I need to get to town."

"Very good sir, how long will you be gone?" Carson's asked while assisting Fitzwilliam with his travel clothes, before summoning a servant to notify the stables.

"I am not certain, but you can send the rest of my things later, if I find that I will be there longer than a week."

"I shall see to it then, sir." He finished assisting the colonel, who had gone to his sitting room to gather some papers. Soon afterwards, he sent Carsons to deliver a message to Darcy. He felt knots in his stomach, worried over what Darcy's response would be.

There was a strong knock on the door. "Enter."

Darcy walked in with an alarmed look upon his face, which Richard knew would grow into one of his cousin's most fearsome scowls."

"Richard, what is it? What is the matter? Has something happened?"

The colonel looked at Darcy with a deep frown and took a long breath." Yes, something has happened, though nothing as dire as you may have imagined. I received a letter from Harriet that contains startling news. It appears that she has conceived, and claims it to be mine. She is threatening to go to the Earl if I do not step up to her."

Darcy drew in a deep breath, "So what is it you intend to do? She must know that if she goes to the Earl, she could be set out, unless she has solid proof that you are the responsible party. I cannot believe she would think to make such threats, unless she does have solid proof. I would also think that she must know that you can ill afford to marry her, and that your father would cut you off if you did."

Colonel Fitzwilliam nodded his head and stared out the window." Yes, she is well aware of all that… she is no fool. She has written as much, but she still begs assistance to be moved from town, and for support of this child. As far as proof, I can think of very few people who are aware of our association… unless…."

"Unless what? Are they a reliable source? Not that it matters, if you truly are the responsible party. You should assume responsibility, though I can see that may be difficult, given your circumstances." The derision in Darcy's voice did not go unnoticed by the colonel.

"As far as the reliability... yes, James is aware of our... relationship. Though I have been the model of discretion, James managed to find me coming and going from her residence more than a few times. As far as being the responsible party... there is a fair chance. Harriet convinced me that she was barren, so we never took the proper precautions." He looked down towards his boots, and then glanced at Darcy with a pensive expression.

"She wrote that if I do not respond soon, she will notify my father...I cannot allow her to do that. I am not yet sure of what to do, but I must be away to town, and soon." The colonel paced to and fro, looking down at the floor, frowning, and trying to think his way through this mess.

Taking a deep breath, he looked at Darcy, and hesitated before beginning again, I know you must think me the lowest sort of rake, but might you be able to allow me to stay at Grovesnor Square when I go to town? I think it might be difficult to arrange these things from Matlock House."

"I do not want my servants exposed to such goings on Richard, though they are very loyal, I should not like to think them feeling as if I support this... this... behaviour!" Darcy looked at his cousin with a sharp glare. I cannot condone your behaviour. I was taught to abhor deceit of every kind. My father lectured me about my responsibilities and to take them seriously! I would never trifle with a lady, nor risk such consequences with a widow no matter her charms."

"No one would *ever* accuse you of shirking your responsibilities, but I am a mere mortal, who does not have the advantage of wealth such as you have. Look I would not have your servants think you are condoning anything, but I cannot arrange anything from my father's house... especially not with my brother nosing around. He always finds things out... and if he did, you can well imagine the results."

Looking pleadingly to Darcy, he continued, "Look, if I can just get things figured out, that is all that I ask of you. I will tell the servants that I have come to town on business matters, and that I do not need the distractions of Matlock House. That is truth enough."

Darcy wore a pensive expression, "Yes, that is only sensible, but you must see to those other issues as well."

"Do you have any thoughts about where I may be able to hide her away... at least for awhile? What about a cottage on your Uncle Darcy's estate? It is far enough away from Derbyshire, and if I need to travel there, it is still close enough not to be a burden".

".A burden to you? Richard, can you not think of anyone else but yourself? Good G-d man, you are acting as if you are the only one put out by the consequence of your behaviour! What of Mrs. Heartherton? Can you not imagine what it is like for her to have to remove to a place wholly foreign to her? To have the person you thought you could trust with such intimacies cast you off as if you were yesterday's newspaper? You should think about that! I cannot believe you! Why should I go to so much trouble with someone who is so very selfish?"

"Yes, I comprehend you, Darcy. I do not deserve your help... but Harriet does. Look... I will not pretend that I do not deserve the punishment I receive for this. You are right, I did not think of anyone else. Now I have to think, and I cannot do it with my parents and James breathing down my neck and looking over my shoulder. I want to at least help her leave town, and I have no other ideas as to where to remove her to. So I beg of you to provide me temporary assistance, and then I will stop asking for more favours from you".

Darcy looked at him as if he was skeptical, I may be able to arrange for her to be moved to one of the cottages on the Lancashire Estate, but mind you, I am only considering this for the sake of the babe, for it is innocent in all of this business."

Darcy fell silent for a moment before shaking his head, I cannot believe I am doing this but... perhaps after we arrange for her removal, we can make other preparations. I shall write to my steward to make the necessary provisions, and I will send you an express when all of the arrangements have been finalized," he said with a scowl.

"Thank you for your assistance, Darcy. I know it is difficult for you to involve yourself in such matters. I do not know how I will ever repay you."

Darcy raised an eyebrow, "The only thing I ask, Richard, is that you endeavor never to repeat such behaviour ... although I doubt you will... change over the long term. If I ever hear about the continuance of such behaviour, the Earl and James will be the least of your worries, understood?"

Richard Fitzwilliam nodded his head, "Understood." He felt thankful that he had managed to get this concession out of Darcy.

Richard and Darcy then parted company.

The Colonel finished packing what belongings he deemed necessary, and within a quarter hour, he had everything he needed in order to start dealing with his mess. Darcy sent a letter to his steward to enlist his help in this debacle as well.

~*~*~*~

Darcy needed to marshal his thoughts as he tried to compose a letter to his steward, Mr. Barker. His first thought was how unjust this was for him to have to clean up after his cousin yet again. *I cannot believe that I am now facing the onerous task of hiding all the evidence to Richard's licentiousness! How has it managed to come to this?* He was not like this before... Finding himself becoming resentful in forming his missive, he began:

18th October 1811

Mr. Barker,

I have need of your services in securing housing for a person needing my assistance. I thought that I could keep them on my Lancashire Estate, Slatemore, for the time being, and that you may be able to open the west cottage there. This would be a good resolution to our concerns regarding the neglect towards that quarter of the property, and I am sending my cousin, Colonel Fitzwilliam, to escort this person as soon as possible to take up this cause. I require that they be well supplied with necessities, as I anticipate need for lodging for some time to come. Please direct any further questions to Colonel Fitzwilliam, as he will be seeing to the arrangements for this person's removal from town.

F. Darcy

There, that should do it, as it says so much yet so little, although I think Barker is intelligent enough to figure out some things. I doubt anyone else who reads this should be able to decipher its meaning.

I will of course, need to give Richard a copy, as he should arrive there before the letter. Barker may think it odd to receive two missives, however, he will at least know enough to resist asking many questions, and will be very discreet while he takes care of business.

Darcy knew that his staff was loyal to him, and would not dare question his motives, but this still galled him as he had no choice but to deceive his staff. He leaned back in his chair with some relief that at last his cousin would now be out of his way. *I did not even have to do anything... he did this to himself! I hope he learns from this...if it was me, I would have never forgiven myself for giving up a chance to earn Miss Elizabeth's admiration!*

Darcy delivered a missive to Richard just before his cousin departed. I hope that you can get things in good order, Richard. Be sure to use the utmost discretion, as I will not endure my staff making speculations about your activities and your motivations for being there instead of staying at Matlock House."

"I will do my very best, after all, it will be my head on the chopping block should this get out." After a brief moment of hesitation, he said, "Oh, and before I go... for what it is worth, I thank you for all that you have done for me, Darcy. I only wish things did not work out this way."

Darcy raised an eyebrow, "Believe me, I would not wish this on anyone, Richard, not even you. Now you must be off."

"Richard nodded, "Goodbye then, Darcy."

Darcy watched his cousin descend in the direction of the servant's stairway, partly to ensure that he was not observed and partly to make certain that he would *finally* be gone from Netherfield. He turned to go to his sitting room and gather his other letter to Mr. Barker to mail today. He had left his rooms in a preoccupied state, and headed towards the main staircase when he ran in to none other than Elizabeth Bennet. He managed to catch her before she fell back, and he felt his heart racing, unsure whether due to fright or the fact that he was holding the woman he had been dreaming of for some weeks in his arms.

"Oh! I am deeply sorry, Miss Bennet. Please allow me to apologize. I failed to realize where I was going."

"I am quite fine, Mr. Darcy. Is everything alright with Colonel Fitzwilliam?" She asked with a hint of concern and a pretty flush. He realized she was still in his arms. He reluctantly let her go.

Darcy blushed scarlet and looked away, feeling uncomfortable with the situation, and a little annoyed that Miss Elizabeth still seemed to show some... feeling for his cousin, "It is at the moment, madam, but he has been called away on some urgent business. I was on my way to post a missive for him when I came upon you. I am very sorry about my lack of attention." He took perverse pleasure in the fact that Richard would be gone from Netherfield for the foreseeable future.

She smiled at him, I thank you, sir, but I am quite alright. I hope it is nothing too serious?"

Elizabeth looked up at him with her bright eyes and he could not help but smile, "Nothing that cannot be resolved with time." He flushed again, "Um, now if you will excuse me, I must see to this letter."

She nodded, "Of course, I shall not delay you."

She curtseyed to him, and they parted ways at the landing. She walked past him towards her sister's rooms as Darcy watched her before he descended the stairs to send off his letter. *Richard, you have no idea what favour you have done me with this.* Suddenly he checked himself, *this is not the best solution though, and I hope no one discovers my previous support of his behaviour!* He shook his head and went to deliver the letter he had been carrying.

~*~*~*~

Two days later, Jane recovered enough from her illness to join them downstairs for a short period of time after dinner. While Mr. Bingley busied himself by seeing to her comfort, both Elizabeth and Mr. Darcy observed his attentions towards Jane. Elizabeth looked over to Mr. Darcy and enquired about his earlier comments, regarding his guardianship of his sister.

"Mr. Darcy, do you see your sister very often?"

"Yes, as often as I can, but we are apart as often as not, as I have estate business to attend to and she has her studies to concentrate on."

She noted how he seemed to regard her, with his soft brown eyes, as the harshness that she would have imagined was not there, "Is she at home, then, in town or at your family's estate?"

"She spends most of her time with her studies in town, as she has easier access to the masters there."

"And, is she all alone there? Or does she have friends there to look after her?"

"She has a companion, Mrs. Annesley, and though she does have a few family friends, I am the one who sees to her needs. You see, she is quite shy, and it is rather difficult for her to make new friends. I do try to ease her loneliness, but it is quite difficult being the guardian to a sister nearly twelve years my junior."

Elizabeth started to feel sympathy for this man, whom she had previously thought of as distant, haughty, and above his company. She supposed that, perhaps, here was a man orphaned at a young age, and left to care for a much younger sister, without much assistance other than hired help. This encapsulated a new side to him that she had not contemplated before. She gave him a compassionate look, and replied, I see, it must be very difficult indeed. I could not begin to imagine what that must be like. I for one always wished to have an elder brother to look after me, but I am quite satisfied with my dear Jane."

She belatedly added, "And my other sister's of course." *Though not so much as Jane.*

"I cannot imagine living in a house with so many sisters. Tell me, Miss Bennet, are all your sisters as close to each other as you and Miss Jane are?"

"Yes and no. We are all quite different, though fairly close in age, we each hold different interests and temperaments. We are, however, fiercely protective of one another."

Smiling he said, I understand perfectly. You seem to have a great many talents as well. Does every one of your sisters have as many talents as you?"

Elizabeth blushed and laughed at his compliments. She was in a fair way towards thinking him as amiable as his cousin. *He is so kind, and ... complimentary. I would never have guessed that there was this side to such a man!*

"Not quite so many 'talents', I do play and sing as does my sister Mary, and Jane is almost as avid a reader as me, but we prefer different subjects for reading material. It does add variety though... May I ask if Miss Darcy has similar tastes to her brother?"

Darcy smiled and said, "We enjoy many of the same things, though our abilities are much different. Georgiana is quite accomplished at the pianoforte as she practices a great deal. We also read about the same amount, however, our interests are different."

Elizabeth felt something akin to delight in his sincere attentions towards her, and could not but be pleased that a man like Mr. Darcy could take such an interest in her...thoughts, and ideas. *He seems so... tender and sweet.*

She wanted to talk with him more regarding his sister and their relationship, and maybe even... other subjects. She started to feel a desire to know this reserved man whom she previously believed to be severe and distant, and so she encouraged Darcy to continue on in the same vein for another twenty minutes, while Miss Bingley stared at them the whole time. They both silently acknowledged her observation of them, while continuing with their tete-a tete. Miss Bingley had a frown plastered to her face as she watched them. This delighted Elizabeth, as Caroline Bingley had been rude to the point of incivility throughout her stay at Netherfield. Their conversation was interrupted when Miss Bingley invited Elizabeth to play on the pianoforte, which she accepted.

Elizabeth felt delighted when Mr. Darcy offered to turn the pages of the music for her, and when he stood next to her, she felt a warm sensation, which she could not explain, given her distance from the chimney. His nearness affected her more than it ever had before, and she could not meet his eyes. She breathed a sigh of relief when the evening came to an end, as she could go to her room and reflect on her reactions to this new side of Mr. Darcy in private, without the glaring eyes of Caroline Bingley.

After a restless night of reflection, Elizabeth was relieved that Jane had recovered enough to take Mr. Bingley's carriage home. She struggled to sort through her newfound sensations while near one of Netherfield's residents, and *Miss Bingley is becoming even more catty, making more and more snide remarks aimed at me. Everyone seems to feel uncomfortable, and Mr. Darcy is acting... different!*

Chapter 9

They had yet to enter the vestibule when Mr. Bennet expressed his relief that Elizabeth and Jane had returned to Longbourn. Elizabeth knew it must have been a trial for him to endure Lydia and Kitty running around talking about soldiers and balls, and Mrs. Bennet shouting about her poor nerves and her 'fluttering heart'. Then, to top it all off, to hear Mary sermonizing about the evils of dancing and lusting after the red coats.

She and her father were of like mind, often amused at the ridiculous, and shared the enjoyment of watching the follies of others. In this kindred spirit, Mr. Bennet shared with Elizabeth, and the rest of his family, the contents of a letter from his cousin, a Mr. William Collins, who would inherit Longbourn upon his death. Mr. Collins had written to inform them that he intended to visit and would be 'offering an olive branch' in commiseration for the disagreement that Mr. Bennet had with his father.

Elizabeth felt both incensed and amused at the man's odd letter. She was curious as to what kind of man he would turn up to be, with such a long lettered apology for inheriting Longbourn, and praise for his 'noble' patroness that he repeated throughout his letter. *This letter demonstrated servility and pomposity in his manner of address. He cannot be a sensible man. I wonder at the name, though. Mr. Darcy said he had a cousin by the name of Anne de Bourgh in Kent. Could it be that father's cousin is the parson to his aunt? What kind of woman would have such a silly man as her vicar?* She did not have long to wait to judge for herself, as he meant to join them within a fortnight.

Mr. Collins arrived and was disposed to talk enough for both himself and Mr. Bennet, who did not wish to talk at all. At dinner that first evening, their cousin proved to be a source of great amusement, particularly when Mr. Bennet asked about his noble patroness, Lady

Catherine de Bourgh. Mr. Collins waxed eloquent on his praise of the woman.

He smiled as he informed them of her attentions to him, "Ah, yes…Lady Catherine has had me to dine twice at least, and has asked me to stay and play quadrille with her to make up a pool. Some people may view her as proud, but I have never seen anything but affability in her address." He stopped to swallow his boiled potatoes, then began again, "She has even condescended to visit me in the parsonage, and has given me suggestions about organizing the closets… she suggested some shelves in the closets upstairs." He exclaimed with great pride.

I wish to ask the man about his patroness and her daughter… what are they like, but, I fear that I shall not receive an unimpeachable opinion, as he seems to think that his position in life means that he should defer his opinions to theirs. He is such a silly man, it is unfortunate that our estate will be wasted on such a man! I will not dare ask him any questions as it would arouse suspicions from papa, or even Jane. Elizabeth did not want to speculate on her reasons for her curiosity, therefore she pushed these thoughts out of her mind.

Mr. Collins droned on, "Mrs. Bennet, I should like to take this opportunity to compliment you upon your fine table, and such a lovely room for which to dine, it is very…elegant, much like that of Rosings Park, yes, yes, that is what this room reminds me of. It is made even lovelier with such… lovely daughters that you have."

"Oh, Mr. Collins, that is so very kind of you to say. I thank you, it does take much planning to have such fine and elegant meals prepared, and I have often spoke of this to my girls. I have been trying to impress upon them that when they find such a fine and eligible gentleman, they will have to be able to manage to plan such fine dinners as well! I think that, as lovely as they are they should have those accomplishments that would make them fine wives as well… do you not agree?"

A smiling Mr. Collins responded, "Oh, why…yes, in fact my patroness…"

Elizabeth fought to contain her mirth as their cousin expounded on about the noble lady's opinions, all the while trying to avoid her father's gaze with his accompanying smirk. She said a silent prayer to help her endure the rest of the evening. *This is enough to predispose mama towards liking him. I wonder how soon it will be before she tries to match one of us with him. I hope it is not me, for I could never tolerate such a silly man, nor could I esteem him! He cannot hide his insincere compliments, and only seems interested in his patroness for her wealth and consequence. What a trial this shall turn out to be!*

She sat at the table listening with a smile, still trying to contain her mirth, which showed in her eyes. Mr. Collins seemed to be winding down with his last praise of his patroness, "...Lady Catherine takes prodigious care of all those in her care." He drawled.

As she listened, she became even more amused at how the man showed himself to be ridiculous. *Such servility, such...such insensibility.*

Elizabeth remained curious to hear anything interesting about the esteemed family, yet dared not ask. She noticed that Mr. Collins seemed to delight in the attention she paid to his conversation. As a result, he directed much of his conversation to her, from there on out until after dinner. He seemed to leer at her, at times during dinner, as he sat next to her at the dinner table. *He is so improper, I wonder that his patroness has him to dinner, but of course, he likely does not leer at her!*

Elizabeth frowned at his attentions towards her, but she had to smile as she thought of her father and understood his motivation. Mr. Bennet made his escape to his study, leaving her with a gleeful smile as Mr. Collins indicated he would be more than happy to read to them. His choice was Fordyce's sermons, after the younger girls proposed novels were rejected. *He reads in such a solemn tone, as if he was at a funeral!*

Mrs. Bennet and Lydia were talking of some gossip in Meryton, and as Elizabeth listened, she laughed, which affronted Mr. Collins as much as their gossiping, and he stopped reading.

"Oh I am sorry sir, I had just overheard my mother and Lydia talking... please continue."

"My dear cousin, it would seem that no one else has found any inspiration in this reading, thus I shall not bother with it any longer. Perhaps we could just sit and... um... talk?"

Elizabeth could think of many things that she would rather do, starting with sticking her embroidery pins in her fingers... multiple times, rather than talk with him. I think you might enjoy some conversation with my mother, as she could describe to you what it is like to... run this household, would that not be beneficial to you, sir?"

His face froze but then he smiled, "Why...yes, my dear Cousin Elizabeth, that is a very good idea, as you are aware that one of these days, I shall be the master here, and what better way to know how things are managed, then to talk with its current mistress." He eyed her before going over to talk with Mrs. Bennet.

Thank goodness, I never thought I would be so happy to hear Lydia and momma gossiping. Maybe with some well placed conversation directed at them, we can keep Mr. Collins sermonizing at bay while he stays here, but how to redirect his attentions?

Much to her chagrin, Mr. Collins would not be deterred from attending Elizabeth that evening. He stayed near her, discussing his parsonage in Kent and his noble patroness until she thought she was neigh on going mad. She thought it a rather high price to have to pay to learn about Darcy's family, but still... she could not resist listening. Her mind drifted at the thought of Darcy's family members. *Are there very many? Would it not be a strange coincidence if they were Mr. Darcy's relations? Why am I still so interested in him... them?* After another thirty minutes, they all parted to retire for the evening.

The next morning, Elizabeth came in from her morning walk, and she happened upon Mrs. Bennet in a tete-a-tete with Mr. Collins. She had little interest in her mother's usual gossip, but when she overheard her name, she did pay attention.

"My dear sir, it is incumbent upon me to hint that Lizzy may very soon become engaged, and we also suspect that my dear Jane may be engaged very soon as well, but of my other daughters I cannot say for certain, but I know of no attachments." Mrs. Bennet said in her louder than normal whisper to a frowning Mr. Collins.

"Ah, I see... well then, I will endeavor to find a suitable bride from amongst one of my other cousins, as my patroness, Lady Catherine, feels that as a man of the church, it is best to show good family values, and in order to demonstrate this, it is best done with a wife." He stopped for a moment, "T'is a pity though, as Cousin

Elizabeth has much good sense, and showed the proper amount of interest in such distinguished personages as the most excellent Lady Catherine de Bourgh. As my bride, she would have much distinction, you know, but... I do have three other cousins from which to choose."

Elizabeth felt relief wash over her when she heard her mother turn Mr. Collins' attentions away from her, but when she heard her mother's proclamations as to her supposed engagement, she was disconcerted. Her mother liked to think that she would make a good match for Colonel Fitzwilliam, but he was now out of town, and there was no way of knowing when, or even if, he would return. Her thoughts wandered back to the drawing room and library of Netherfield, and then settled on another gentleman.

At the breakfast table, Elizabeth noticed that Mr. Collins paid her less attention, and instead directed his attentions towards Mary.

"Cousin Mary, Mrs. Bennet tells me that you have been studying Fordyce's Sermons. Do you read other similar works as well?"

Mary sat there staring at him before acknowledging her preferences. "Yes, sir, that has been my lifelong work, to seek the word of the lord through many different works, and I feel that is one of the best published volumes, as it relates to proper conduct of the fairer sex."

Elizabeth wanted to roll her eyes at Mary's declaration, but fought the urge as she thanked her maker for diverting their cousin's attentions away from her. Unfortunately, she still would have to tolerate the man's company, as Mr. Bennet asked their cousin if he would like to join the girls on a walk to Meryton. Mr. Collins was quick to accept this invitation and they were soon off to the main road towards the town.

It would seem that Mr. Collins has found a kindred spirit in Mary, as they both prefer the church teachings and stories with a moral base, even preferring Fordyce's Sermons. She even seems to defer to his opinions about certain passages in her texts and I am almost certain no woman of sense would defer to that man's opinions... about anything. Elizabeth watched as they walked side by side and talked... animatedly about various church doctrines. They seemed to enjoy themselves. Elizabeth, with the rest of her sisters, walked past the pair towards town, as they talked and lagged farther and farther behind.

They arrived in Meryton before Mr. Collins and Mary caught up with them, and by that time, they met up with Mr. Denny and a new friend who was to join the regiment. When the regiment came to town, they were one of the first families to be introduced to all of the officers, mostly due to Mrs. Bennet's urgings, and so they knew every one of them. The gentleman that arrived the day previous was introduced as Mr. George Wickham. She noted his tall, handsome figure and pleasing manner of address, as well as his engaging conversation. They entered into a light discussion of the county when she noticed Mr. Bingley and Mr. Darcy come riding through town.

Mr. Bingley stopped when he came upon them and engaged Jane in conversation. "Hello, Miss Bennet, Miss Elizabeth, Miss Mary, Miss Catherine, and Miss Lydia."

They nodded their heads, and Mr. Bingley dismounted his horse to come over to where Jane stood. "We were just on our way to Longbourn to enquire on your health Miss Bennet, when we came upon you, were we not, Darcy?"

Mr. Darcy nodded his head in acknowledgement to Mr. Bingley, and then looked at Elizabeth, but when his eyes landed on Mr. Wickham, his face paled and he frowned. Elizabeth happened to glance at Mr. Wickham as his face was very flushed while he looked towards Mr. Darcy. *They obviously are acquainted, and from the looks of it there must be some unpleasant history.*

~*~*~*~

Darcy dismounted from his horse when he saw who it was that stood by Miss Elizabeth, as a sudden protective urge came over him. *That profligate has the audacity to tip his hat to me! And what the devil is he doing here? Of all the places to meet him again! Why is he standing next to her?*

Realizing that Elizabeth saw the reaction to their meeting, he took a few more steps towards her and barely acknowledged Wickham, who backed away as Darcy approached. He advanced to

Elizabeth's side, and placed himself between Wickham and her, causing Wickham to step closer to Miss Lydia.

He turned his attention towards Elizabeth, "Miss Elizabeth, I hope we find you well today." He stole a glance at his old enemy.

She looked back at the two gentlemen and raised her eyebrow, "Ah...yes, Mr. Darcy, we are all well. We were just walking into town with our cousin when we came upon Mr. Denny and Mr. Wickham."

He felt the tension leave him, as he realized she had not known him as anything more than a passing acquaintance. *At least he has not had a chance to tell her his tale of woe, and poison her against me! I see. Were you enjoying your walk?" Why is it that I cannot find the words to engage her in an interesting conversation as easily as that scoundrel is likely to?* He chastised himself.

"Yes, we came for a little shopping and to show our cousin, Mr. Collins...." She nodded towards the gentleman.... "the town. He has come from Kent. He is the parson to Lady Catherine de Bourgh."

Darcy regarded the man, *he does not seem too sensible, though Aunt Catherine prefers her clergy to be odious, cloying, and servile... wait, did she say he is her cousin?* Darcy said to her, "Really? That is quite a coincidence, as Lady Catherine is my aunt. She resides at her estate, Rosings Park, in Kent." He threw another glance toward the greasy looking man.

When he looked back to Elizabeth, she appeared to be studying him and Wickham, and he could not help but be pleased that she had rested her eyes upon him.

"Our cousin has a great deal of respect for Lady Catherine. He tells us she takes prodigiously good care of all those under her charge, and is quite attentive."

He smiled at her teasing conversation, more than happy that she focused her attentions solely upon him now, *I have no doubt about that, she is quite attentive to everyone under her supervision."*

She has such a delightful expression, with so much amusement written in her eyes.

"Yes, he says she has even condescended to give him advice as to how to arrange his closets. Now that *is* quite attentive, would you not agree, Mr. Darcy?"

Darcy could not break his gaze into her eyes, and he could see her dark pools, staring at him with so much merriment. He was about to respond to her when Bingley addressed him.

"Well, Darcy, we should be on our way back to Netherfield, so these lovely ladies can get back to their shopping before luncheon."

Bingley mounted his horse and Darcy glanced at him, before returning his gaze to Elizabeth again and said softly, "It was good to see you... all of you, this morning. Good day."

He bowed low to her and less to the others, then mounted his horse. As he rode away, he chanced another glance back to see her watching him, and he felt such a swell of pride in his breast. *So much loveliness before me... yes Sir William, you were correct about that!* Suddenly, he saw Wickham regarding Elizabeth with interest. It took all of his self control not to turn around and ride back and thrash George Wickham for even looking at her. Darcy vowed right then to see to Elizabeth's safety from the rogue one way or another.

~*~*~*~

George Wickham regained his bearings after coming face to face with his former childhood friend. After he had left Ramsgate, he did not think he would ever see Darcy again. He was relieved that Darcy did not run him through, after the last time they met in the same manner.

That was when he had left the Darcy's in Ramsgate, after the disastrous Georgiana elopement scheme was thwarted. *Of all of the places to meet with Darcy! Of all the luck, and just when things were getting interesting!* Wickham thought he would be lucky not to be called out right then, while he was standing next to Elizabeth. *What is that about Darcy, standing between the lovely Miss Elizabeth and myself? It is not like you would deign to pursue such a country nobody.*

Wickham feared that Darcy would reveal his past behavior to all of Meryton. *Would he dare tell her about Ramsgate? He would not say such things, though, as it would involve exposing his dear Georgiana!*

He regretted not getting his hands on her thirty thousand pound dowry and avenging himself on Darcy. That had occupied his thoughts for a long time. I *should have succeeded with the elopement. It was such a good plan too. Darcy always did have impeccable timing, always showing up at the worst possible moment!* Still lost in thought, he missed part of Denny's question.

"What was that Denny? I was thinking about last summer."

"I asked what you thought about the Bennet ladies? Really! You must be lost. I have never seen you turn down an opportunity to wax eloquent on such fine specimens of womanhood. I should say those ladies are quite fine. What say you?" Denny asked with his eyebrows moving in a suggestive manner.

Wickham laughed, I should concur with your assessment, Denny, especially Miss Elizabeth." He took a deep breath, then let it out slowly while shaking his head. "Now that is one fine young lady! Have you ever seen such liveliness, or such playful manners? And, oh my, those eyes! Such expressive eyes, and that light and pleasing figure, not to mention her more than ample bosom!"

"If I did not know you better, Wickham, I would say that you are in a fair way of losing your heart to the lady."

"My heart, Denny, shall remain unengaged. She is, however, pleasing enough to find amusement while I pass the time here."

They both laughed, but then Wickham fell silent. *Why must I allow Darcy to spoil my fun? I may enjoy the company of whomever I wish! He was always looking over my shoulder at Cambridge, and he was ever the prig. He should have been intended for the church, not me! Why, he could not enjoy his wealth and privilege as it was meant to be enjoyed!* Wickham resented the unfairness of it all.

Now here they were again, face to face, and in the unlikeliest of places. Wickham had noted the party of beautiful young ladies approaching him and Denny. He was hardly the sort of man, who would turn away an opportunity to socialize with ladies, much less ones that were quite pretty. He thought the two oldest Bennet ladies were exceptional beauties, particularly Miss Elizabeth. *She is a most singular young woman.*

Darcy was ever protective of her. He has never stood so close to a lady... well, maybe Georgiana, but then she is his sister. He continued to muse about the encounter on the walkway, pondering it from another view. He stopped walking, however, when another thought hit him. *Darcy would never have stood so close to another female, not even in town, with all those rich heiresses with all their wealth and consequence. He did not need that though, as he has a fortune and connections. Why would he care to stand so close, unless...? Could it be that the imperturbable Darcy had a tender regard for this country Miss?*

Wickham had seen the looks that Darcy and Elizabeth exchanged and felt it unusual as Darcy had never before acted in such a way with a woman. He also knew that Darcy would stop at nothing to attain what he wanted, as he could afford the finer things in life. *What a lark, Darcy falling for a country Miss, when he could have the best the ton could offer! Though I cannot fault him for his taste, she is lovely.*

Wickham did not fail to notice Elizabeth's light conversation and teasing manners. *She nearly had Darcy laughing in public! Could she also have some regard for Darcy? Well of course she would! What woman could resist a man worth as much as Darcy? She would be a fool to refuse such a wealthy gentleman! Ah, but what if Darcy was denied this?* With this last thought, Wickham walked happily towards the militia's encampment plotting his next course of action.

Chapter 10

Elizabeth reflected upon the 'chance' meeting of Mr. Bingley and Mr. Darcy, as she made her way through the shops in Meryton. Though she was not one to listen to idol gossip, she very much wished to know what had happened between Mr. Darcy and Major Wickham. She thought back to their discourse, and tried to make some sense of the unspoken gestures the gentlemen gave each other during their encounter.

~*~*~*~

She watched as Mr. Darcy and Mr. Bingley rode towards Netherfield, before she turned her attention back to Mr. Wickham, I am sorry for having neglected you, Mr. Wickham. I find it difficult to attend to so many amiable conversationalists. My mind often wanders in several different directions, and it is difficult to concentrate on them all."

"I could not agree with you more, Miss Elizabeth. I too find it difficult to attend more than one conversation at a time myself. I try to concentrate on the most interesting conversation and attend to that speaker." He directed a thoughtful gaze at her.

"I also found it interesting to see my old friend, Fitzwilliam Darcy, in Hertfordshire. May I ask, do you know if he has business here in Hertfordshire?"

She looked at him with great interest, but did not dare offer more information than she felt was prudent. "Nothing in particular, other than lending a hand to Mr. Bingley, with the running of his estate. He leased Netherfield Park."

"I see. Then, Darcy is still the ever attentive friend to those worthy few."

Elizabeth was taken aback by his response, but chose not to show her surprise at such an insinuation. "Yes, he is quite attentive to his friends, and I should say that Mr. Bingley is a worthy man. Mr. Bingley, I think, is lucky to have such a friend as Mr. Darcy." She showed no offence as she responded to Mr. Wickham's pointed remark with her playful manner and a raised eyebrow.

The party broke up soon after, and Elizabeth joined her sister and Mr. Collins. *Well that was very interesting! But what to make of Mr. Darcy's and Mr. Wickham's reactions to each other? They must be acquainted with each other... Mr. Wickham acknowledged as much, but Mr. Darcy seemed to want nothing to do with Mr. Wickham.* She walked along side Jane, and did not attend to anything but her thoughts until Mr. Collins addressed her.

"Cousin Elizabeth, did my ears deceive me? Was that gentleman, Mr. Fitzwilliam Darcy, the distinguished nephew of my most noble patroness?"

"Yes indeed, sir, he is..."

"I did not even acknowledge him as is most fitting of a most distinguished personage as Mr. Darcy! What will Lady Catherine say if she finds that I did not address him? Why did you not interrupt me when we were talking with those other gentlemen?" Mr. Collins said in obvious distress.

"Mr. Collins, I am sure that Lady Catherine will over look your lack of address to her nephew. You see, he told me that he had some other business to attend to," she lied, "so I am sure you will be forgiven."

"Dear me, I hope this is so, Cousin Elizabeth. I would not want to inadvertently offend Lady Catherine or her nephew. That would not do." He fretted, shifting from one foot to the other.

"I am sure you will continue in her good graces, sir." She said, hoping that would end this ridiculous conversation.

Mr. Collins is such a fool! Why would anyone think to ingratiate themselves to their patroness' nephew? It would make sense to do so towards someone closer to her... like her son or daughter, but not a nephew! I am relieved that he stopped paying his addresses to me. I cannot think what I would have to endure of mama's ranting, should

I have to turn down an offer from him. They continued on towards the milliner, and then the book shop before heading home, all the while Elizabeth tried to avoid being addressed any further by their cousin.

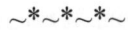

~*~*~*~

Darcy rode in silence towards Netherfield, not paying any attention to Bingley's chattering about his 'angel'. Finally, after Bingley said to Darcy, I say, Darcy, I think Caroline is planning a private dinner with you and her tonight in her sitting room." Darcy looked up in surprise.

"What? Bingley you are not…?" Darcy sputtered with alarm.

"No, I am not serious, Darcy. I just wanted to see how long it took for you to acknowledge the rest of the world." Bingley laughed.

Darcy took a deep breath of relief, I am sorry for my distraction. I just happened upon someone whom I never wished to see again: George Wickham, who has been a thorn in my side these last few years, and recently caused some difficulty for myself and my family."

"Oh, yes, I remember you talking about him. So that was the rogue who caused so much trouble at Ramsgate. You would not know it from his engaging manners… Oh lord… Darcy, you will not believe this, but I have issued a general invitation to all of the officers for the ball next week. I wonder what can be done now, to keep him from attending? Do you think I should…?"

"Do not trouble yourself, Bingley, he knows that we are friends, and I am sure he knows that I am staying at Netherfield. He will not dare show his face, as he knows that I shall deal with him should he be so foolish." Darcy looked straight ahead with cold fury.

"Well, if you say so. I will trust your judgment."

"Yes, he knows better than that. If he does not, he will *never* forget the lesson I will teach him."

"Now look here, I do not want any trouble…"

"Do not worry. I will not cause a scene. I know how to deal with him. After all, I have had years of experience."

Why was George Wickham, of all people, standing on the walkway talking to Elizabeth? Darcy was all too aware of Wickham's mannerisms around women, and what he saw did not please him. That is why he approached her. He felt the need to separate her from Wickham, for he recognized that feral look in Wickham's eyes as he gazed upon Elizabeth. It infuriated him and all he could think about was how much he wanted to strangle him.

I must find a way to warn Elizabeth about him, but how? I do not dare risk exposing Georgiana to censure. How can I get her aside from everyone to warn her away from him? She must be informed about Wickham's profligate tendencies. I cannot allow him to harm her or her family, especially the younger girls! They have no sense, and will be easy targets for Wickham's seductions!

As he rode on towards Netherfield, he thought about Elizabeth morning walks. *Perhaps we can meet while she is out on one of her walks; she is alone during the early mornings.* He then resolved to ride out early the next morning and chance another tete-a-tete with her.

Prior to the chance meeting in Meryton, they had met several times the last few weeks while he rode out in the meadows of Netherfield Park, and she walked through the timber. It was not intentional, not at first anyway, for when he saw her, he would acknowledge her, and they would engage in conversation about the weather, or their exercise.

They met more and more frequently, and their talks became more involved, growing deeper than a passing conversation. He came to anticipate their unintended rendezvous, and when the weather was inclement, he would sulk and behave with incivility towards his hosts. Their last conversation occurred two days ago, when they were again at the edge of the trail between the timbers and the meadow. *Yes, tomorrow, I will ride out with that one purpose in mind... to see Miss Elizabeth Bennet.*

The next morning he rose extra early, dressed, and went down to the breakfast room before the rest of Netherfield's occupants had risen, and usually did so to avoid Caroline, not that she would ever get out of bed before nine o'clock in the morning. Taking a hot roll, he proceeded to the stables. As he approached the line between Netherfield and Longbourn, he spied Elizabeth coming out from the trees on the path. He kicked his horse in the side, urging him to move in Elizabeth's direction, slowing his pace as he approached her. "Hello, Miss Bennet, how do you do this lovely morning?"

"Hello, Mr. Darcy, I do quite well, and how do I find you this bright and sunny autumn morning?"

He smiled, I am quite well, madam."

"You look as if you are deep in thought, sir. May I ask if it is from thoughtfulness or from forgetfulness?" she asked in a playful manner.

Laughing lightly he said, .I have been thinking about our last conversation. Do you remember it?" he prompted. "When we were discussing our preference for a walk as opposed to a ride? I have come to the conclusion that it is much more pleasurable to ride as it affords me the opportunity to view those on foot much sooner from the higher vantage point atop my horse, and although they may see me, I may be able to either join them sooner, if I wish, I can ride off before they address me."

She tilted her head, arching her right eyebrow. "Are you saying sir, that you do not mind addressing me? Or perhaps I was too hidden for you to spot me and then make your escape?"

"I would not deny myself the pleasure of your conversation, Miss Elizabeth, for whom else would I find to discuss the merits of walking verses that of riding? Certainly nobody at Netherfield!" They both laughed about his implied jest towards the Netherfield ladies, and their dislike to walk where they can be driven to any given place.

He found their conversations grew more profound and engaging over time. He had never in his life been able to converse with a woman as he did her. *This is so refreshing. I wish we could talk like this forever.*

"Yes, I can well imagine that there are people who do not share the propensity to enjoy nature and the beauties it has to offer."

"Yes, I agree. My sister feels that walking is a good means to clear her mind, too… while enjoying nature. She might even be able to keep up with you, Miss Elizabeth."

"Oh? And how does she feel about horseback riding? Would you say that she also feels that it is a means to meet or avoid those whom one wishes to or not to converse with?"

"No, Georgiana is quite shy. She would never even think of such things. She struggles to start conversations as she is quite timid," he smiled. "Unfortunately, many people get the wrong idea about her mannerisms and see her as aloof, instead of seeing the truth about her shyness. That is one of the reasons she doesn't have many friends. Conversing is very difficult for her." Amazed at having divulged such personal information, Darcy looked at Elizabeth to see how she received it.

She wore a sympathetic look upon her countenance and smiled. I see. It is unfortunate that she did not join you here, Mr. Darcy, for I would like to meet her."

"I think that would be nice, Miss Elizabeth." He paused, I hope that she will have the privilege of becoming acquainted with you, Miss Elizabeth… and with Miss Bennet."

Elizabeth raised her eyebrows, "Oh? You do not think that I might turn her into one of the savages here, sir?"

Darcy blushed at her reference, I do not think that *you* could do such a thing, Miss Elizabeth. You and your sister are far too eloquent.

Elizabeth blushed and Darcy could not help but admire her loveliness, despite the danger of scaring her off, "Please forgive me, Miss Elizabeth, it was not my intention to make you uneasy."

She smiled at him through her eye lashes, "I…am not uneasy sir, and I… thank you for your compliments." She halted, "Pray, may I ask what other pursuits your sister is apt to enjoy? Does she like to be out of doors or does she play and sing all day?"

Darcy, realizing her discomfort and noting her change in subject, answered, "When Georgiana is in town, there is not much to see out of doors, thus she spends most of her time practicing her music. When we are at Pemberley, however, she does spend a great deal of time walking, gardening, and riding. There is so much to see there as opposed to town."

"It must be lovely there… My aunt grew up in Lambton. Is that anywhere near your home?"

Hearing the name of the nearest town and that her aunt grew up there, surprised Darcy, "Ah, yes, Lambton is but five miles from Pemberley. In fact, it is the closest town to my estate. You say your aunt grew up there?"

"Yes, she did. She has often times lamented the fact that she was brought down to the lowlands when she grew up, and now that she is married to my Uncle Gardiner, they reside in London. She has spoken often about returning to visit, as she says the Peaks are lovely."

"Indeed, I should have to agree with her. The sights are magnificent. Much of it is untamed and wild, but that is nature and beauty, it is at its best. Nothing could compare to the hilltops, the grit stone, and the limestone formations. Many people are impressed by the massive timber and the pastures as well... but then I guess one could say that I am biased." He smiled.

Elizabeth had been looking at him while he spoke of his home with much attention, and smiled at his descriptions of his home. "You must be proud to call such a place home. It makes me want to see it as well, especially since my Aunt Gardiner tends to say much the same about her former home."

Darcy could not be more pleased to hear her say such things. Suddenly, he wished that he could be the one to show it to her, and he wanted to talk to her forever about the landscapes surrounding his home.

Their conversation led from the serious to the mundane, and when they had conversed for nearly a half hour, they parted company and headed their opposite directions. His thoughts, however, remained in that pasture on that very spot where she stood just moments ago. *She is such a wonderful woman. I cannot think of anyone else who compares to her. I would give anything in the world to have such loveliness with me forever.*

She would be so good for Georgiana too, and maybe bring her out of her shell. He could almost feel an ache in his chest at the loss of her company. I *never wish to be parted from her. What shall I do? Could I marry her...?*

~*~*~*~

Charles Bingley and Mr. Darcy arrived back to Netherfield, and Caroline, being in a very good mood earlier in the day, greeted the gentlemen most pleasantly. She observed both of them carefully, but her eyes rested upon the beautiful body of Mr. Darcy. She caressed his form as if she were examining a prize horse. Darcy looked at her questioningly. She addressed him without her usual simpering, and watched his every move.

"Mr. Darcy, how was your morning ride? Did you enjoy the countryside? Or have you found much for Charles to improve upon these grounds?" She saw that Mr. Darcy looked puzzled for a moment. They had told her that they were going out to survey the grounds. She observed Mr. Darcy recollect himself.

"Yes, I did enjoy my ride through the country, and though some fences may be in need of repair, and an embankment dug out a bit, I did not find need of any significant repairs upon the grounds."

He is being evasive today. In fact...they are both avoiding me. If only I could get up as early as they, and go out riding. I am sure I could impress Mr. Darcy with my riding skills!

Nodding her head, she said, I see."

Turning her attention to her brother, she asked about his plans after the Ball. "Charles, are you still planning on going to town after the ball? You know you should just stay in town afterwards as there is likely to be nothing of interest here. The harvest is nearly finished, and I am sure the weather will become much worse. We could even be snowed in for a long time."

"I have some business in town that I must see to, but I am still planning to return afterwards, and I am sure that we will not have as many difficulties here as we have had up north. The winters here are much milder. Besides, I find I have enough to do with planning for the next spring's planting. You may stay in town, if you wish. Perhaps, Reginald and Louisa will have you in their townhome."

Caroline became more displeased and unhappy, but she made no further arguments, excused herself, and left to attend to some details pertaining to the ball. *There is so much that a lady has to attend to when planning these things, I am sure I could garner appreciation in Mr. Darcy's quarter when I prove to him how much of an asset I will be to Pemberley.*

She was very unhappy about her brother's refusal to accommodate her wishes to stay in town, as she knew that if he stayed in Netherfield, Mr. Darcy would be more than likely to join him. She also realized that she would not have many opportunities to visit him if

Charles left for Netherfield, and Mr. Darcy stayed in town, as her brother was their main connection. Another thought struck her momentarily, but then left as quickly. *I could visit Georgiana, but that little chit will not bother to make conversation. She feels so superior to everyone. She barely talks to anyone but her brother! They are so close, those two. Maybe Mr. Darcy will stay in town if both his sister and cousin are there. Then he would at least be away from that chit Eliza Bennet!*

She knew that there was still some chance that Darcy may stay in town, since Colonel Fitzwilliam was staying at Darcy's home. Observing the two gentlemen over the last six years, she knew he was close to his cousin, and that the two of them shared much of their lives with each other. *They were as close as brothers and ever since the colonel left, Darcy was in a distant and distracted mood. I do wonder at what Colonel Fitzwilliam's missive was all about... doubtless something to do with the army... perhaps Mr. Darcy is worried about his dear cousin being sent off to war again? I could help to calm his nerves, and make him forget about all that!*

The colonel's assistant had packed up all of the colonel's belongings about a week following the arrival of an express. It appeared that he did not intend to return to Netherfield for the ball. Caroline did not wonder at his reasoning. She could understand why he would not return to Hertfordshire. *Why would a man of the world want to come to a small country shire when he has all of the delights of town? If I had any choices, I would never have come here in the first place. I must try to convince Mr. Darcy to go to town when Charles goes, and then try to convince them they should both stay. It is obvious that Mr. Darcy is missing something here anyway!*

Caroline continued the musings in the ball room until the upstairs maid handed her a letter she found under the bed in the guest rooms used by Colonel Fitzwilliam.

Chapter 11

*T**he day of the Netherfield Ball has arrived!* Thought Darcy. Rain and other distractions kept Darcy and Elizabeth from meeting again in the meadow by the timber for two weeks, which did nothing to alleviate Darcy's anxieties. He was looking forward to dancing with Elizabeth, something that had been denied him before. His valet, Baxter, arrived to his rooms early this morning to help Darcy ready for the day. He intended to ride out to the meadow and perchance meet Elizabeth, and then he would talk to her about George Wickham's past. Though he desired to avoid the subject of Georgiana and Wickham, he knew in his heart that if there were anyone he felt safe to discuss that issue with it would be her. Somewhere deep inside him, he also wished the only man for her to dance with would be him.

This morning the weather cleared up and allowed for a rendezvous, and Darcy felt his mood grow lighter than it had been for days. Wanting to look well if he should happen to find Elizabeth on her morning walk, and not wanting to chance missing her, he implored his ever efficient valet to hurry things along.

"Baxter, I need good riding clothes today. Perhaps the tan trousers and the green coat... oh yes, and my brown Hessian riding boots. They are polished, are they not?" He asked while sorting through his bedside drawer. He searched for his 'good luck charm' to give him the courage he needed to talk to Elizabeth about what he needed to disclose to her.

Baxter smiled and responded, "Yes, sir, they were polished last evening, and your clothes are laid out here. Shall I shave you now, or do you wish to summon me in a few moments when you are ready?"

"Ahhh, yes, I wish to shave as soon as you are ready. I want to avoid any unnecessary dilemmas if at all possible." *Such as Caroline*

Bingley, and Louisa Hurst, and Bingley too, for that matter. I cannot have them dragging my mood down or Bingley wanting to go out riding while I would rather be left alone with Elizabeth.

Baxter nodded sharply, "Very good sir, and will you be wanting to ready yourself earlier this evening than your usual?"

Darcy glanced up at his valet then back down, finally finding the item he was searching for buried deep in his drawer, "Yes, I will need to start readying myself around six o'clock this evening, Baxter."

Servant and master finished the task of getting Darcy ready for his early morning ride, and Darcy left his dressing room with a spring in his step as he headed towards the breakfast parlour.

Oddly enough, he saw Reginald Hurst in the breakfast parlour. Upon seeing him there this early in the morning, Darcy started.

"Good morning Hurst. What brings you down here so early in the morning?"

"Morning Darcy, I came down early as I slept ill last night. I was listening to all that tittering between Caroline and Louisa in the sitting room, until damn near one o'clock this morning. I ended up asking Caroline to leave so I could get some rest!" Hurst went back to reading the racing sections of his paper, as Darcy finished his coffee and grabbed some toast and jam.

This is rather odd that Louisa would have Caroline in her sitting room that late at night. They should have just stayed in one of the parlours to chat, if that is what they wished to do. Quickly finishing his breakfast and coffee, he left for the stables after excusing himself.

When he reached the edge of the meadow, he spotted bright flashes of colour moving towards the edge of the timber. Within a few moments, Darcy could see Elizabeth coming through a clearing. As he came closer, he felt his pulse quicken and his heart beat wildly when he saw a radiant smile upon her face.

"Why good morning, Mr. Darcy. If I did not know better, I would think that you were waiting upon someone." She looked up, her eyes roaming over his form.

She is so mesmerizing with her brightened eyes and flushed face. It took him a moment to come back to the present, and he dismounted.

When he stepped off his horse, he faced her, then approached her. Nervous about the subjects he wanted to broach with her, he slowly gained his wits enough to address her, "No... I mean yes... Miss Elizabeth, I was hoping to catch you this morning on your daily constitutional." He took a few more steps towards her, I wanted... actually needed to talk to you about...our encounter earlier this past fortnight... with Mr. Wickham."

He thought she looked rather crestfallen when he stated his purpose, to which he felt a sort of perverse pleasure in.

"I see, and what is it you wish to discuss with me about Mr. Wickham?"

"I believe that you may have observed the... cool reception between myself and ... Mr. Wickham," He spat out the name, "That day, when Mr. Bingley and I came upon you and your sisters in Meryton." He took a deep breath and ran his fingers through his hair, I feared that you may have received the wrong impression about that, and..." He twisted his ring upon his finger as he looked away from her, I feel that I needed to explain some things... about his and my history." He paced back and forth in front of Elizabeth, but then he stopped himself and took another deep breath, "You see, I did not expect to see him here... in Hertfordshire... and I am afraid you may have..." He began pacing again, "viewed it... our meeting in a poor light." He stopped again and looked at her, willing her to understand him.

"Yes, I had noticed that you and that... gentleman... appeared as though you were not on good terms, but I fail to see what that has to do with me."

Darcy became concerned, "He did not do something to you did he? If he has done anything, I will..."

She interrupted him, "No sir, he did not. I must say that I did not have any negative opinion of you, sir. Mr. Wickham appears upon first acquaintance to be amiable and charming, but he has, upon further acquaintance, displayed a hint of rudeness."

Darcy let out the breath he had been holding, and nodded his head, "What did he do?" He searched her face, "Forgive me, Miss Elizabeth, but George Wickham and I go way back, and what you are telling me comes as no surprise. I must know, though, if he has harmed you in any way." Filled with anxiety and nervousness, he turned the ring on his finger.

"He has not harmed me, Mr. Darcy. My first impression of him could not be regarded as anything other than unfavorable. After you left with Mr. Bingley, Mr. Wickham made a few unbelievable comments about you. He said that you were 'a friend to those worthy few', which surprised me as I was a stranger to him. I did not think it proper for someone whom I had just met to say such things... well anyone for that matter, to say such things."

Darcy could not help but admire her good sense, and wanted to explain his past with George Wickham, "Yes well... we lived together as roommates in school, and I became all too familiar with his ways. In fact, that was what I wanted to talk with you about... this morning." He continued to study her, nervous about opening himself up to her.

Yes sir, I am all attention." Elizabeth's face appeared open and willing to listen.

Encouraged, Darcy began, "Miss Elizabeth, you must understand that I do not perceive you as just another casual acquaintance. I count you as a dear friend... and because of my regard for you as a friend. I feel I must overcome my reticence about speaking of my private matters."

Noting her blush scarlet at his last declaration, Darcy continued, "That is why I wanted to warn you about George Wickham. He is not to be trusted. He has ruined more women than I could bear to mention. He has had many unpaid debts to the shopkeepers around my estate, and I am certain that anywhere he ends up, he will accumulate gaming debts.

I had to send him away from my home five years hence, when he refused to take orders for the living my father intended for him. He denied wanting to take orders, and wished for financial compensation instead. I knew he would not be fit for the living, and so he was compensated and we parted. A year after that, he came back and demanded the living, but he was denied as he had already been compensated. He left in anger when I would not give that to him, and we parted, thinking never to see each other. Unfortunately this last summer, we again crossed paths."

Darcy looked down into her face as she was staring up into his, and their eyes met. She had a soft look about her that made him feel that she could be trusted." Miss Elizabeth, what I am about to reveal is very personal, and though I do not believe I should have any fear of you, I must beg for your secrecy as it involves someone I care about deeply."

Elizabeth nodded her head, "Of course sir, you have my promise."

Taking a deep breath, he continued, "George Wickham conspired with a woman, a Mrs. Younge, to pose as a candidate for my sister, Georgiana's, companion. Mrs. Younge then convinced me and Georgiana that she should go to Ramsgate to study, to which we both agreed. Once there, she met George Wickham, and he persuaded her that she was in love with him. He convinced her to agree on an elopement. His purpose was to get her dowry of thirty thousand pounds. Fortunately, I came unannounced to visit her two days before the intended elopement and she, unwilling to grieve a brother she sees almost as a father figure, confessed about the elopement."

He paused for a moment to see how Elizabeth took all of this information.

She stared at him with her mouth opened and her eyes glimmering in disbelief, "How fortunate she is to have such a brother to protect her. She must be grateful that you came when you did, otherwise she may have been lost."

"Yes, she and I are both grateful. Had George Wickham succeeded, he would have had his revenge upon me. The reason I wanted to see you this morning, was to warn you about him, and put your family on guard, but I beg of you not to reveal the mistake of my sister. I trust your powers of discernment, Miss Elizabeth, but felt you needed to know what he is capable of. "

He watched as Elizabeth was silent for a moment, I thank you sir, for thinking about us, and about sharing your sister's story too. I will not disclose such personal business, but I can let it be known that I have heard it from a very reliable source that he is not as trustworthy as he may seem. The people here tend to believe it when one of their own, whom they trust, tells them things of this sort."

"I have the utmost faith in you Miss Elizabeth." Darcy studied her, trying to gauge her mind set. He took a deep breath, rubbed his hand over his 'charm' that he had placed in his pocket, and said,

"Um... there was one more thing... that I would like to discuss. I was wondering... may I request a dance with you at the ball? Perhaps even the first... that is if it has not been spoken for?"

Elizabeth smiled and laughed, "No, sir, I am not spoken for yet in any of the dances, and yes I would be happy to dance the first set with you. Oh, that reminds me I have to go to Meryton this morning to pick up a few last minute things, and it is getting rather late."

She looked at him again, but this time it was with a very warm, intense look... as though she were studying him.

"I shall look forward to dancing with you this evening, Mr. Darcy.

His heart skipped a few beats. He stared at her as their eyes locked. He replied, I shall very much look forward to our dance Miss Elizabeth," With that he bowed to her curtsey, and she walked back towards Longbourn. As he watched her walk down the path, he noted her turning to look back at him. With jubilation, he leapt onto his horse and rode towards the manor house.

~*~*~*~

Elizabeth arrived back at Longbourn a little later than usual. She decided that she would discuss her early morning tete-a-tete in the meadow with Jane. The truth was, she wanted to discuss her new and unusual feelings whenever she was around Mr. Darcy. She felt his absence keenly, while their early morning meetings were interrupted by the weather, and this feeling about him surprised her. She joined her father and Jane for breakfast, and their usual light morning chatter, but before she could sit down, their party was joined by Mr. Collins.

"Good morning to you all, I trust you are well this morning?" He bowed in his servile manner.

"Good morning to you, Mr. Collins, I trust you rested well?" asked Mr. Bennet.

"Yes, indeed I did, sir, and awoke this morning very well rested. In fact, I believe I will be in ready condition to dance at the ball."

"Forgive me sir, but is it proper for a man of your status to go to a ball? What would your patroness say?" Piped in Elizabeth.

Smiling in his condescending way, he replied, "My dear Cousin Elizabeth, it is gratifying to think you are concerned for my patroness Lady Catherine's opinion, but yes, I believe that she would agree that a ball tended to by some many genteel persons -why... even Mr. Darcy, my patroness' nephew, is to be in attendance at the ball -- so I do not believe she should have any problem with me attending the ball, or dancing. Which brings me to another subject; I would like to take this opportunity to ask both my fair cousins to dance."

Elizabeth cringed, and then chastised herself for mentioning the ball to her senseless cousin. "Ummmm...yes...that would be..."

"Good! Good! I am very much looking forward to the ball and to dancing with the both of you Cousin Jane, Cousin Elizabeth."

Elizabeth and Jane looked at each other in dismay and then continued with their breakfast as their father looked on at them with a smirk on his face, I wonder at Mr. Darcy's dancing, though as I understand he does not like that activity."

Mr. Collins replied, "That, I suppose, is a good thing as his intended is not of the healthy constitution to enjoy that activity."

Elizabeth choked on her coffee. She regained her breath, as everyone was looking at her, and apologized, I am sorry, I must have swallowed my drink down the wrong direction."

"Obviously." said a concerned Mr. Bennet, as Jane sat across the table and stared at her.

"I am fine." She froze in place, unable to move for a few moments. Elizabeth finally asked, "Excuse me Mr. Collins, did I hear you correctly ...? That... Mr. Darcy is engaged?" She asked, feeling disturbed.

Mr. Collins, still stuffing his eggs in his mouth, matter-of-factly replied with a smile, "Ah, yes, to his cousin, Miss Anne de Bourgh, Lady Catherine's daughter. It is her fondest have her dearest nephew and her daughter united in matrimony..."

As Mr. Collins droned on about his patroness, she felt herself feeling cold. For a few minutes, her mind was spinning, and she could not hear what that ridiculous parson was gibbering about. *Surely, though, Mr. Collins should know well, who his patroness daughter was* engaged to, but I can hardly credit it. He does not even act as a man who is betrothed.

She had so many thoughts and questions running through her mind all at once, and suddenly she was struck by a sharp pain in her temples. Her head felt as if it would explode. Mr. Bennet and Jane noticed her paleness, and Jane enquired with concern, "Lizzy, are you alright? You look rather pale."

Elizabeth looked at her sister with distress, I have a sudden headache. May I be excused?" She directed her gaze at her father.

"Yes… are you sure you are alright, Lizzy?."

"I shall be fine after I lie down. I think, perhaps I spent a little bit more time out of doors than usual." She arose out of her chair and nodded to the room before making her way to the entryway.

Just before she left the room, however, Jane asked, "Shall I help you upstairs, Lizzy?"

"No, I am sure I will be well after I rest for a while." She made it to her own room. She sat down hard on the side of the bed, and by that time her headache grew to excruciating levels. She could feel the stinging sensation in her eyes, and was frustrated with herself for being so tearful.

Why did Mr. Darcy lead me to believe he was unattached, if he is indeed engaged to his cousin? What to make of his discussion from this morning! She tried to make sense of this newest piece of information, and put all of the pieces in the puzzle together. *But nothing makes sense! He seems so warm and sincere. Why would he act as if … as if… he wanted to become better acquainted? He even asked me to dance the first set at the ball. Nothing makes sense! Surely he would not believe that he could have me as his… his… mistress!* The more she thought about Mr. Darcy, the angrier she became. *Teasing, teasing man.*

Elizabeth heard a knock on the door followed by the sound of Jane's voice, "Lizzy? Are you alright? Can I come in?"

She was roused out of her anger. "Yes Jane, you may come in."

Jane walked in and stopped in the middle of the room. Elizabeth suspected her cheeks were tear stained and her eyes were reddened and swollen.

"Lizzy, what is the matter? What has you so upset?"

Shaking her head, Elizabeth answered, I am not certain, Jane."

"I saw the expression on your face Lizzy, you cannot fool me! You seemed rather... umm... surprised ... when Mr. Collins mentioned Mr. Darcy being engaged to his cousin."

Elizabeth gazed out of her window, I do not know how to explain it. Whenever I have been out walking, he seems to be there and we have over the last few weeks had meaningful conversation. He treated me as if he had some interest in what I had to say, and it made me feel... I do not know... I cannot explain it. This morning, I came upon him again and after we discussed serious matters, he asked me to dance the first set at the ball. When I heard this news at breakfast I was ... very surprised to hear that he is engaged." She gave Jane a distressed look.

"It sounds to me as if your heart is engaged, Lizzy. But do you credit it? You know sometimes Mr. Collins is rather... misguided when it comes to meaningful information. Perhaps there has been a misunderstanding on his end."

Ignoring her first statement, Elizabeth responded, "How can I not credit it? Mr. Collins could hardly misunderstand that his patroness' daughter is engaged to Mr. Darcy! Besides, these sorts of arrangements occur all of the time with the very wealthy. What I do not understand is, why he would lead me to believe he was unattached? And why he would give me such... gazes anytime we are together? Or why they, his gazes, made me feel almost... desired?"

Elizabeth noted Jane's blush. "Lizzy, I cannot account for his gazes, but as for yours, I believe it could be that you are in love with him, because that is the way I feel when I am with Mr. Bingley."

Elizabeth looked away.

"Lizzy, perhaps you should ask Mr. Darcy about this. That is if you are still planning to attend the ball. You are engaged to him for the first dance."

"I..." Elizabeth took a deep breath, I may do that

Jane... There is another matter that I should divulge to you. It concerns Mr. Wickham. When I went out this morning and met Mr. Darcy, he informed me of the character flaws in *that* gentleman, as he has known him for many years. Mr. Darcy informed me that he has known Mr. Wickham for almost his entire life, and they are no longer friendly due to Mr. Wickham's ungentlemanly behaviour..

Elizabeth went on to inform Jane of all of the tales of woe that Mr. Wickham had perpetrated. Jane seemed very shocked, not wanting to believe anyone could be so cruel.

"I do not know what to think. I have seen nothing but his amiability and charm, but it must be true, else why would Mr. Darcy go so far as to reveal things about his childhood friend?" Jane frowned.

"Yes, I too believe him, but what is to be done... I mean about Mr. Wickham?"

"I believe we should discreetly talk to those that know him, and if there is anything unusual, then we can discuss it with our father before going any further."

"I think so too, though even if we go to father, there is still a chance that Mr. Wickham will be foisted upon society here." She knew that Jane understood that should they go to Mr. Bennet, he may not bother to follow up on that information.

Elizabeth sat in silent reflection in her room for some time. Jane eventually managed to coax her to join her, and their other sisters to run some errands before the ball. Soon enough, they were on their way to Meryton, giving Elizabeth some time to think about this morning's occurrences without being observed. Though try as she may, Elizabeth could not stop thinking about how Mr. Darcy made her feel. A subtle thought then dawned

upon her consciousness... *I am in love with Mr. Darcy!* She was not sure if she should welcome this or regret it, but she could no longer deny her feelings for him.

She continued to be plagued by other thoughts, however. *What shall I do if he is engaged to another woman? And why would he continue to pay me such attentions as he has unless... no, I shall not let this take me over; he is too decent to do such things...right?* It was with this resolution that she readied for the Netherfied Ball. *I shall get to the bottom of this, even if it means my own disappointment.*

Chapter 12

Darcy waited for the Bennet's carriage to arrive, and when he spotted it coming up the drive to Netherfield, he felt his heart start beating rapidly. He headed down to the front hall where the guests were coming through before they entered the dance hall, as he wanted to greet Elizabeth as soon as she arrived. When he laid eyes on her, he was mesmerized by her beauty. *Good Lord, Elizabeth, you are a handsome woman!*

She wore a pale yellow satin dress with a braided trim and embroidered flowers, with her hair in an upswept cascade of curls, pinned with a beaded butterfly design. She looked like a fairy princess. Darcy stood in the hall, envisioning her at his side while he worked on his accounts in his study at Pemberley, and showing her the great hall where many generations of his ancestor's portraits hung. He could imagine her portrait hanging there as well. *You are breathtaking, with such a graceful manner, and so much beauty! Elizabeth, you possess my heart.*

Where did that come from? He started at the direction his thoughts took him. Approaching the reception line, he greeted Mr. and Mrs. Bennet, then Miss Bennet. Finally turning to Elizabeth, he greeted her with a formal bow, taking in her whole essence. When he looked up, he saw that she studied him with an intense and guarded look. *I wonder what idea would put that look on her face. She seems ill at ease compared to our last meeting.* The rest of her party continued into the ballroom, and he took the opportunity to talk to her so as not to be overheard by anyone else. "Are you well this evening, Miss Elizabeth?"

Nodding her head, Elizabeth replied, "Yes, I am well, sir, I believe that I have had a hectic day. I have much information to reflect upon from this morning." She gazed into his eyes as if she were lost and looking for some direction.

"I hoped that you were not too overwhelmed. I apologize if you were offended in any way." He became worried that he imparted too much information to her this morning.

"It is not that..." She hesitated, *I have other information given to me today that I was... rather... surprised to hear.*"

He nodded his head, not completely understanding her meaning. "Perhaps I can clear up any questions..." He looked around to ensure that nobody could overhear them, "Perhaps this evening I can answer your questions?"

She nodded her head in acquiescence and curtseyed to him before exiting to the ball room. Watching her leave his side, Darcy felt a sense of foreboding in his stomach. *This does not look good. I wonder what else she could have heard today to make her so apprehensive of me tonight? Surely she believed me; she could not but seem to believe in what I have said to her this morning... But what else could it be?*

~*~*~*~

Caroline surreptitiously attempted to listen Darcy and Elizabeth's conversation. She noticed that Darcy looked at Miss Eliza differently... with a warmth and brightening of his face when he gazed at that chit. *He has never looked at me like that! What can he mean? Of course she would be a fool not to want what such a man who could provide for her, especially with such connections! What does she have that I do not?*

Could he possibly mean to make her the next Mistress of Pemberley? Surely not!

This shall not be allowed to happen! I have to do something to put a stop to this! Perhaps I should ensure she does not want him. But how? He is such a desirable match; she would be silly to turn down such a man! Caroline was determined to keep a close eye on the couple this evening, *and if an opportunity arises I will not hesitate to act.*

As she followed Darcy into the ballroom, Caroline approached the subject of her thoughts. "Mr. Darcy, I have yet to see any guests that it would not be a punishment to stand up with, do you not agree?"

"Actually Miss Bingley, I see perhaps, a half dozen it would not pain me to stand up with."

"Really?" She purred with a smile, "And which are the other five ladies here you would not mind standing up with, if I may be so bold as to ask?" She said as she slid her arm through his.

He looked down at their intertwined arms and extricated his from hers, I will keep *my* opinions to myself for the moment. I prefer to leave them in suspense for a little while longer, if you do not mind, Miss Bingley." Nodding quickly at her, he then side-stepped away from her.

She watched him move through the crowded room closer to where that little country nobody, Miss Eliza Bennet, and a friend of hers, Miss Lucas stood. I *must do something before he gets mixed up irreparably with that chit! Suddenly, as she thought of the note from the day before, a thought came to her. Yes, I may be able to save you yet, Mr. Darcy!*

~*~*~*~

In another corner of the Netherfield Ball room, several of the invited guests were mingling with the militia's officers; one them was Major Wickham. He had planned to go to town when the officers were invited to the ball, but decided to stay and attend; he felt that he may be able to gain more intelligence on the status of Darcy's apparent attraction to Elizabeth Bennet.

He walked throughout the room, scouting out potential dance partners, certain that he would ask the lovely Miss Elizabeth. While he mused about what he wanted to do with Miss Elizabeth, her two youngest sisters approached him. Miss Lydia flirted with him, "Major Wickham! Why, we have been looking for you since we arrived, why have you not come to greet us yet?"

Wickham bowed to both Lydia and Kitty, smiled, and said, "Miss Catherine, Miss Lydia, how are you ladies this evening? I was just making my way through the room to greet you. Tell me that you ladies have not filled up your dance cards already? I was hoping that at least one dance was saved for me, with each of you?"

Both Miss Lydia and Miss Kitty giggled at his pretty speech; however, it was Miss Lydia who answered, "La, you are so amusing, Major. Of course we shall each dance with you, for I am quite sure we will be able to provide more fun than some of the other ladies here." She glanced towards Miss Bingley.

Wickham laughed, I do not doubt that, and may I claim the first dance from you Miss Lydia, then the second from you Miss Catherine?" He made sure to turn and smile at each.

The two girls looked at each other, and then giggled. Miss Lydia spoke for both of them, "Of course we shall dance with you, but I am engaged for the first, perhaps I can dance the third and you can claim Kitty for the second?"

"I suppose I shall have to suffer the company of another lady for the first sets." Wickham said. I suppose I should go to find her. I look forward to the following sets." He bowed to them with a rakish grin and walked towards Miss Maria Lucas. He could still hear their giggling as he made his exit. *That Miss Lydia is ripe for such a young country miss. I would not mind discovering the taste of that fruit!*

As he was talking with Maria Lucas, the music began for the first set. Observing the pairings for the first set, he sighted his principal object. Darcy paired up with Miss Elizabeth Bennet, then Bingley matched up with Miss Bennet, that odd cleric, Mr. Collins, stood opposite Miss Mary Bennet, and Caroline Bingley paired with some unknown gentleman, whom he later discovered to be Frederick Lucas. Wickham saw that Miss Bingley eyed Darcy, almost as much as he eyed Miss Elizabeth. *This is getting interesting!* He mused as he observed Mr. Darcy's pensive look. *What is going on through your mind, Darcy?* He laughed as much to himself as he did out loud.

~*~*~*~

Darcy started to relax into the dance when Miss Elizabeth suddenly asked him, "Mr. Darcy, are you very close to all of your cousins?"

Surprised, he replied, "Yes, though more so to Colonel Fitzwilliam and to an extent, his brother, the Viscount Matlock." Darcy tensed. *Elizabeth could not have heard of Fitzwilliam's mistress... as no one here knows about her. Does she ask because she cares for him and is missing him?*

She nodded before they separated in the set, then when they rejoined she added, I understood from my cousin, your Aunt Lady Catherine's parson, that you are also quite close to your cousin de Bourgh."

Caught by surprise again, Darcy stopped before beginning the next move with a distressed appearance, I cannot imagine how he could assume such things. I had never met him before that day in Meryton."

"I had understood from him that Lady Catherine has announced her daughter's engagement to you, sir." She glared at him.

He took a deep breath, I can well imagine what my aunt proclaims to those in her service; however, the truth is quite different. You see, she has proclaimed this ever since we were both in our cradles, but I have never desired it to be so, and I am not inclined to oblige my aunt simply to placate her wishes.

To his relief, she looked more relaxed, and she flushed while looking away from him. Darcy wanted to clarify her concerns, "Was that what you meant when you said that you had 'much information to take in this morning'?"

"Yes, I confess that I was quite... taken by surprise when my cousin made that declaration."

Smiling to himself, he met her eyes and held her gaze, "You seemed troubled when you arrived. Would it have bothered you had it been true?"

She did not answer immediately, but then whispered, I do not know how to respond to that question sir... I must confess I was..."

"Was what...Miss Elizabeth?"

"I was... disillusioned when I heard my cousin's proclamation." He smiled at her, "And why was that... Miss... Elizabeth?"

Unable to break their gaze, he stared into her eyes as she replied, I cannot say for sure, sir, but perhaps after being called one of your 'dearest friends', and having discussions such as we have had, I felt as if I had been betrayed by one of my 'dearest friends'."

Taking a very deep breath and continuing with their dance, he held her gaze. I would never disappoint you. In fact, I think of you as even more than a very good friend, Miss Elizabeth."

If it were possible, he thought she may be blushing even more, and her lips turned up as she answered, I believe I could say the same for myself, sir."

~*~*~*~

They finished the rest of their set in silence, unmindful of the other dancers around them. He took her hand and led her to the side of the room where her father stood. The couple was joined thereafter by her sisters and two officers from the militia.

Elizabeth and Darcy were still conversing with Mr. Bennet when Major Wickham came to their gathering to claim Kitty's hand for the next set. Elizabeth felt uncomfortable upon recognizing the interloper. She glanced at Mr. Darcy, concerned about his reaction to being in the company of the man who had caused him so much grief throughout his life. She noted that he stiffened, and glared at the man.

Major Wickham addressed the group in general, I do beg your pardon, but I believe I have the next dance with Miss Catherine, and I have come to claim my next partner." She saw that man smile towards Mr. Darcy.

Kitty and Lydia giggled at his attentions, then Lydia proclaimed to no one in particular, "Yes, and then you shall have the next with me. You will not be bored with our assistance, Major Wickham."

"Indeed not, Miss Lydia. I shall look forward to the evening…" Elizabeth could not help but notice him smirk towards her and Mr. Darcy's direction, "Indeed."

Both Elizabeth and Mr. Darcy frowned, and Elizabeth noticed how Mr. Darcy flushed and glared in Major Wickham's direction. She asked with concern, "You do not suppose he has come to make trouble with you tonight do you, Mr. Darcy?"

"I should think he would know better than to cause trouble, but one can never know what goes on in such a man's mind."

Just then, Major Denny approached her for the next set. Soon her other sister's, aside from Mary, were joined by their next dance partners, leaving Mr. Darcy alone with Mr. Bennet. They conversed with some animation as they seemed to be watching the other couples dance. When the second set finished, Elizabeth rejoined the two gentlemen, and both greeted her with more pleasantry than their norm.

"Lizzy, tell me that you have another partner for the next set, for if you do not, I shall have to talk with Colonel Forster." Mr. Bennet teased.

Mr. Bingley came up to the group and gallantly offered, "That should not be necessary, Mr. Bennet, I shall be delighted to dance with Miss Elizabeth, if she would accept my hand for the next set." He smiled his usual friendly smile.

Mr. Darcy then said, "And, I shall take this opportunity to ask Miss Bennet for the next set as well. That is, if she would care to dance?"

Jane accepted his hand, and the two couples headed for the dance line. Elizabeth noted how Mr. Darcy conversed with Jane during the first set, who seemed to be enjoying herself with him. She felt a warm sensation spreading through her as she viewed Mr. Darcy take pains to engage Jane in discussion.

Darcy and Elizabeth sat close by each other for supper, both enjoying light conversation with their fellow diners. They exchanged glances, but did not talk much to each other. Mrs. Bennet exclaimed about the expected engagement of her daughter Mary to their cousin Mr. Collins. As she elaborated upon her joy, Elizabeth blushed then blushed again due to her mother's effusions. She saw Caroline Bingley watching the show as she exchanged conversation with Mrs. Hurst, which made her furious with her mother's lack of decorum. She stole a glance at Mr. Darcy. A deep frown graced his face. *It is impossible to wish that he has not heard mother! Oh, if only she had sense to know when to cease speaking, or at least lower her voice!* She shot a silent look of apology towards Mr. Darcy, who looked back at her with an unreadable expression.

~*~*~*~

"Louisa, can you imagine that Charles wants to attach himself to such a family? Mrs. Bennet is positively vulgar! I could not imagine having to suffer her presence much less her conversation for many evenings, and I fear that Mr. Darcy may be infatuated with that conniving chit, Eliza Bennet. Who does she think she is? He could not be thinking her an adequate mistress of Pemberley...!" Caroline stopped suddenly, thinking of an idea.

Her sister, who had been nodding her head the whole time said, "What is it? What are you thinking, Caroline?" She asked with rapt attention.

"I just thought of an idea... to dissuade Miss Eliza from wanting to form an attachment with Mr. Darcy. Do you recall our conversation last night?"

"Indeed I do, but what of it? How will that dissuade her from wanting to form an attachment with such a man as Mr. Darcy?"

"Just follow my lead when I cue you in." She looked at Louisa with a wicked gleam in her eye.

Louisa smiled back at Caroline with the same wicked look. They went to their places and sat and conversed with their neighbours until the end of dinner, when their brother implored them for some music. They were happy to acquiesce and the assembly appeared to enjoy their entertainment.

~*~*~*~

As the assembly attendees returned to the ball room, Major Wickham took the opportunity to approach Miss Elizabeth to request a dance. Though she loathed the idea of dancing with him, she could not refuse, and there would be no chance to dance with Mr. Darcy again if she did so, thus she accepted him.

"Yes...Major Wickham, I am available for the next set." She forced a smile and followed him as he placed her arm upon his.

They walked past Mr. Darcy to the dance floor, and Elizabeth could see a frown upon his face, his eyes following them. She looked at him apologetically.

Once they were lined up in the set, Major Wickham addressed her. I take it that Darcy does not approve of your dance partner, Miss Elizabeth?" He stared into her face.

"Ah, but you may not dance any further if you decline, can you? Now, that *would* be a tragedy, Miss Elizabeth. I have seen you dance and can honestly say that you do yourself credit." He laughed.

"I thank you for the compliment, Major Wickham, and I did not say that I was induced by propriety to accept your offer to dance." She smiled her disarming smile with a raised eyebrow.

"Well then, I am grateful to be flanked by such beauty as this evening is a dream come true, Miss Elizabeth, especially considering that I have managed to catch one of Darcy's lovely ladies, even if it is just for one dance."

Elizabeth was taken aback by his statement, and countered, I cannot imagine that Mr. Darcy thinks of anyone as his possession!" She became angry, "Besides, I very much doubt that he would see me as me as a subject of his great concern!"

The major smiled, "That may be subject for debate, Miss Elizabeth. I have known him a long time and have seen how he uses his money and influence to have his own way about things… or people." She could feel his eyes caress her.

"I have understood that you tried to use undue influence to gain something that did not belong to you!" She looked challengingly at him, I have also heard that it involved someone who was without proper protection, and that you toyed with the emotions of a very young, very fragile person." she said in a low accusing voice.

"Touché, Miss Elizabeth, but we are not discussing my motivations, now are we? I believe that there is a great deal that you do not know about Mr. Darcy. He could have any woman he wants, and for whatever purpose, without thought to the consequences to himself, but as others…well… please understand my concern is only for you. He is well connected, and I would hate to see you come to any harm."

"I thank you for your concern, but I think it is rather misguided."

"Think what you will, Miss Elizabeth, I was only thinking of your welfare." He glanced at her with what she felt to be a forced smile.

The set ended by the time Wickham concluded his assault on Mr. Darcy's character. He escorted her to her family party, to which Mr. Darcy joined shortly thereafter. Upon seeing her countenance he asked, "What did he say to you, Miss Elizabeth? You look distressed."

"He said nothing of consequence. Major Wickham was just voicing his opinions, that is all."

"I do not suppose that they are very flattering, but I do hope that you will consider the source."

"You need not worry, sir. I understand his opinions come from disappointed schemes, and that clouds his judgment." She glowed with a as their easy conversation continued through the next dance set. They did not seem to register the other people around them as they were enjoying each other's company far too much. As the evening drew to a close and guests began to leave, she decided to step out of the warm room, and onto a cool balcony.

~*~*~*~

Caroline Bingley, along with her sister Louisa, had been watching the couple and took the opportunity to step out to the opposite side of the balcony, pretending not to see Elizabeth standing off to the side. Caroline began their conversation in tones just loud enough to be heard at a short distance, I say Louisa, what do you make of our dear guest's missive? I must say that I was shocked! And to think that *he* kept this mistress right under our noses!"

"I know, Caroline, Mr. Darcy seemed to be so upright, so straightforward! To allow such behaviour, I cannot imagine. And then to send this woman to his estate in Lancashire, while she is in her confinement! Who would have guessed? I would never have thought it of him."

"Yes, well that is not the least of it. I do believe that he had sent his cousin, Colonel Fitzwilliam, to town to help… deal with things, and ensure that this mistress is removed to Lancashire. It is so good to have such an obliging ally in such business, is it not?" Caroline Tittered.

She and Louisa continued with their tete-a-tete for a little while longer, throwing in gossip from their circles in town as well, and when they noticed Elizabeth's shadow moving towards the door, they looked at each other with self satisfied smirks.

~*~*~*~

Elizabeth entered the room feeling warm and flush, but worst of all, she felt like a fool. Uncertain of what to make of the conversation she had heard, she knew the voices of the women well. *Who else would know of Colonel Fitzwilliam's exit from Meryton, but them? Only those at Netherfield knew in what haste he left, and I know those voices too well! But... why would they discuss something like that within earshot of another person? Women are not supposed to know of such subjects! I could not imagine asking a man about such things! Surely they know it would harm a person's reputation to speak of such things! Then again, since when would people of that ilk care for another's reputation? What were they implying though, about a mistress... and a child? It is all too terrible to think of him!*

Suddenly feeling waves of nausea, Elizabeth wanted to go home immediately, and tried to convince her father to take her and the rest of the family home. She wanted to avoid Mr. Darcy after what she overheard on the balcony, and needed some time to think those accusations through. Desperately wishing to acquit him of cruelty, but unable to entirely dismiss the facts of the conversation out of hand, she started to feel the beginnings of a vicious headache.

On their way back to Longbourn, Elizabeth dwelt upon what she had learned that evening. There is a mistress whom he is supporting who is now with his child and he is keeping her in his estate in Lancashire.

Her father looked at her in sympathy, "Ah, my Lizzy, I see you are tiring of such frivolity. I sympathize with you my dear, in fact I wish I had thought of such a maneuver earlier, and then perhaps I would be spared from the tedious conversation with Sir William." He laughed.

Not wanting to divulge her real reason for wanting to leave, she allowed her father to think what he would, and then resolved to avoid talk of a certain gentleman for a while. She felt a need to be away from all of the gossip and deception, and resolved to write to her Aunt and Uncle Gardiner to petition to stay with them at their home on Gracechurch Street. *Yes, town will be diverting enough to not think on such things!*

Chapter 13

Morning came all too soon for Elizabeth. She hardly slept. When she finished her breakfast, she headed towards Meryton with Jane to post her letter. Elizabeth could sense Jane was concerned about her, for her sister kept glancing at her. Elizabeth, however, tried to focus on the path, preferring to think about last evening.

Jane broke the silence, "Lizzy, what happened last night? I had thought before that you had found a positive resolution to your questions with a certain gentleman. Is that not so?"

Pausing, Elizabeth looked away, then said, "Mr. Darcy and I spoke last night. In fact, he told me that he wished we would be more than friends. I felt... no, I think that... he was implying he wished to court me. Not in so many words, but he said it so earnestly as if..."

"As if what, Lizzy?" Jane prompted.

"As if he was really speaking from his heart... he spoke like he meant it."

"Why, then, are you so sad, dear sister? Should that not be a good thing? After all, I do believe that you care deeply for him. In fact, I think you are, or soon will be, in a fair way to being in love with him." Jane stared intently at Elizabeth.

Elizabeth glanced up the road away from Jane, and took a deep breath, I thought I was, but then last night I went out to the balcony at Netherfield and heard... well I am certain that it was Miss Bingley and Mrs. Hurst, talking about personal issues in regards to Mr. Darcy. They insinuated that he had... has a ... a mistress! I could not believe it, but they did not seem to be talking in jest, in fact, they said that they had found a letter. I can only surmise that it was written by this woman." Shaking her head, she continued, I could not live with a man, who keeps another woman while he proclaims to love, honour, and respect me. That goes against everything that I hold true…"

Elizabeth could feel the stinging sensation of tears forming in her eyes, followed by their hot sensation upon her face.

Jane took Elizabeth's hands as she turned to face her. "Lizzy, do you really believe that he would do such a thing? Mr. Bingley has the highest regard for him, and I cannot believe that he would condone that, let alone be very good friends with Mr. Darcy if that were the case. Perhaps there was a misunderstanding about the letter. You said that it was implied. Could it not be that they have the facts wrong? I daresay letters can be misconstrued to mean one thing, but say another."

Perhaps, but Jane, you were not there, you did not hear them. Why would anyone say such things in a place where there is a chance to be overheard? That would be unconscionable, to repeat such untrue rumours."

"Yes, I agree, but I cannot offer any excuses for that behaviour, other than they may not have believed that anyone else was within hearing of their conversation. You know how gossip is here, Lizzy, and I am sure it is no different in town."

"Jane, you cannot believe that I have so much naiveté as to believe that the men from certain circles in town do not… keep women, for I have heard stories, though I should not like to think it of Mr. Darcy. It is just… well… the other corroborating details that I heard as well. Colonel Fitzwilliam left in great haste, and according to Miss Bingley and Mrs. Hurst, the reason he left was to 'deal with' the issue of Mr. Darcy's mistress and… her… confinement!" Elizabeth's eyes became bleary. Gasping, she went on, I do not know what to think, but I do know that I do not wish to become a subject for gossips. Oh Jane, I need to get away from Meryton, and think about all that has happened these last few months. I cannot think clearly with his presence." She begged of Jane, "That is why I need to get away. It would be so much better if you were to join me."

Jane looked at her sympathetically, "If you are resolved to go, then I shall consider it."

Elizabeth thought she could see a hint of disappointment and remembered Mr. Bingley, "Oh dear, Jane, I am sorry. I seem to be only thinking only of myself. I should not wish to take you from your Mr. Bingley."

"Nonsense, Lizzy. You are very important to me as well, but yes you are right, I would miss him." Jane paused then started again, "But wait, Mr. Bingley will be leaving to town today, he thought he might be gone for several days. Perhaps, I could send a letter to Miss Bingley to inform her of our journey, and then she could inform her brother."

I doubt that Miss Bingley would be so eager to relay anything about us to her brother... or Mr. Darcy. Elizabeth wore a doubtful look as she responded, I am not so certain she would be willing to do so, but perhaps... if we were not gone too long." *Yes, then perhaps I can have another voice of reason to help sort through this... news.*

"Oh Lizzy, I am sure you are mistaken about that, as well as the other about Mr. Darcy, but I will go to town with you as I do not want you to despair, and we can return back then when Aunt and Uncle Gardiner come to Longbourn for Christmastide."

It was now settled. They would go to Cheapside until just before the Gardiners would be coming to Longbourn to celebrate Christmas. Elizabeth could not forget her concerns though, no matter what she resolved to do. *I cannot say for certain how I feel about this information. It is too much to take in at once! I cannot really believe that he would behave in such a way, but how can all of the details be explained? Why would he keep a woman at his estate, if she were not his?*

Distressed and confused, she resolved to think no more about it at present, and concentrated on her trip to London.

~*~*~*~

Darcy awoke later than his preference, but felt satisfied about the results of the ball. He felt some disappointment last night at not being able to see her out to her carriage. Mr. *Bennet would have granted me the opportunity to see her out... after our discussion last night about my coming to see him this morning, I was certain that he would understand.* He intended to ask Elizabeth's father for permission to court her, and he also wanted to talk to him about the dangers of

George Wickham. For now, though, he dwelt on more pleasant subjects.

Elizabeth shall be mine! And very soon we shall come to know one another better... Since the time she stayed at Netherfield, he had dreamt about Elizabeth as his wife. As he lay in bed thinking about them, he wanted to run his fingers through her mahogany silky curls as it cascaded over her ample bosom. He closed his eyes and imagined himself caressing her shoulders and her lovely breasts, and then moving downward, kissing the trail his fingers left... and then what he would like to do... afterwards.

He stopped himself, before he became miserable from his thoughts and his growing arousal. He got up and went about dressing in a better mood than the previous day. Baxter had him ready in record time. Shortly thereafter, Darcy made his way to breakfast. When he arrived, Bingley nodded to him in greeting.

Bingley noted his cheerful manner and behaviour, I say, Darcy you are uncharacteristically cheerful this morning. May I ask if a certain young lady is responsible for this odd behaviour?"

Darcy frowned but then shook his head and smiled, "You may say that I had a delightful evening, Bingley, and you were right about giving a ball. I was amused, and I did find a companion for whom it was not a punishment to converse with."

"I was right for a change! I believe you found someone for whom it was not a punishment to stand up with, am I correct?" Bingley laughed.

"I will admit that I enjoyed dancing with Miss Elizabeth. She is an excellent conversationalist, as is her father, and yes, I had some good company..." Darcy stopped when he remembered Wickham's presence. He had enjoyed Elizabeth's company so much that he nearly forgotten about that rogue. His face turned grim with a frown, I did not, however, enjoy the presence of a certain militia officer. It seems that he could not help himself, and wanted to taunt me with his presence. I do intend to discuss this matter with Mr. Bennet this morning, though."

Bingley's face lit up at the mention of going to Longbourn, "Then, may I join you on your ride to see the gentleman, as I do not leave for town until twelve o'clock?"

Darcy smiled, "Of course, I could not deny you a chance to see your lovely 'angel', besides I would not mind visiting the gentleman and some of his daughters."

The two gentlemen finished their breakfast in short order, and made their way to Longbourn with much anticipation. As they rode, they discussed their thoughts on the needs for Netherfield Park, and possible improvements to the stables. Darcy hinted to Bingley, I wanted to take a few private moments to talk to the gentleman about some issues that are rather sensitive…"

Bingley interrupted with a broad smile and a winked. "Ah, I understand. I believe I can find *some* way to entertain myself for a while."

"I do not want you to think that I am rushing into things. I just do not wish to lay open my private affairs to everyone, and it is difficult for me to do so with an audience."

Sighing, Bingley conceded, "Yes, I know that you will *never* rush into anything, Darcy. It is not your nature, but am I right in guessing that you will at least want to ask for a courtship with Miss Elizabeth?"

"I will not comment on that right now, but I do think that we may soon be closer than we had ever hoped." Darcy replied with an enigmatic smile.

They were soon at Longbourn, and being led to Mr. Bennet's study with the master greeting them, "Well, hello gentlemen, I must say I did not think I would see you today after such a successful ball. Why, I would have thought you would want to rest before your trip, Mr. Bingley."

Bingley smiled, I could not go until I took leave of my neighbours, and I felt that this was the best place to start." He winked at the elder man.

Mr. Bennet chuckled. I suppose I am not the only motivation." Mr. Bennet looked towards Darcy, who had not joined in their banter.

Darcy began, "Sir, might I have a word with you?" Darcy stepped forward. I wanted to talk to you about some concerns I have with a certain… gentleman from last night, who seemed to be paying your youngest daughters' much attention."

That was the queue for Bingley to make his exit. "If you do not mind, sir, I believe I will make my leave now."

Mr. Bennet opened his mouth as if to say something to Bingley, but the younger man left before he got a word out.

Darcy watched as Bingley left the study, "When you say 'a certain gentleman', I assume you are referring to Major Wickham, sir?"

"That is correct," Darcy answered. "You see, I have had a long history with Mr. Wickham. We grew up together, but I hope that you understand he and I are nothing alike."

"Yes, Mr. Darcy, I have noted the Major paying particular attention to my daughters, Lydia and Kitty, though I do not understand what allure they would hold for such a man. I must ask why you have taken the extraordinary step of coming all the way here so early the morning to discuss this with me?"

"If I may explain some of Major Wickham's and my history, it may become easier to understand. I must, however, request your secrecy on the specifics I reveal as I am not a man who discloses his private business without very good cause."

Mr. Bennet was all earnestness. "You have my word that I will not repeat anything you say to me. I must say that I am very curious now as to what you have for an explanation."

Darcy sighed and walked over to the window, looking out for a moment before beginning, I am not certain of his motivation, but I believe that it may be due to me. Furthermore, he is not a man to be trusted with your daughters, sir. I speak from knowing what he has done. Once he tried to seduce a young lady into believing she was in love with him so that she would agree to an elopement in order for him to gain her sizeable dowry. He and my family go a ways back, and I have known him for quite some time."

Darcy paused for a moment, catching Mr. Bennet's gaze and holding it. "My father was his godfather and sponsored him in Cambridge in the hope that he would take a living in the church, but his behaviour was not suitable for a man in the clergy. I never said anything to my father out of respect for him, and when he died, he left a living for Mr. Wickham. At the time, he refused to take orders and was duly compensated in turn for the intended living, but he spent his inheritance, and when the living became vacant, he wished to receive it. I did not grant it, and he was not pleased with me, to say the least.

After he left my estate, I had not heard from him for quite a while." Darcy answered.

"Now that is quite a story, Mr. Darcy. But, what, sir, would *you* have to do with him now taking an interest in my youngest daughters?"

"I believe that Mr….Major Wickham sees my attentions towards Miss Elizabeth, and I believe he may be trifling with them. He may even try to compromise one of them, thinking that I would cease my… attentions towards… Miss Elizabeth." Darcy explained.

Mr. Bennet asked, "And why would he think that in compromising one of my daughters that it would have any effect upon your paying or not paying attentions towards Elizabeth?"

Darcy paused and looked out the window then back at Mr. Bennet, "Mr. Wickham knows that I do not pay my regards to any woman, much less dance with her. I almost never dance if I can help it, and Mr. Wickham is aware of this. Thus, my marked attention to Miss Elizabeth at the ball last night must have been noted by him."

Darcy took a breath and continued, "We had also met when he first came into Meryton, which, as a matter of chance, was when he first met Miss Elizabeth, and she and I conversed while her sisters were in conversation with the other members of his party. Sir, I believe that you should know that I have the highest regard for Miss Elizabeth. In fact, I also wanted to come here today to ask your permission to court her, so you see, I have honourable intentions towards your daughter."

Darcy looked pleadingly to Mr. Bennet, who was full silent for a few minutes.

"I see," he said quietly, "And what does my Lizzy have to say about that, sir?"

"I have not yet asked her. I wanted to ask your permission first, so that you understood my intentions are sincere."

Mr. Bennet nodded his head. I see, well then, Mr. Darcy, if Lizzy will have you as a suitor, I see no reason to deny you."

Darcy left Mr. Bennet's study shortly thereafter to join Mr. Bingley, who was cornered in the sitting room with Mrs. Bennet and her younger daughters. Upon seeing no Elizabeth or Jane, and not wanting to listen to Mrs. Bennet's effusions any more than he had to, he and Bingley took their leave, all the while listening to Mrs. Bennet exclaiming how unfortunate it was that those ladies walked into town to post a letter.

~*~*~*~

Elizabeth and Jane returned home later that morning.

Elizabeth managed to avoid her mother's admonitions for not being available when the gentlemen from Netherfield were visiting Longbourn. She resolved to avoid one particular gentleman until she could remove herself to Cheapside. For the most part, the weather aided her in this resolve, as it rained for three days straight and on the fourth day she received an accommodating and concerned letter from her Aunt Gardiner:

Thursday 28th November 1811

Gracechurch Street, London

Dearest Elizabeth,

Your Uncle and I were surprised to receive your letter from the other day, but we are happy that we are able to accommodate your request to come visit us these next few weeks before Christmastide. I must admit that your sudden request was worrisome in regards to getting away to think about recent issues that have arisen within the neighbourhood. I am sure you know we would always be willing to take you in any time as you and Jane are a joy to have around. I have no doubt that it is not easy to think clearly with the many distractions of Longbourn. Hopefully, this issue is nothing too serious?

Perhaps, when you come to town we may shop for the Christmas, and give you a reprieve from your troubles. Surely, we can manage to get everything ready with you both here. I must confess it will be helpful to your uncle and me. I must end this letter now, as the children are begging for my attention, and I have to discuss dinner plans with cook. I will, therefore, conclude with the hope that we shall see you and Jane within this next week.

Take care with love,

Mildred Gardiner

Elizabeth was relieved to know that she would soon be traveling to town. Now all she had to do was wait until Monday.

Chapter 14

Six days after the ball, Elizabeth and Jane headed towards town in the carriage. When they reached the Inn at Hatfield, they changed coaches to their Uncle Gardiner's carriage. Comforted by the gentle rocking of the conveyance, Elizabeth reflected upon the past few weeks. She recalled the numerous times she met Darcy in private, when she walked through the timber. Her mind attempted to reconcile the man with the many faces of his personality, who could be strong and reserved, yet soft and vulnerable at the same time.

She could not comprehend the vicious gossip she had overheard. It sounded incredible. Could he be capable of dallying with a woman? Would he keep a mistress? Why is this not making any sense? Why does he seem to hide himself away in his inner fortress? And why will he not share himself with me? Why, why, why... indeed, so many questions... and yet so few answers to this puzzle of a man!

I wish that he would have warned me about this other woman, not that I approve, but at least I would not have been taken by surprise. Would I truly want to know though, and would I have reacted differently if he had informed me? She wallowed in confusion and torment. Sighing heavily, she leaned back against the cushions and glanced to her left. Jane slept as Elizabeth contemplated everything that had happened. It is painful to imagine him in another woman's arms. As she thought about it, she became angry and hurt. Could I forgive him his past, if I am his future? Not sure of how she felt, but knowing that if he was a respectable man, then he would take responsibility for his actions, as he seemed to be doing in taking his mistress off to his estate in Lancashire.

Try as she might, Elizabeth could not remove Mr. Darcy from her thoughts, despite the pain and confusion it caused. He is a handsome specimen of a man. Such dark warm deep pools of brown, with thick eyelashes, dark unruly curls, a noble mien, with such height, and... oh... the warmth I feel when he is near. *What I would not give to at least know what it would be like to be in held in his arms.* She felt herself becoming warm in her lower regions and flushing throughout her body. *How could I still have feelings for such a man, and how could my body still respond to him, knowing what I now know of him?*

Just then Jane woke up, "Are you felling unwell, Lizzy? You look feverish."

Elizabeth startled out of her woolgathering and flushed before she replied, I am well, Jane, just a little warm from being inside a carriage for most of the morning." She dropped her gaze for a moment and tried to reassure Jane with a forced smile.

Jane raised an eyebrow and tilted her head, "Are you certain, dearest? I would not like to see you become ill before we arrive in town."

"Jane, I assure you, I am well. There is nothing the matter with me. I will be fine, once we get to Gracechurch Street." She frowned at Jane, then glanced out the window to the passing scenery. *At least, I hope I will be fine when we get to Gracechurch Street.*

~*~*~*~

After failing to see Elizabeth for two days, Darcy could no longer contain his anxiety. He had expected to spot her on one of her early morning walks. Certain that she understood his intentions, and feeling as if she returned them, he thought they could form a closer acquaintance. By the end of the evening, he was ready to share his world with her, his life, and his heart. After his discussion with Mr. Bennet, he thought he was on the road to his own happiness. Then he heard, courtesy of Caroline, that Elizabeth intended to depart in the morning for her aunt and uncle's in Cheapside.

Miss Bennet sent a note to inform Miss Bingley that she and Elizabeth would travel to town and stay there until Christmastide. Caroline read the letter to him and Louisa Hurst, explaining it as a shopping trip for the season. After she read the letter, Charles' sister became more attentive to him than usual, which was more than decency required. He tried to ignore her, but she insisted on paying him every notice. He felt as if she would leap upon him at any moment. Having enough of her, he retired to his rooms.

I could not have been mistaken that Elizabeth accepted my attentions? Surely I have not misunderstood I know that Elizabeth happily accepted my attentions. No... but could she doubt the veracity of my words? He was heartbroken after he heard the news. Has she rejected me? But why? What could have happened after the dance? Unable to bear his disappointment, he sat down on his bed, and took a deep breath as he tried to fathom what had transpired over the course of their acquaintance from these last few weeks. *She danced with Wickham, but that conversation seemed benign, from what I could discern. She looked at me as though she wanted to accept me. Would Mr. Bennet try to talk her out of accepting our courtship? But why would he do that? I am, perhaps, the best offer she or any of his daughters could hope to have, and Mr. Bennet said that he would allow Elizabeth to accept or decline as she wished.* As he thought of all of this, he recalled their first meeting near the timber.

She also asked about my cousins. Surely she does not still have feelings for Richard? The thought of his Elizabeth with his cousin drove him mad. Thinking about Richard at the moment made him angry. *Richard could charm any woman he chose with his easy manners, but then he had taken up with a mistress! Though all the better for me,* he mused

Darcy paced the room, trying to reason everything out, but nothing made sense. *Why would she not at least say goodbye? That does not seem like her, she would be honest with me.* Thinking again of their conversation, he recalled her asking about Anne. *Perhaps she did not believe me, and now thinks that I am trifling with her? No... no that will not do. She gave every indication that she believed me at the ball, so what could have changed her mind? I must speak with her, but how? Will she speak with me, if she believes me to be trifling with her?*

Resolving to go to London in the morning, he called for Baxter to pack his things. He needed to talk with her before all was lost.

When Baxter arrived, he instructed, I need you to ready my things, for I am leaving first thing in the morning for London."

"Very well, sir. Oh, and sir, here is a letter for Colonel Fitzwilliam." The valet handed the missive to Darcy. Looking puzzled, he remarked, I thought it rather strange though, sir."

Glancing at the letter, he asked, "How so, Baxter?"

"Well..." The man hesitated, "The maid said that she found it on Miss Bingley's dressing table sir, and..." He paused again, "And this is even stranger, for she said she believed that it was the same letter she had given Miss Bingley before the ball."

Darcy frowned and took several deep breaths before he said, with his usual 'Master of Pemberley' manner, "Who is this maid, Baxter, and might I be able to have a word with her?"

Baxter bowed, I believe the girl is named Gertrude, sir. I shall see to it directly." The valet exited the room and headed towards the servants' hall.

Darcy looked down at the letter, opened it, and saw that it was indeed what he had feared Fitzwilliam's letter from Harriet and his other copy of the letter to his steward instructing him on the needs of his cousin inside of it. A sudden feeling of dread came over him. He wanted to wretch at the thought of this information in the hands of one of the ton's biggest gossips. Fear washed over him as he sat down, lest he faint. Leaning over and putting his head between his knees, he tried to clear his mind.

I must forewarn Fitzwilliam before this goes too far. This could not have happened at the worst possible moment! Now resenting Fitzwilliam for putting them both in this situation, Darcy knew he needed to make haste before the situation was exposed to their entire circle of acquaintances. "D-mn!" He said out loud. He rose and moved towards the wash stand to wash his face and cool himself for all of a sudden he was diaphoretic. As soon as he finished, Baxter knocked on his door.

"Come." He commanded.

"Sir," Baxter replied, "The young maid is in the back hallway. Where shall you like to talk with her?"

Darcy took a deep breath, I think it best that you bring her to my sitting room and stay there with us while I talk with her Baxter, for the sake of propriety."

"Very well, sir." Baxter left through the back hall door, returning to Darcy's sitting room door a few moments later.

"Yes, Baxter. Come!"

Baxter entered with a little slip of a girl that Darcy assumed was Gertrude. She looked no more than sixteen and was petite, with mousy blonde hair and pale blue eyes that swept the floor in apparent apprehension. He looked at her curiously, thinking it unusual for such a young servant to be able to perform the tasks of an upper maid, let alone read. He attempted to make her feel less fearful, which only seemed to have the opposite effect. Finally he grew impatient."I understand… Gertrude is it?" At the young maid's nod he continued, I understand, Gertrude, that you found a letter just before the ball. Is that correct?

Gertrude nodded again, "Yyyyes ssssir." She did not dare to look up from the floor.

"And where did you find this letter?"

"I… I… I… ffffound iiit in the rooms used for Colonel Fitzwilliam, sir. Theys under th bed but as th mistress requires everthing ta be gone over right spiffy, I's cleanin under theres well an found 'em ther letters sir, an I's gave 'em ta th mistress then, sir… ifin' I seen 'is 'er Mr. Baxter, sir I'd given 'em ta him right away , sir."

He softened a little while watching the frightened maid, I understand, and you did the proper thing by giving it to the mistress, Gertrude." He sighed, "Now then, I understand you saw the letter again on Miss Bingley's dressing table. What made you remove it then, and give it to Baxter?"

The maid glanced up for a moment then her eyes fell, "Well, sir, I seen th' same letters as before when I give it to th' mistress. I was spectin' she give it ta the right proper person sir, but I seen it there on er dressin table an know it shoulda been given ta someone thas knows th colonel better, an I tho tha since you was 'is cousin you shoulda been given it sir."

Darcy nodded at her and gave a smile of reassurance, "You did the right thing Gertrude, and I thank you for returning them to me. I am sure your mistress is thankful to have them in the hands of the rightful owner." Dismissing both Gertrude and Baxter for the evening, he went to his bedroom to his writing desk and immediately composed a letter to be dispatched to his cousin at once. *Well that explains a few things! Should I find Caroline responsible for Elizabeth leaving Hertfordshire, she will not be able to move far enough away for what I shall like to do to her!* He hastily wrote to his cousin.

Netherfield Park, Hertfordshire

Sunday 1st December, 1811

Fitzwilliam,

I hope this letter finds you and your 'friend' well, as I have alarming news to relay. It seems that your letter from Harriet and my letter for you to give to Barker have been found at Netherfield in your rooms, under the bed by the maid. They were initially given to Caroline Bingley. I thought I should warn you about this so that you would not be caught unaware, should things start unraveling.

I am not sure what kind of mischief she can cause with this, as her primary goal has been to entrap me all these years, but knowing her as a desperate woman, she may go to desperate measures in order to use this to her advantage. You must, therefore, watch yourself wherever you go. I will be away to town tomorrow, as I have unfinished business to attend to. Should you need to be in contact with Harriet, you should have your missives directed to Barker. I must emphasize that discretion must be followed, especially now. Should word escape, then it would appear as a rumour and be duly ignored. I will write to you later when I have any more information.

F. Darcy

After seeing to it that the letter had been sent express to his cousin, Darcy sat down on the edge of the bed, taking up his glass and filling it with port. He could not be certain, but felt a sinking feeling that all of these events, along with Elizabeth's exit to town, were not a coincidence. He would get to the bottom of this and when he did, there would be hell to pay.

He stared into the fire for several minutes, thinking on this day with great anxiety and pain. After finishing his glass of wine, his last thoughts remained on Elizabeth; he lay there imagining her with him as his wife in his arms after he made her his. Nothing, nor anyone, would separate them again if she would have him.

When Darcy awoke in the morning, he dressed and made ready to travel. Last night, he had left word with Grimes that he would be away early and did not wish to alarm Miss Bingley, therefore Bingley's butler could notify Caroline that he had urgent business to attend to in town and needed to leave very early. He also wished to avoid her, insisting that he take her and the Hurst's back to town with him. Spending another moment in that woman's presence was the last thing he wanted right now. *In fact, if I see her this morning, I may not be able to restrain myself from doing her bodily harm.*

After pushing his breakfast back and forth on his plate, he boarded his coach. *I will unite with Elizabeth and explain everything.*

Chapter 15

Elizabeth watched as the Gardiner's carriage rambled through the busy streets of London. She hoped that this trip would relieve her feelings of uneasiness. *This is all so unsettling, to feel as if I am... hollow and vacant inside. No matter where I go or what I do, I cannot get over this emptiness, as if something is missing!* She continued to gaze out the window, lost in thought. As the carriage came to an abrupt stop, Elizabeth was startled. For a brief moment, she did not realize where she was. They had arrived in good time at Gracechurch Street.

The Gardiners and their children greeted Elizabeth and Jane effusively, though the children were much louder than their parents. Both the Bennet ladies had always thought of the Gardiner's home as their second home, so coming to town seemed more like a homecoming than a visit. Once they were settled in their rooms, they joined the Gardiners in the parlour.

After exchanging pleasantries and family updates, Mrs. Gardiner asked, "How was the Netherfield Ball? Your mother was quite excited about it four weeks ago, and she had me send her the latest magazines with the latest fashions along with fabric and lace." She chuckled.

Jane managed to reply, "It was the nicest affair that I have ever attended! The flowers were lovely, and the music excellent. And there were many pretty dresses... Miss Bingley, Mr. Bingley's sister, did all of the planning, and she did a most admirable job... I wish I had the talent to plan such events."

Elizabeth felt sympathy for her sister, as she knew Jane would be forlorn without Mr. Bingley, and yet she had come to town in support of her. She did not want to discuss the ball, as she would be forced to think about what she heard, and how it made her miserable. Frowning at Jane's last comment, she said, "Nonsense, Jane dearest! You would do an excellent job of planning a ball and many grand parties as well. You need to be given the right setting and you will see; for I am quite sure you can do just as well as Miss Bingley... probably even better." Smiling at her sister with a raised eyebrow, she looked over to her Aunt Gardiner, "*Mr*. Bingley was a most wonderful host."

"So I understand, according to my sister Bennet. Your mother wrote to me that you both enjoyed two dances with two different gentlemen." Mrs. Gardiner prodded.

Jane flushed and smiled, but Elizabeth looked down into her lap and sighed before answering, "Jane has an admirer, but then who could not admire her?"

Her sister glanced between Elizabeth and her aunt, "And who could not but admire our dear Lizzy? I do believe that Mr. Darcy is in a fair way to admiring you as well."

Mrs. Gardiner set her tea aside. "Mr. Darcy? Did you say Mr. Darcy, my dear?"

Jane nodded, "Yes, he is a dear friend of Mr. Bingley, from Derbyshire, and he has been staying with him at Netherfield Park since around Michaelmas."

"I have heard the Darcy name from the area where I grew up in, as Lambton is just five miles from that family's estate, Pemberley! Old Mr. Darcy was one of the best landlords in the country... I would imagine that his son has kept up the tradition of benevolence to his tenants as well." She smiled to Elizabeth, and then stared at her. "Well, Elizabeth, what have you to say about this young man? Is he a kind and generous man?"

Elizabeth felt wretched, she came here to escape from any discussion of Mr. Darcy, and it seemed that would not be the case. I would have to answer yes, aunt... he is a most kind and generous man."

Jane and Mrs. Gardiner exchanged glances and drank their tea. After concluding the subject of balls and Mr. Darcy, they moved on to other topics.

It was after dinner, that they joined Mr. Gardiner and the children, reading tales and discussing their stay in London.

~*~*~*~

For the next two days, Mrs. Gardiner noticed that Elizabeth seemed more quiet than usual. On the first day that the sisters were in town, they planned to go shopping near the area of shops that Mr. Gardiner owned. They each had their own money, and of course, Mrs. Bennet had a whole list of things she wanted them to obtain for her while they were in town.

Their Aunt Gardiner knew what her sister-in-law was like, and it was another reason she would acquiesce to either of their requests to come for a visit in town. Understanding Fanny Bennet to be difficult to live with, she often wondered how her brother-in-law had endured twenty years of listening to her ranting on such trivial things. It was a topic of amusement for them to discuss, but today she only half paid attention to the conversation. *Where is that amused laughter in your eyes, Lizzy? Your mind has wandered off somewhere else. But where else could it be?*

She had always been closer to the two oldest Bennet girls, and found them a joy to have around. Madeline Gardiner was the first person that they would go to, when they had no other responsible person to approach with their problems. It was easy for her to read both of them, and she could see for certain that Jane was smitten. Elizabeth's feelings, however, were puzzling and difficult to discern.

Usually lively with the Gardiner family, Elizabeth seemed more reserved during this visit. When she suggested that Elizabeth take her cousins out to the nearby park for some fresh air, Elizabeth agreed, but not with her usual enthusiasm. *This is not at all like the Lizzy I know. Something is the matter and she is shying away from discussing the events of Hertfordshire prior to their removal from there. I must talk with Jane to see what is amiss.*

While Elizabeth went to the park, Jane stayed behind. Mrs. Gardiner sat with Jane in the sitting room, where they made themselves comfortable. Mrs. Gardiner began, "My dear Jane, what is the matter with Lizzy? Why is she so melancholy?"

Jane looked up then down at the garment she was sewing before replying, I cannot say for certain, Aunt. Since the ball at Netherfield, she has been distant and sad. She, I believe, has very strong feelings for Mr. Darcy. I also believe she overheard a conversation near the end of the ball that upset her. Elizabeth has not confided completely in me everything, so I am unsure of the particulars."

"That is a most singular happenstance for her, for I do not believe that I have ever seen her to be so indifferent, and over things that were said at a ball! Do you know who the source of this information was dear?"

"No, I do not know for certain." Jane looked up, "Lizzy said that she thought it was another of the guests at Netherfield, but she could not say so for certain. Apparently she overheard a bit of gossip and it has her distressed greatly."

"Well, I have an inclination that it is better for her to discuss her troubles, rather than run away from them, pretending that they do not exist. I cannot bear to watch our dear Lizzy suffer so, for that is what is happening here." As she looked on, the relief upon Jane's face was evident.

"I, too wish I knew how to console her, but I have no idea how that is to be done."

"Do you suppose that she would open up to me a little more?"

"I… I would hope so, but she seemed a bit short with me when I tried to talk to her. In the carriage ride to town, she was very quiet and distracted, hardly making any conversation. That is so unlike her."

"Then it is settled! I shall have a heart-to-heart discussion with her." She smiled at her dear niece, "Tonight, I shall talk with her and see if I can come up with a solution." She laughed. "After all, your mother sends her girls to me to resolve her problems, so we may safely say that I am attending to my duties, as your host!"

When Elizabeth and the children returned from the park, she came into the sitting room to report on their activities. Mrs. Gardiner noticed that Lizzy's trademark sparkle in her eyes was absent. *I will not allow her to mope about, making herself even more miserable! I must get to the bottom of this once and for all! It is for her own good.*

~*~*~*~

After Elizabeth went to her room for the evening, she sat in front of the looking glass and dwelled on her conversation with Mrs.

Gardiner and Jane from two days earlier. In her mind, she pictured a certain gentleman atop his horse when she heard a knock at her door.

Expecting it to be Jane, she answered, "Come in, dearest." She was surprised to see her Aunt Gardiner.

"I came to wish you good night, as I fear you may have had trouble sleeping, my love." Mrs. Gardiner held a look of concern on her face. "Do you want to talk about it, or is it too private?"

Elizabeth hesitated, glancing away momentarily. Returning her gaze to her aunt, she said, I do not know how to explain this... my feelings... right now, well... I am not certain of them myself."

"Well my dear, the best place to start is at the beginning. I assume this has to do with a certain gentleman from Derbyshire?"

Elizabeth nodded, "I... I guess I should say that I have known him for a few months, but we were not what you would call on friendly terms when we met." She laughed at the recollection of their first meeting.

"He almost ran me over with his horse, and we exchanged heated words... but then I began to see him more often, when I went walking, and we would also see one another when we went to the same gatherings. While Jane was ill at Netherfield, he and I came to know each other better. Afterwards, when I went on my walks, we would stop our activities and talk... about anything. I found him quite... interesting. It is as if there are two sides to him; one severe and serious, and superior, and the other soft, kind, and thoughtful. I saw hints of this before, but then I came to know him better; he thought of me as a 'very dear friend'. At the ball, when we danced, he said he felt that he wanted to be 'better than very dear friends'." She looked up at her aunt.

Mrs. Gardiner's eyes widened, "You do not mean that he asked you to marry him, dearest?"

Shaking her head, Elizabeth reacted, "He did not say that, although he spoke with papa the next day about courting me." She looked down again into her lap.

Mrs. Gardiner took in a deep breath, then examined her niece, "Oh my dear Lizzy, why such sadness? Is this not what you wanted?

"Yes but...the night of the ball... well actually the whole day of the ball, I must have been destined to hear alarming accounts of him." Elizabeth went on to tell her aunt about her concerns after what Mr. Collins and Mr. Wickham recounted to her before the ball, then how Mr. Darcy had explained it away, allaying her fears.

After describing those events, Elizabeth paused for a long moment. Mrs. Gardiner waited silently. Finally, the younger woman spoke, "Later, just before our party left Netherfield, I overheard two ladies talking about his having a mistress and... and that... that she was with his child, and he was keeping her at one of his estates. I could not imagine such a thing! How could I have come to be so... so vulnerable to such a man?"

Mrs. Gardiner listened, and seemed concerned. "Lizzy, you sound as if you discussed the supposed engagement with him and he answered your concerns, and then you again doubted him on the word of two gossips that have nothing better to do? If you cared to ask him about this rumoured engagement, why would you not ask him about this conversation you overheard?"

Elizabeth thought about her aunt's statements and felt unsure, "I... I am not sure how to explain it. I thought that I have always been such a good judge of character, and then suddenly I did not know myself. I felt so fragile... vulnerable, that someone could hurt me like that should it be true..."

"And so, why did you not confront him with the facts of the conversation, so that he could respond in his own defense?"

"I was just...just so afraid."

Mrs. Gardiner took a deep breath, "Well, my dear that is because you care. Only those that we love and care about can cause us to hurt so. You do, however, owe it to the gentleman to be able to explain how such gossip could come about with reference to him."

Elizabeth sat up on the bed, contemplating her aunt's sage advice, looked down at the covers smoothing out imaginary wrinkles on the bedspread, "Yes, Aunt," she answered in a near whisper.

The lady directed a pointed look at her niece. I should also tell you that this feeling... this caring will make you a stronger person, if you take the chance to open your heart to him. Then, you could have so much to gain, and I do not mean just materially! It sounds to me as if he had your respect, and I am certain that the Lizzy I know can judge a character very well indeed. And if he is so foolish to trifle with you in such a way, then you will have us to help you through it. I, however, doubt that to be the case. As I have said before, I grew up near Pemberley, and I cannot imagine that he would have been raised in such a way."

She brought Elizabeth's chin up with her fingers and looked into her eyes, "And you, my dear, should consider all of these circumstances, and then decide if you think he is worthy enough to give him a chance."

Elizabeth smiled and nodded her head. "Thank you, aunt, I will."

Mrs. Gardiner smiled, "Good! And good night, dear. I think we have a very busy day planned for tomorrow, so get some rest." She kissed the top of Elizabeth's head and left her to her thoughts.

The next morning, after breakfast they were sitting in the parlour when there was a knock at the door. The housekeeper came in to announce, "Mr. Fitzwilliam Darcy and Mr. Charles Bingley, ma'am, to see the Misses Bennets."

Chapter 16

Elizabeth felt her heart drop when she heard the maid announce Mr. Darcy and Mr. Bingley.

Catching Jane's eye, she picked up her handiwork. Suddenly, she felt more interest in her needlework than she had at any other time in her life. She dared to glance up for more than a second as the gentlemen entered and she caught a glimpse of Mr. Darcy.

What she saw startled her. It was the same sad look she had noticed when she had last seen him in the timber. *Has he been this sad this whole time, or have I never noticed it before?* Lost in thought, she neglected to pay attention to where her needle was aimed, and thus stuck it into her finger. She winced as she whimpered her discomfort, and shook her finger in pain. Everyone's attention was directed towards her.

"Oh, I am sorry. I must have lost my concentration." She blushed as she brought it to her mouth.

Glancing up, she encountered Mr. Darcy gazing at her with a mysterious intensity mixed with concern.

Mrs. Gardiner raised her eyebrow, "My dear," she chided, "are you all right? Do you not think that you can spare an introduction to your friends?"

Jane and Elizabeth looked at each other, the former with an unmistakable look of excitement, and the latter with apprehension.

"Ah... yes... Aunt Gardiner... um... may I introduce... Mr. Fitzwilliam Darcy and Mr. Charles Bingley? Mr. Darcy... Mr. Bingley, may I introduce our Aunt, Mrs. Edward Gardiner?" She was breathless when she said the last. *What are they doing here, and how did they find us here? Jane! She must have sent word to Netherfield!*

Everyone exchanged their courtesies and greetings, with Mr. Bingley starting off with his typical enthusiasm, "We have been looking forward to meeting the Miss Bennets' family here in town." His eyes focused on Jane.

As Mr. Bingley glanced between his friend and Jane, Darcy stepped forward, "Yes, we did..." he responded uncomfortably.

Mr. Bingley picked up where Mr. Darcy left off, "As it has been eight days since we had last seen the Miss Bennets, we had hoped we might be permitted to walk to the park nearby... that is, if that is acceptable to all of the ladies?" Bingley could not keep his eyes away from Jane.

Mr. Darcy glanced towards Elizabeth and then lowered his gaze, while shifting from one foot to the other. Mrs. Gardiner looked between the two young couples and smiled, I am afraid I have to talk with the governess, but of course, it seems like a waste if there is such pleasant weather and no one is to enjoy it. Besides, the park is not very crowded at this time of the day."

Elizabeth lowered her lashes for a moment, placing her handkerchief on the sewing basket, and then she and Jane arose silently. As they passed by their visitors, they each looked at the gentlemen and walked to the cloak room to retrieve their outer wear. Elizabeth whispered, "Jane, please stay nearby."

"Lizzy, I will be close by. In fact, Mr. Bingley and I will stay close. Do not worry, dearest, you are one of the most courageous people I know. You will be fine! Mr. Darcy is a good man, and he at least deserves a chance to explain himself. Besides, would he be here right after you left Longbourn, if he did not feel you were worth his effort?"

Before Elizabeth could respond, the gentlemen joined them in the foyer. Mr. Bingley offered his arm to Jane and Mr. Darcy offered his to Elizabeth. "Shall we, Miss Elizabeth?"

Walking down the steps, she wondered at their sudden appearance in Gracechurch Street. *How on earth did they manage to find us? Did Jane tell Mr. or Miss Bingley where we are staying?*

Then, Elizabeth thought better of it, as Jane would not be so forward and Miss Bingley would not divulge such information to her brother or his friend. *But how did he get this address?*

She accepted his arm and turned to gaze upon him. *He looks thoughtful and unsure of himself.* She said, I was… am… surprised to see you sir, and your friend too, so soon after you must have left Netherfield. There is no urgent problem to bring you to town so soon, is there?" Curiosity overcame her, and she ventured, "Was it Miss Bingley that gave her brother the address to our aunt's home, perchance?"

Mr. Darcy held her arm close, tightening his embrace. "To answer your first question, I believe that there is a very urgent problem that brought me to town, which required me to request this address from your father." He turned to face her and looked into her eyes. "Miss Elizabeth, I became concerned when you left the ball, and did not make an effort to say goodbye to… to the party at Netherfield, and then you were not out on your usual walks of a morning. I once thought that I had seen you in the timbers, but then you were gone. All this seemed so out of character for you. I felt a need to come here after I had heard some…" he took a deep breath and wrinkled his nose and brow, .rather distasteful news at Netherfield. Thus, I went to see your father to discuss these issues as well as to talk with him about our prior discussion at the ball and our discussion the next morning at Longbourn, about…" he took a deep breath, "my request to court you." He took her hand and brushed her gloved palm with his fingers.

She felt an odd fluttering deep in her belly. "And what did my father say to you, sir?"

"He said that he discussed my request to court you, and that you had reservations… even more reservations than the last time we talked at the ball, and you came to town to try to get away and think more clearly… to sort out your feelings. He was very reluctant to give me the address, but after I explained my reasoning for wanting to come see you, he sympathized… he would not deny me a chance to explain myself to you… to try to improve your feelings towards me."

"I do not know what to say sir, I am flattered… honoured at such a display of constancy."

Darcy paused, but his eyes darted around the street and park. I think, Miss Elizabeth that you know why I am here. You must know that I…" He looked away from her, "still meant what I said the night of the ball, and…" Looking back at her, I believe I know why you are avoiding me, but you must allow me to explain. It is very difficult to discuss this, for I am not in the habit of discussing my personal business."

Elizabeth stopped at the edge of the park and peered into the tree lined walks, I had …" *This is so much more difficult than I thought.* "I… felt as if I needed time to think about all that… everything that I heard in reference to you, sir, your rumoured engagement and… having less than honourable intentions towards various… women. Although, I must admit I was never privy to the ways of the men of your society, but what I heard surprised me. I supposed you felt an obligation to support the mother of your child." She glanced up to his face and caught his alarmed expression.

"What… What do you mean 'support the mother of my child? And I have never…" Mr. Bingley and Jane turned to look at him. Darcy took a deep breath and calmed himself, scanning their surroundings, before he began, I am sorry for my outburst, Miss Elizabeth," He sighed, I can imagine what you have heard from various people, and I would not, under normal circumstances, discuss such topics, but since you have breached those subjects, I feel as if I must address them. I assumed that you would know better than to trust the word of a man like George Wickham, but honestly I…"

Elizabeth interrupted, "Sir, it is not just the word of Major Wickham, but others who spoke in confidence to each other in regards to the woman whom you have sent to your estate in Lancashire, and who is with your child!" She stared at him with an accusatory look.

Darcy's face flushed. He took a deep breath, I do not know how you came to hear this tale, but a tale it is, madam. I can assure you, I do not have a mistress in Lancashire or anywhere else, much less one with a child! Furthermore, I would never entertain the idea of having a mistress!" He paused for a moment, his eyes widening, "Did you happen to 'overhear' this the night of the ball, by chance, Miss Elizabeth, from Miss Bingley and Mrs. Hurst?"

She had been avoiding eye contact, but when he paused, she looked at him without comprehension.

He repeated his question more insistently, "Madam, did you hear this information as if in confidence the night of the ball from a discussion between Miss Bingley and Mrs. Hurst?"

She nodded, "Yes… yes I did, I had been cooling off outside, on the balcony. They came out and mentioned a letter from your alleged mistress, which revealed that you had your cousin, Colonel Fitzwilliam, send her to a cottage in Lancashire when you discovered she was with child. I would not have thought that they would discuss such things within hearing of anyone else."

"I think, Miss Bennet, that we have both been victims of Mr. Bingley's sisters' plotting!" He looked at her closely. I think I should… I need to explain some very embarrassing circumstances regarding a family member of mine, whom you are acquainted with, my cousin Fitzwilliam. You see he… he has had a mistress for a couple of years. They had both believed her to be barren, until he discovered that she was with child. In fact, he received her express while we were at Netherfield. Do you recall when he left abruptly?"

Realization slowly dawned upon her, and she regretted making accusations without allowing him the chance to explain himself in Hertfordshire. Elizabeth was shocked about Colonel Fitzwilliam's behaviour… *he seemed so amiable… but then vices are better concealed under the manners of amiable men.* I do not know what to say, Mr. Darcy. I am very sorry to have ever thought such things about you. My only defense must be that I relied on what I heard about you, not having known you as well as… as well as…"

"As well as what, Miss Elizabeth?"

Elizabeth hesitated, and with a flush creeping up from her neck to her face, she looked into his eyes and summoned all her inner courage, "As much as I would … like." As she stared into his eyes which were dark burning pools, she felt a shiver go through her.

"I think, Miss Bennet, for your willful misunderstanding of me, for running away to London, and for not giving me a chance to explain myself, I shall have to demand that your punishment… and retribution will be…" He stopped.

"I…I do wish for you to know that I am heartily sorry for all that I had thought, and for leaving without … giving you the chance to defend your character, it was most unkind and thoughtless of me." Elizabeth felt saddened and disappointed in herself for causing them both so much distress.

He smiled as widely as she had ever seen Mr. Bingley smile, his features softened and he said, I wish for you to know me so much more than as an acquaintance or a friend, Elizabeth. I cannot express how much I admire and love you, and I have done so these past few months. I never wish to be parted from you again."

After all that she had learned from Darcy, and her Aunt Gardiner's wise counsel, she knew deep within her heart that he was telling her the truth. She felt her armor melting. Tears formed in her eyes, but they were happy tears. Her heart leapt out of her chest, and she found herself breathless. She finally managed to state, "That may tend to raise some eyebrows, sir." she said with amusement written in her eyes.

His brows furrowed, then he grinned, "Not if you were to be my wife… that is… if you will have me." His serious mien reappeared, along with that same burning look she had grown to love.

She flushed and took a deep breath then smiled, looking up into his face while nodding, "Yes, yes, Mr. Darcy, I would be honoured to have you, sir."

He could scarcely contain his joy, "Please Elizabeth, if you are to be my wife, you must not address me as 'Mr. Darcy'."

Emboldened, she asked, "Then how shall I address you, sir? Fitzwilliam… Darcy…or dearest?" She smiled and he returned it.

"I rather like 'dearest', but I doubt that propriety will allow that… at least, not yet." Looking down into her face, he spoke softly, .Perhaps, Fitzwilliam, for now." He reached into his pocket for a small box and held his hand out to her. "This was my mother's wedding ring," he slipped the large, sapphire and diamond flanked golden band from the box and placed it onto her left ring finger. "She gave it to me just before she died, and told me to give it to the woman whom I had the courage to give my heart to, and who would return hers in exchange." He looked at her tenderly.

With tears in hers, Elizabeth stared into his eyes. She looked at her hand, but her eyes could not be removed from his for long, and so she was forced to return her gaze to him, "Oh, it is lovely… I do not know how to thank you for such a beautiful gift." The tenderness in her eyes told him that her thank you was not just for the ring, but for everything, his love, his forgiveness, and his never-ending patience with her.

The pair stood there, staring into each other's eyes, unmindful of their surroundings. She turned her face to his as he bent his head down and their lips met in a tentative first kiss, followed by a deeper kiss then another, until their mouths were united in an endless string of kisses. Eventually, they realized their untenable position and stepped back to catch their breaths, still staring into each other's eyes. Finally, they found themselves at the park entrance.

They smiled at their contentment and walked on through the park, not realizing that they had lost Jane and Mr. Bingley, but thankful for the privacy, until they had been gone for nearly three quarters of an hour. Upon seeing Bingley, Darcy made a mental note to talk with him in regards to Caroline, but at present he wished to enjoy the moment in the park with his dearest, loveliest Elizabeth. For now, he did not want the unpleasant thoughts or talk of Caroline Bingley to ruin this happiest day for him. Within a short while, they rejoined the other couple who seemed to be almost as contented as they were.

Chapter 17

Darcy and Bingley left the Gardiner's home after having made dinner plans with the family for the evening. Both gentlemen seemed to be in better spirits than when they had left Darcy's town home. They rode along in silence. Darcy noticed a silent contentedness about Bingley that he had never seen, and Darcy felt certain that his complaisance matched Bingleys.

The sound of Bingley's voice boomed through the coach, shattering the peace held within it. "Darcy! What an amazing morning! No! What an amazing day! Did you not think that the Miss Bennets looked especially well today?"

Darcy smiled and said in a low voice, "They looked very well indeed, Bingley."

Bingley glanced twice at his friend, I take it Miss Elizabeth is warming up to you, aye?"

Darcy took a deep breath before turning in his seat to reply, "You could say that … and I take it that Miss Bennet is finding *your* company more tolerable as well?" He stared at Bingley before facing the street again.

Bingley laughed, "You may say so. As a matter of fact, you may say that she finds my company tolerable enough to want to spend the rest of her life with me!" He grinned.

"May I be the first to offer my congratulations, then, Bingley?" Darcy turned the corners of his mouth up and raised an eyebrow.

"You certainly may! I can scarcely believe that Jane has accepted me! Is that not wonderful?"

"Yes, it is, but then I did not doubt her acceptance after hearing her mother's ravings about four thousand a year," Darcy said with a cheeky grin.

Bingley rolled his eyes and countered, "Do not think, my good friend, that I had not noticed you and Miss Elizabeth looking quite close and, I dare say, contented. Do you have anything you would like to tell me, Darcy?" He prodded, waggling his eyebrows.

Darcy smiled again, "You might say that Miss Elizabeth and I have come to an understanding."

"Have come to an understanding?" Bingley huffed, "Come to an understanding!" He raised his voice, but then lowered it, sounding more hopeful, "What *kind* of an understanding, Darcy? It would not include becoming closely related to me through my Jane, would it?"

"It may," he laughed at Bingley's baffled expression. "Alright then, yes we are, it seems, bound to be brothers, my good friend. Elizabeth has accepted me, so I think I may be as happy as you... probably even more."

"I do not think so, Darcy, although when Jane and I joined you two after losing ourselves in the park, you both seemed quite flushed and breathless."

"We were walking at a rapid pace and were flushed due to the exercise... we were, after all, trying to catch up to you."

Bingley snorted, "Right, I suppose those swollen lips came from pressing your fingers to your mouths as well, hmm?"

Darcy feigned offense. "Certainly not!" The corners of his lips betrayed his happiness at the remembrance of Elizabeth's lips upon his.

Bingley stared at him and laughed, I see you are in much better spirits now my friend... so how was it, hmm?"

Darcy preferred to think on the taste of her delicious lips in privacy, and glared at Bingley to let him know he would not discuss the matter any longer.

He wanted to change the subject and now was as good as any to address the information he had learned. "Bingley, on a serious note, we must discuss the behaviour of you sister, Caroline."

"What about Caroline? I suppose you think she may have a few things to say about our future marital status, though yours may cause her more grief than mine, especially after reading yours and Fitzwilliam's letters." He said, frowning at recalling their previous discussion.

"That is the problem. I have heard why Elizabeth left Hertfordshire, and I must say I am most displeased! It seems that she had heard Caroline and Louisa talking on the balcony the night of the ball... talking about me... *me*... having a mistress who is with child, who I have been keeping at one of my estates!"

"*What*? Why... how... I cannot fathom what would cause her to say such things...and about you! Oh my, are you... I mean is she absolutely certain the speakers were Caroline and Louisa, and they had spoken of you in these terms?"

"Yes Bingley, she recognized the voices as Caroline and Louisa, and there was *no* mistaking it! As to why, I am sure you know exactly why. Caroline will not stop hoping that I will marry her. You need to rein her in before she does irreversible damage. For if she had ruined my chances with Elizabeth, there would be no place for her to hide from my wrath. As it is, I must forewarn you that I shall not welcome her to Pemberley after this."

Bingley took a deep breath, I can understand... are you sure...?" He shook his head, " Never mind, I am sure you are, she has never given up on her unrealistic hope of marrying you... but, yes, you are right in not welcoming her to your and Miss El... I mean, the new Mrs. Darcy's home. I have tried to rein her in before, but now she has grown worse. I fear only one thing works with her. Do not worry though, I know how to deal with her now."

They arrived at Darcy's town house and parted at the front entrance with plans to meet later in the evening, where they would take Darcy's coach to Gracechurch Street for dinner. Darcy glided to his study to work on the mounting papers on his desk that he had been neglecting. I *cannot believe it. Elizabeth is mine! And what a woman!* He warmed at the thought of how wonderful and plush her lips felt upon his, as he stroked her back and shoulders. *She is so soft and fragile, yet, so passionate... and womanly.* He found it difficult to concentrate on his work, and stood up to walk to the back courtyard.

As soon as he entered the garden, he saw a familiar face. His cousin, Fitzwilliam, had made it to town. Darcy was surprised at his appearance, thinking it would be another week before he would be in town.

"Fitzwilliam, you made it back in good time! How are things in Lancashire?" He shook his cousin's hand.

The Colonel brushed off the dust from his travel, "As good as could be expected. Harriett is settled and waiting... well, we both wait for now." Darcy could not help but notice the creases in his cousin's forehead and the tangled web of wrinkles surrounding his eyes. He looked as if he had aged a decade since Darcy last saw him. "So what is this about the letters being found in my rooms and... found by the maid?"

Darcy grimaced, "It seems that you misplaced two letters before you left Netherfield. Mine was damaging enough, but the other from Harriett was worse! Then, to have them in Caroline Bingley's hands! You cannot imagine the damage she has done with that information already." His scowl deepened as he spoke, "Why did you not keep them in a safe place, so as not to get them lost? That was very irresponsible of you!" He shook his head at the contrite look on his cousin's face.

"I know it was irresponsible, Darcy. You cannot imagine how awful I feel about this... well about this whole mess. I put those papers into my case, but they must have fallen out when I went to retrieve my other papers. You must admit I was quite distracted."

Darcy sighed, I suppose that is a reasonable explanation, but still... I think we ought to go into the house, as there is no need to risk servants overhearing our conversations."

Fitzwilliam followed Darcy into the house and down the halls to his study. Darcy offered his guest a glass of brandy, and then paced back and forth in front of the hearth as he looked down at the floor in a vain attempt to gather his thoughts. *Of all of the times he has to show, why does he do so now? This was meant to be one of the best days of my life, but now I have to deal with this... disaster!* Darcy's resentment increased due to all of the circumstances that had separated him from Elizabeth, and now that he had gained her hand in marriage, he had to take care of Fitzwilliam's problems, compounded by Caroline's interference and snooping.

Feeling all of the unfairness of it he lashed out, "You cannot imagine the chaos that you have wrought upon me.

First, I had to fund your reprehensible proclivity for 'women's attentions', then I had to accommodate *your* mistress, when she found herself with *your* child only to have that fact uncovered, twisted, and thrown in my face. It was bad enough when I had given you support in the first place, and I can only think that the heavens saw fit to punish my part in the endeavor by nearly costing me my happiness with the woman I love." His eyes shot daggers at Fitzwilliam.

"I cannot say how sorry I am to have caused so many…" He stopped, "Wait a moment… Darcy, what are you talking about, 'costing you your life's happiness with the woman you love'? What woman is this?"

Darcy took a deep breath, suddenly conscious of his unintentional confession, "I… I… am in love with Elizabeth Bennet," he said quietly, "In fact, I have asked her to be my wife, and she has accepted me, which you should be thankful for because if she had not, I would never have forgiven you or Caroline Bingley for spurring the only woman I have ever loved to reject me."

"Why would she reject you? You are one of the richest men in the country! It is not as if she would be stepping down in society by marrying you! She would have all the riches and the best position she could ever desire."

"Ah, but *that* is the difference between her and everyone else. She cares not for my money or position, or her lack of consequence. She cares for me… she loves me… and I love her. I do not expect you to understand that. Most people would not. I should also tell you that because of your irresponsible handling of those letters, and Caroline's getting her hands on them, it nearly cost me her trust! It appears that Caroline, being Caroline, decided to use that information and twist it to imply that I have a mistress with child and I am keeping her on one of my estates, while I rely on you to help bail *me* out."

He gave an ironic laugh, "She proceeded to 'discuss' this in feigned discretion on the balcony at Netherfield during the ball; with the intent, I assume, to frighten Elizabeth and tear her away from me."

"I can imagine why. She has been after you for years. I doubt she gives up easily when she believes the prize is worth the effort. Now, the other question is what do you believe she is capable of doing?"

"That is the question. I think she is capable of many despicable actions. It depends on how desperate she is, and how successful Bingley is in reining her in. I discussed with him the issue of Caroline's being given our letters prior to the ball. I also informed him that she kept them for several days afterwards. That alone would keep me from ever offering for her, not that there was ever any chance of *that* happening."

Fitzwilliam nodded, "And when did you discover that you were in love with Miss Elizabeth? Was that before or after she came to Netherfield?"

"Almost from our very first meeting, and before you ask, nothing untoward happened while we stayed under the same roof." He retorted, seeing the unspoken question in Fitzwilliam's eyes. "You are welcome to stay here, but I am going to Gracechurch Street tonight to dine with my fiancée." He said, smiling at the sound of that.

"I congratulate you, Darcy, on engaging the heart of such a fine woman. You have all of the luck; fortune, position, consequence, and now a very singular and lovely fiancée. If she had had a decent dowry, you would be singing a different tune, old man."

Darcy scowled, "Richard! I could not imagine having a woman like Elizabeth, and keeping a mistress. I would never do that to her! I love and respect her too much, and I honour the sanctity of marriage too much to violate the trust she has in me. That is why I am the lucky one. After all she has heard about me, from all sorts of different people... oh, yes! By the way, I ran into one of our old acquaintances in Hertfordshire... George Wickham! He has joined the militia of your friend Colonel Forster."

"What? That devil! What could he want with joining the militia...? Ha! He may find it becomes tougher after a while. He did not try anything while you were there, did he?"

"Nothing out of the ordinary. He attempted to drive a wedge between me and Elizabeth, telling her tales, which did not help our situation after she heard Caroline and Louisa talking about *my* mistress."

"I am so very sorry about all of the mess I have caused. I will try to make it up to you someday, I promise."

The gentlemen spent the rest of the morning discussing the needs of Mrs. Heartherton; and the damage control resulting from her circumstances. Darcy then attained the freedom to anticipate his evening with Elizabeth. He had begun writing his proposal for the marriage articles to present to Mr. Bennet. Heading downstairs to ready for his departure to Gracechurch Street, he was stopped by his butler, who handed him a letter from his uncle, the Earl Fitzwilliam. Frowning, he moved to his study to read the letter in privacy. A sinking feeling settled in the pit of his stomach. This was not a simple note welcoming him back into town.

Matlock House, London

4th December, 1811

Darcy,

I need to discuss news of a most alarming nature regarding you, which I have heard earlier today. I need not remind you that I do not usually require such attention on such short notice; however, this is of the utmost importance. I will expect your attendance this evening at Matlock House for dinner, and then we may discuss this rubbish, and settle it once and for all.

J. Fitzwilliam

Darcy went cold, breaking into a cold sweat by the time he heard Bingley being introduced at his study door. Bingley started, "Are you unwell, Darcy? Can I get you something? A glass of wine perhaps?" He hurried over to Darcy, pouring a glass of wine and handing it to him.

Darcy shook his head, letting out his frustration, "D-mn! Can I not have at least one day to enjoy my happiness without someone trying to interfere?"

"Why? What has happened? Has Caroline caused you trouble already?"

What are you talking about, Bingley? What would Caroline have to do with anything right now?!"

"Oh... Well, she came back to town this morning with Louisa and Reginald. I thought for a moment she may have come here to make some trouble."

Darcy stared at Bingley in non-comprehension for a moment.

Chapter 18

When Grimes informed Caroline Bingley of Mr. Darcy's departure from Netherfield, she lost her composure and wanted nothing more than to leave for town in order to put her plans into place. She had planned to request the use of Mr. Darcy's coach, but since he had already departed, she would have to impose on that sod of a brother-in-law of hers to have his coach made ready. However, since neither he, nor his wife arose early, it would be unlikely that they would be able to depart as quickly as she wished.

She intended to remove Bingley from Hertfordshire permanently, with Mr. Darcy's assistance. She had other ulterior motives, however, which were more important than their family's removal from the small shire. Her objectives were formed when the upstairs maid had given her the letters intended for Mr. Darcy. Unfortunately, this morning she found them curiously misplaced. *Arggh! What else could go wrong today? I need to get to town before Charles and Mr. Darcy pay their compliments to those little country nobodies!*

Caroline Bingley's hopes were to arrive in London two days after Mr. Darcy and her brother. It took great effort to prod Louisa and Reginald to leave the rest of their packing to the servants in order to leave earlier than they had planned, but in the end she did manage to coerce them into agreeing. Louisa Hurst had always been more than happy to accommodate Caroline's wishes, especially when she pointed out to her sister that they would both prefer the society in town to the God forsaken country shire of Hertfordshire.

Caroline had much planning to do in short order, and she needed to find those letters. *They will be instrumental in persuading Mr. Darcy of his need for discretion in maintaining his family's good name, that and keeping him from forming a connection with that chit,*

Eliza Bennet! But where have those letters gone? That incompetent maid! She must have misplaced them.

She summoned the mousy maid, "Gertrude, where are the letters that I had left on my dressing table last night?"

"Them letters from th' other day, ma'am?"

"*Yes*, those letters from the other day, Gertrude! *What* have you done with them?"

"They's been give ta Mr. Darcy ma'am," the maid responded with a slump to her shoulders.

"What? Why were they given to Mr. Darcy?" She frowned and shook her head, making the feathery plumes decorating her head bob in a ridiculous manner.

"Cause, they's 'is ma'am. I jus figure yous too busy wi th' ball an all to get 'em ta th' gemen, a thot wi 'em be an 'is at 'e shoul 'av 'em."

Caroline's face reddened with fury and she let off an explosive sequence of angry words towards the maid, ending with the dismissal of her from the manor, much to the girl's dismay. The teary eyed maid left through the doors flanked by two footmen to gather her belongings. Upon her exit, Caroline paced back and forth until Louisa came to join her.

Together, they devised a plan to travel to town and gain an appointment to see Lady Fitzwilliam, in order to impart sensitive information regarding that lady's nephew. Their mother, the late Mrs. Bingley, and the Countess had known each other since before their marriages, and on a few occasions the two ladies dined with each other. Miss Bingley was certain that once she heard what they had to say, she would be willing to do whatever it took to gain their silence upon the matter.

She may be able to influence her husband into persuading Mr. Darcy to make a more prudent match, especially if she knows how he has behaved towards that country nobody! His family will never accept such low connections... not if I can help it! She decided to throw in a few derogatory words about Miss Eliza Bennet as well. *They will never receive her! Not if I have anything to do with it!*

The Hurst's coach traveled to town too slowly for Caroline's tastes. Upon her arrival at the Hurst's town home, she attempted to procure an appointment with the countess. Two days later, Caroline received word that the Countess of Matlock would be able to see her and her sister at two o'clock that afternoon. When the butler at Matlock House announced Caroline and Louisa, they entered the upstairs sitting room to find Lady Matlock, whose frown did not escape Caroline's notice.

"Mrs. Hurst, Miss Bingley, have a seat." She pointed to the settee across from her. I will not bandy words, or waste time. I have allowed you time during my busy schedule due to the nature of your note, Miss Bingley. I understand there are alarming developments that have come to light in regards to my nephew?"

Caroline shifted in her seat, "Yes, your ladyship, I tend to turn a blind eye towards some occurrences with the gentlemen of quality here in town, however, I gained possession of a few incriminating letters, one from... Mr. Darcy and another from a woman here in town. She had written to Mr. Darcy at Netherfield, informing the gentleman that she had a 'situation' develop due to certain...well... shall we say, 'activities'? And is... expecting a child, as a result of said activities."

The countess raised her eyebrow, but remained silent. Caroline continued with a frown, "You can imagine my shock... our shock, at such news and we felt it should be kept discreet but, unfortunately there were other activities that had occurred at Netherfield, involving your nephew and a certain country squire's daughter." Caroline leaned in, "Mr. Darcy, I am sure, would have been able to dismiss such an insignificant young lady, but I am afraid that he may have fallen for her arts and allurements, and thus may wish to take up with her, or even connect himself with her in order to be able to keep this mistress and raise the child. I felt it to be my duty to make sure that his closest relatives were apprised of this situation, and could try to dissuade him from such a course. What are intimate friends for, after all?"

The Countess appeared disgusted, Caroline noted with satisfaction, certain that Mr. Darcy's relatives agreed with her. That lady took a moment to respond, "Miss Bingley, I do not suppose it would be too much of an imposition to show me these letters?"

"Ah... your ladyship, unfortunately the maid I had at

Netherfield saw fit to give the letters to Mr. Darcy's valet, so I no longer have the letters." She said with a shake of her head and a hissing noise muttered under her breath.

"So... what you are telling me then is that my nephew Mr. Fitzwilliam Darcy, has a mistress who is in a family way, and he is keeping her where? And you discovered this by reading his letters... his *personal* letters?"

Caroline listened to the Countess, but her subterfuge in regards to keeping the letter without an apparent intent to return them did not sound good even to her ears, especially when she noted the look of skepticism in the older lady's countenance. "Ah, well ma'am, I had every intention of returning them, but at first I had to discern to whom they belonged. The servants, "she tried to smile and said conspiratorially, "you understand, are not literate, and one must be careful to return someone else's property to the correct person. I could not imagine the embarrassment that could have ensued if someone else would have found them."

Louisa nodded in agreement while she took a bite of her biscuit, as Caroline went on to further explain, "He seems to have sent this woman to his estate in Lancashire. This matter of the... country lass is also alarming madam, as there seems to be mounting evidence that he may try to connect himself to her. His intention must be to marry her to be able to keep the mistress and the child... I dare say to raise the... child with this country miss. After all, what could a country nobody say to a man such as Mr. Darcy about such things? She would be a fool to turn down such an advantageous match!"

The Countess sighed, "Miss Bingley, Mrs. Hurst, I have heard all I need to hear. I... thank you... for bringing this matter to my attention, and I am sure you *will* keep your discretion in regards to this matter, am I correct?"

Caroline realized this was said as more of a command than a request.

"Of course, ma'am. We would not think of spreading 'gossip' regarding your family about town, as we know how damaging it can be to one's reputation." She hastened to reassure the countess.

The Countess continued to stare at them until it became unbearable to both Caroline and Louisa, and they begged their leave.

After they left the Countess, the sisters chose to ignore that hostile stare and instead focus on their sense of triumph at having gained an ally in their cause to prevent Darcy from becoming engaged to Miss Eliza Bennet.

~*~*~*~

Lady Matlock watched Caroline Bingley and Louisa Hurst leave from the front window of her parlour. She had never liked those two ladies. To her, they were insignificant social climbers. She knew their mother to be one as well, however, that woman only succeeded in scaring all of the men in their set off, and she married a tradesman. Her daughters had a reputation for being cruel and catty to the younger women of their set.

It is too bad that their brother is saddled with such women for sisters and Reginald Hurst for a brother-in-law! This does not bode well, for Caroline Bingley to have had access to any personal letters of Darcy's! I can scarcely credit it. He of all people is the man least likely to engage in such activity, and to be so careless is out of character for him! That sounds more like something James or Richard would do. And, what of this country lass? The gossip about the country girl disturbed her less than anything else Caroline had to say. *So what if he does attach himself to a country squire's daughter? That could be no worse than connecting himself to the daughter of a tradesman, or to a mistress that bears an illegitimate child!*

She resolved to get to the bottom of this issue by informing her husband of the risk of an impending scandal, the likes of which her family had not seen before. Finding her husband in his study she greeted him, "James, I just had an alarming visit with a Miss Caroline Bingley and her sister Mrs. Louisa Hurst. According to them -our nephew, Darcy, received a letter from his mistress, and she is with child! They also said that he has been keeping her at his estate in Lancashire! Then, they alleged that he is about to become engaged to a country gentleman's daughter to try to make this situation tenable." she explained, pacing in front of his desk.

With a look of skepticism, her husband replied, "Wait one moment, Margaret. Why would Fitzwilliam tie himself up like that?

George lectured him for many years about women who scheme in such ways, and Darcy would never put himself at such risk."

"There must be something of merit to bring Miss Caroline Bingley, and Mrs. Louisa Hurst to my doorstep to request an audience. I cannot imagine that they would have the nerve otherwise!"

"No, there must be a rational explanation, but I cannot figure it out while sitting here. Regardless, we need to keep this from making the scandal sheets, which is what will happen if there is any shred of truth in it and Caroline Bingley has any real knowledge of it. She has been trying to get her claws into Darcy for ages, and I fear she will stop at nothing to get what she wants. I will send a note to him, and have him come to explain any such alleged letters."

~*~*~*~

When Bingley arrived home, after his visit with Jane and his side trip to Boodles, he found both of his sisters awaiting him in his sitting room. Apprehensive whenever they were together in his home without company and sans Reginald, Bingley knew he was in for an argument. Putting on the most pleasant smile he could muster, he began, "To what do I owe this precipitous visit into town? I had thought you would stay at Netherfield until at least after the New Year."

"Charles," Caroline began, "we need to discuss that situation. Do you really believe that it is a good idea to keep such a place, where you have little experience, and where you will not be near anyone who has significant experience to guide you?"

"Caroline, I know you are not fond of the country, and lack faith in my judgment, however, I must remind you that I have only leased Netherfield Park for one year, and may soon be looking into an estate closer to Derbyshire."

Caroline's eyes brightened and she purred , "Really? What brought this on? Have you decided to give up on your country crush, and find a decent society lady?"

Bingley resented his sister's insinuations, and wanted to wipe the smirk off her face, but he thought better of it, I have made decisions about my future, and what would constitute my happiness, and yes, as a matter of fact, I have decided to take a society lady as my wife.

Ladies, it pleases me to announce that this morning I have seen my angel and asked her to be my wife, and she has accepted me!" He said with a look of pure joy in his eyes.

Caroline and Louisa responded, *"You did what?"* Caroline then exclaimed, .You cannot be serious, Charles! You realize the only reason she would accept you is because of your wealth, and at her mother's insistence. You will be played the fool!"

Bingley's anger grew by the minute. I do not think so. Jane Bennet is the sweetest, most beautiful, and sincere woman I have ever had the privilege of knowing, and I will not stand here and listen to the two of you disparage her character! She is to be my wife, and I will not tolerate your insinuations, catty remarks, or slights towards my future wife! Do I make myself clear?" He glared at them, I have tolerated your rude, selfish, and mean behaviour before, but no more! I have had enough. I am not so dim as not to see what you are about, especially you Caroline!" At her look of indignation he went on, "Oh, and do not play the victim here, I know about you having personal correspondences of Fitzwilliam and Darcy's." He laughed at her, "Yes, Darcy informed me that you had their letters before the ball, and did not plan to return them to him. The maid, however, had enough scruples to do the right thing."

"Charles, let me explain... I... I... had not the time to think to give Mr. Darcy those letters, and you can be assured that..."

"*No! No!* Do not try that with me. You had no intention of returning those letters, but that was not the worst of it, was it? You and Louisa discussed those letters out on the balcony with every intention of distorting the truth. You twisted the facts and insinuated that Darcy was a cad, and had such low morals as to keep a woman and send her off in disgrace, and as if that was not bad enough, you did it with every intention of '*allowing*' Miss Elizabeth Bennet hear the whole of it!"

He shook his head at their gaping mouths, "Do not play *innocent* with me, I have heard it all now, and *if* I hear that either of you has come to cause Darcy *or* me any trouble, I will send you up to our family in Scotland. As for you, Caroline, I have kept track of all of your expenditures, I know how much you have overspent your money, and I have been covering it thus far out of a misguided sense of sympathy. However, one more misstep, and I will demand those expenses be repaid, and you will be supporting yourself!"

Bingley was breathless when he finished his tirade. Feeling proud of himself, he turned on his heel without awaiting any response and walked to his study to spend the rest of the afternoon working on his marriage settlement papers.

I have never felt so liberated in my life. Perhaps married life will agree with me! He thought when he sat down at his desk. When the time came to ready himself for dinner with the Gardiners, the Miss Bennets and Darcy, he took great care of his appearance, wanting to make a good impression on his soon to be family. He could not wait to get to Darcy's house for the ride to Gracechurch Street.

When he arrived at Darcy's house, he was shown to the study and found a very pale Darcy holding a letter. Seeing the look upon his friend's face, Bingley stepped in to offer whatever assistance he could. *Oh my, I hope this is not something that Caroline has instigated!*

Bingley concerned himself with ensuring that Darcy would be all right, but he still had a nagging feeling about Caroline's sudden appearance in town coinciding with his friend's difficulties. *If she has done anything to jeopardize our happiness, I swear Scotland will not be far enough away from either of us!*

"I have been summoned to Matlock House. Apparently, there has been some news... gossip... reported about me... that has found its way to my Uncle Matlock! I cannot believe this!"

Bingley turned almost as pale as Darcy, I do not know what to say... I swear to you that I have had a serious discussion with my sisters today, but I am afraid it may be too late to keep this under wraps with your family, and for that, I am prodigiously sorry, Darcy."

Darcy struggled to regain his breath. "Little good that does me," he hissed. "However, I must away to Matlock House to figure out how to clear up this mess, and in the mean time, I must require you to give my sincerest regrets to my fiancée."

"Of course, I will." Bingley was about to say something else but shook his head. I will see you later then, Darce. You will let me know the details, so I may know how to deal as well?"

Darcy nodded his head and saw Bingley out. Darcy seemed angrier than he had seen him in a very long time, and Bingley knew his sister must be set straight once and for all.

Chapter 19

Elizabeth anticipated this evening with Mr. Darcy throughout the day. She and Jane talked of their feelings for their fiancés, and how they had once wondered if they would ever find a suitable match for themselves. Earlier, Jane had confided in her, revealing that Mr. Bingley had proposed to her before that morning, but gave no specifics.

"Truly? Oh, that is wonderful news, but why did you not tell me before we left Hertfordshire?" Elizabeth had asked.

"Charles and I wanted to keep it between ourselves, until he could obtain our father's consent. Do not be alarmed, we only wanted to relish our mutual secret."

"Well... I think I can understand, and I shall tell you that Mr. Darcy proposed this morning in the park." Elizabeth's face lit up with her brightest smile.

Jane gaped, "Really Lizzy? Oh, how wonderful! We could get married together. Would that not be wonderful?"

"Yes it would be."

"But dearest... why do you look so fretful? Is there a problem?"

"No, not now. It is only that I feel terrible about coming to town without taking leave of him. Part of the reason I left, as you know, was to sort out my feelings, and now I find that I have acted foolishly. I should have asked him about what Miss Bingley and Mrs. Hurst had referred to, instead of running off like some ninny to hide her head in her pillows. It was compelling though, as Mr. Wickham added his information. With so many rumours and insinuations stirred up at the same time, I felt rather overwhelmed!"

Jane said with sad regret, "Yes, it is shocking that people would behave so. I can scarcely believe that they are of the same family as my Charles, and I do regret that they made you feel so terrible, so… helpless. It is distressing, is it not?"

Elizabeth nodded her head in agreement, "Yes, but now all is well, and we shall be the happiest couple in the country!"

"Perhaps one of them," laughed Jane.

Elizabeth did not wish to tell her sister about her and Darcy's improper behaviour in the park, however. Her wanton acts still shocked her, and she worried that he might think poorly of her for her complicity in submitting to such impropriety.

After dinner, Bingley and Jane talked between themselves in a corner of the Gardiners' parlour after dinner, while Elizabeth sat alone and worked herself into a state of anxiety, wondering if Darcy thought twice about marrying her after this morning's activities.

~*~*~*~

It concerned Elizabeth when Mr. Bingley arrived at the Gardiners' residence without Darcy. After the maid took his hat and cloak, he addressed his host. I came here, in part, to relay Darcy's deepest regrets for not joining me, as he wished to visit the Misses Bennets and their family this evening. He was called away by his uncle the Earl of Matlock quite abruptly." He turned to look at Elizabeth with an apologetic expression.

"That is unfortunate, as my wife told me how lovely a visit you all had, and I had looked forward to meeting the gentleman," Mr. Gardiner said.

"Indeed, uncle, we were eager to introduce you to Mr. Darcy." Elizabeth hoped that Mr. Bingley would elaborate on Mr. Darcy's absence.

Jane made introductions between Mr. Gardiner and Mr. Bingley, and then took Mr. Bingley away from the gathering to a corner of the parlour.

The dinner bell rang, interrupting further conversation, and they left the parlour for the dining room. Elizabeth felt trepidation over

Mr. Darcy's absence. *I hope that he has not changed his mind due to my allowing certain liberties in the park this morning, and this is just an excuse.* She did not cease chastising herself for her earlier behaviour, and could not pretend to be hungry at the table.

Involved with her thoughts, she failed to hear her sister tease her about her silence. When she realized the party had been focused on her, she tried to excuse her absent-mindedness, "Forgive me, I was thinking about a discussion this afternoon. Jane and the rest of my family can attest to my habit of woolgathering, Mr. Bingley."

"I understand, Miss Elizabeth. I have found that as of late, I have also been caught 'woolgathering'. There are many pleasant thoughts to dwell on." He looked towards Jane.

Elizabeth took pleasure in Bingley giving her sister the amount of attention that a man in love ought to give. *At least dear Jane will be happy, for she is someone who deserves her good fortune.* She found it difficult to dispel her uneasiness though. *Something is the matter, as I am sure that Darcy would be here, if everything was all right. Perhaps he is trying to find a way to disentangle himself from this, and lacked the courage to come tonight for that reason.* Those thoughts made Elizabeth miserable not only throughout dinner, but afterwards as well.

Elizabeth noticed during dinner, how Mr. Bingley avoided eye contact with her, and seemed to want to avoid any discussion of why Darcy had not joined him. Mr. *Bingley is usually an affable, talkative gentleman, but all he is doing now is making small talk with Aunt and Uncle Gardiner, and making moon eyes at Jane! Why could Darcy not have sent a short note? All it would have taken was a scribble or two, which would have explained something!* She could only manage a few bites of food as she thought of his reasons for not coming tonight. *Surely word has not gotten out already of our engagement somehow, and now his family is trying to prevent us from marrying?*

After they finished the meal, the gentlemen retired to Mr. Gardiner's study, and Jane and Mrs. Gardiner joined Elizabeth in the parlour. Jane voiced her concern, "Lizzy, what is the matter? Why do you look so upset?"

Elizabeth took a deep breath, .I do not know how to say it, but I do not have a good feeling about Mr. Darcy's absence. I know he was… or at least seemed to be looking forward to this evening and then to suddenly have 'urgent' business does not sound right."

Jane reached over and touched her sister's hand, I am sure that he would not stay away on purpose, unless something significant occurred. You must not worry, I am sure that he will explain his absence when they come again tomorrow."

"Tomorrow?" She looked askance at Jane, "What do you mean by, 'tomorrow'?"

"Ch… Mr. Bingley said that he and Mr. Darcy would pay us a visit tomorrow, so I am sure that you …that we will learn of the severity of the reason for his delay."

Elizabeth took another deep breath, allowing herself to calm as she tried to overcome her sense of dread.

~*~*~*~

Darcy rode along the short route to Matlock House, still unsure of what to tell his uncle. He guessed the subject matter of this urgent missive, and felt confident that it involved Caroline Bingley. If she made matters worse for him, or Richard, he would find a way to have her locked up for the rest of her life. *She will never be accepted or welcome in polite society again*, he vowed.

Upon his arrival at Matlock House, the butler showed him into his aunt and uncle's small parlour. There, he noted the presence of his cousin, the Viscount James. When the doors closed, his aunt and uncle greeted him curtly. Sighing, Darcy tried to quell the feeling that he stood in front of a firing squad.

His cousin gave him a smirk as he greeted the Earl and Countess.

The Earl began, "Darcy, how long have you been in town?" Darcy noted his uncle's curt manner.

"I came to town two days ago, sir. I would have called sooner, but I had business to tend to." He heard his cousin snort.

"No doubt, Darcy." James sniggered, but stopped at a withering look from the Countess.

"There is no point in dickering about. I have been the recipient of alarming news in regards to you, involving a Mrs. Harriet Heatherton. We have heard her name bandied about here in town, however, never had I expected to hear that name in connection with yours." The Earl's face appeared flushed with anger.

Darcy grimaced. "You cannot believe everything you hear in the way of rumours, sir, and I have never done anything dishonourable in my life."

"Nonetheless, this is a serious matter. One misstep and this sort of problem can get out of hand. What I really need to know is how this could have come about?"

"I do not know, sir. As I have said, I have not done anything dishonourable. Perhaps, if I knew more of how this information' came to you, I might be able to accommodate you." Darcy stalled for time to think of how he could extricate himself from the situation unscathed.

"This afternoon, I learned that this Mrs. Heatherton had written to you about her 'situation' and pleaded for 'assistance' to help take care of that 'issue'. I also heard that you had written a letter to your steward to aid this... this... woman, and that she is living in your estate in Lancashire." Darcy suspected that the Earl was trying to be as delicate as possible in front of the Countess.

"Sir, what evidence is there of this... letter, did this person give you these letters? Where are they?"

"No,. interrupted the Countess, .they did not give me the letters; they implied that a maid had given them back to you, and that you are still in possession of them. I was very skeptical of this information considering... the source. Your uncle and I, however, felt it was imperative that you allay our fears. Furthermore, I... we felt you needed to be aware that there are people out there that may cause a stir -should this information, whether true or not, get around town." She looked him in the eye.

Darcy felt emboldened by his aunt's offering, and directed his response to his uncle, "Sir, I have not been in collusion with this Mrs. Heartherton. I have never met her, and I doubt I ever will. As to the other matter, all I can say is that I have no such letters in my possession, and I would challenge anyone to produce evidence to the contrary." *I am not lying to them. I did not have any contact with that woman, nor will I ever and those letters have been burnt, as they should have been in the first place.*

The Earl examined his every feature with keen eyes and formal pose. Darcy waited. He desired to appease his uncle for now, but he knew that his cousin would not be so easily fooled. He also thanked the heavens that Richard was his mother's favourite, although at present, he wished that Richard was his father's favourite child, not that conniving son and heir of theirs, James.

A servant alerted them that dinner was ready, with that the Earl said, I will trust that you ensure this does not go any further, as you know what kind of trouble there will be on this end of the family, not to mention your Aunt Catherine. Humph, but then that may be another idea..." He seemed entertained by a thought, "Catherine would move heaven and earth to dispel any rumours of that sort to suit her own purposes. I dare say she would venture to shoot the messenger who bears such news."

Everyone but Darcy laughed. He did not find it amusing to make sport of his alleged alliance with his cousin. In all the years that he could remember, his aunt would toss about the ridiculous notion of him marrying his cousin, and that news almost cost him Elizabeth.

As they sat down to dine, they discussed lighter topics. Darcy kept thinking of Elizabeth and the meal that he should have been enjoying with her and her family. He resented that Bingley was at Gracechurch Street, while he had to deal with this situation of Fitzwilliam's. He thought about his encounter earlier and hoped for a repeat soon. Darcy resolved to go there with Bingley tomorrow to make an early call, and perhaps he could gain an audience with her uncle.

Elizabeth's aunt seems to be a well bred person... I am most pleased to have made her acquaintance. I should like to invite her and her husband to Derbyshire, as I suspect they would enjoy it. Georgiana will like them as well. He realized that his sister had yet to meet Elizabeth, and he vowed to introduce them as soon as possible.

He consumed his meal in silence, but realized the viscount had been observing him. Adjusting himself in his seat, he tried to make as polite a conversation as he could muster. "So, James, what are you planning for after the holidays? Have you decided whether or not you shall stay in town or go to Matlock?"

James paused and raised his eyebrow. I have yet to decide, cousin. I had thought to stay in town, but now that I think about it, going up North may be more appealing than I had previously thought".

Darcy frowned, failing to hide his consternation, and changed the subject. "Have you been over to the club? I hear there is a new fencing master, and he has remained undefeated since he has come here."

"I have not been there to fence, but I have heard about the man, and seen him do his best upon you friend, Stone." He laughed a little, "But the man was so busy that I had to stand around the club awaiting my chance to prove my skills, so I end up chatting with the other members. Oh, by the way, I have heard something quite unusual. I heard that Richard has been in town a couple of times these past couple of months and I found it strange… very strange that he has not once paid us a visit."

Darcy almost choked on his soup. After regaining his composure, everyone at the table stared at him with curiosity.

"Indeed? I believe he came at some time or other to attend to some business, but then I am sure that there are many things he needs to attend to due to events occurring over on the continent." He diverted everyone's attention to something else, as his relatives bemoaned the possibility of Richard having to go to battle on the continent.

Darcy did not linger at Matlock House for long, as he wanted to collect his thoughts. After directing his driver to take him back to Darcy House, he reclined against the seat of his coach and breathed a sigh of relief. He felt a need to communicate to Richard about his meeting with the earl and Countess. He knew that Richard would be back, and he needed to let him know that unless he went to visit his parents, he would be putting himself at risk of exposure.

Darcy felt that this near disaster of a dinner would be fair punishment for missing a dinner in Elizabeth's presence. *Soon my love, very soon we will not have to deal with these separations.* He thought of when he could bring Elizabeth back to the Darcy House as his wife, or better yet Pemberley. He grew most uncomfortable as he rode.

Chapter 20

Darcy felt a sudden compulsion to see his beloved Elizabeth, by the time he neared his town home. He needed to see her in order to settle himself for the battles he knew were coming. He felt that there was no reason to suffer any further tonight, and he resolved to go to Gracechurch Street. Rapping on the roof of the carriage, Darcy directed his driver to turn the coach around and head towards the Gardiner's residence. When he arrived at his destination, he felt a lifting of his spirits.

As he came through the door, he saw Elizabeth's face lit up as their eyes met. A warm sensation grew within him. He thought he detected a look of distress in her countenance, but it disappeared as quickly as it appeared, replaced with a happy smile. *How beautiful she is, looking at me with her bright eyes and her face all aglow. I have to be one of the luckiest men alive.* His attention diverted from his betrothed when he greeted Mr. Gardiner and Bingley, who made introductions between the two gentlemen.

"At last I have the privilege of meeting you, Mr. Darcy, and it is a pleasure." At Darcy's questioning look he explained, "My wife has told me of her enjoyable visit with you this morning sir, and I must say that Mr. Bingley and my nieces have praised your character as well." He said with an easy manner and genuine smile.

Darcy paused before responding, I assure you sir, that the pleasure is all mine. I think highly of Mrs. Gardiner and your nieces…and of course I need not mention my friend's good character as well." He tried to give Elizabeth's Uncle a good first impression and put in a good word for his friend.

"Sir, we understood that you had urgent business to tend to and so were unable to attend to us earlier. We are, however, delighted to have you in our home sooner than we had been told."

"Ah, yes... I had been called on some... matters of business that required my immediate attention, and I cannot tell you how it pained me to be absent for the earlier part of the evening," Darcy said with a meaningful glance at Elizabeth.

He noticed that she watched him carefully, and blushed as she listened to his conversation. *If you only had an idea of what you do to me Elizabeth, you would be frightened by the violence of my affections.* He struggled to keep his admiration in check, fearful that his body would betray him. *This will not do, to be thinking of such things in a room full of her relatives.* He thought about his meeting earlier and instantly felt chastened.

Mr. Gardiner replied to Darcy's comment at face value, I understand, as a businessman I find that there are times when you must take care of your interests when you would much rather spend time with friends or family." He said, nodding his head towards Mrs. Gardiner.

Bingley entered the conversation. I have found that to be the case many times in my life, as I would much prefer to spend time with my friends and family rather than tend to business matters, but sometimes it cannot be helped." He glanced in the direction of Jane.

Conversation soon withered as the evening grew late, and the two suitors soon bid their beloveds and their family good night.

Bingley walked to the front foyer with Jane as Elizabeth followed with Darcy to a secluded corner of the foyer, giving the other couple a chance to have privacy. Darcy wished to resume this morning's activities, but knew he would create a scandal if he did so in the front foyer in front of Elizabeth's sister and the servants, so he settled for light conversation as his eyes caressed her form, causing her to produce yet another one of her lovely flushes.

"Do you realize, Elizabeth, that I adore you when you blush like that?" He said in a low voice.

"I had not realized until this evening sir, however, hence forth I shall expect to have need of a fanning device in order to protect myself from the discomfort that it produces. Perhaps, I should insist that I take your visits in a room without a lit fire in order to ensure my continued comfort." She replied saucily.

He recalled her look of what appeared to be distress and asked, "What distressed you earlier when I arrived, did Bingley not tell you that I had an urgent matter to deal with?"

Her smile faltered, "Yes, however... I... I... I thought that you may have viewed my collusion with our earlier activities a little differently once you left, and you..."

He smiled at her with his piercing, burning stare, "Do not concern yourself about that, for I was the initiator of said activity and was... mmm... quite thrilled with this morning's activities, in fact I thought of little else all day. I shall endeavour to strive for your continued comfort for an eternity, Elizabeth..." He said in all seriousness, I can scarcely tell you how much I loathed being called away earlier and missing your company during dinner. That is why I came here right after I left... my uncle's house. Do not worry dearest, I shall join Bingley tomorrow, and perhaps if we can walk out again I may be able to explain my need to meet with my uncle."

She looked at him passionately, I shall look forward to it then, sir, until tomorrow..."

"Yes, until tomorrow, my dearest, loveliest Elizabeth." He took her hand and placed a kiss upon it, then turned it over and kissed her palm before placing one last kiss upon her inner wrist again, enjoying her reaction to his attentions. Finally, he made his exit and boarded his coach. He had the pleasure of seeing Elizabeth frozen in place with such a look as he took leave of her. *This bodes well for our future!* His carriage pulled away.

For the first few moments after their departure, the gentlemen were silent until Bingley broke their reveries, "Darcy, I did not expect to see you again tonight, after our earlier meeting. Tell me what happened at the earl's home?"

Darcy sighed then frowned at having to give up arousing memories of Elizabeth, "Well, I am convinced that Caroline has been to Matlock House, trying to stir up trouble, no doubt, with regards to a circumstance that she has a poor understanding of."

Bingley returned his frown, "Why? What has happened? Did they say that she came there? What was said?"

"It was not so much what was said, but what was *not* said. I did not, in fact, hear Caroline's name mentioned, but what the Earl and Countess repeated had every indication of coming from someone who would have intimate knowledge of the contents of those letters, and no one would have access to them other than Baxter, your maid Gertrude, *and* Caroline. I am certain that your maid would be able read much less devise some nefarious scheme to besmirch my character, and I could not think that my own man would do such a thing. Unfortunately that leaves us with only one other person…"

"Caroline." They said in unison.

"I cannot tell you how sorry I am about this Darcy. I hardly know what to say, except that I will ensure that there is no foul business from that quarter anymore. I plan to deal with Caroline and give her no room for a misunderstanding."

"What shall you do?" Darcy asked, curious to see if Bingley could deal with his wretched shrew of a sister.

"I shall make arrangements with our family in Cumberland. Then I shall cut her off… she will have her money, however, she will have to make do with shortened funds. You see, she has overspent, expecting me to cover her overages. No more! I cannot tolerate this when she intends to injure my good friend's happiness, and the happiness of my dear Jane's sister!"

Darcy reflected on everything that had happened during the day. *So much happiness, yet so many complications! And here I am tangled up in the middle of a mess not of my making!* When Darcy broke out of his reverie, he realized they had arrived at the front of Bingley's town home, where Bingley's horse was led from the back of the carriage to the stables as Bingley made his way to his front door.

~*~*~*~

Caroline waited for her brother to arrive home. She found out that he had spent the evening with Jane Bennet. She did not fail to notice that Mr. Darcy's carriage had pulled away from the front of the house, as she looked out the window when Charles arrived. Upon seeing

Charles, she knew that he had a discussion with Mr. Darcy, which likely included a reference to her and those damnable letters. *If only that twit of a maid had not taken them and given them back!* She moaned to herself.

Finding her in the front parlour, Bingley began, "Caroline! We must speak. As I am sure you can figure out, I have just had a most interesting and distressing conversation with Darcy!" He looked at her sternly which surprised her for her brother did not lose his temper very often."

"I am sure, I would not know to what you refer to Charles! How could I possibly know? I have done nothing to earn your ire!" Caroline felt that the best defense was a good offense.

"Do not try that on me Caroline! I have had it with your lies! I know your character too well to be deceived by your subversions, especially when coupled with evidence that you are lying!" Charles face turned beat red with fury.

"You have no proof of anything! It is the word of a simple, stupid maid!" Caroline stopped with a realization, and then gasped.

"Aha! There, you have given me the proof yourself dear sister! I have not spoken a word about any maid, however, Darcy mentioned that Gertrude was the one who found Darcy's and the Colonel's letters and that she gave those letters to you. You did *not* give those letters to Darcy, but kept them for yourself, and to further your transgressions, you slandered Darcy where you knew that Miss Elizabeth would hear it! I cannot tolerate such behaviour under my roof! Within a fortnight, you will be

on your way to Scotland to see Aunt Dugan. If I were you, I would stay far away from Darcy, as he is livid with you right now. In the meantime, while you are still here under my roof, you will conduct yourself with discretion and avoid prattling to *anyone*! If you behave, I may condescend to allow you to come to my wedding." With that final word, he turned on his heels and marched out of the room.

Caroline sat on the sofa, with her mouth agape while pondering the day's occurrences. *Well I never! You cannot do that to me, Charles!* Then she recalled their earlier conversation in regards to her finances, realizing that she needed to tread carefully in respect to her next actions. She sat for a long time contemplating her options.

How to unravel this without losing face? To have such lowly relations as the Bennets! No, this is not to be borne! I must do something, but what can I do? Darcy cannot be in his right mind to consider associating with that country nobody! I am the rightful Mistress of Pemberley; it should have been me dining with him tonight. He should not be at some despicable place like Gracechurch Street!

Caroline rose from her seat and began pacing back and forth, thinking about all of her connections that could come to her aid in convincing Bingley and Darcy of their poor choices for wives. She ran certain scenarios through her mind, but a headache forced her to give up her plotting for the night.

~*~*~*~

After depositing Bingley at his residence, Darcy arrived home with a better attitude than when he had left it earlier that evening." That changed when he was greeted by his cousin Fitzwilliam, who ran into him as he met him at the door with an anxious look on his face.

"Darcy, it is about time you arrived! I heard that you have been to Matlock House in response to a command?" Then he realized that he stood in the front foyer of Darcy's town home with the butler standing right there and a footman not five feet away.

Darcy directed him to his study and closed the doors. He walked to the sideboard and grabbed a canter of port and poured himself a glass, then looked to his cousin and lifted up the glass in silent invitation.

"I could use some of that right now." Fitzwilliam replied, looking anxious.

"I cannot say that I have ever had a more horrible meeting with the Earl than I did this night, Fitzwilliam." At his cousins questioning look he continued, I have been accused of having a mistress, one Mrs. Harriet Heartherton, and I have also been credited with fathering said woman's child, and that I am keeping her at Slatemore."

At Fitzwilliam's attempt to speak, Darcy held up his hand, "Do not try to say anything to me on that account. I can only be ashamed of keeping your mistress on my estate," He looked down and shook his head, "Although there are some who would say that I am as guilty in this whole mess as you, and at present I am about to concede my culpability in your scheme. Right now, however, I must provide damage control and inform you that your parents and James, are aware of your presence here. Unless you are prepared to face the lion's den later, which would be worse, I suggest that you go to them as soon as possible and give them whatever story of your choosing. I will, however, require you to leave me out of these dealings as this has nearly cost me so very dearly already."

"What do you suggest that I do, Darcy? I cannot afford to keep this charade up, and marry Harriet. I would be ruined, and James is unwilling to do anything but finish me off, should I even think to do such a thing."

"You chose the wrong time to consider all this, Richard! I shall have a hard enough time convincing Elizabeth's father to grant me consent to marry her as it is"

At Fitzwilliam's questioning glance, Darcy continued, "Oh yes, by the way Miss Elizabeth Bennet has consented to be my wife today, and that was the pinnacle of my day... well, my life really, and should word of this rumour get out, I am not sure that anything short of elopement would allow us to marry, and that would not help our family's standing in decent society! He shot a look of disgust towards his cousin.

At that moment, they were interrupted by Mr. Humphrey's knock on the study door, "Viscount Fitzwilliam to see you and the Colonel, sir."

Chapter 21

"Well, hello there Darcy…Richard." James Fitzwilliam said as he entered Darcy's study later that evening, and nodded to each of the gentlemen. I would normally wait for your permission before visiting you so late in the evening, but I am in a hurry. I must confess I am not surprised at seeing you here, Brother." He held an ironic smile on his face.

Darcy started as James entered the room, and then realized that Fitzwilliam looked surprised as well.

Darcy regained his equanimity first, "What brings you here so very late this evening, James? Do not tell me it is because you cannot sleep or do not have other activities you prefer. I doubt you could be missing my company!" He crossed his arms and raised an eyebrow at his new guest.

"Yes, James, do tell us what brings you here so late tonight? Surely, you did not come for a simple social call!" Fitzwilliam added.

James sauntered towards them and smiled, "Do not think that I have been fooled by your skulking around, trying to avoid the family Richard!" At their puzzled expressions he continued, "It has come to my attention that you have been running about the countryside on some not so official business, and that it is due to some rather… umm… how I shall put this? Reprehensible purposes?"

Darcy interrupted, "What is your purpose, James? You did not come over here to just taunt…?"

"Would I do that?" James replied as innocently as he ever could.

"Yes!" Both gentlemen replied in unison.

James gave them a haughty look. "What? Have you come to stir up more trouble, James?" Darcy said.

"No, no indeed not. I came here to offer my assistance..." He saw both of their perplexed looks, "And silence. In return, I want assurances that when the time comes, I can expect your assistance in... negotiating with a certain person of our family... business dealings." He looked expectant as they put all of the pieces together.

Darcy solved the puzzle after pondering James' words, "What you mean is, that you want us to promise to back you in whatever dealings you have in reference to our aunt, Lady Catherine? With what 'business dealing' are you referring to James?"

"In a few words... the Welsh estate, and of course, the mining that is going on around there. Think about it, we would all stand to profit, and there is not much over there other than sheep and small crops..."

Darcy interceded, "And why would we need to do that? How would we do that? Your father has a say in this as well, and I am sure he would protest. Why is that so important to you?" He became leery.

Darcy felt strongly about preserving the land, and had long been against blighting the countryside with mines, but the viscount pled on, "It is a matter of profit. If Lady Catherine supports it, and we all agree to it, then he will have to listen. I have a few connections that could assist us and make more money for the estate..."

"You mean you have debts to repay, and you want us to help keep those creditors off of your back." Darcy knew about his other cousin's propensity toward gaming and was furious over the quandary his relatives' actions placed him in.

"I shall not deny that there are outstanding debts that need to be repaid, but this has nothing..."

"Nonsense, this has everything to do with it! You and I... We all know that, and Lady Catherine would never allow such a thing! What makes you think that she would even listen to such a plan? Neither of you will have anything to do with it until you father is gone!"

"True, but you do have a say, and Lady Catherine will listen to you, especially after you and Anne are..."

"*No! No! No! No!* I am *not*, nor will I *ever* be engaged, or married to Anne. That is a delusion of Lady Catherine's. Anne would not make a proper mistress of Pemberley, nor a proper wife! Her health is too fragile to carry out the requirements of producing an heir! I should also take the time to inform both of you, Richard and James, that I am engaged to be married, and it is not to Anne!" Darcy exhibited more emotion than he had ever displayed before, causing both of his cousins' to stare at him with surprised expressions.

"I see, and may we be privileged to know who this lucky lady is?" James asked.

"I am delighted to say that it is Miss Elizabeth Bennet of Longbourn in Hertfordshire, and she has done me the honour of accepting my hand today." He smiled at the thought, but then frowned when he remembered their present conversation.

"That is why I will *not* be marrying Anne, among other reasons. I will have to deny my influence now, as I will soon fall out of her good graces. Perhaps, you ought to leave me out of this."

"I do not believe that I have ever heard of her…" James started.

"No, you would not have. Her father owns a small estate called Longbourn, in Hertfordshire, and before you ask, she does not have much money or connections. That is, not any that you would know."

"I am all astonishment! How is it that a man who prides himself on his family's connections and consequence is taken in by a country nobody? She must be quite extraordinary!"

This comment brought Fitzwilliam into the conversation, I assure you James, she is," then with a look of resignation at Darcy, he continued, "Miss Bennet is all that is charming and wonderful in a woman. If I were in Darcy's place, I'd like to think that I would be so lucky."

Darcy shot an alarmed glance at his cousin, and raised his right eyebrow.

James continued, "Well then, I congratulate you Darcy, but does Lady Catherine know about your engagement? I mean… is there still time to take care of this business? I am sure you can wait, before you make any hasty announcements…"

"As far as making any announcements, no I have not told anyone, other than you two and Bingley. I will not make further announcements regarding my engagement, until I speak to Miss Elizabeth's father. After that, I will make my plans according to my betrothed's and my own inclinations. You two may do as you see fit. I will caution you, though; I will not stand for anyone making a mockery out of the Fitzwilliam or

Darcy names. I have behaved with consistent propriety, and I will not tolerate anyone dragging me through the mud because of *their* behaviour." He glared at his Fitzwilliam cousins.

"From here on out, I suggest that you leave me out of your troubles, and find another way to pay off your debits, then quit the behaviour that has caused all this mischief. Now, I am quite tired from all of this running amuck, and am going to bed." He turned toward Fitzwilliam, "You are welcome to stay here for now, but as I said, leave me out of further dealings. I will not risk my happiness for this misery." Darcy turned on his heel and walked out of his study and up to his private rooms.

~*~*~*~

The two Fitzwilliam brothers were left staring at each other in the study. Fitzwilliam recovered from his brother's sudden appearance, "Well then James, it seems that you are always one step ahead of me when it comes to subversion. You know, you would have done quite well in the army, what with all this sneaking about."

His brother raised an eyebrow, "Indeed, however, I seem to recall that I am the elder brother, and that would not do, now would it? Besides, you were doing quite well in hiding Harriet up at Darcy's Slatemore estate… at least for a while. You do realize… no, I will not do that… not now that there is bound to be… issues arising, besides, I have other things I need to do right now." He sighed and bowed his head to his confused younger brother, I bid you a good night, Richard." Then he walked out to the hall and retrieved his coat and walking stick from Humphreys.

Richard stood there with many unanswered questions and a full blown headache from all of the news of the day. *Now that opportunist of a brother is trying to hold all of this over our heads. How on earth did he find out about Harriet?* He also remembered that Caroline Bingley was aware of their situation and could exacerbate the situation by one slip of the tongue. He rubbed his temples and headed towards his own rooms. *This just keeps getting worse and worse.*

~*~*~*~

Feeling much more relieved and relaxed than earlier that evening, Elizabeth dwelt upon Darcy's attentions to her just before his departure. She wanted to remember everything about this day. When

Elizabeth went to bed, she felt as if she were floating on clouds. When she woke up, she felt refreshed, as though waking from the best night's sleep she had in a long time. She remembered having vague dreams of her and Darcy, alone in a grand room dancing around an enormous bed, and then suddenly she found herself in that same bed alone with Darcy, and they were naked, but then she awoke from her sleep. She felt warm and nervous at the same time as she recollected that part of the dream. Her remembrance of his naked body back at Brooks Pond crept into her mind, and she felt the need to wash her face with cool water. *Today I will see Darcy again, and we may walk out in the park and...*

Her thoughts were interrupted by a sudden knock on her door. "Come in."

Jane answered, "Lizzy, how are you this morning? You had better prepare, for I believe Mr. Bingley said that he and Mr. Darcy would be here as early as was acceptable."

They both laughed at their jubilation with the prior day's events as Elizabeth readied herself for the day. "It is a very fortunate circumstance that you and I became engaged about the same time, for I am sure that I could not withstand all of this joy alone. I believe that I shall be the happiest creature alive!"

"I think you may be the second happiest creature alive, as I think I may own that title dearest, but then we may have competition when our mother learns of our joy!" They both laughed.

Elizabeth retorted, I would not like to imagine our Mother's raptures at having two daughters so well married! There will be no end to her joyous effusions."

They smiled knowingly at each other then Elizabeth turned to fix her hair before she turned around to ask Jane, "How do I look? Am I presentable?"

"You know you look very well Lizzy, and Mr. Darcy will fall more in love with you than ever. Now shall we go down to breakfast and strengthen ourselves before our walk?"

"Yes." Elizabeth replied with enthusiasm.

They went down to breakfast and enjoyed a quiet meal with Mrs. Gardiner and the children, and once the children were sent up to their parlour for their lessons Jane, Elizabeth, and Mrs. Gardiner went to the main sitting room to converse before the gentlemen's arrival.

~*~*~*~

As soon as the gentlemen were announced, Elizabeth and Jane looked towards their betrotheds with pretty blushes. The gentlemen greeted Mrs. Gardiner, before directing their attention towards their ladies. Darcy stared at Elizabeth with his burning look, which made her feel self conscious. *At least now I know he does not do that to find fault.* After a brief conversation about the weather, and their lovely dinner last evening, Mr. Bingley requested permission for them to go to the park to enjoy the scenery.

Elizabeth could scarcely believe that today was so much improved from the previous day. *So much has changed! So much will change!* She felt impatient to spend time with Darcy quasi-alone, and could not imagine a better combination than Darcy and the outdoors. She remembered him as God made him at the pond, and blushed at the visions. Elizabeth started her light banter as they entered the park in order to distract herself from those visions, I believe you had left me last night sir, with a promise to explain your absence during dinner. She looked at him through her eyelashes and tilted her head.

Darcy looked down at her as if he were startled, "Yes, I did. I was a miserable wretch before I joined you last night and, as I said, it was business that could not be delayed. My uncle had heard alarming news, no doubt from the same source you had heard that same distressing tale." He looked into her widened eyes, I have great reason to believe that Caroline Bingley visited my uncle's home and spouted off that same tale to cause trouble, perhaps to cause you or your father to deny me your hand in marriage."

Elizabeth answered his concerns, "You do not believe me to be so inconstant as to take back my word on the basis of what I now know as idle gossip? And as far as my father is concerned, I believe I know how to deal with him. So there you have it! You may have a reason to repine one day sir, when you figure out that you have taken a bride who will not be gainsaid once she makes up her mind!" She smiled coquettishly.

He laughed, but his good humour faded, and he gazed at her with a grave expression, "You will never cause me to regret taking you for my wife, my dearest. I must say this though, as far as the rumours being mere gossip, I am afraid it may be worse than that."

Elizabeth felt a knot forming in her stomach; she did not like to think that those things Miss Bingley had said were true.

"Why would such things be worse than you had said prior? Did you not say that those rumours were false?" She could feel herself go cold for an instant.

Darcy stared at her with silent intensity and stopped walking. He took her hands in his and looked down at their joined hands. "Elizabeth, there is something that I need to tell you, as it may get out, and I do not wish for you to hear it from anyone else. Now, while I did tell you that I do not… nor have I ever had a mistress, I have enabled a family member to carry on with a mistress with my help… in the way of monetary supplements. I will not pretend to be innocent. I have turned a blind eye when other members of my circle have chosen to take that route." He took a deep breath, "Dearest, please understand, I did not know the value of passionate love, until I met you. My adoration for you spurred me to tell my cousin Colonel Fitzwilliam last night that I will no longer support his habits, and he must deal with his mistress as he sees fit."

Elizabeth reeled in shock at Darcy's admission, but she later found her voice and looked up to his face, "Colonel Fitzwilliam? You mean he has not provided for his mistress, and his child?"

Darcy nodded, "Yes, and that is why he left Netherfield in such a rush. It was not false, however, that she remained at my estate as we… he and I… felt that it would be best that she leave town for a while, until this dreadful business could get sorted out. I do not have to tell you that it would be most difficult for him to marry a woman of her station as a colonel, and I have supplemented his income to help with his… 'other expenses'. He, as the second son, will only inherit minor funds from my uncle when he passes, and even then that may be in danger should the Earl learn of his mistress, much less her being with child."

"Then that is the letter that Caroline referenced, but how… why…?"

Darcy shook his head, I do not know why she intimated it was me, or my mistress and child, other than the fact that I sent a note… or rather meant to send a note with Richard, to my steward, who takes care of my Lancashire estate. When he left, those two letters were found together."

He studied her for a moment, then said, "Elizabeth, I *promise* you that I shall not support such behaviour in the future. Right now, however, I feel that I must right this situation. I felt responsible for this mistress, as I gave Richard the funds to... well, to enable him to do such things."

Elizabeth's head swam in jumbled thoughts as she tried to absorb this new information. *He is the very best of men! Most gentlemen of his society would not give it a second thought.* She developed the need to relieve Darcy's anxiety. She looked around, and seeing that they were in a secluded part of the park, she reached up on her tip toes and kissed him.

His face brightened, "What did I do to deserve that?"

"Well, sir, you looked so miserable that I thought that you needed something to distract you."

"I see... I do not suppose that, at intermittent times, I may be able to persuade you to repeat that, may I?"

Only if you can convince me that they will cure you of your need to carry everyone else's burdens, yet neglect your own."

"That, I most assuredly can do." With that he pulled her close to him, and his lips descended upon hers, softly at first, then a little more demanding until their tongues met as fervently as a well matched fencing bout. Elizabeth could feel his caresses of her back and waist, and she wrapped her arms around his neck. He then dragged one hand up alongside her ribs, until his hand rested just beneath her breast, and she gasped as she felt his hand there.

Darcy pulled his hand back and apologized to her, "Oh, Elizabeth please forgive me. I do not know what came over me. I did not mean to offend you it is just that..."

Elizabeth managed to interrupt his unnecessary apologies and grabbed his hands while she gazed into his face, "Darcy!"

He stopped his groveling as Elizabeth continued, "My love, do not apologise for our actions. I was not offended, and I do feel that, while it may not have been in the most appropriate of places, our behaviour was most natural. Is that not what two people do when they are so violently in love?"

Darcy paused with a look of relief upon his face and then smiled. "Indeed, I believe that you are correct." He took a deep breath then exhaled, I hope though, that I did not manage to frighten you."

"No," she smiled, I was not frightened... In fact I felt rather..."

"Exhilarated?" She smiled, then nodded, "Yes, I believe that would be one word for it."

"I hope that you continue to feel this way as we grow closer my love, for I fear that you may become even more exhilarated after a while."

She saw a fire in his eyes that made her shiver, which Darcy noticed. "Are you cold my dear? Shall we go back to the Gardiner's so you can warm up?"

Not wanting to admit the reason for her body's involuntary betrayal, she agreed to go back with some regret, so they found the other besotted couple and returned to the house. When they had arrived back at the Gardiner's, Elizabeth found it difficult to attend to the general conversation, as she noted Darcy still looking at her with his burning gaze as if he were studying a statue in a museum. She recollected herself enough to see him out when it was time for the gentlemen to depart, and still felt chills running through her as their eyes met just before he disappeared into his coach.

~*~*~*~

Caroline Bingley had half a night's rest, as she tossed and turned, trying to think her way through this mess of Charles and Darcy's engagements to those country nobodies' from Hertfordshire. *This cannot be happening! I must do something to bring them to their senses and stop this madness!* She felt only half certain that Charles would send her to their Aunt Dugan's home in Scotland, but felt sure that she did not wish to be there when she had much rather be in town. *Surely, there is someone who can help bring them to earth!* Reviewing all of her acquaintances in town and any mutual relatives of Darcy's, at least one person she felt certain would know how to act.

In the morning, after she had dwelt upon the last few weeks and possible allies, she felt she knew who would be most injured should Mr. Darcy make a disadvantageous match. *Georgiana! That's it! She would be loath to be associated with country nobodies. Hmm... but she is* under the protection of her brother, and he will ensure that she bears no opposition to his plans! Who else is there to enlist though?

Suddenly a thought struck her and she went to the writing desk and penned another missive. *This should do it; he would not dare to trifle with such iron willed, intelligent, and well connected personages!* She began her letter, thinking that another mode of insurance would be beneficial as well, and as soon as she finished with her first letter, she penned a second and sent both post haste. *That will fix them for certain! Then Darcy will come to his senses and realize what he was about to do to himself!* She went to the side table with a smug smirk on her face, and took up some brandy, coughing violently as it ran down her throat. When she looked at the bottle, she saw that the brandy was really scotch. *D-mn!*

Thus she penned two letters; one, she sent to Kent, Rosings Park and began thusly:

5th December, 1811

Dear Madame,

Please excuse my presumption in writing to you in such a forward way; however, I think that you will agree that it was most prudent to do so, as it involves your nephew Mr. Fitzwilliam Darcy. You see my dear lady, it has come to my attention that he has come under the influence of a lowly country maid, who has neither money nor connections, and has relations that are most indelicate and obscene in their conduct in public. I must also inform you that one of the lady's relatives is in trade and lives in Cheapside, and another is a country attorney Under these circumstances, I am sure that you must feel the need, as I do, to ensure that he removes himself from this unfortunate connection before it is too late.

I felt that you, being one of his closest living relatives, ought to be informed of this proposed alliance, as you could have enough influence to avert an announcement of an engagement before it could harm your families' good name.

With warm regards,

Caroline Bingley

Caroline felt some relief at doing something, but not so easy as to feel complete relief, thus another missive was sent to Hertfordshire, with a different tone, and a different angle. *That should take care of that little baggage. Now, Miss Eliza let us see if he shall want you after this.*

Chapter 22

As the Viscount Fitzwilliam made his daily rounds about town the next day, and met an acquaintance whom he would rather have avoided. Lord Blake sat at his usual tables in the back room of one of the fashionable men's clubs. James cringed at the realization that his number one creditor had already arrived. He greeted the man, and put on his most pleasant persona. "How are you, Blake? In good spirits today after last night?" I *hope*.

"Come now, Fitzwilliam, you know better than that! After you left, I defeated Windslow, and won another fifty pounds! I should say I am in much better spirits!" The man eyed this new addition to the party's offering,

"What say you to joining us for another round here, old man? I am sure we can make some room for one of our regulars at this table." Lord Blake said with a raised eyebrow.

"No, I… thank you," James looked around the room, I do not believe that I will indulge right now." He looked towards the exit.

Unfortunately, his colleague noticed his movements as well, and motioned to some footmen to guard the exits. James started to feel ill. He turned and heard some laughter behind him as Lord Blake's hand forcefully grasped his shoulder, turning him back around.

"Fitzwilliam, just where do you think you are going? You did not think that I had forgotten about my ten thousand pounds, did you?"

"Of course I have not forgotten, Blake; it has been rather difficult to get my hands upon such a large sum all at once and…"

"Fitzwilliam, you know how I feel about excuses and I have been very patient with you. Now, however, that patience is starting to wear thin and I am beginning to think that you need to be reminded of your obligations."

James' face lost most of its colour, and he felt perilously close to fainting when Blake added, "What about your cousin, Darcy... hmmm? I am willing to bet he would pay a hefty penny to keep his family's name out of the papers. Perhaps, though, you have discussed our little venture with your kinsmen?"

The viscount thanked heaven that he had not eaten much breakfast, for it would have reappeared in a most distasteful fashion. I have discussed the mining with some of them; however, I still await a response from others... but I know I can persuade them to allow your operation to open up there and then..."

"And then I will consider your down payment on your debit paid in full." He looked meaningfully at his colleague and continued, "You should have learned to walk away from the tables sooner, Fitzwilliam, you are a terrible bluff, and you can hardly hold your liquor. In case you have not figured it out, I do keep my eye on those who owe me a great deal of money, and I am none too pleased with what I have seen of you. I could be easily pleased to have bought all of your debits at the other gaming houses and now I am the sole owner of them all."

He laughed at the look of horror on his companion's face, "Oh yes, I have an insurance policy that you will do as I say, and there will be absolutely no protest, otherwise you and your family will be exposed for this... hmm... charade of propriety that they put on." He looked into James' face and ordered, I will give you no more than one week to come up with the twenty five thousand pounds... or... your assurances of my rights on your family's estate." He then let go of James shoulder, turned on his heel and walked towards the table to begin his next game.

James slowly regained his breath, and a little colour returned to his cheeks. He walked towards the door from whence he came after collecting his coat, gloves, and walking stick. He knew he needed to get assistance from his family, but the question was from *whom* and *how*? He headed towards his family's home. I *would be disowned should I approach my father. D-mn! Why did my family have to go and make a mess of my plans? Anne... Hmmm... well there may be hope yet.*

~*~*~*~

Lady Catherine was taking her tea in her grand sitting room with her daughter, Anne, and Anne's companion Mrs. Jenkinson, when

Mr. Jeffers, their butler, arrived with the mail. She imperiously dismissed her butler and glanced momentarily at her letters. Her eyes narrowed at finding one written in a hand that she did not recognize. She decided to put that particular letter aside until she drank her tea and continued on with her previous topic of conversation, before the arrival of the butler and the mail. In a loud voice, she resumed her monologue about how the tenants to the north of her property failed to produce sufficient crops to maintain a 'proper' income befitting the tenants of the owner of Rosings.

After she exhausted herself and her listeners with the topic, she then dismissed the other two and stated that she will now tend to her correspondences. Once Mrs. Jenkinson had taken Anne upstairs to rest, Lady Catherine was free to peruse her mail beginning first with the letter marked urgent business. *Of all of the presumptions! To mark a letter 'urgent' then not send it express... humph... what bad manners... such simpletons!* She opened the letter and read the contents. She froze with alarm.

"Jeffers! Jeffers! *Jeffers!*" She called to the bewildered butler. Once the man appeared, she glared furiously at him, I must go to town immediately! Have the carriage readied and have the maids pack our things, I know not how long we will be gone, but ensure that we will be ready to depart within the next two hours!" She watched as the servant nodded smartly and bowed out of the room.

She was furious. *How dare anyone try to get in the way of my plans! This is not to be bourn! I shall see to it that Fitzwilliam does no damage by making any hasty foolish decisions!* Pacing back and forth, she thought hard about what she needed to do, suddenly remembering some papers she had stowed away years ago, she went to her study to retrieve them from a locked drawer and tucked them into her portfolio. She then headed towards the upstairs to see to the packing as she knew for certain that the maids were not adept at proper placement of garments within a valise.

Within a record hour and a half of preparation, the great lady headed off to town in one of her finest coaches. She brought along her daughter, Anne, who looked even more pale and sickly than usual, as their hasty journey prohibited adequate rest or provisions. Lady Catherine became more infuriated at the incompetence of her staff, as she felt they did not leave in good time. Mrs. Jenkinson fussed over her charge as they barreled through Kent, and bore the brunt of Lady Catherine's wrath. She shifted restlessly as she thought of the stable hands not getting the fastest horses hitched to the carriage. She ensured that everyone knew of her displeasure.

I shall have a word with the stable master! I will not tolerate such inefficiency! They should know that when I have an urgent need to travel they must be ready upon the instant! I never waste my time on trivial pursuits! She had worked herself up into a lather by the time they arrived in the outskirts of town. The whole party looked relieved at the sight of their London home, as the lady had finally seemed to calm a bit, for now anyways.

~*~*~*~

The next few days at Gracechurch Street were marked with daily visits from Darcy and Bingley, with the couples often times separating for a while in the park before joining back together at the Gardiner's home. Both Jane and Elizabeth shared their plans for a double wedding, for it seemed to make sense to do so with such close sisters and such close friends as they were. The next step though had to be obtaining Mr. Bennet's consent.

Should it be done in person or could we write a letter? As they both had a great deal to accomplish in such a short period of time. Their solicitors needed to be consulted, and the marriage articles written and then signed in town, they opted to write a letter requesting that, at Mr. Bennet's earliest convenience, they wished to meet.

Since Bingley admitted that his handwriting left something to be desired, Darcy wrote to the gentleman, and both he and Bingley signed the letter. Elizabeth had the idea of both of them signing it as Mr. Bennet would be more than curious at such an unusual letter and would likely pay at least some attention to it. She also requested that Darcy's letter be sent with one from her, as she knew her father would be leery of giving his consent in light their previous conversation before she left for town.

Now, they had to await Mr. Bennet's response, and then, hopefully, an announcement could be made. Darcy and Mr. Bingley experienced a growing intimacy with their betrothed's family; they were both comfortable with Mr. Gardiner enough to ask his permission to court the ladies, pending final approval of their engagement and wedding plans by Mr. Bennet, in light of the fact that he was their nearest male relative in town. Of course, he gave his permission readily, for he had no cause for complaint, and was delighted to see that his nieces were happy regarding their present situation.

As for the ladies, they had gone shopping with their Aunt Gardiner and found some accoutrements for their wedding dresses, and other garments they could wear after they were married. Darcy could not stop imagining some of the articles that he knew they purchased, in order to obtain a sufficient wardrobe for Elizabeth.

He would brook no argument for Elizabeth's hand and knew that, if he had to, he would take her to Gretna Green in order to marry her. No one wanted a long engagement and they planned to be wed by the end of January. The gentlemen would have loved to be with their beloveds much more to make plans, but it seemed as if each man had his issues involving his own family that required his time.

Darcy wanted Georgiana to meet her soon to be sister, and finally had brought her with him to visit Elizabeth, who was also excited, and eager to make her acquaintance.

~*~*~*~

When the maid announced the Darcy's and Mr. Bingley, Elizabeth felt a little fluttering in her stomach as she expected this visit with Georgiana Darcy, and was anxious to please, as well as be pleased. She looked intently at Darcy, seeking a clue as to what he may have told his sister about her and how to proceed, but she discovered he was staring at her with that increasingly familiar expression in his eyes that caressed her no matter where she stood. It disconcerted her to feel so flushed as she greeted his sister.

Upon greeting Georgiana, the ladies of Gracechurch Street discerned that she was a very shy young woman with no pretensions and very likely in need of reassurances. Elizabeth glanced at Darcy again then smiled at his sister, I am very pleased to meet you, Miss Darcy, how do you do?"

Georgiana murmured, I am well, thank you, Miss Be... I mean Miss. Elizabeth, I am pleased to make your acquaintance as well." She had dared to let her eyes come up momentarily before dropping again. She lifted her gaze to Elizabeth's face again, and then smiled ever so slightly.

Elizabeth glanced towards her aunt and Jane, and then invited her to sit next to her, in order for them to chat for a while. I hear that you are much favoured when it comes to playing the piano forte, Miss Darcy. I do hope I will not be made to sound so paltry in comparison." She teased.

Georgiana's eyes darted up to Elizabeth's with surprise, I should think not, Miss Elizabeth. My brother has told me that you play most wonderfully."

Elizabeth looked up with laughing eyes at Darcy, I cannot believe that he could think my playing anything but poor compared to the many other ladies I have heard play."

"But, Miss Elizabeth, my brother never lies. I am sure if he said that he thought you wonderful, then it must be so."

Elizabeth found humour in Georgiana's naiveté and looked warmly at this young woman, I do not doubt that he has said such things, however, I believe him to be partial as well."

Georgiana looked at Elizabeth at the same moment that she looked at Darcy, and suddenly the young lady blushed scarlet and looked down to her lap with a small smile. The couple recovered from their momentary distraction and Elizabeth said, I hope that you do not believe everything that you have heard, Miss Darcy, I am afraid that I may have some very high standards to live up to."

"Oh no, Miss Elizabeth, I am sure I could not be disappointed in your abilities, as my brother is most discerning with regards to whom he gives praise."

Elizabeth could feel herself flush, and she knew that not just her face, but her whole body must be crimson. "I... do not know what to say to such a compliment, but that I hope to continue to earn his praises for much time to come."

Georgiana appeared less tense and more relaxed in the Gardiners parlour with the present company, and she and Elizabeth carried on their tete-a-tete with Darcy silently looking on, a small smile upon his lips and a glow to his eyes. Mrs. Gardiner attended Jane and

Mr. Bingley for the time being, only occasionally looking to the other group with a smile about her face. It seemed as if the group as a whole had made a decision to allow the two future sisters to converse privately as much as possible for the time being.

They talked of books and music, as well as their love of walks, which led to the subject of Pemberley. Elizabeth found a subject that this young shy woman could wax eloquent on. *Apparently their home is a magical place for both Georgiana and her brother*, she thought, *both talk endlessly on the natural beauty of the park and the peaks.* Elizabeth's curiosity increased about her future home, and of what awaited her when she became Mrs. Fitzwilliam Darcy.

This thought occupied her until her guests began to take their leave. Unfortunately, she could not say the goodbye in the manner that she would have liked to Darcy, but the lingering kiss to the back of her hand, and the blazing look he gave her before his carriage lurched forward made her shiver, and she felt certain it was not from the cool late autumn air.

She and Jane had decided to join the Gardiner children in the park; it became more and more of a habit where the sisters could discuss their betrotheds, and how it felt to be so much in love with someone. On one such day, as they still waited for Mr. Bennet's reply, they went to the park again.

"Lizzy, do you think that our father will have any reservations about granting his consent?"

"No, Jane." Then Elizabeth thought of her and Darcy's situation before they came to town, "at least he seems not have any reservations about you marrying Mr. Bingley."

"But, you do not think that he would deny your hand to Mr. Darcy, do you?"

"I would think not, but that is why I wrote to him along with Fitz… Mr. Darcy's letter. I wanted to let him know how much I have come to adore Fitzwilliam, and how happy he has made me with his offer." Elizabeth also thought of other visions from long ago, but checked herself.

"Do you think that we shall be good wives for our husbands?"

"Jane, you shall be the perfect doting wife, and hostess for your Mr. Bingley, you have nothing to fear. As for me…"

"Yes? Lizzy, what is it? Are you unsure of yourself as a wife?"

"No… well… yes… and no. I hope that we should be the happiest couple in the whole world, and I shall be the perfect wife, and I am almost certain that it will be so with Mr. Darcy by my side. I also take comfort in the fact that we have spent so much time with our Aunt Gardiner. It has done so much more for us than to watch our own mother as a wife. Although she does set a 'good table', we learned many more skills that we shall need for our new lives from our Aunt." Elizabeth still wondered at her other pleasing abilities though.

Elizabeth remained unsettled, however. *Why do I feel a burning sensation within my lower belly when I am in Fitzwilliam's arms, and why is he so reluctant to be alone with me? Is this just pre-wedding nerves?* She knew not how to discuss such a subject, but then she was never one to shy away from her curiosities either.

She and Jane had taken a ramble through the park, and when the time to go back to Gracechurch Street arrived, they were greeted by an unexpected guest.

Chapter 23

"Papa, whatever are you doing here?" said a very surprised Elizabeth to her father.

"I came to see to my daughter's welfare, and discuss some business with your uncle. Besides that, I felt the need for more... stimulating conversation."

Elizabeth and Jane laughed at their father's response. Still, Elizabeth became curious as to her father's sudden appearance at the Gardiner's home, as he tended to delay his responses to most correspondence. *This is so unlike him. What is he up to?*

Jane interrupted her musing, "Papa, we are very glad for you to join us, but had you planned to come to town all along, or is there something the matter?"

As Mr. Bennet looked to his older daughter, he seemed weary, "No, nothing is the matter, I have just had some correspondence that necessitated my sudden departure to town."

Mr. and Mrs. Gardiner observed Elizabeth with apparent concern, and she shot them a questioning glance. "Will this 'business' take much of your time, or will you have time to spare for leisure as well?"

Mr. Bennet smiled at his favorite daughter, I hope to have some free moments to spend in leisure, but for now I wish to speak to you alone Elizabeth."

Elizabeth nodded her head in acquiescence, and followed her father to Mr. Gardiner's study. Mr. Bennet paced back and forth in front of the hearth, which did little to relieve Elizabeth's anxiety. He turned as if in realization of her anxious thoughts, placed his hands gently on both of her shoulders and said, "My dear, it was not my intention in coming to town to frighten or alarm you, however, when

I spoke earlier of an important piece of correspondence, it was in fact a letter that I received from a most unusual correspondent... Miss Caroline Bingley."

Elizabeth's jaw dropped, and for a full minute she remained speechless. Her father noted this and continued, I was as surprised as you are now to have received any such thing from such a... lady, but there you have it. Furthermore, I can tell that you are burning with curiosity now, as to what she could have to say, concerning you?"

"Yes, I am very curious, Papa. Please do not keep me in suspense. I wonder why she has taken the trouble to write to you, of all people?" She raised an eyebrow in concern.

The last statement had not been missed by Mr. Bennet, and he smiled wryly, "Well, it concerns you and Mr. Darcy, and her purported... umm... concern for your virtue and his intentions towards you."

"She dared to write to *you* and speak of her 'concerns' for *my* virtue...? And Mr. Darcy's intentions towards me...?"

Elizabeth looked at her father with flashing eyes, "Papa, I understand that you may be concerned for me after our last discussion, before I left for town. However, I should take the time to inform you that I have had the opportunity to see the gentleman in question and have discussed my concerns with him to our... mutual satisfaction... and to her decided *dis*satisfaction."

"And what does the term 'mutual satisfaction' mean?" Her father's voice was on edge, and his eyes narrowed suspiciously.

She shot a quick glace to him, "Sir, Mr. Darcy and I have come to an understanding, that is to say he has asked me to be his wife... and I have accepted him."

Mr. Bennet let out a deep sigh, I was afraid of that my dear girl, but all may not be lost, as I have yet to give my consent."

At her look of alarm he continued, I have received some alarming information about some... rather... unsavory details of the 'gentleman's' past, and wanted to ensure that you are protected from such scandal..."

"Papa..."

Her father held up his hand, "No, let me finish Lizzy, you see there are some things that occur in his circle that you would not be aware of…"

"Such as having mistresses?" she interrupted, to his shock. "Yes papa, I am aware of what has been said about him, but I have heard his defense, and before you ask, no I have not been compromised in any way by the *gentleman*."

She said with hesitation, and continued, "In fact, he has been everything that is charming, and I am not going to repine my choice in mate due to some unfounded, and malicious rumours circulated by a woman, who has been disappointed that her schemes have not worked!"

"I see, well then," Mr. Bennet raised his eyebrows, I will await any further judgment. Hopefully, I will have a chance to discuss my concerns with your Mr. Darcy, and will be as satisfied with his 'explanations' as you seem to be."

Elizabeth felt only slightly relieved and responded, "That is all that I ask, Sir." They stared at each other, waiting for the other to make the next move. Elizabeth lost her patience and spoke, "And I thank you for your concern. Papa, I think you will find that Mr. Darcy is a most wonderful man, and he has done nothing to deserve anyone's censure. The rumours you have heard are all due to an enormous misunderstanding."

Mr. Bennet forced a smile, I hope so…I sincerely hope so."

~*~*~*~

Lady Catherine and her entourage arrived at Matlock House and found nobody there from the family to greet her. Knowing the woman's propensities, the servants showed her to her suite of rooms. The earl and countess had previously instructed their servants on what needed to be done whenever the earl's

rather… difficult sister would arrive unannounced, as was her tendency from time to time, especially when she wanted to vent her spleen.

The butler had the footmen take up their things; while the great lady scrutinized the management of how her valises were being handled. One unlucky young man bore the brunt of her walking stick at one point, "Careful with that you simpleton, those are antiques, and are quite expensive!" she exclaimed while poking at his back.

Once she arrived in her rooms, she rummaged through her papers and sat at the chair by the hearth. Since the death of her dear father, she had not set her eyes on these documents. As she perused the papers, and sorted through the specific details of his will, she was concerned with a particular segment:

I, Richard James Fitzwilliam, herby bequeath my estate in Wales, 'Cantrell Hill' to the second male heir of my son James Andrew Fitzwilliam, should he have said heir. If this shall not come to pass then the property shall revert to the daughters of said son. Furthermore, should there be no children resulting from my son's issue, said property will revert to my remaining daughters Catherine Isabella Fitzwilliam and Anne Elizabeth Darcy.

Lady Catherine knew that this will existed and had found it shortly after the earl's death. She did not dare share the contents with anyone, for she had feared she would be left with little in the way of resources should she never marry, as she had not yet been introduced to her husband Sir Lewis de Bourgh at the time of her father's demise. As the Fitzwilliam family grew and her siblings' children came, she continued to keep the contents of the newer will to herself as she felt there was just that minor adjustment from the original will, it would make little difference anyway.

This last missive she had received was, to say the least alarming. *A mistress! And what is this messy business of carrying on with two such young men and the other dealings! Heaven forbid, James, what have you wrought upon us!* The letter had been sent from Lancashire, from a Mrs. Heartherton, who had become aware of some alarming business involving her two lovers who also happened to be the Lady Catherine's nephews.

4th December, 1811

Dear Lady Catherine,

I do not intend to be presumptuous in writing this missive to you; however, I feel that it is imperative that I communicate some news of VITAL importance to your family. I must first assure you that it is not my intention to cause discord among the Fitzwilliam's. I wish to redeem myself for what I need to communicate. I have known your nephews, James and Richard for some time, in a more than casual acquaintance. I have been brought with child and it is the viscount's. However; James, as I am sure you can guess, has not, nor will not accept any responsibility for his part in this situation.

He has encouraged me to deceive his brother, for he knew that Richard and I have also been 'involved', and he correctly surmised that Richard would be more likely to see to my needs as well as support the babe. I am sorry to say that I consented to this deception, and thus far, Richard believes that he is the rightful father of my child.

You may question what this has to do with you. To answer this, I shall continue further back in time before I knew either of your nephews. I had a patron, Lord Blake, who has had some business deals involving the mining industry. He has recently conducted business with developers in Wales who were interested in mining on your family's Cantrell Hill estate. Apparently, there was some wish to buy this property, but factions of your family rejected the proposal and would not relinquish the deed for any cost. I am sure you know that Lord Blake does not back down easily and thus was determined to ensure that he would acquire what he desired by deceit, if necessary. He then lured your nephew, James, to the gaming tables, which were less than above board, and as a result the viscount found himself with a rather large amount of gaming debt. Lord Blake's intent was to force the viscount to act for him, however necessary, to acquire the property in lieu of his gaming debits.

And that was where I came in. I met the viscount through Lord Blake, while the latter entertained at his tables. Keeping your nephew distracted was my job, and after a while it became more of an 'arrangement' between us. Eventually, I met the colonel through the viscount. I found the younger gentleman infinitely more agreeable than his brother, which was probably another reason that I was so willing to deceive the colonel into believing his brother's child was his.

Now I come to the point of the reason I write to you, which is to warn you that Lord Blake had finally succeeded in luring the viscount to significant debt to the amount of twenty five thousand pounds. Lord Blake is, even now, planning to call out his debts unless the estate in Wales will be surrender to him. I am sure that I do not need to warn you of the damage he intended to inflict upon your family's reputation if he is thwarted in his plans."

I will end this with saying that I truly did not intend to do harm to your nephew Richard, despite all of my misdeeds.

Sincerely,

Harriet Heartherton

Lady Catherine read through her letter again, her other letters from the morning had been forgotten with this horrid piece of news. She knew that she had missed some information to make her family members appear less culpable than it would seem that they were, but to no avail. *This is a disgrace! What if this should get out? We would be ruined! Brother, where are you when you are most needed, and why have you not controlled these children of yours? At least Darcy is an exemplary young gentleman. Yes, he will make a fine son-in-law for me and husband for Anne.* She continued to muse over the letters, and the situation at hand trying to find a solution for damage control.

An hour later, the earl and countess had returned home to find that their sister had arrived.

~*~*~*~

Caroline Bingley strolled on her way towards Darcy House when they literally ran into each other.

"Oh, I am terribly sorry madam; please forgive my lack of attention. I hope you are quite alright?" He looked at her with more frustration than anything else.

Caroline seemed as if she were about to vent, until she recognized to whom she spoke to, "No... I mean yes, I am fine, sir. I was just on my way to see someone whom I believe is a relation of yours... Miss Darcy?"

"Yes... Miss Bingley is it?"

"Yes, and you are Viscount Fitzwilliam?" Caroline Bingley said as almost a statement more than anything else, as she prided herself on knowing who was who in town, what their rank was, and how much income they had. Naturally she reminded herself she had to be on her best behavior with the gentleman in front of her... *just in case things did not work out with Lady Catherine or Mr. Bennet. One must remember to cover all of their prospects after all and a viscount who will one day be an earl would do nicely as well. Hmmm...Viscountess Fitzwilliam, or better yet Countess Fitzwilliam.*

"Ah, yes ma'am, how are you doing this fine day?"

Caroline smiled, I am very well, Sir. I was just on my way to see our dear Georgiana and make my usual call upon her. She is such a dear girl, is she not?"

"Indeed she is... and so very accomplished."

With this subject, Caroline could wax eloquently, and she quickly grasped onto it, "Oh yes she certainly is. It is one of the advantages of rank, to be able to develop those accomplishments as well to do you not think?"

"It certainly helps."

Disappointed at the lack of response from Darcy's cousin, she tried another vein, I hear that your cousin, Mr. Darcy, has been in town for nearly a week, sir. I am surprised that he has not come to see us at my brother's townhome. He is such good friends with Charles."

James snorted, "Yes, I believe he has visited Gracechurch Street daily with your brother, however."

She rolled her eyes, "That is rather unfortunate, is it not?" She said, mortified that her brother had been connected to that area of town, discomfited with the thought of his cousin going to the same place.

"It appears there is something to be said for the company there. I, however, would be more careful if I were them. It is a tragedy to see such wealth wasted."

"Indeed sir, I could not agree with you more."

They stood there, eyeing each other in seeming contemplation before they bid each other goodbye. Caroline headed towards Darcy House and James headed towards Matlock House. At least one of them had contemplated meeting the other again in the near future. *And soon.*

Chapter 24

When James arrived back at Matlock House, the butler greeted him, and told him that his parents awaited him in the earl's study. James felt an immediate surge of uneasiness. He walked slowly down the corridor and paused before the door of the study to collect himself. Upon entering, he saw not only the earl and countess, but Lady Catherine as well. His uneasiness increased.

"James, we have been expecting you for some time now. Where have you been?"

The viscount swallowed hard, and croaked out, I had some errands to attend to, and then I visited some friends.

"By 'friends' I… we hope you do not mean Lord Blake, and his ilk." The countess joined the conversation.

James looked away briefly, and caught a glimpse of Lady Catherine's glare, I had not thought… that is to say, I do not believe that there is so much wrong with Lord Blake." He cringed inwardly, thinking he sounded unconvincing, even to his own ears.

"Do not try to lie to us, James!" demanded the earl.

Everyone turned to look at the Earl, whose emotions escalated to a rare and full lather, complete with flushed face, and near bloodshot eyes. I have had enough of your lies, and of your bootlicking to me and your mother, only to go behind our backs to make a mockery out of us!"

"Father, I do not know of what you are speaking."

"Do not pretend with us, James. We are onto your game! We have proof of your misdeeds, yet you stand there and lie to me to my face! How dare you? How dare you come in here and tell me that you did not have a mistress who, by the way is with child?" James' face paled, but the earl seemed not to have noticed. "And, as if that is not bad enough, then you compiled it with... with gaming debts! What in the h-ll were you thinking?"

"Father... papa, I still do not know what you are speaking of, if you will allow me to understand, perhaps I can explain." He tried to stall for more time.

"I do not believe you! You stand here in my study and have the audacity to tell me that I do not know of what I am speaking, and yet here is a letter from one who has intimate knowledge of your scheme, and you allowed your brother, your brother for G-d's sake! To take the blame for this! How do you sleep at night?" The earl glowered at him.

Backing up a couple of steps, James raised his arms into the air and offered, "Father, I can explain..."

"Explain? Explain what? This... this mess? No, no, no, I do not believe even you can explain this away." The earl shook his head. "To think that I accused your cousin of being responsible for your misdeeds! I hope to goodness he is forgiving! I have also found that you and this woman tried to ensnare your brother into this mess..."

Glaring at James, he took several deep breaths all the while shaking his head. I have heard that this Harriet woman was, for a time, trying to convince your brother to take on your responsibilities, and that your cousin was... was helping him with putting this woman up on his estate in Lancashire. Oh, but that is not the worst of it is it? *No*, you went to those gaming dens and racked up an enormous debt, to the tune of... what was it Catherine?"

"To the amount of..." She pulled out her letter, "Twenty five thousand pounds! Where on earth did you think to get those funds, James?" She looked at him pointedly, "Surely, you did not believe that we would let you off the hook for such a sum... why that is the amount of some of the wealthier ladies' dowries. Did you think that you could just marry it off and hope that word would not get out?"

She stepped closer to her nephew, "Or did you think that you could get your hands on some *property*, and dispose of it without us noticing? Oh yes, now we know it all, but perhaps you did not realize that you were also played for the dupe? It appears that your *dear* lady was in collusion with Lord Blake, and you were set up from the beginning."

James felt as if he would faint, so he sat down and bowed his head while grabbing his knees with his arms. He felt ill from his family's knowledge of his misdeeds. They fell silent for a while as they watched his eyes tear up and his shoulders shake. The countess looked almost sympathetic towards her eldest son. Seeing his mother's expression, James rallied and smiled inwardly. *I shall have them eating out of my hands again in no time.*

"James, you do realize that, should the news about this get out, we would be ruined. I, however, think that you are not the only culpable party," The countess looked up at the two senior members in the room, I believe that we, as a family, can work through this but you will be on a very tight leash, and will not have nearly the freedoms that you have had in the past. And as for the child... if it is still one of your... our blood... you cannot evade your responsibilities, however, why you set your own brother up for a dupe as well... I cannot fathom that kind of behaviour, and it will not be tolerated."

James looked up at his mother, I am... I cannot tell you all how sorry I am that this happened. It grew so out of hand and I... I forgot myself." *That and how well Blake likes to load up his opponents at the tables.*

The other family members gave a collective snort. The earl began, "You do not appear as though you are sorry enough... yet!" The earl gave him a challenging glare.

"I do not know what you mean, sir. I cannot tell you how much this has weighed on my mind... and conscience. It has been a terrible cross to bear."

Lady Catherine growled, I do not think that even Richard would stoop so low as to demean the Fitzwilliam name in such a way! You have put us all in jeopardy with your carelessness, and loose rakish ways!"

James despised his aunt's hypocrisy, as she only seemed to show up just to start trouble, but usually it did not involve him. He had always found a way to off load his misdeeds to others-namely, Darcy or Richard.

The earl leveled another glare at him, "You do realize that you will be under my protection..." He began, but Lady Catherine interrupted.

"You cannot be serious, Brother! To overlook such misdeeds! It should not be borne! I would certainly..."

James glanced at Lady Catherine with contempt. The earl said, "You do not think that I would allow such a scandal to occur, do you? H-ll this does not affect only you, James; this affects everyone in this family. I hate to think of what it could do to your cousins, Darcy and Georgiana, or even Anne. It could not only ruin their reputations, but it could even affect the next generation!"

"What... what are you... are we going to do?" James asked his father. His mind was whirling with schemes on how to get out of this. He knew that family honour would take precedence over whatever trespasses, he committed, so he did not fret too much, but still... *to be duped by Blake, and then to have that trollop Harriet all but call me out! I will have to be more careful to hide my tracks in the future.*

"We are going to cover your debts to Blake. Then as to this Harriet business, you are responsible for bringing a child into this world. But *it* would not be accepted into polite society, nor would marriage to a kept woman... to many different men I might add. The only solution is to see to its upbringing, and perhaps, if Darcy were forgiving enough... he may allow her and the babe to stay on at Slatemore. We will have to some groveling to do there, I think".

The past hour of family confrontations left the viscount drained. After a long pause, the earl and countess excused him with the understanding that he was not to leave the house unless they knew his whereabouts, and trusty footmen or drivers escorted him. They had an understanding that he would be covered by them, so long as he did not fall out of line.

~*~*~*~

Once James left the study, the earl and countess turned to Lady Catherine to finish off their family conference.

"So what is this new 'bit' of information that you were speaking of Catherine... in regards to father's will?"

His sister gave the earl a defiant gaze, "James, I was doing the Christian thing in..."

"Do not give me that sanctimonious tone, Catherine! You know what I am talking about! You have some of our father's papers…and have had them for some time… what for nearly thirty years! And to think that Richard could have had his estate…his estate, Catherine! Instead, he had to go into the army and face Napoleon and his troops over there, and was nearly killed! You cannot know how much we have worried about him! To think that he could have been home all this time… out of harm's way, and yet for your own selfishness you did nothing, and took away his rightful inheritance!"

"Oh, but James, I did not allow that to happen after I discovered James' wrong doings, did I?" She said as if to exonerate herself. "In coming here, I am preserving Richard's rightful inheritance, after all." She pointed out.

Both the earl and countess stared at her incredulously. James Fitzwilliam had always known that his sister, Catherine, had a tendency to be overbearing, and was many times selfish, but that paled in comparison to what Richard had almost lost. It took all of his self control to maintain calm, even as all of his nerves screamed to throttle his sister.

"Oh no, but you did wait all this time to disclose it. You waited until our family is embroiled in a catastrophic incident. Catherine, I really do not know how you sleep at night knowing this!" The earl seethed. He glared at his sister, as if daring her to give him a reason to lose his temper again, before he turned on his heel and stormed out of the study. He had the butler gather his outerwear and informed him that he would be *walking* to Darcy's House. *Yes, a bit of fresh air would do me good right now.* His only guilt lay in leaving his wife to deal with his sister.

~*~*~*~

Darcy made it over to the Gardiner's home at his usual early morning hour, and now with his more than ever constant friend Bingley. Upon the announcement of their arrival, the party gathered in the Gardiner's sitting room, they were greeted by the unexpected sight of Mr. Bennet. Darcy felt less at ease with Elizabeth's father's presence, as the last time that they spoke, he had not attained the man's final approval to court his beloved Elizabeth, much less marry her.

"Mr. Bennet, how do you do, sir? I must say, we were not expecting to see you so soon."

"No, I do not expect that you did, Mr. Darcy, but I am here none-the-less." Mr. Bennet had an unreadable expression on his face.

Darcy shifted where he stood and looked over at Elizabeth, whose comforting smile reassured him.

"Papa, perhaps you and our visitors would like to visit in my uncle's study?" Both gentlemen gave her a grateful look.

"Yes," interjected Mr. Bingley, "we have not seen our neighbour for at least a week, I believe." He looked between Darcy and Mr. Bennet with a nervous smile.

Mr. Bennet acquiesced to this request, and Darcy and Bingley followed their beloved's father into the study, with hopes of emerging successful in obtaining the gentleman's permission to marry his two eldest daughters.

When they were settled into the study, Mr. Bennet sat behind Mr. Gardiner's desk and allowed the younger gentlemen to start the conversation. After a few minutes of silence, Darcy began, "Sir, you can have no doubt as to why we have come to this house to see your two daughters…"

Mr. Bennet interrupted, "On the contrary sir, I believe that Mr. Bingley here has said that he has called to extend his neighbourly greetings even as we find ourselves here in town and no longer quite so close."

Darcy cringed at the older man's biting wit. *This is where Elizabeth gets her liveliness and sense of humour… although I have to say that hers is much kinder.* To Mr. Bennet, he answered, "Sir, I believe you know that we… that is to say I, have come to ask for your daughter's hand in marriage…"

Mr. Bennet held up his hand, I understood that, sir, but I also understood that you were to give my Lizzy some time to think about her feelings for and about you, before you came seeking her here."

Darcy became frustrated with the man, and hoped that he had not blown his chance to prove his merits in obtaining Elizabeth's hand in marriage, "Sir, I believed that I had found the source of Eliz... Miss Elizabeth's distress before she left, and it was my intention to come to town and try to relieve that distress by coming here to explain myself. I wanted to personally defend myself against some untrue... very untrue statements about my character." He frowned with the remembrance of what Elizabeth overheard the night of the Netherfield Ball.

Bingley joined in to assist him, "Yes, sir, I can vouch for Darcy's character, and that there was some terrible misunderstanding, but I do believe that Miss Elizabeth has started to understand Darcy's character as well." He gave Darcy a nervous grin.

"And you succeeded in defending your character to my Lizzy, sir?" Mr. Bennet asked, in a far too incisive manner for Darcy's liking.

"*Yes*... yes sir, I had understood that some person or persons," He looked over towards Bingley, who seemed to be following their conversation intently, "had accused me of behaving in a very ungentlemanly manner with a member of the opposite sex, and in such a way as to insinuate that this was not an isolated incident. Mr. Bennet, I can assure you that I have explained this to Eli... umm... Miss Elizabeth, and she has understood that there was never such an indiscretion on my part nor, sir, will there ever be. I promise to you, sir, that I will treat her with the utmost respect for the rest of my life, and I love her with all of my heart, so I ask you to allow us to marry."

"And why, Mr. Darcy, did this 'misunderstanding' occur to cause that sort of gossip? How am I to know what you truly are? I have, after all only known you for what... two or three months. What if I allow this, and then come to find my daughter in a loveless or faithless marriage? How can I be assured of her comfort and affections?"

Darcy's heart raced, for in front of him stood an obstacle that could grant or deny his future happiness, and he had to choose his words well. He loved Elizabeth more than he could express, and felt her very existence could keep him for an eternity. With those thoughts in mind, he soldiered on and decided to speak directly to the point, "Mr. Bennet, I cannot but swear to you that I have *never* taken a mistress, or done anything as despicable as that. I can apply to Bingley to vouch for my faithfulness and constancy, and if you wish I will bring all of my friends and acquaintances to meet you to vouch for me as well. I assure you that I am a reliable and constant companion and, as I said... I love your daughter with all my heart. I would feel as if I were dying inside without her by my side." Darcy pleaded as he paced across the study.

Darcy was reluctant to reveal his cousin's culpability in the gossip, however, he felt that this was important enough for him to do so. He also knew that he could trust Mr. Bennet with such information. "Sir, I also think it imperative that I reveal to you some information that will at least partially explain all of these rumors you may have heard. I must request your word of secrecy on this, Sir."

He paused examining Mr. Bennet's demeanor as he nodded his acquiescence, and Darcy continued, "Though I am not proud of this, I have allowed my cousin, Colonel Fitzwilliam, to carry on an affair with a mistress, even aiding him with funds from time to time. I was not, nor have I at any time, involved myself in a personal manner with this woman. I am also not proud of my part in this affair. I must also add that I have informed my cousin that I will no longer be supporting his... um... *lifestyle choices*. This is the result of my everlasting devotion to Elizabeth, and respect for her rightful indignation at my previous behavior." Darcy stopped and looked at the elder man.

Mr. Bennet watched Darcy as he pled his case, and after a few moments of thought, he sighed, "Sir, I believe you when you say that you love my Lizzy. I had talked to her earlier, and she had said pretty much the same thing as you have. With that in mind, I suppose I have no other choice than to allow you two to marry." His voice had almost a sad quietness to it.

Darcy stood silent for a moment, allowing the words to set in, I cannot tell you how much this... she means to me, sir. I promise not to ever abuse the trust you place in me."

Mr. Bennet smiled and waved his hand, "Yes, yes, now I believe that Mr. Bingley may want to add his two pence to this conversation," He looked at Bingley, "Am I correct, sir, or was I mistaken?"

Bingley looked up, "No, oh, I mean yes, Mr. Bennet, I to wish to ask you about... um... about obtaining your permission to marry your daughter, Jane, sir."

Mr. Bennet smiled at him in his teasing way, "The previous gentleman said all sorts of pretty words, and expressed all sorts of valuable sentiments... are you telling me that you do not have the same sort of feelings...?"

"Oh no, sir! I mean to say I do love Jane and I do so wish to have her as my wife, sir..."

The gentleman smiled a genuine smile, "Well then Mr. Bingley, that was much improved... I suppose I have no other choice than to allow you to take one of my other daughter's away from me."

"Thank you, sir, I cannot tell you how much I am relieved to have that taken care of."

"Indeed, Mr. Bingley. Do either of you know when you would like to start the settlement..."

"Ah... I believe, sir, that Mr. Bingley and I have taken the liberty to have the marriage papers done just for this Mr. Bennet's eyebrows shot up, "Have you now, Mr. Darcy? That was quick work, and so very presumptive." He looked teasingly at both of the gentlemen.

"I... we had thought that we should be prepared for any possible last minute trips out of town to Hertfordshire, and did not wish to waste any time... of yours of course so we took that liberty... sir."

He and Bingley could tell that the older gentleman found amusement in their discomfiture, but because he was their betrotheds' father, and they were now in such a good mood, they chose to overlook his amusement at their expense.

"I suppose that it is a bit too early to drink to our good news, so perhaps we should get down to business, and have a look at these papers... or would you rather delay that and let Jane and Lizzy know of the outcome of our friendly early morning visit?"

They all agreed that the ladies must have grown quite anxious by now, and went out to inform them of their good fortune.

When Darcy came out, he saw Elizabeth sitting within easy view of the door to the study, and he noticed the relief in her eyes at his calm and encouraging smile.

He joined her on the sofa, where she worked on a piece of embroidery, and observed the pattern. She smiled and looked lovingly into his eyes, "These are Sweet Williams, for my sweet William." She bit the corner of her lip and blushed.

He wanted to take her out to the park again and taste those sweets lips, but instead settled for a cozy conference with Jane and Bingley, with an occasional adage by Mr. Bennet, and Mrs. Gardiner. They had a very pleasant visit, despite their lack of privacy in the Gardiner's sitting room, and left in much better spirits than they had arrived. As they said their goodbyes,

Darcy exacted a promise from all the ladies to attend his house on Grovesnor Street, for tea with his sister. *Perhaps I may be able to manage a few moments alone with Elizabeth?*

Chapter 25

When the earl walked towards Darcy House, he noticed a young woman leaving that same residence. As he drew near, he recognized the woman as Caroline Bingley, and frowned at the sight of her. To his annoyance, Miss Caroline Bingley had seen him and made a point of greeting him.

"Lord Fitzwilliam, it is good to see you. May I ask how you and Lady Fitzwilliam are?" He thought her smile was insincere.

"Miss... Bingley is it not?" He struggled to civilly acknowledge this social climber yet intended to ensure that she did not get too familiar with him.

"Uh... yes sir, it is. I was just leaving after visiting with your niece Georgiana..."

"Is my nephew here as well?" He did not want to stay there and discourse further with this woman, who was known as 'Pining Caroline' in his own private circle.

"Um... yes I believe that he is, but I must forewarn you that he has been in his study most of this afternoon, and seems to have much work. He has not left the study as of yet sir, and well... I was told he was in a poor mood." She leaned in as if she were telling state secrets.

The earl frowned, and backed away, I shall keep that in mind, Miss Bingley. Now, if you will excuse me, I must be off to... to tend to business." He walked past her and looked down his nose at her, giving her the message that he had no further intention of addressing her.

He left Miss Bingley standing on the walkway with a puzzled look upon her face and knocked on the door to Darcy House.

Mr. Humphrey received him and led him to Darcy's study after he obtained admittance.

His nephew stood to receive him and bowed graciously, all the while he was studying him, the earl noted. "What brings you here uncle... and upon foot? Is there a problem?" Darcy asked, then frowned.

"No...well, yes and no." Upon Darcy's questioning, look he elucidated, "It appears, my dear boy, that I owe you my most humble apologies."

Darcy stood there with a questioning look, without speaking a word.

The earl sighed, I am sure you know to what I refer? I believe that you have taken on great responsibility in protecting our family's honour in reference to James'... well Richard's and James' mistress." At Darcy's surprised look he continued,

"Oh yes, you have not heard about the latest family scandal."

"No... sir, I guess that I have been kept in the dark about some new developments." Darcy raised an eyebrow.

"I suppose I should start from the beginning; it appears that both of your cousins, my son's, have had the same woman as their mistress."

A horrified expression appeared on Darcy's face at this bit of information.

"Ha! I can tell that you felt the same astonishment and disgust I did upon hearing this, but it only gets worse..." The earl related the sordid tale about James and Richard and the situation with James and Lord Blake including that man's plan to force the family to sell him the Cantrell Hill Estate. He explained Lady Catherine's deception in regards to that estate.

"It appears that many years ago, before you children were born, or at least before most of you were born, my father... your grandfather had made out a new will. It was not disclosed until today by Catherine."

"*What*? What do you mean a '*newer*' will? Where had it been? Why did she just *now* disclose this?"

"That was what your aunt and I wanted to know. She had been keeping it to make certain that she and your mother were protected. You see, when your parents married, your mother was desperate to conceive, but she had much difficulty and at that time your Aunt Catherine had not yet married. She feared that their interests would not be protected from me should Catherine never marry and Anne not conceive. As you can see those fears were unfounded, and I can honestly say that I have never been so offended to hear her accusations of my possible neglect of any member of my family."

The earl began pacing around Darcy's study, I knew that George Darcy would not leave your mother in a lurch, should something happen to him and she not conceive a son… or a child for that matter. As to the other explanations as to why now," he shook his head, I have gathered that she repented that she now had no basis to hold on to the will as she had been married many years and widowed many more, and then there are you and Georgiana as well. When she received the letter from Mrs. Heartherton, she knew that should anything happen to her or I, Richard would be left in the lurch… well at least by James, it appears. If he was willing to sacrifice his own brother to evade the consequences of his sins, she could not imagine what would happen after we were all gone. She knew that you and Anne would take care of him, but also knew that that would be unfair to both of you, so she 'remembered' this newer will, and brought it to our attention."

With a deep frown, Darcy asked shortly, "*How* can you be so *calm* when…when someone has cheated your son out of his rightful inheritance?" Darcy shook his head, I could not fathom being so forgiving after all that has happened to Richard… he faced Napoleons army for G-d's sake!" Darcy's face flushed.

"Yes, I know." The earl said quietly, glancing out the window as Darcy spoke, "But at least now, he will not have to and… umm… furthermore, he will not be forced to marry where he does not wish, though I must say that after I have seen James' behaviour, I am not too impressed with either of them. Richard is no better than the average gentleman of our society, but that does not give me any comfort. I need to thank you though, as I understand that you have been instrumental in helping him… well, them with this mistress. I shall not be able to thank you enough for that, and I do not wish to impose but…"

"You need me to keep her there in Lancashire until other arrangements can be made for her and the child." Darcy completed his thought.

The earl had enough grace to blush at the admittance, "Yes… if it is not too much trouble…"

Darcy let out a big sigh, "No, however, I do not expect to have to answer for this woman with child…"

"No, no my dear boy, you shall not have to. We have devised a plan to 'bequeath' her with some 'inheritance' from her 'recently' deceased husband. This husband is, of course, one of our relatives from Wales." He looked at Darcy pointedly.

They silently acknowledged that this would mean a possibility of a reemergence to polite society after some time. Nothing further needed to be said between the two gentlemen on that subject. At least one of them was more than uneasy with this proposal, but they agreed that it was the best solution, for now.

Darcy paced back and forth from the desk to the window a couple of times before he stopped and turned to his uncle, "There is something that I should tell you uncle and it is very *good* news." He smiled, .I have become engaged to a most wonderful woman…"

"Why Darcy! Catherine did not say anything about your engagement! Congratulations dear boy!" *I never would have imagined him to finally cave to Catherine's demands.*

Darcy looked puzzled for a moment, "How would she know about my engagement to Elizabeth?"

The earl looked up in confusion, I do not understand, Darcy. I believed you and Anne had agreed to marry…"

"No, no we have not uncle! I do not speak of my marriage to my cousin, but to Elizabeth… Elizabeth Bennet. I never had any intention of marrying Anne. That was only a dream of Catherine's. It had nothing to do with *our* desires, but with hers to unite Rosings and Pemberley." He gave the earl a defiant look at, and the earl shook his head, smiling slowly. *Thank goodness, the boy has some sense!*

"I should have guessed that. You never were easy to bully into doing something you did not wish to do. Now, tell me do I know of her family? What connections does she have?"

Darcy looked thoughtfully at the man, "You have probably never met any of her connections before in your life, much less her family. Her closest relatives are... well, suffice to know that they are not of your station. She is, a gentleman's daughter, and that is good enough for me. I do not need to worry about consequence... that is, unless my cousins continue their foolishness, and as far as her family is concerned, there has been no major scandal associated with them."

Lord Fitzwilliam put his head down then looked up to Darcy with a sad smile and nodded. They had an unspoken agreement to respect the other's decisions from then on, as it became more apparent whose counsel held more merit, and which decisions were none of the other's concern.

~*~*~*~

Darcy looked forward to this morning as he had his carriage sent to Gracechurch Street to fetch Elizabeth, Jane, and Mrs. Gardiner. He had also made arrangements for Bingley to join him later in the morning to meet with Jane. Georgiana watched his pacing and commented, "William, by the way you are pacing back and forth, you will wear a hole into the floor."

He stopped, as if unaware of his own actions, and flushed, I was not pacing... I was... checking to see if the carriage has arrived safely."

She giggled at his response, "If you say so, Brother."

He frowned at her, but his response was cut off by a noise outside the house. His carriage had arrived with Elizabeth and Jane, and he ran to the front door to greet his guests. Georgiana followed him with a more sedate pace. Looking up to her brother, she said, "William, are you suggesting that I cannot handle guests?"

He looked at her apologetically, "No dearest, I just wanted to... well... see to it that they felt most welcome."

"I do not think that any of your guests would be made to feel unwelcome... even Miss Bi..." She stopped mid sentence and blushed.

He broke out laughing, which brought a smile to her face.

"That is quite alright, dearest. Those are my sentiments as well, but we must remember that she is still Bingley's sister, though she does not deserve such notice," Darcy said.

Their guests had arrived and upon seeing Elizabeth, Darcy wanted to pull her into his arms, but satisfied himself with an overlong kiss to the back of her hand. He felt most pleased with the pretty blush to her cheeks. It took him a few moments to realize that their party was shy of one person.

"Aunt Gardiner was detained at home as our cousin Nathaniel has come down with a fever, and she felt it best to stay nearby incase he became worse," Elizabeth explained.

Darcy had a genuine look of concern for the small Gardiner child, "Will he be alright? Does she need anything to...?"

Elizabeth smiled, "No sir, I do believe she has everything in hand. She has dealt with these things before, and I am sure it will soon pass, with none the worse for wear."

He nodded and stared at her until he recalled himself at the sound of Georgiana clearing her throat, reminding him that he had not greeted Elizabeth's sister. "Oh, I am so sorry Miss Bennet, I... we welcome you to Darcy House."

Jane smiled with understanding, "That is quite alright, sir. I am sure you have other things on your mind at the moment."

Darcy glanced at her quickly before looking back at Elizabeth, who was now blushing even more scarlet. He felt warm for he suspected it spread beyond her face; he had glanced down at her chest.

All too soon for him, the ladies adjourned into the sitting room, and Darcy was left staring at a closed door from the hall. He decided to try to get some work done in his study until he could join his betrothed, but he was finding it more difficult to concentrate when he thought of Elizabeth sitting in his sitting room, with his sister and so very close to him. He began thinking of where else he would like to see her in his house... the dining room, the music room, his library, his study, his... bedroom.

I must stop this, else I will never finish these crop contracts! It did not take long for him to lose himself again in his thoughts about what he wanted to do with her in certain rooms of his house. *My Elizabeth, you are so beautiful with your pouty luscious lips, your light figure, your lovely chestnut curls, and your... pert full breasts.* As he sat at his desk, he found himself growing uncomfortable with each passing thought. He felt the front of his breaches grow tighter, and thought he would go mad, if he did not find some way to stop these thoughts.

Suddenly, he looked down to his desk at some papers to his steward, which reminded him of his uncle's conversation in that very room. Thinking about what Fitzwilliam endured at the hands of his own brother managed to distract him. He remembered how they were all deceived with Lady Catherine's withholding of the newer will.

He recalled his uncle's assumption of his marrying Anne as well... *that would never have happened anyway! Ah, but I have yet to tell Lady Catherine about my engagement. I must send a message to request an audience with her at her earliest convenience, which, unfortunately, will certainly be of no convenience to me.*

He had made an agreement with the earl that Darcy should be the one to announce his engagement to his aunt, but he would have preferred her to learn it from the newspaper. *That would serve her right for all she has done. She will be furious, but I will not let that affect my decision!*

As he mused over these concerns, he heard a knock at his study door, "Come."

Bingley arrived, and was ever eager to see his beloved Jane, I am so very glad that you thought to invite the ladies to tea Darcy, as I am sure Mr. Bennet would likely not even consider them coming without their family, and after yesterday I am not yet ready to face him again."

Darcy laughed, "You must know how much Mr. Bennet loves to tease, Bingley. He had his fun at our expense."

"Yes, I understand that now, but it was not so amusing to me, and if I am not mistaken, you seemed discomfited when the gentleman had his go at you."

Darcy snorted. They began their routine conversation about why they were to be the happiest couple on earth and enumerated the merits of their ladies; then the topic unfortunately moved to Caroline.

"Bingley, did you know that your sister, Caroline, was here for a little over an hour yesterday, and it took me 'reminding' Georgiana that she needed to practice for the music master to hint for her to leave."

Bingley wore a genuine look of surprise, "Oh dear. I have told her to quit her foolishness, as you are to marry Miss Elizabeth, but she seems not to understand that it is final, and there is absolutely nothing she can do to change that. I have even instructed her to pack for a trip up north, but I cannot send her until…"

They were interrupted by a knock on the door. Mr. Humphreys had come to announce that Georgiana had sent for her brother. The two gentlemen arose and walked to the sitting room to join their fiancés. Each taking a place by their respective lady.

"William," Georgiana whispered, "Miss Elizabeth has expressed an interest in seeing the house… I thought that… well… that we could show her new home…"

"That is a most excellent idea. "Eliz…Miss Elizabeth, would you like to see your soon-to-be new home?"

Elizabeth agreed, "Yes, sir, I believe that I would, as I do not think it would be a good idea for me to come to a house as its new mistress, and get lost only to become a wandering spirit."

He smiled with great delight, "Well then, shall we?" He said to the group as a whole, but was decidedly looking at Elizabeth and offered her his arm.

They could hear a slight giggle from Georgiana's direction, but chose to ignore it for the present. As they began the tour, Georgiana followed her brother and Elizabeth, with Bingley and Jane trailing everyone. The first leg of the tour was on the main level with the parlour and sitting room, followed by the dining room then the library.

As this was one of Elizabeth's favourite rooms, she stayed to examine his extensive collection of books upon books.

"I do not believe I have ever seen so many books in the whole of my life."

Darcy was pleased with her first impression of his home, "Well then, madam, you shall be overawed when you are at Pemberley, for it is two stories high and has at least ten times the volumes." He smiled down into her face; intensely interested in her response.

She looked into his face and swallowed hard. "I... I... hardly know what to say."

"I cannot wait until I can bring you home to find out what you will say."

She smiled at his blatant flirtation, and looked down before looking back at him through her thick eyelashes. They then realized that Bingley and Jane had joined Georgiana to complete their tour. He saw Elizabeth blush prettily and noted that it started well below her chin, for his eyes settled on her heaving breast as she breathed. Looking up to her face, he saw her watching him with intent interest, and noticed her lips parted.

Unable to withstand the temptation, he bent down and laid claim to her lips. He could feel her soft breath upon his cheek and smell her lavender scent. It overwhelmed him, and he deepened their kiss. Darcy brought his hands to her waist, and began caressing her back and shoulders. Feeling her acquiesce to his touch, he deepened the kiss further and parted her lips with his tongue. Hers then met his in a delicate duel of passion. That kiss led to more and more of its kind, leaving Darcy feeling unable to control his passions.

He caressed her harder and harder, until his hands moved to her rib cage and moved up to cup her left breast, which caused her to gasp. Darcy broke their kiss, pulling back to look into her passion fogged face. She said to his silent query, "No, do not stop."

That was all the invitation he needed, and he claimed her lips again with even more fervour, caressing her shoulders and breasts until he removed the sleeve from her right shoulder, pushing it down while he held her tiny waist with his right hand. He slipped his left hand under the fabric of her bodice, and felt her grasp at his lapels and slipped her hand under his coat. He gasped at her bold move and picked her up, moving them over to a settee in the corner of the library and placing her slight frame across his lap while continuing their never ending kiss.

As he slid his hand to her back, he felt for the buttons to her bodice in the front of her gown and began working on them all the while as she unbuttoned his coat and then started on his vest, trying desperately to slide her fingers and hand through the fabric separating them. He nearly had the last button undone when the side door opened unnoticed, and they stopped their attentions to each other when they heard a loud gasp.

Chapter 26

Darcy and Elizabeth jumped away from each other when they heard a loud gasp. Their eyes darted towards the source of the noise, but only saw the door close. They looked at each other in a panic, both panting from their activity. Darcy let out an expletive, then realized whom he was with and quickly apologized, "My love, I do not know what came over me, I must beg your forgiveness… for my behaviour. I have never acted in such a way with any woman. It is just that… when… when you are near, I feel so very strongly for you that I cannot help myself."

Elizabeth managed to find her voice, I am not harmed sir, and I think that you are not any more culpable than I as… well… as I feel… the same." She blushed and looked down then glanced up to observe his face through her eyelashes.

He took a deep breath, exhaled, and grasped her hands, which were busy rebuttoning her bodice. I cannot tell you how much your affection means to me." He looked down at his state of attire and came back to their current predicament, "We had best hurry and right ourselves, as I fear we have been discovered." He buttoned his vest and coat, covering the flush that crept throughout his body.

Elizabeth frowned at him, I do not… that is I… I did not see who happened upon us sir, I…"

Darcy caressed her face and brought her chin up to meet his eyes, "Elizabeth please, when we are alone you do not need to call me sir, you may call me by my name, especially here in my own home. As to who interrupted us, I have not a clue." He feared it may have been Georgiana, and wondered how he could explain his behaviour if it was.

She glanced at him shyly, I suppose that would be in order considering my previous behaviour. I… I guess we shall learn soon enough… Fitzwilliam… or is it 'William'?"

"Elizabeth, you could call me anything, and I would respond to you. Now, we had better go and join the rest of our party before we stir up more suspicion."

He rose and assisted her, feeling dizzy from this morning's activities and discoveries. Putting on his most serious expression, he guided her through the door, and out to the parlour. They found Georgiana there with Bingley at Jane's side. Everyone looked up when they entered the room.

Georgiana said, "We thought you may have gone lost William. We went looking for you shortly after we noticed Elizabeth's and your absence." She smiled at him and raised an eyebrow.

He realized that his sister's calm behaviour immediately ruled out Georgiana as the witness to his impropriety earlier. *What of Bingley and Jane?* He observed them throughout the rest of their visit to see if he could determine the intruder's identity, but could only discern Bingley's doting over Jane. *I will get to the bottom of this, and keep our reputations intact.*

He noted that Elizabeth appeared more quiet than usual as she observed her sister with some interest. He felt badly about his part in their tryst in the library, but another part of him rejoiced in his intended's newfound passion.

After another fifteen minutes in the parlour, the Gracechurch party announced the necessity to return to the Gardiner's residence, as Mrs. Gardiner would be requiring relief from tending a sick child.

Darcy assisted Elizabeth into her pelisse as Bingley did the same for Jane, and both gentlemen regretted the ladies need for departure. Before Elizabeth stepped into his carriage, Darcy leaned into her ear and said, I will try to send word later on today if it was Bingley who had… come upon us, and perhaps you may be allowed to come tomorrow, and we shall discuss it… you can bring Jane as well." They both blushed.

Elizabeth replied, I fear that if it were Jane, then I shall be forever ashamed of disappointing her… but in another way I… well I… just think that it happened as a natural occurrence between two people who love each other. It is very hard to explain."

Darcy nodded, I know." He took her hand and kissed the back of it overlong before handing her into the carriage.

Both he and Bingley watched as his carriage took their beloveds away from them. *Soon my love, very soon I will not be sending you away, wondering when I will see you next.* He went into his study and Bingley followed. As soon as he came into the study, Bingley frowned. He sat in a nearby armchair and seemed as if lost in thought.

Darcy studied him, before Bingley realized he was being observed. "Oh sorry Darcy, I was contemplating Jane's behaviour after we left the music room. She seemed upset about something, and I hope it was not what she and I had discussed earlier."

Darcy started, And what did you discuss Bingley? If you do not mind my asking."

"Oh, I told her about Caroline. I will not be able to send her to the Dugan's until I hear from them. Hopefully it will be soon..." He sighed, "Jane seemed very upset about it... I mean, about sending Caroline away so soon. She felt that Caroline was just misinformed and intended to protect Miss Elizabeth."

He laughed and glanced at Darcy, "You and I know better than that, but Jane... she is so very giving and kind. Perhaps I should..."

"You should what, Bingley?" Darcy looked at him suspiciously, "Oh no, no, I do not think that it would be a good idea to give her another chance, Charles. It seems that she will not give up pursuing me. She has gone to my aunt, the countess, and started spreading lies about me, and *do not* pretend that you do not feel disgusted about her attempts to keep you from your Miss Bennet."

Bingley looked away sadly and nodded his head in silent acknowledgement of the facts. Darcy felt secure that it was not Bingley who happened upon him and Elizabeth, but now had the uncomfortable idea that it was Jane. *Why could we not have some respite from all of this turmoil? And why did it have to be Jane who happened upon us instead of Bingley? At least then I would be the one taking the brunt of it instead of Elizabeth.*

~*~*~*~

Elizabeth noted that Jane had acted odd all afternoon. She could not so much as catch her sister's eye, and Jane seemed to be avoiding her. She guessed the source of the problem, and came to Jane that night. Jane sat on a stool brushing her hair, facing away from her sister,

"Jane, I…wanted to talk to you today about… well about… well about recent events."

Jane stopped brushing and looked down before turning to face Elizabeth and raised her eyebrow without looking back up, "What events, Lizzy?"

"I fear that… no, I am afraid that I may have given you a poor impression of me today."

"Whatever do you mean?" She asked with a high pitched voice.

Elizabeth looked away, I think you know what I am talking about dearest Jane… in the library?"

"Oh… that. I… well… I do not know what to think, Lizzy. I mean we were all together, then you and Mr. Darcy disappeared for a while, and we went looking for you. I thought of the most likely place to find you and I was correct, only I found you and Mr. Darcy, and …well…" She looked accusingly at her sister.

Elizabeth had the grace to flush, I do not know what came over us, dearest Jane. I do not know how to apologize enough for embarrassing you like that…"

"Lizzy, it is not for me to feel the offense, however, in light of all that has been said here in town about… well about Mr. Darcy and all…" Her voice trailed off as her sister looked back to her in concern.

"I realize this, Jane, but it all happened so suddenly. I really do not know what came over me…well us. I cannot explain this feeling; it is almost as if we are alone in our own world. I do know, however, that it is most… enlivening." Sighing, she looked at Jane, I only wish I could explain it more."

"Yes Lizzy, I understand those feelings, but you must realize that should it be someone else who walked through that door, Miss Darcy, or some other family or friends, it would not help his situation… or yours for that matter."

Elizabeth looked down and nodded, "Yes, I guess you are correct. I shall endeavor to protect my virtue from here on… that is until we marry," She said, regaining her sense of humour.

"And I shall endeavor to ensure that you do," Jane replied with gravity.

Elizabeth and Jane smiled at each other in silent agreement and parted with a better understanding.

~*~*~*~

The next morning, Darcy had a note sent to Gracechurch Street under the pretext of inviting his fiancé to meet with Georgiana again for tea; He also used the excuse that the future Mrs. Darcy needed to meet with the Darcy House housekeeper and some of the senior staff. He felt that all of the ladies should be invited, in light of what happened the day before, for he knew that he may not be able to be trusted with his passion towards his Elizabeth.

He had spent the night tossing and turning with the recollection of his few stolen moments with Elizabeth in the library. It was bad enough to have a raging erection while trying to sleep, but he also had a hard time with it while with Elizabeth. All he wanted to do was to rush over to the Gardiner's residence and bring Elizabeth home with him to take her... well just to take her.

We will have to be wed soon, else I may be driven mad with desire for her. D-mn! This will not do! I must find a way to convince her of the need to set the wedding plans in motion. Then I... we will not have to worry about being found in compromising positions! Now if I can only get through tonight!

~*~*~*~

When three o'clock rolled around, he paced in the front foyer awaiting Elizabeth and Jane. The Darcy's had received word that Mrs. Gardiner was again unable to attend them due to a sick child. He noted that Georgiana watched him with a hint of amusement and delight glimmering in her eyes, but made no comments. When the carriage came towards the front of the house, Darcy ran out to greet his fiancé. As Elizabeth stepped out, she smiled at him and raised her eyebrow, which gave Darcy some comfort that no serious repercussions had befallen her after their being 'discovered' yesterday. He then turned to assist Jane down from the carriage.

He led Elizabeth and Jane into Darcy House one on each arm and explained to Jane that Bingley would join them later, as he had the day before. She smiled in response. Georgiana greeted her guests with less shyness than the day before and again led them to the parlour.

"How did you enjoy the ride here today Miss Bennet? Miss Elizabeth?"

"Oh it was lovely coming over, but I think it is getting a bit cloudy, and perhaps we may get some precipitation a bit later." Jane replied.

"Yes, but the temperature is unseasonably warm for this time of year, perhaps instead of snow we will have rain." Elizabeth said.

"Shall we sit and take tea?" Georgiana motioned towards the sofa, and both guests sat down with their host and hostess.

They were all engaged in small talk about town life versus country life and their favourite books, but they stopped talking when they heard a knock on the door. The butler, Mr. Humphreys, announced the presence of a visitor.

"Miss Bingley, to see Miss Darcy."

Jane and Elizabeth looked at each other when Caroline was announced, and watched as the lady herself waltzed in. She started as if she had not expected to see the Bennet ladies there, "Oh, I… I came to visit today, Georgiana. I had not realized that you had company, and to see my… future sister Miss Bennet, how do you do?" She gave a false smile.

"I am fine Miss Bingley, how are you this afternoon?" Jane replied politely.

"I am very well, very well indeed!" It was not lost on the group how she barely acknowledged Elizabeth, "Miss Elizabeth." She said with a slight nod to her head in Elizabeth's direction.

"I wanted to say what a lovely time we had yesterday Dear Georgiana, and I had hoped to discuss plans for the summer. It is never too soon to start planning these things you know." She directed most of her conversation towards Georgiana, with the apparent intent to slight the other ladies present.

"Miss Bingley," Georgiana began timidly, "Our plans may change, as we will have Miss Elizabeth to consult as well, since she will in all likely hood be married to my brother by then." She nodded her head towards Elizabeth.

"Ahem… yes I suppose that is correct…" She droned on, trying to avoid that particular point and steering the conversation to the most recent fashions.

It annoyed Darcy that Caroline was only addressing Georgiana as she was referring to bridal wear and trousseaus.

"Dear Georgiana, have you seen the latest bridal fashions from Madam Chauveaur? I do believe she get's many of her lovely ideas straight from Paris."

As if Georgiana has any interest in bridal wear and trousseaus, Caroline! Do you not know how obvious you are?

Darcy frowned at Caroline, and noted Georgiana's confused look as she answered Caroline politely.

"No… Miss Bingley, but… I am sure that Miss Bennet and Miss Elizabeth would be most interested to see them."

Darcy noticed that both of the Bennet ladies had an odd expression on their faces. When Georgiana tried to redirect the conversation to more general topics, Caroline still tried to continue on in the same vein.

At that moment Darcy heard a loud knock all the way from the front door followed by the very distinguished voice of none other than Lady Catherine de Bourgh, who sounded as if she was ready to vent her spleen. *What now?*

There was no way for Darcy to avoid his aunt. He excused himself to tend to her fits lest she make a scene in his own home, and within earshot of Caroline Bingley.

"I fear I must attend to my aunt, Lady Catherine, if you will excuse me?" He gave Elizabeth a nod, and bowed to the room full of ladies.

When he came out to the foyer, the butler, Mr. Humphreys, informed him that Mr. Bingley had just arrived right before Lady Catherine came, and he was in Darcy's study. Darcy knew that it would be a disaster should he have Lady Catherine anywhere near the parlour where Elizabeth and Caroline Bingley were for very different reasons, however. He knew that he could trust Bingley, and therefore led his aunt to his study, thinking it safer to have the matron vent there instead of closer to the parlour. He was not surprised when she started her tirade either.

"*Darcy*! What is this news in the Times of an announcement of your engagement… to… to… to Elizabeth Bennet? This must be a mistake! It must be the work of that… that Lord Blake to defame us!" She stopped when she noted that Darcy gave no reaction at all as he moved past her. "*Well?*" She demanded.

Darcy sat at his desk, shot an annoyed look at his unexpected guest then turned toward his friend, "Bingley, could you give me a moment with my aunt?"

Bingley held the expression of a startled man. He moved out of the room and headed towards the parlour, shutting the study doors firmly behind him. Darcy glared at his aunt, and stood up, never taking his eyes off of his aunt. He began to speak in a controlled voice, "Lady Catherine, there is no mistake or any subterfuge by anybody with that announcement. I am in fact engaged to be married to Miss Elizabeth Bennet, so you must not be alarmed on my account, madam. I hope you would wish me joy." He did not smile, however, as he disapproved of her intrusion into his study and venting her feelings in front of Bingley.

"*Wish you joy? Wish you joy? Are you mad?* Is it this nonsense with James and Richard? If it is, let me assure you that it shall have no effect on my feelings about you marrying Anne. No one needs to know about the near scandal that was avoided!"

It was not lost on Darcy that James and Richard were as much Anne's cousins as they were his, but he chose not to fight that battle at this moment. "It has nothing to do with James, Richard, or anyone else but myself. I have asked for her hand and she has accepted me, and our minds will not be changed-not by you, not by the earl, nor even her family if they so choose to challenge us".

"*Darcy*, you are forgetting your dearest mother's wish for you and her namesake. You and Anne were…"

"*Enough!*" Darcy had reached the end of his patience and wanted to be done with this conversation. I will *not* marry Anne, or anyone else who is *not* Elizabeth Bennet! I will *not* accept a delusional dream of anyone that we were 'formed for each other from our cradles'! It is ludicrous to assert such notions and…"

He held up his hand to stem his aunt's venting,

"And I have had it on good authority that it was more of a one sided demand by you than anything else. Furthermore, you will treat my wife with the utmost respect, or else I will see to it that you are no longer accepted into my household. Now, if there is anything further you wish to discuss then I suggest you make your business known, otherwise I have guests to attend to and other matters to take care of."

Lady Catherine did not allow her apparent shock to stop her anger, "You have not heard the last of this young man! I will see to it that this atrocity never takes place! Whomever this… woman is she has obviously put you under some sort of spell and…"

She wore on his patience and he raised his voice.

"*Madam! You forget yourself!* I will not tolerate your disparagement of my future wife, as you have never met her before in your life! Do not forget that I have the authority over my own personal and business matters, and I have made my decision! *Nothing*, and I do mean *nothing*, you say or do will change that! Now if you *do not mind*, I have *other*, guests to attend to!" Darcy stomped past her to the parlour, leaving a silenced Lady Catherine.

As he walked down the corridor, Darcy heard her call for her coach and outerwear and leave the house the next moment.

Darcy joined the group gathered in the parlour and was surprised to see Caroline Bingley still sitting amongst them. He gave that woman a cold glare. She did not bother to say much to anyone beyond what could be considered civil. It annoyed him that of all of the people to show up at such a time, it would be Caroline Bingley and she might have heard his heated discussion with Lady Catherine.

It seems as though she knew that my aunt would be showing up here. I wonder what other reason she would have to come here, besides to witness the spectacle that Lady Catherine caused? To him, it seemed that everyone besides Caroline Bingley tried to ignore the brouhaha that just took place down the hall.

"Mr. Darcy, was that your aunt, Lady Catherine de Bourgh, that we heard come in? Will she be joining us?"

He noted Caroline's wicked gleam.

"No! No, Lady Catherine had to leave rather abruptly."

"I hope there is not a problem, sir? I thought she sounded rather… excited."

Darcy was debating upon throwing Caroline out of his home, but thought better of it as her brother was his good friend, and he did not want to alienate him. He therefore, changed the subject, and directed his attention to Elizabeth.

"Miss Elizabeth, how is Mr. Gardiner today? I am sorry I had forgotten to inquire about him earlier."

Elizabeth smiled at him, "He is fine today, I thank you. It seems he managed to avoid what has afflicted our cousin."

Before Darcy could formulate another response to Elizabeth, Caroline injected herself in their conversation. I believe that you are quite fortunate Miss Eliza, that your uncle has a warehouse with stores of fabric inventory. It must be so very convenient to have such connections."

Elizabeth responded, "Yes it is, Miss Bingley, after all, he had been known to be a supplier to some of the Royal Houses, and I cannot think of a better connection. It is indeed fortunate, is it not?" Her eyes were alight with amusement.

Caroline frowned and wore a surprised expression, "Yes, I suppose it is." She sneered, I suppose then that we should expect some rather 'dignified' guests at your …wedding?"

Caroline's attacks aimed at the Gardiners did not sit well with Darcy, and he was about to respond to her viciousness when Elizabeth fought back.

"We do not *pretend* to be on an intimate basis with all of those whom we do business Miss Bingley, but we do pride ourselves on being able to supply things of finer quality."

Elizabeth's defense caused Caroline to fall silent.

Bingley joined the conversation, steering it to more neutral topics. I say, we should be discussing our weddings, or should I say 'wedding' as we were discussing a double wedding, were we not Darcy?"

Darcy was still preoccupied with stewing over his aunt's hateful words, and Caroline Bingley's intrusion, when his thoughts were interrupted by Elizabeth's amused questioning, "Sir, I believe we are awaiting your response…"

Darcy turned a questioning look to Elizabeth, I am sorry, madam, I did not hear the question…"

He heard a most delightful throaty giggle from Elizabeth, I had not noticed. We were discussing the plans for a double wedding perhaps in mid to late January?"

He grew alarmed, "Uh… I had thought rather late December early January… but of course it is up to you."

He was a little disappointed at this, and was soon lost in his thoughts until Bingley announced that he needed to go to his house for some errand.

"I believe that Caroline and I should be going now. Perhaps I may be able to see you all tomorrow?" It was obvious he was speaking to Miss Jane.

"Of course, Bingley. We shall hopefully meet again tomorrow, though I will have to send you a note to inform you of when, as I may have some business to tend to." He looked meaningfully to Bingley, who took the hint.

"Yes, yes, of course. I shall look forward to it then." Bingley said nervously. He confided to Darcy on his way out, that he would attempt to come back again as soon as possible to join his beloved.

Jane and Darcy waved farewell to the Bingley's from the door. Almost immediately after they departed, the clouds opened up with lightning and thunder claps. Darcy thought it was fortuitous, for now, at least his beloved would be safe at home… his home. In fact, as it became later in the evening with no sign of the rain stopping, the Gracechurch ladies were forced to concede they would not be going anywhere until at least morning. So at the Darcy house they would have to stay.

Chapter 27

When Caroline arrived back at Bingley's townhouse, she felt humiliated from the whole debacle of sitting in the presence of the woman she scorned. She knew that she should have been the one crowing about capturing Darcy for a husband. She planned on attending as many balls and parties as possible, in order to ensure that she would meet other eligible gentlemen. She knew her plans for capturing Darcy were not flawless; therefore she wanted to have options in case the first choice fell through. She had wits enough to know that she needed to secure a husband to avoid being sent away by her brother, but still needed to find a groom. And she had just the man in mind.

The day prior, she had run into Viscount Fitzwilliam near the park and had a decent chat with him. He had seemed interested in her conversation, which indicated an alteration from his prior indifference. She did not wonder at his previous lack of interest, because she had neglected him in the past, inclined to believe him to be less desirable than his cousin, Darcy. The engagement of Fitzwilliam Darcy to a country nobody... *that Miss Eliza Bennet*... did not become a serious possibility to her until she read it in the London Times, and saw the public acknowledgement of the travesty.

Caroline had always preferred Darcy's looks to his cousin's, but she could now accept that the viscount had a decent, though not quite handsome, appearance. It did not hurt that he came with a title and a family of wealth and privilege. These were necessary qualities in a man in order for her to consider them marriageable. She decided overnight to activate a plan to secure the viscount.

If the viscount and I married, then I could watch Darcy and his little country chit fall flat on their faces in society, while I would be the height of fashion and in due time hold the title of Countess Fitzwilliam.

Ah yes, that will teach him, and Darcy will regret having passed me over for that... that country nobody! Now all I have to do is show the viscount what a real woman of quality is and he will be mine.

She embarked on a letter writing campaign to all of her acquaintances to ensure that everyone of her set knew of her presence in town and that she would be available to attend all of the balls and parties that the viscount would be likely to attend. Caroline finished writing her letters, sealed them, and sent them with her maid to be sent out in the morning.

~*~*~*~

Unfortunately for Bingley and Jane, the weather did not cooperate with their plans to reunite. Jane had been in a gloomy mood since her betrothed left Darcy House, and Elizabeth tried to cheer her by eliciting Georgiana to play with her at the piano forte. Soon, however, Elizabeth found that she needed a distraction from focusing on Darcy, because she saw his darkened sultry eyes that sent her spine tingling. She had difficulty concentrating on the music and missed a note. Her mind wandered to yesterday, and the memory of the feeling of being in Darcy's arms in a secluded part of the library.

She did not know how they could sleep under the same roof. She wondered what it would be like when they lived under the same canopy. She considered what he may expect of her as his wife. Elizabeth had always been known as one of the better readers in her family; however, some books were not accessible to a young maiden of a certain upbringing. These last few weeks had roused a curiosity within her about certain subjects. *Perhaps there might be some informative books in that vast library of Darcy's.* She would take this opportunity to continue her investigation.

She stole a glance towards Darcy, finding a most curious expression on his face. His lips were turned up and he had a glazed look about him, as if daydreaming. He noticed her glance and gave her a questioning look. She tried to concentrate on the music, but Jane expressed a wish to retire for the night. Elizabeth conceded and they all left the music room to go to bed. *This shall be a long night! Maybe I shall find some tedious books to read... or maybe not.*

Darcy and Georgiana escorted their guests to their respective rooms, which Jane entered after glancing towards Elizabeth and wishing her a good night. Darcy took Elizabeth to the best guest bedroom, and wished Elizabeth a good night, "If there is anything… anything at all that you need, Elizabeth do not hesitate to ask. I shall see to it that you are comfortable. After all, it would not do to have the future mistress wanting for anything, would it?"

Elizabeth stared into his eyes and flushed, but managed to reply, "You have quite an attentive staff." She tried to lighten the mood but went distracted from the passionate looks by her fiancé.

"You are not entirely correct, there are a few requests that the staff may not be able to accomplish."

She searched his eyes and felt an unusual burning within her lower abdomen. She looked away, then turned back to him with a smile, "Well, then, I hope that you shall not go wanting for anything, sir, as that would be most distressing for the master of such a household."

He smiled at her slowly "Indeed." Darcy held her hands, caressing the back of each with his lips, and then stroked her palms and wrists before relinquishing her to the room. He backed away and headed to his own suite, leaving her standing on the other side of her door breathless, remembering the feel of his lips on her hands, wishing that he had also placed them on her lips. She wanted for *something*, but she remained unsure of what.

Soon after looking around the room, she heard a knock from the servant's entrance and called for whoever it was to enter. A maid came in and helped her ready for bed. Elizabeth dismissed the girl only to be disturbed from her quietude by another knock on the other door. Suspecting it may be Jane, she turned to answer it finding her future sister behind it.

"I am sorry to disturb you so late Miss Elizabeth but I was wondering…" Georgiana hesitated.

"It is quite all right, Miss Darcy…"

"No, Georgiana…" She blushed, I mean to say you do not have to call me 'Miss Darcy', as we are to be sisters, you may call me 'Georgiana'." The girl smiled.

Elizabeth felt touched by her sweetness, "Then you must call me 'Elizabeth' or 'Lizzy'."

Georgiana gave her a grateful look, I was just thinking... well wondering if I may talk to you about my brother... and my aunt?"

"Of course, my dear. What would you like to discuss?"

Elizabeth burned with curiosity about this subject since Lady Catherine left this afternoon, but after their confrontation, Darcy had such a dark countenance that she did not as yet broach the subject with him.

Georgiana moved towards the chairs by the fire as Elizabeth had indicated. They each sat while studying the other. "I... I wanted to discuss what we heard this afternoon. I know that you are not the kind of person that my aunt has insinuated you are. I have much faith in my brother's choice for a wife. My Aunt Lady Catherine, though, does not believe that there is anything else to a marriage other than the uniting of fortunes."

She looked up to see Elizabeth's encouraging smile, and continued, "She has been saying for... all of my life that our cousin, Anne and my brother were 'destined for each other', but no one really ever believed it, besides her. She has been known to say that it was our 'mother's fondest wish', and even that is disputed by our uncle the Earl of Matlock. So... I wanted to make sure you knew that not everyone sees you and my brother's marriage as a disappointment." Georgiana wore a nervous expression.

Since Elizabeth had already heard this story, or at least part of it from her cousin, Mr. Collins, she did not fret over it, and her only concern now was to reassure Georgiana. I must confess that it was unsettling to hear that... commotion this afternoon, but I have already heard this story so I am not that surprised to hear it has caused your aunt such turmoil. And I must also say that when he asked me to marry him, I did have some reservations about that... well, that and other things, but he was so very reassuring that I am no longer concerned about it."

Elizabeth saw the girl relax, I am glad to know that. I wanted you to know that I am glad he is to marry you... I want to see my brother happy in his life. It has been he and I alone for so long that... well we have just had each other to comfort for as long as I can remember, and he has comforted me while I... while I did not do so for him as much as I should have. It is likely due to our age difference, but I always felt that there was something... well... I am not sure how to say this... 'missing' is perhaps the best word. Yes perhaps that is correct, you see William has been the responsible brother and master ever since father died. He took his duties very seriously, and he threw himself into taking over the estate business even before our father became ill. He has never had anyone to look out for him."

The young girl looked at Elizabeth as if willing her to understand. Elizabeth gave her encouragement to continue, as she really wanted to know about Darcy's life before they met. Georgiana began again, "He had seemed so sad for so long... as if something were missing. That is until recently... until, I believe, he met you."

Elizabeth smiled at the compliment, I do not know what to say, Georgiana. Other than I hope to continue providing him happiness. I do believe that is the purpose of falling in love."

Georgiana smiled wider now, I am very happy that you are to marry him. I must confess that I had feared he may end up with the likes of Miss Bingley..." She flushed and said, "Oh dear, that was unkind of me, I did not mean... that is..."

Elizabeth reached over to put her hand on the girls shoulder and tried to contain her mirth, "That is quite all right, my dear. I can safely say that I am as relieved by that as you. I do not think she would have made him happy either."

"It is just that there have been so many 'society' women, who valued him only for his possessions without caring about him. I dearly hoped he would find someone deserving of him and... and I am glad that it is you. The two of you seem so right for each other."

Elizabeth felt her heart swell to a great affection for this dear girl, "My dear, there is nothing in this world that I would like more than to make your brother the happiest of men, for he has made me the happiest of women, and I hope to share our lives with you. I have every intention of keeping your lives as normal as possible... well there may be a few changes..." At Georgiana's questioning look she added, "...a very few changes, but only as it relates to the married state of things."

They both laughed and enjoyed another thirty minutes of conversation before Georgiana expressed a need to retire to her room. Elizabeth noted the time and knew that she should also go to bed, but found herself too energized to sleep. She glanced at the clock and knew Jane would be asleep by now, then thought that it may help to go to the library and find a boring book to aide her to sleep.

She made her way to the still warm room and found some religious books. She chose 'Fordyce's Sermons', thinking it may be just the thing to aid her rest. As she returned to her room, she realized she had not paid as much attention to her room's location as she should have. She tried to recall the location and convinced she had found the correct door, then knocked to ensure its vacancy, and entered when there was no reply.

Thankfully she had found the right quarters, but she no sooner sat down in a chair by the fire, than she heard a knock on her door. She opened it to see none other than Darcy.

"Elizabeth, I wanted to talk to you about earlier… with my aunt… What? Does it amuse you?"

"No, but you are the second person this evening to come to my room to discuss it."

"The second person?"

Elizabeth sighed and nodded, "Yes… it seems Georgiana was worried about me as well, so she came to reassure me of her support."

He nodded while staring at her, I am happy to know that she has more sense than some of the people in my family. I… I wanted to apologize to you as well, Elizabeth, for my Aunt's poor manners."

"My love, you have no more control over your family than I do mine. I learned years ago that if I went around apologizing for *my* family members, I would scarcely get anything done."

They both laughed.

Standing in front of the fire, they looked at each other with a deep intensity. Elizabeth was speechless for a moment, but she recovered from her reverie when Darcy said, "Is there anything that you have need of, dearest… any concerns? If not I shall just… um… wish you good night, though I know not how I will be able to." He looked up and down her form, clad only in one of Georgiana's nightgowns and a robe. I must confess, I came earlier but you did not answer your door. I wanted to ensure you had everything you needed."

Elizabeth flushed, "Ah... no... I... I could not sleep after I spoke with Georgiana and... well I just..." She stared at his naked neck and the opening to his shirt, as he had removed his coat and vest, and stood in front of her in just his breaches with his shirt unbuttoned from the top. She swallowed hard, trying to speak but finding all words had left her. Darcy looked down at his state of undress, and grasped her hands, pulling her towards him.

She startled, "Sir, what are you doing? What if we are discovered like this?"

Darcy looked down into her face, "Then we shall be forced to marry sooner, and I would be a very happy man.

Unfortunately though, I fear that there is no one here to witness us as such and my staff is either already abed, or unaware of my presence." He looked at her and said, "So, my love, you have not answered my question... what really keeps you up so late in the evening? Might I hope that you missed me as much as I missed you?" He raised an eyebrow.

She smiled at him, "While I have missed you this last hour, I was talking with your sister... about you...and..."

"And?"

"...And she expressed concern about my feelings regarding your aunt and told me how happy she was that you will marry me instead of Caroline Bingley."

"Well then, that makes two of us, as I am happy I am to wed you and not Caroline, but that still does not explain your being awake this late at night, my lovely Elizabeth." He bent down to give her a light kiss.

She reached up on her tip toes and began again, I could not sleep and went to the library to find a book that would help me sleep, only to find that when I came back, my wonderful betrothed came looking for me." Her eyes shone with mirth as she gazed into Darcy's eyes.

He frowned, I see… so it was not your burning desire to see your betrothed…?"

"It is not that I did not wish to see you, sir, I did and that explains why I could not sleep."

He smiled and pulled her towards him with a growl, wrapping one arm around her waist and another around her shoulders, and then pulled her up towards him to kiss her, starting slowly, then becoming more demanding. She was not averse to this as it was what she had wished for earlier, and she met his demands with her own. Soon they found themselves breathless and senseless with desire.

Half of Elizabeth knew that they were playing a dangerous game and the other half did not care, as she had desired it ever since… to be truthful, ever since she danced with him at the Netherfield ball. It felt so right as he caressed her back and waist. She gasped as she felt his hand move up her rib cage and cup her left breast. She gasped and he stopped suddenly, looking at her with concern but still holding her, "Oh dearest, I am sorry I did not mean to frighten you with my desire…"

Elizabeth raised her fingers to his mouth to silence his self castigation, I do not object to your touch sir… it is just…"

He grasped her hand, "Just… what my love?" He then kissed her hand.

She blushed and looked down. He placed his fingers under her chin to look into her eyes and she flushed more, "What would you think of me, if I were to tell you that I did not mind it at all? In fact… I rather enjoyed it." She raised her face up to look at him.

He fell silent for a moment and then a huge smile came over his face, I would say that I shall be the luckiest man alive to have you, my dearest. I cannot tell you how much I love you, and think you so irresistible."

They smiled at each other with the realization that their union would not just be one of love, but passion as well. They attacked each other's lips. Her hands went to his back and neck, while he pulled her tighter to him and ran his hands up her back to her shoulders, then moved them back to her breasts and lowered them to her buttocks as well.

She could not form any words to explain how well this felt to her, other than 'exquisite'. Darcy's fingers teased her breasts and nipples, and as he caressed her, they became hard. He continued to play with her breasts, squeezing them and kneading them, rubbing her nipples between his thumbs and forefingers eliciting a low moan from her. He became emboldened and quickened his attentions, and found her writhing in is arms. She could feel his firm manhood pressing insistently against her hip, and found herself growing in anticipation as to how he looked naked.

Feeling every bit of the ecstasy created by his attentions, she did not fail to note that his manhood seemed to be pressing even more insistently against her. She moved her hand down to investigate the object and as she caressed his bulge, he gasped suddenly and moaned her name.

Further emboldened by her ability to elicit such a response, she slid her hands across the object again and again ever so softly to find him writhing in her arms. Suddenly he grasped her hand and pleaded, "Oh, Elizabeth, you are torturing me. You have no idea what you do to me."

She became concerned she had done something to harm him, "Oh I am so sorry, I did not mean to..."

He silenced her with his deep, probing kisses and she felt herself lifted into his arms and carried to the bed. He laid her down upon the comforter and joined her upon it, reclaiming her lips, caressing her breasts and bottom again and again with insistent and demanding caresses.

She met each with caresses of her own to his back, boldly moving towards his bottom. She felt him slowly moving to the sleeves of her gown, kissing his way down along her jaw and neck then yet further down to her bosom. He became bolder yet, and shoved the sleeves down her arms to reveal her pert lovely breasts. She flushed with maidenly modesty, but soon forgot that in a passion filled fog.

Without much thought, she pulled at the tail of his shirt and brought it up to reveal his firm muscle laden chest, with its soft downy dark hair and let her hands wander on his skin as she felt his quick shallow breaths upon her as she gazed at his godlike physique. He took one of her hands in his and rubbed it up and down his chest. She was fascinated at his body and wished to see all of it. As if reading her mind, Darcy rolled to the side of her and finished pulling his shirt up and over his head.

He looked at her in silent contemplation of his next move, and she nodded to him in silent agreement as he unbuttoned his breaches and slid them down his finely muscled thighs, past his calves and threw them to the floor.

Elizabeth held her breath, knowing what would come next. He moved slowly towards her and started to caress her breasts moving his hand to the gown which was by now around her rib cage. He leaned in to touch the tip of her nipple with his tongue, lapping around it then finally taking it into his mouth and suckling causing her to arch towards him. He took this as an invitation to continue, and gently caressed the other breast before moving down. Her gown was shoved slowly down to her waist, caressing her, and finally past her hips to her thighs. He raised his leg to catch the fabric with his toes and pulled the gown completely off of her.

They lay upon his bed caressing each other, he suckling her breast and caressing her around her waist, daring to move to her nether regions, until he felt her womanly portal and gently caressed her there. She moaned from his attentions. She joined him in that activity again caressing him on his hardened manhood, stroking him to near oblivion, until he stilled her hand with his begging her to have mercy upon him. He lay there staring into her eyes pleading, "Dearest Elizabeth, if you do not cease then you will be compromised."

She bit her bottom lip and slowly stroked his lower belly seductively, I know my love, but I do not think that I want to stop."

He looked intently at her while he lightly ran his hand down from her breast to her navel, and said, "Then I must tell you that… this may not be too comfortable for you the first time… but I will be gentle with you."

She slowly nodded her acquiescence and he moved over her as she reflexively opened her thighs to him, and stared into his eyes as he gently probed her entrance and slowly slid his hardened manhood into her, careful not to cause her undue pain. She could feel the fullness of him as he entered her and with a final thrust, she gasped as he tore through her final barrier. She felt a sharp tearing pain, which gradually let up.

He paused for her to accustom herself to his body, and when her felt her relax he began a their slow intimate dance, increasing his pace until he felt her tight womanhood contracting around his manhood, she never imagined that she could feel such ecstasy and pain all at once. She thought of how wonderful it felt for them to be joined as such, finally losing herself to the carnal pleasure he gave as he thrust harder she could feel her nether regions squeezing around his member and she felt her release again. Darcy felt her flesh tighten around him and with a final, forceful thrust he released his seed deep inside of her. Elizabeth could feel a warm sensation deep within her as he finished moving inside her, and felt blissful and complete at that moment.

They lay there breathless and in awe of what had just happened, until Darcy feeling heavy upon her, rolled off and lay on his back with his arm over his face. Elizabeth came out of her passion filled haze and realized what they had done. Part of her was mortified at her brazenness, and part of her overjoyed at what she had just shared with her beloved. She stared up to the canopy then looked towards her fiancé, who was just finding his breath.

He turned towards her again and embraced her, tightly kissing her forehead. Resting his head upon hers, he spoke, I am so sorry, my love. I did not mean to compromise you in such a way." He searched her face for an indication of her reaction to what just occurred.

She looked up to him and caressed his face, smiling gently, wanting to reassure him, "Do not be concerned about me, dearest, for I was just as much a party to it as you. Do not regret it for it was…"

"Wonderful." He finished and smiled at her.

Elizabeth had been studying him, looking up and down his body.

"My love, what is it that holds your interest?" Darcy said.

Elizabeth flushed, not wishing to reveal that she had already seen him nude a few months ago at Brooks Pond. In truth it fascinated her that his… person seemed so different then, than it did tonight.

When she did still did not respond he prodded, "Lizzy? What is it? Come now, you can say anything to me. I think now there should be no secrets."

Elizabeth buried her face in his shoulder and shook her head, and Darcy brushed her hair back to look at her face, "Well? Can you not tell me?"

She hesitated, .I must confess something... that I saw... a few months ago, before we met at Netherfield, in the meadow that first time you saw me."

Darcy puzzled at what she referred to but encouraged her to go on, "Yes?"

"I... I saw you before. In fact I saw *all* of you before that day. I had gone to Brooks Pond the afternoon before we met, and I wanted to cool off in the water..."

Realization dawned on Darcy as he came to understand that their party from town had been seen by none other than Elizabeth. Thinking further he remembered that both Fitzwilliam and Bingley were known to her eyes as well, which nearly made him nauseous. "You... you mean to say you saw us..."

"In the nude." She finished for him.

Darcy swallowed hard, "And what did you see... exactly? I mean did you see..."

"Everything. I did not intend to stay when I heard that there were people there, but I was drawn to stare..."

"At what? Did you... did you see...?"

"My love, I saw three men playing like schoolboys in a watering hole. I assure you that I did not find anything to keep me there, other than..."

"Other than what?" He almost demanded.

Elizabeth felt put off until she saw his worried look, and she wanted nothing more than to assure him then, "Dearest, I did see three men naked, but I have seen statues in museum pictures, and it did not surprise me. Besides that I have seen boy babies, and I know that men are different from we women, but what drew me there longer than was proper was a dark haired gentleman that was... disproportionately larger than the other two." She blushed at her admission, to which Darcy had an overspread smile gifting his features.

If she could have only known how well such a compliment sat with the gentleman she would have been well pleased. Though Darcy worried that she may have been attracted to his cousin, knowing that it was *him* that kept her there filled his spirit with what could only be called an instinctive manly pride and he laughed. "So you were not shocked when we…?"

"No, not exactly shocked, but… I did not know that you men change shape there, I mean I may have been more frightened if I had not seen you already." She confessed.

Darcy could see the humour in her confession and admitted, I can see how it could be a surprise to a maiden such as you, but yes indeed, that 'changing shape' makes the… the prospect of mating more feasible."

They laid there embracing each other until he came to a realization, "As much as I do not want to cloud this moment over, I feel that we should discuss something… that is… what we did Elizabeth… you do realize that now there may be…'consequences' to our actions?"

Elizabeth did not say anything for a while and sighed, "I… I do realize that that… may be the case… but do you… do you really think that it… that is to say… do you think that we need reveal that?"

Darcy looked away from her up to the canopy and sighed, "My love, I *prefer* not to reveal any of our private… activities to anyone, however… dearest, please understand that if we wait… well suffice to say that if you are not now brought with child… then you may soon be. I fear that I cannot stay away from you now that we have known each other in such a way."

She flushed at the idea of carrying his child, and of engaging in more of said activities, though not due to embarrassment, but from excitement. I see, so what do you propose sir?"

He studied her, smiled rakishly at her, and said, "Well, for right now allow me to demonstrate upon my proposal. I shall deal with the other issues in the morning."

They set their concerns aside for the moment enjoying each other's attentions and tried to put aside any apprehension they felt until morning.

Chapter 28

Darcy had numerous ideas to propose, several of which involve them remaining in bed. "My love, I propose in the way of our marriage... now you must realize that you are mine... and I am yours." He kissed her swollen lips and noted her dilated pupils with great pleasure.

She kissed him back and smiled. I know dearest... I know... but how will we explain why we wish to wed so soon? Do you not think that our families will question us on our reason for haste?" She raised an eyebrow.

Her hand caressed his chest as her fingers seemed to hold a fascination all of their own for the hair that rested in the middle of his musculature. Comforted by the sensation, he leaned forward and laid his forehead next to hers as he kissed her jaw line, thrilled with her attentions to his... person, while he caressed her breast and brushed his fingertips down to her soft hair below her navel. As he did so, he could feel her shiver.

This is heaven. He teased her with his touch before he kissed her with passion, their tongues dueling as he felt her arms snake around his neck. He drew back, breathless, "We *must* marry soon... surely you see that. I understand your apprehensions about your father, however, it is unwise to wait. What if something terrible happens? What if we wait and you are with child or worse yet, something should happen to me? There would be no one to protect you."

She hesitated before acknowledging the truth of his statement. I know... it is not just me though... there is Jane as well... and Mr. Bingley... I had so hoped to marry with her, and now I feel as if I have interfered with their happiness... I mean, is it right to push them so soon into this? Then there is also... well I do not.... She touched him again, caressing him down his chest, following his fine hair and rubbing his shoulders. Her soft brown eyes pleaded with him.

He could feel his heart melting again and his other parts... well were hot but definitely not melting. "You mean to say you do not want your... family to know that we... we anticipated our vows?" He sucked in a sharp breath as he caressed her shoulders and back, intrigued by her smooth skin.

She nodded her acknowledgement, returning his favours with her affectionate touches.

"I *promise* not to reveal that if I do not have to... You *know*, however, that I abhor deceit and will not lie to your father in order to protect myself. No, I accept my responsibilities. Though I may elicit Bingley into assisting with that endeavor for I believe that he may be as impatient as I."

He smiled down at her.

She showed her gratitude by pulling him down and kissing him passionately as she wound her fingers through his curls. Then she moved her attentions down towards the hollow of his neck, tasting his musky scent, licking his jaw line and nibbling upon his ear.

He let out a groan in response. "Love, do not tease me..."

Looking her in the eye, he felt a burning sensation arising from his lower abdomen. She seemed not to hear him as she continued her attack upon his chest, leaving the sensation of her warm breath upon his skin as she moved from his neck downwards.

"Oh Elizabeth," he moaned, I knew as soon as I had met you why I fell in love with you... it was your passion for life... your vest for living... Please darling, I cannot wait much longer without going mad... I am not even sure after tonight how I will manage to get along without you with me every night." He pleaded, and then leaned forward to kiss her, wanting to take her again.

Elizabeth fell quiet for a moment. "You are right, and it is not fair to you, and... I should confess that I will miss your touch after this ... but may we just say that... that..."

"That we enjoy each other's... mmmm... 'companionship'... and you will marry me as soon as feasible?" Darcy prompted with a smile.

She smiled and nodded, then looked at him under her lashes, which elicited another response in him. He redoubled his attentions, wanting to entice her into an encore. He assaulted the area behind her ear and moved down her jaw with his soft lips, which caused her to give a loud moan.

She began to caress his shoulders then traverse downward along the lean planes of his back, landing on his firm buttocks, driving him senseless with desire as her fingers stroked and messaged. She moved to the front area without thought and stroked and caressed his erection further exciting him. He dangled on the edge of his self control. As she attended him, he moved towards her breasts, caressing and suckling her firm tips, bringing forth another low moan from her throat.

"Umm, William... that feels so wonderful...," she breathed out.

When he heard her response, he gave her a more concentrated effort as he felt his manhood throbbing with desire. He then began moving down her abdomen towards the center of her desire and kissed her near her core, which caused her to take a deep breath.

"My love, dearest, please I am in agony... please..." She cried out as she tried to bring him up towards her.

Resisting her pleas, he became bolder and pried her thighs apart to move down her body. She looked down questioning his intentions, and he began, "Just relax and let me give you pleasure, my love... let me love you," he said on a soft whisper.

She was reluctant, but allowed him to place his mouth upon her core, and he began stroking her softness with his velvet tongue, making her senseless. "Mmmmm... my lloooovvve... oooooooh..." She cried out.

With his tongue, he caressed her pleasure zone until he heard her moan in a hymn of pleasure. He could tell that she had reached her climax as she arched her back and twined her fingers through his hair as he attended her. He had discovered one of the most potent aphrodisiacs for him, making him unable to resist her siren call.

He moved to place himself where they could enjoy this same pleasure together and entered her. The feeling of her womanhood enveloping his throbbing member was pure bliss, and he barely heard her moan out again, "*Ooooohhh... yeeeeeeesss...*" This was sweet ecstasy.

They began a delicate dance of pleasure as he intensified his movements to the rhythm of her moaning encouragement. With each moan, he thrust harder and deeper than the last. He could feel her excitement growing as her sweet femininity began to squeeze and contract around his excited shaft and was able to bring her to a thrilling orgasm of deep satisfaction. He crested a moment later, spilling inside of her. They lay in her bed with Darcy still on top of her in exhaustion, yet he had never felt so happy in his entire life.

Elizabeth smiled up at him in a passion- filled fog, her eyes bright. He could not resist and kissed her again until he was ready to faint due to euphoria.

They parted after several moments of gazing at each other in silence, and he lay on his side while he grasped her to him and nestled her neck, wrapping his arm around her waist in a protective embrace. They fell into a peaceful slumber under the spell of Morpheus… until morning.

~*~*~*~

Caroline Bingley was a woman on a mission as she set her mind to entice the Viscount James Fitzwilliam. She intended to finagle an invitation to the Shetler's Ball, which she knew the Earl and his family would attend. She had learned that Darcy would be there, and felt it would be an excellent opportunity to show up his little country tart. I *will make sure he regrets his choice, and he will wish that he had never seen the likes of Hertfordshire.*

She had decided to walk to the Hurst's and then go to the park to be seen and possibly *see* the Viscount. *This shall be wonderful… delicious … money and a title, too!* Giddy with her plan, she hurried out into the midmorning mist. It had rained throughout the night, creating an environment which was most unpleasant. If she continued with her current plan, she would have to be extra cautious from all of the puddles she would have to navigate, and she did not want to appear muddied when she met up with the Viscount, so a different course of action was needed. Therefore, she decided to call for the carriage, and when it was readied, she headed for the coach, but upon seeing the very man she had been thinking of, she stopped to address him.

"Lord Fitzwilliam, how do you do this fair morning?" she asked in the sweetest voice she could muster.

The Viscount looked at her and seemed surprised, but recollected himself, I am well and you, Miss Bingley, how are you this *dull* morning?"

"I am quite well, sir. Were you taking your morning constitutional? It is cool is it not, after all of this rain…?"

"Ah, yes, but then that is to be expected at this time of year, but no… I was headed towards… Darcy House… to see my cousin."

Caroline smiled and felt the need to put her two pence forward regarding Miss Elizabeth Bennet. "Yes, I would imagine he appreciates your continued support … what are family for, after all?"

"Indeed, but I had no notion that there was anything amiss with him. Is there something that I should know of…? Is there something wrong, Miss Bingley?"

She said in a low voice, "Have you seen that he has announced his engagement to that… to Miss Eliza Bennet, sir?"

He pulled his head back and nodded.

"Well have you met this… Miss Eliza, sir?"

"No, Miss Bingley, I have not had that pleasure as of yet, but perhaps I may soon enough."

She smiled as if pitying him. I … should not say, but I rather think that I should prepare you for the … lady. She is a simple country squire's daughter, and has been known to roam the countryside alone… unescorted! I could hardly believe such behaviour, and she traipsed three miles in mud just to come see her sister who had a trifling cold, and was being well cared for at Netherfield Park! Can you imagine the frightful sight she presented, sir?"

By the look on his face it was evident that he could, but he respectfully replied, "Indeed? That would be something to have beheld. It shows affection for her sister, however."

"It *was* a sight to behold, after all. Indeed it was! And who among *our* set would behave in such a manner? I hope that Mr. Darcy is able to tame his little country creature." She laughed.

The Viscount raised an eyebrow. I shall soon be able to meet her. I believe that I heard Darcy intends to marry soon. I rather feel that he would know what is in his best interest…" He stopped.

Caroline leaned in. "Yes… I suppose you are correct. Perhaps there are less obvious reasons for him to marry so… suddenly."

"I suppose that is true, however, if that were the case, then he could have done that at any time he wished as, I am sure that you know, the Darcy family has *very* high connections, and if he really needed to, there is nothing that could stop him. He has privileges that many people cannot afford."

She smiled at this innuendo, as it was one of her favorite subjects. "Yes, that is true, but I must confess I am astounded that such a country…" She leaned forward again, "nobody could catch his eye… she has nothing to offer. Goodness, she has no dowry even!"

"I see, so he has fallen for someone with lowly connections and no fortune? That is unusual for *him*."

"I am certain that he will bring her to the Shetler's Ball, and then you can see for yourself. I have seen very few people as opinionated and impertinent as Miss Eliza Bennet. But like I said, you will meet her soon enough."

"Miss Bingley, I do not suppose you would be able to arrange for introductions to the lady, would you? I mean, so that I may be able to see this apparition for myself?"

Caroline purred, "Well of course sir, anything for you. If nothing else, I may be able to entice her and her sister to walk in the park, and arrange for you to meet them both. Then you may see her at her boldest." She sneered, "And you can see what a hoyden she shows herself to be, as she is a 'excellent walker'."

"I thank you, madam. That is most generous of you. May I ask if you are planning on going to the Shetler Ball, Miss Bingley?" He smiled.

Caroline glowed, "Why yes, sir, I plan to attend. I am looking forward to seeing some of my distinguished acquaintances there."

Her innuendo was obvious, but she had not failed to notice that he had stopped paying attention to what she said. They soon parted as neither had much to add to this conversation.

Caroline boarded the coach and rode to the Hurst's residence, only to find that the couple would be unable to attend her, as they had spent the evening with some friends and had not yet readied for the day. She was still frustrated with her earlier lackluster encounter with the Viscount, but would not give up her pursuit. *This calls for serious effort. But just how far do I need to go to secure him?* She *was* a determined woman.

~*~*~*~

Lady Catherine de Bourgh woke up in an even fouler mood than when she went to bed. Having vented on the upstairs maid and a footman who were not quick enough for her tastes and still angry about her afternoon encounter with Darcy, she vowed to see to it that he never married that country upstart. She had tried to elicit her brother's assistance but to no avail.

He has no intention to save this family from disgrace! It is up to me to preserve the bounds of decorum and make Darcy see reason! He must marry Anne, for he has been promised these many years to her, and I will not let anything stand in the way. But what to do?

She did not join the rest of the family until later than her usual. *Perhaps if I could find something against the woman?* Suddenly she felt as if she may have come upon a solution. If she could not find anything on this Miss Bennet, she would ensure that there would be something 'to be found' before they were wed. *Yes, then Darcy would be forced to end this engagement, and he could marry Anne.*

She summoned her nephew, James, to attend her in her sitting room.

"You sent for me, ma'am?"

"Yes, James, sit! I have been thinking of these 'problems' we have had as of late within the family, with *your* disgrace, and Richard being pulled into it. Then there is the situation with Darcy and that... that woman! Something must be done! There is no resolving your troubles easily, but I think I have come up with a solution."

"Indeed, madam? And what would that be... and why am I being told about it?"

"Because it involves you! I see that you still do not comprehend my meaning! Your involvement in this affair. You are to help me separate Darcy from that woman... it would be the ruin of us if *he* does what he is planning! *We* must stop him... make him see come to his senses! And since you have no scruples with interfering with certain kinds of women, your assistance is required..."

"I beg your pardon, madam! You... you seem to think that I should involve myself with your plan to... to what?!"

"*That* is simple! If he will not see reason, then we must *give* him reason, and then he will not wish to marry such an amoral woman! In the mean time, you may get your pleasure..."

"Get my pleasure? I am *not* some thug who would do such things, madam! Besides, why would I involve myself with such a scheme? What do I have against Darcy?"

"My dear boy, do not be so dense! This could ruin our family's reputation as much as the reprehensible things *you* have done! It is our duty to protect that, and as I recall *lately* you have not done *your* duty! I am a very resourceful woman, and I have inquired into your habits, and what I have discovered is that you not only owe Lord Blake twenty-five thousand pounds, you owe another of your gaming 'associates' five thousand! And to have cost your dear father so much money... why, if you were my son, I would have put you out! Now here is a chance for you to redeem yourself... and perhaps... I may be willing to provide you with compensation, for your trouble. As a matter of fact, that is what I am willing to do... that is if you cooperate, I will not mention this to my brother."

He paled at the sight of his aunt. "What do you intend for me to do?"

Lady Catherine smiled. "We must be able to arrange for you to meet this woman, and become friendly with her in order to elicit trust. I believe that you are to attend the Shelter Ball with your parents...?"

James nodded in acknowledgement.

She smiled widely for the first time in weeks. I shall ensure that Darcy and his... this woman are invited, and once they are there, you shall draw her away from the common rooms and out to a secluded area, then you may do whatever you desire to make it look compromising. In the meantime, I shall bring Darcy away on some pretext, and we shall find you and her in such a situation. He will be infuriated and thus would end this farce of an engagement! It is quite simple you see."

James frowned. I am not certain that this is a good idea Aunt. After all, Darcy helped with this other... situation, and I am not so cold hearted as to do such a thing to him. It seems too cruel... I mean to my own cousin!"

"Oh pish-posh, James! This is not *against* him, do you not see? It is *for* him... we would be doing him a favour in the long run, and you will redeem yourself as well. It is to be expected that Darcy is bound to feel some remorse for his decision in the first place, but he will soon come to realize what a mistake it would have been. He will get over her in a matter of days, and she will soon become a distant memory."

James paced back and forth. "How are you so certain this plan of yours will work? Have you even met this Miss Bennet?"

"Oh do not be ridiculous! She must be the same as the other women of her society... seeking a man of means to secure her future! I do not have to meet her to figure that out! This would save him from his poor decisions, and then your dear cousin Anne would have her rightful place as the Mistress of Pemberley! You must do this to save this family. I will brook no opposition, and now you shall be on your way young man, you have your duties to perform!"

With a terse wave of her hand, she dismissed James from her sitting room and stepped out of his presence.

Chapter 29

Darcy readied for the day while preparing for his discussion with his soon-to-be father-in-law. Not sure of what he wanted to say, he thought of a plan to coerce Bingley into helping him convince the older gentleman to allow both of them to marry sooner, and in London as opposed to Longbourn. He had the resources to accomplish this in a short period of time. He felt certain that Mrs. Bennet would be more than happy to crow about having a society wedding in the most fashionable part of London, and if she wanted friends to come, they could easily ride to town.

With that thought to tide him over, he sent a note around to Bingley, inviting him to Darcy House for breakfast, reminding him that Jane was staying there. *That will bring him here faster than anything else!* And he was correct, as Bingley not only accepted but arrived there within twenty minutes of receiving his invitation.

Darcy brought Bingley to his office as soon as he entered. Taking a seat, he stated his case. "Bingley I know from personal experience that a man in love would not wish to wait for a long time to take his wife, and I find myself impatient to be at Pemberley before the weather turns foul, as you know it can be treacherous…"

"Yes, I know how dangerous the roads can be, but what are you saying? Is it that you are just as anxious to 'have' your bride as I am? Because if that is so, then I am open to your suggestion, for I am sure you have one, otherwise you would not trouble yourself with sending out a request for my presence so early."

"You are correct, Bingley, I do have a thought as to how to bring our intendeds to the alter sooner, but I will need your help." He looked at his friend speculatively.

"Well? Out with it man! I am all ears!"

Darcy smiled with a gleam in his eye as he rose from his seat and began to pace the floor as if in thought. Finally he spoke. I had thought that a double entreaty to Mr. Bennet, along with his daughters' pleas, may help us accomplish our goal. We should be able to convince him using Mrs. Bennet's propensity to want a 'fine' wedding with all of the trimmings. As far as the special licenses, I may be able to arrange that with the archbishop. I just need to speak with my solicitor, but I will do all that it takes to accomplish this. And that, my friend, is why I have called you here so early in the morning."

Bingley smiled widely at his friend's innovation and single mindedness. I see that you have thought this out. So, when shall we start to implement this plan?"

"Immediately."

"Well then, shall we go to announce our plans to our ladies?"

"Naturally," he answered with a self satisfied smile as he headed for his study door and led the way to the breakfast parlor.

During their meal, they discussed their thoughts and plans with each other, while Georgiana looked on with apparent excitement. She had indicated that she was nearly as impatient as her brother to have Elizabeth join their household. The group made plans to travel shortly to Gracechurch Street.

~*~*~*~

Mr. Bennet had just finished breakfast when his daughters were escorted into the room by their respective fiancés. After exchanging brief pleasantries, they requested an audience with him. Once they were ensconced in Mr. Gardiners library, Darcy began, "Mr. Bennet, I would like to take this opportunity to request that my and Bingley's wedding date be set. That is, trusting that everything is to your agreement in the marriage articles, sir?"

Mr. Bennet appeared taken by surprise, but knew that such a man as Darcy would have a plan, and tried to sound neutral when he made his requests known. Nonetheless, he would give him a dose of his humor. I have, sir, and everything looks in order as far as pin money and the like, and I am sure that we can have things arranged to everyone's liking by April—if that is what you desire." He could tell that the gentlemen were none too enthused when he mentioned the spring. Their expressions made him chuckle.

"Um sir..." Bingley began, "Ah... we had rather thought that we might be able to wed sooner rather than later." He looked to Darcy for encouragement. "And as a matter of fact, we had hoped that... well that we might be able to plan things by the end of the year..."

Now it was Mr. Bennet's turn to be surprised. "Excuse me, Mr. Bingley...?" He frowned and looked toward Darcy. I thought that I heard you say... the end of the year? This year?"

"Ahhh... yes sir, I did say the end of the year..." Bingley reiterated as Darcy frowned at him.

"You mean the end of..." He cocked his head to the side and raised an eyebrow. "*Next* year sir?" He asked hopefully. *Why such a hurry to be wed? Are they that impatient?*

"*Ahhh*, no sir, no not at all. I might bring to your attention that Darcy... lives up north and..." Bingley tried to finish but Darcy cut in.

"Mr. Bennet, you are aware that my estate, Pemberley is further north...and... the roads can become quite treacherous during the winter, and I am sure you can sympathize. *We...* meaning Mr. Bingley and I, would like to be married sooner rather than later."

He added, I am sure you can understand, as a man who has farms to tend to, during the planting season things get very busy. That is why I have planned to request this... what one may tend to think of as a hasty arrangement, but I assure you that I will do everything within my power to ensure that nothing is wanting for our wedding, or for your daughter's happiness. In fact, that is another reason for me to make this application, as I think it would be in Miss Elizabeth's benefit to begin her transition as Pemberley's mistress at this time, as it would be far less... hectic...sir."

Mr. Bennet was speechless. He knew the day would come when he would give away Jane and Elizabeth and... the other girls, too, but now he faced losing them both at once. He sat and thought about his best response to such an entreaty, and said, "You will forgive me if I seem to be at loss for words. This is quite sudden." Pausing for another moment, he offered, "Why can we not entertain the idea of waiting after planting is finished, Mr. Darcy? That way you would have enough time to get things ready at Pemberley, including redecorating Lizzy's rooms, and there would be no rush. It would be much less stressful for planning."

Darcy and Bingley each looked to the other as if expectant that someone else would know how to respond. Finally Darcy began, "We realize that this may cause some hardship for you, sir, and we are cognizant of the amount of work it may take. However, we are willing to have our staffs assist with any and all plans to ensure that nothing is wanting. As a matter of fact, we are each willing to apply to the archbishop for special license, and I have here a draft of what I should like to send to him in order to expedite this process."

"You are assuming, sir, that everything is in order, and that I would agree to such a scheme…"

Both gentlemen looked alarmed. "You mean you will not allow us M… M… Mr. Bennet?" Bingley cried.

Mr. Bennet felt sympathy for of him, but quickly recollected himself and continued, I have not thought about that, but this is all so quick… and why all of a sudden has it come to light that we need to proceed so hastily? I mean why, if that were part of the plan the entire time, why was it not made known, then I could have saved myself the trouble and denied such requests."

"But, Mr. Bennet, we only wanted to do what we felt would be in our… everyone's best interests, and felt that this was the most practical solution. If it is such a problem, we may go to Hertfordshire and make arrangements as you like, but please understand we are loyal to our cause, and think only of the Eliz… ahh, Miss Elizabeth and Miss Bennet." Darcy pleaded.

"And, how… exactly is this in everyone's best interests, Mr. Darcy?" Mr. Bennet requested.

Darcy froze, and his lack of timely response caused Mr. Bennet to feel uneasy. "What is the urgency… sir?" He directed a pointed look at Mr. Darcy.

That gentleman stood up to his full height, pausing, as if debating a response, then turned towards his friend.

"Bingley, would you give Mr. Bennet and me a moment? I would like to discuss some… issues with him privately."

Mr. Bingley gave a look of confusion and then frowned.

"All right Darcy, but I would like to know what this is about. Call for me when you are finished." At Darcy's nod, Bingley left the room but paused as if to add something, then shook his head and closed the door after himself.

"Mr. Darcy, what is so important and so secret that you have requested your friend to leave? Is there something *else* that you need to discuss?"

"Sir, Mr. Bennet, I did not want to be so forceful with the issue about when we wed, but it is impossible to wait for a spring or summer wedding."

"Impossible you say? Why it is *impossible*...?" The idea then came to Mr. Bennet of what Mr. Darcy referred to. "You are saying that you *cannot* wait?"

"Yes," is all that his daughter's fiancé offered for an answer.

For a few moments, Mr. Bennet sat in stunned silence. At first, his eyes widened then narrowed. He never thought that his Lizzy would ever be put in such a situation. His two youngest daughters, he could not vouch for. It made him feel ill as his failure as a father. *Nothing can be done now... he has taken away my Lizzy, and they must marry. At least, he is an honest man and does not drag on a charade in order to save face.* "You can very well guess what I should do, and would like to do, Mr. Darcy! It does not please me in the least to have to agree to such hasty arrangements, but then there is nothing to be done about it! I hope that you have enough sense to value your prize, sir, for she has been the jewel in my crown all these many years. I would hate to see her liveliness and talents wasted." He glared at Darcy with silent fury.

The gentleman in front of him looked contrite. "You have my word, Mr. Bennet. I will endeavor to make every effort to see that Miss Elizabeth is happy for as long as I shall live."

Mr. Bennet nodded in approval, and since Darcy had been so honest with him—more honest than most men in his situation would have been, he ceased his interrogation. He called in Mr. Bingley and said, "Well gentleman, it looks as if you are to help Mrs. Bennet with her mission in life… to marry her daughters to well situated gentlemen." He chuckled with a smile that did not reach his eyes.

Both gentlemen looked surprised, until they seemed to realize that Mr. Bennet was demonstrating his dry wit on them, and they relaxed. After a few moments they began again with all of their planning, until finally Mr. Bennet ceded to their request on a date for their wedding. They went to the sitting room where the ladies were visiting to announce the happy news, as Mr. Bennet walked away from the library, listening to all of their effusions of happiness.

He was saddened by this turn of events. Though he knew in his heart how happy his daughters had become, and how happy they were made by these gentlemen, and yet, he would miss them. It was difficult for him to accept that they would soon be under the protection of other men, and he would not want them to have to worry over their futures should something happen to him. The other concern that he had stemmed from the revelation of why they were to leave him so soon. He fully felt the guilt of not tending to his duties as a father and husband.

With that last thought he grudgingly went to the writing desk to pen a letter to Mrs. Bennet. *The storms will be coming with a vengeance, gentleman, you had best hold onto your bootstraps. You have no idea what kind of a ruckus you will have unleashed now.* Finally discharging his duties, he regained his old habits of avoiding company, sitting back in the study and reading, happy to know that all of the arrangements would be made with little effort on his part.

~*~*~*~

Back at Matlock House, Richard made his appearance after getting things settled with his troops, and by pushing through some paperwork at the War Office, he was finally free to attend his family. At least now, he knew about Harriet's deception and the paternity of her child. In truth, he was disappointed at the turn of events since the autumn. Most of all, he was saddened that it had prevented him from knowing Elizabeth Bennet better, but that was for naught as she was now betrothed to Darcy.

His parents had learned that he stayed with Darcy and sent a missive for him to join them the same day they had learned of James' treachery. He felt unsure of what would befall him during this meeting, but he was relieved that he no longer held the title of the black sheep of the family—or at least not the blackest one.

"Sit down, Richard. You need not be afraid of your own parents." The Earl commanded.

Richard looked at both of them apprehensively and did as he was told. The Countess added, "Why had you not contacted us when you came to town? You know that your family home is always open to you."

Richard looked down and raised his eyebrow. I had rather thought that after you heard that I had done something so foolish and irresponsible, that I would not be counted among 'family' again, ma'am."

His mother looked sympathetic.

The Earl offended, "Why do you think that we would cut you off, dear boy? What? Because you made a mistake? Heavens! If that were the case, then we would have sent your brother off to India by now!" They all had a laugh once the ice cracked beneath them.

The Earl began again in a more serious vein. "We do, however, have some business to discuss that involves you,

Richard. It involves that estate in Wales that we had… which we were led to believe belonged to myself and Darcy as well as your aunt… Lady Catherine." He hesitated at this, knowing Richard to be the offended party and would rightfully be angry at having been cheated all these years. "Well, I am not sure how to say this, so I will just come right out and say it: that estate was willed to you by my father shortly before his death."

Both he and the Countess observed their son for signs of his anger, but all that they saw was surprise.

For a few moments, Richard was unable to comprehend what they told him, and then realization struck him. He was an independently wealthy gentleman, and had been for some time. The injustice of it all suddenly struck him. He stood up and went to the window. Collecting thoughts, he took a deep breath. "So, what you are telling me is that I have been denied all of these years…" He frowned before continuing, .And for what purpose? What reason can you give me… and *why* now all of a sudden have you *finally* chosen to tell me this?" His anger rose as the seconds passed.

The Earl begin, "We are terribly sorry, and please believe us that had we known," he indicated himself and the Countess, "we would have ensured that you were installed as the rightful owner. Unfortunately *we* were not made aware of this until recently."

"*How recently?*" Richard demanded.

"When Lady Catherine came to town, and brought a newer will from your grandfather. *Apparently*," he cleared his throat, "she had had it for some time and felt that should she never marry, and should Darcy's mother never have produced him, then they would be at a disadvantage, but still…" He lost his voice.

"*Still*, she should have brought it about much, *much* sooner! My G-d, is there no end to her selfishness?! She has tried to interfere with Darcy's and Anne's lives, and has been doing so all along with mine… only unbeknownst to anyone!" He angrily paced back and forth in the study, shaking his head.

No one said anything for a while, then the Earl began, I am very sorry that you have had to endure all of the injustices that you have, and now that I see what James has done to himself… well, let us just say that I think all the more proudly of you, son. I am only sorry that you have not known it up until now."

Richard finally calmed. It was the first time his father had ever said such a thing to him, and he felt truly… touched by the sentiments. "Well, what now? I mean what to do about this whole mess?"

"If you mean the Cantrell Estate, it is yours and has been these many years. I must say that you are quite a wealthy gentleman." His father smiled wryly. "As to the deception by Lady Catherine, I am not sure. I can understand that you may be bitter about all of this, but I am not sure at her age, what could or should be done. You will receive the past income from the time you should have inherited, and as to your position in the army, I am sure you know our preferences to that."

Richard stood still in a fog- like state. I appreciate that, but you never did say why she now has come forward with this information? Was that the reason?"

"*No*, no, you see, Mrs. Heartherton wrote to *her* to explain all of the underhanded dealings; and let us just say she saw that you had much more to lose by not inheriting it now. I believe that she did say that she 'intended' to will the estate to you her death but still, it should *all* have been yours long ago," the Earl said with a distasteful look.

Richard pondered the situation, imagining what else could have been his not so long ago should he have known about his good fortune. *Elizabeth should have been mine, if I had known about this. She would be mine now. Hell, we could have been married and living... wherever. Instead I have been running around the countryside with this whore of a woman thinking that I was soon to be the father of this illegitimate child, and my own aunt has deprived me of this as well? There will be some justice here. I shall see to it!*

The Earl and Countess allowed him some time to contemplate all of these new developments, and felt a need to see to it that Lady Catherine was nowhere near Richard.

~*~*~*~

Within the hour James arrived his family's home. Richard had already left for the War Department, and everything seemed more quiet than usual. When he found his parents, they were sitting quietly in the front parlour. They barely acknowledged him as he entered the room. He inquired about their invitation to the Shetler's Ball, and when they said that they had received an invitation and, that they would attend, he felt relieved. His parents did not seem to be in a talkative mood at present, thus he sat down to read the Times. He thought it would be in two and a half weeks, and that should give him plenty of time to arrange assignations with Miss Bingley and meet up with this Miss Elizabeth Bennet.

He was not able to meet with Darcy or his new fiancée before they had left Darcy House, but he did catch a glimpse of the two women who had joined him and Bingley in front of Darcy's home, and now felt more enthusiastic about his assignment from Aunt Catherine. *It would be easy to see how a man could fall under the spell of the Miss Bennet's... for they are the most beautiful women I have ever laid eyes on.* He even thought that it would not be such a hardship to do a double fete in seducing Charles Bingley's fiancée, as she looked to be such a lovely creature as well. With that thought, he sat down to plan his strategies for accomplishing his mission.

~*~*~*~

When Mrs. Bennet received the express from her husband in the form of a private messenger in the Darcy coach, she nearly fainted. Never had Longbourn seen such a flurry of activity, even from this woman. Once she had regained her bearings, she had such flutterings of her heart, and such palpitations.

"Oh Hill! Hill! We need to pack for town immediately! Girls! Girls! Come! Come!"

"What is it mama?" Lydia asked rather petulantly.

"You will never guess! Oh! Oh my... your sisters! *Both* of them are engaged... and to such wealthy gentlemen! Oh and they are wanting to wed immediately! And, of course they need their mother in town to help arrange such things..."

Lydia and Kitty stood in their mother's sitting room doorway with their mouths a gape, staring at Mrs. Bennet when she turned round. "Well what are you standing there for? Get to it. You must pack for we are off to town as soon as may be... hurry, hurry!" She shooed them away towards their rooms.

She could hardly believe her good fortune with two daughters engaged to such rich gentlemen. They would be in a position to put her other daughter's in the path of other rich men. "Goodness me, I shall go distracted!" she said aloud to no one in particular. She knew exactly how to plan such elegant arrangements. She had also been informed that she would be given free rein to plan this opulent occasion, all thanks to Mr. Darcy. She began throwing as much as she could out of her drawers and closet for Mrs. Hill to pack. It took no more than an hour and a half to pack everything that Mrs. Bennet deemed necessary for such an endeavor, and they were soon on the road to Gracechurch Street.

Chapter 30

Elizabeth dreaded this day as her mother was due to arrive from Hertfordshire in the afternoon. Tomorrow morning she would bring her mother, along with her sisters, to Matlock House for tea, and the thought of her mother exposing their family to censure within the ton did nothing to assuage her nerves. It had been three whole days since Darcy discussed their reasons for wanting to marry so soon, and her father had said very few words to her since then. Needless to say, it sat heavily upon her heart to cause him such trouble.

Luckily, her Aunt Gardiner and Jane distracted her enough for her to only think upon it half a dozen times a day. She also had good news from Darcy; the archbishop approved their application for a special license, and he approved one for Mr. Bingley and Jane. At least, that part of their plans had not been disrupted by her and Darcy's anticipating their vows. With this bit of news, she began to enjoy planning the ceremony, as she and Jane had gone out with Mrs. Gardiner to the finer warehouses for their wedding clothes and trousseaus. Both her father and her fiancé gave her leave to purchase whatever she desired, although Darcy encouraged discretion.

Elizabeth had never been one to dwell upon fripperies, but she knew that her intended socialized with the upper tiers of society and she, as his wife, needed to dress the part. Having the ability to shop without regard for cost was a novel experience, and one she could become accustomed to.

The concept of becoming the wife to such a man as Fitzwilliam Darcy, and the mistress of such a great estate as Pemberley, began to unnerve her. Darcy reassured her that he wanted her to ease into her new role, and felt she would best be served by getting to know his aunt, the Countess. As a woman who knew about the society in which Darcy had been raised, Lady Matlock could assist her in many ways, helping to welcome her into his social circles, and introduce her to key members of the ton.

Normally, introductions did not cause such an uproar for Elizabeth, however, her mother and younger sisters would be a trial on her nerves in Lady Matlock's sitting room. She consoled herself with the fact that Jane and Mrs. Gardiner would be there, as well as Georgiana, and of course Darcy. She was also leery about meeting Lady Catherine, but she understood that Darcy's other aunt would be away for the day while she and her family visited, which also helped her courage immensely.

If the afternoon were to be any indication as to how this meeting would progress, Elizabeth would not be likely to sleep at all. As soon as Mrs. Bennet arrived and saw her *now*, two favourite daughters, she began her effusions over their conquests of being married to such 'fine and rich' gentlemen. The next item on her mother's agenda, it seemed, was to drag them again to all the 'finest' fabric warehouses and pick out the 'very best' materials. Both she and Jane blushed as they were shown the finer fabrics, and tried to take the odd looks from the salesclerks in stride, as these were the same ones that had attended them before, with Mrs. Gardiner.

Upon reaching the last shop of the day, they managed to come upon Caroline Bingley. It seemed she also had need of the 'finer' fabrics, as she expressed her intention to attend the Shetler's Ball two weeks hence. Jane initiating the conversation. "Miss Bingley, how are you today?"

Caroline looked at Jane and Elizabeth, then the rest of their party and addressed them all condescendingly. "Miss Bennet, Miss Eliza, and Mrs. Bennet, how do you do? I am looking to find fabric for my ensemble for the ball. I assume Charles and Mr. Darcy have already mentioned it to you. It is really quite exciting, and of course, all of the *ton* shall be present."

"Yes Miss Bingley, they have informed us of the Shetler's Ball, however, we have been quite busy these past few days shopping for our gowns and trousseaus as the wedding shall be upon us very soon." Jane responded sweetly.

Caroline looked at Jane with a false sincerity, "My dear Jane, you do want to look your very best for this occasion. All of the quality will be there and there shall be plenty of time to plan for the wedding afterwards."

Elizabeth narrowed her eyes. *She is the rudest, most obnoxious woman I have had the displeasure to know. To think that poor Jane will have to deal with such a meddling conniving wretch!* Before she could speak a word, though, Jane replied to the woman dressed in bright orange.

"But have you not heard, Miss Bingley? We will likely be married sooner than the first of the year. I am surprised that you were not aware." Jane looked surprised at Caroline's ignorance. Elizabeth took some satisfaction in being able to witness the genuine disappointment of the woman who had taunted her before in Hertfordshire.

Caroline's eyebrows shot up at this statement and she said in honest surprise. "Indeed? I had…I had not heard… It seems that my brother was remiss in informing his own family about his plans to wed."

That did not surprise Elizabeth, as she had rather thought that Mr. Bingley was wise to his sisters' ways. If she were aware of it too soon, then she might try to disrupt his plans, but as they were to be married in less than a fortnight, it seemed that there could be very little that she could do to cause any problems in that vein. With Jane informing the woman about their plans, they would have to be diligent in regard to what they said to Miss Bingley. She still wanted to taunt the woman, though, "That is surprising, although not much so, as he had been planning to accomplish many things in this short time. He likely has not had the time to notify all of his family."

Caroline seemed to be avoiding her in favor of Jane and addressed her, "Well Miss Bennet, it seems that we are to be related sooner than expected, how… wonderful." She finished insincerely.

Jane, being Jane, acted as if this was as good as any compliment, and heartily agreed. "Yes, is it not? Char… I mean Mr. Bingley and I are quite thrilled to be able to do so with all of our beloved family so near, and during the holidays to! This shall be a magnificent Christmas, and with my new family as well!"

Elizabeth kept an eye on Caroline as Jane continued, noting with amusement the many shades of white passing over Miss Bingley's face. When Jane finished, Caroline was able to half heartedly issue an invitation to the Bingley Townhouse to see, and presumably inspect, the place for Jane's benefit.

"Perhaps tomorrow you may join us at our townhouse to have a look at your new quarters." Elizabeth could see the bile rise in the woman as she continued on. "And then you may make requests as to your preferences for the interior decor of the house..." She looked towards Elizabeth. "We also have a park not too far away, Miss Eliza, which we can walk to if the weather permits and you so wish it... I remember after all that... you are *such* a good walker."

Elizabeth met her. I would certainly be happy to join you, Miss Bingley, however, we cannot do so tomorrow morning as we already have another engagement with Mr. Darcy's aunt... Lady Matlock."

Caroline eyed her for a moment and then said, .Ah yes, such an *elegant*, and *noble* lady. I do hope she does not overextend herself as she is keeping Lady Catherine de Bourgh and her daughter *Anne*, as well at her home." She stared intently at Elizabeth.

Elizabeth paled slightly at the mention of Darcy's unpleasant aunt, but was still of a mind not to give Caroline what she so obviously wanted... seeing her fret. She resolved to think on that later... when she was not in such a public place. "Well, then I will have the privilege of meeting more of Mr. Darcy's family, as I believe that it is good to form a close bond with those who should support you the most..." she smiled and qualified, "Your family."

Caroline gave small sneering smile. "Yes, well perhaps you may then want to join *us* for tea tomorrow afternoon. If you would like, I could even introduce you to the *best* modesties in town..." she looked Elizabeth up and down, "That is, of course, if you would prefer not to travel so *far* back to Cheapside between visits."

Jane ignoring the slight towards them and eagerly accepted the invitation. "Oh you are so kind Miss Bingley. It would indeed be wonderful to spend time with my new sisters so that we can get to know each other better."

Elizabeth immediately went into her protective mode and decided that if Jane was going with the 'superior sisters' as they were called, she would be there to protect her, and with that, they parted company. They soon traveled back to Cheapside to prepare for diner with their fiancés which had become the norm. Mrs. Bennet could not help crowing to the ladies in the shop about what 'advantageous' matches her daughters had made. That was the final catalyst for Elizabeth to remove them from there.

How am I ever to get through tomorrow without the Countess insisting that Darcy end our engagement due to our most unfortunate relatives? She dwelt upon this the whole ride home and then some.

~*~*~*~

Caroline Bingley wanted to scream. *How can this be happening? Why is Charles doing this and so rapidly as well? It seems as though he is trying to bring our whole family to ruin at the devil's pace!* She thought about this last encounter her entire ride home. When she finally arrived, she was so out of sorts she did the unlikely and went for a walk in the nearby park. She had been enveloped in her own thoughts so that she did not hear a familiar voice call to her.

"Miss Bingley, what a pleasant surprise to see you. I thought that you preferred to ride." Viscount Fitzwilliam seemed glad to see her.

She smiled at the thought of a person such as him actually addressing her. "Yes, well, I do at times tend to take the exercise for I am told that it… brightens one's eyes and complexion. She batted her eyelashes at him and smiled almost ridiculously.

He smiled and further offered, I do not suppose you have had a chance to bring your lovely… um soon to be family here to show off this part of the neighborhood…?"

She felt a little deflated with this line of questioning, but continued nonetheless, "Yes, well, I had actually seen them today. In fact, I made the invitation for them to join me tomorrow morning, but it seems as though your family has already claimed them for that part of the day. However, they will be joining me and my sister, Mrs. Hurst, afterwards." She smiled at him thinking that they both felt the family beneath them. I suppose that we may be able to persuade Miss Eliza to come to the park as she is such a great walker." She sniggered.

The Viscount seemed to relax with those words, "Then hopefully we will have fine weather and I may be able to join you for your walk in the park, Miss Bingley."

He stepped back and bowed gracefully, then excused himself, leaving a fluttering Caroline in his wake. She stood for a few moments seemingly frozen to the spot where he issued those words, before hurriedly returning to the Bingley townhouse. She determined that she would have to wear her best outfit, not only to be seen among the most fashionable, but also to be seen as a most attractive prospect for the Viscount. *I'll be damned if I will allow that little upstart trollop to outrank me! She will see what it takes to get ahead here in society, and I shall relish seeing her bow to me, and make Mr. Darcy wish he had made a better choice of brides.*

~*~*~*~

As James ambled towards Matlock House, he began to make plans of his seduction of Miss Elizabeth Bennet.

Perhaps if I am very good, I may be able to help myself to the other fine beauty as well! Mmmmm... would that not be delicious? Two for one! It is too bad that I cannot get more out of Caroline Bingley, as she seems ever so eager to get rid of her brother's fiancée too. Oh well, this will probably be one of the easier duties I have had to perform.

When he arrived home, he headed towards his rooms to plan for his rendezvous with the Misses Bennets. *It does not hurt that they are to come to my family's London town home for tea.* He would first slip in rather nonchalantly and be introduced. Then he would linger for tea and later offer to escort them to see Caroline Bingley.

He spent the last few days dreaming of the lovely brunette with the chestnut curls and those beautiful eyes, *and the lithe blonde with the sapphire eyes... both so gorgeous in their own way.* He had not seen such loveliness in all of his life, and to be from the same family was beyond his greatest expectation.

James knew that special care would be needed, and he planned to slowly draw them in, taking great care as he wanted to keep his options open. *Perhaps one may work better than the other for a seduction; then again, does it really matter?* He laughed to himself.

Aunt Catherine will surely pay either way, whether it is Miss Elizabeth or the other Miss Bennet, as they will be ruined just the same, and my debts will be paid. Such a pity really, as they are lovely additions to this society, but then this will really not affect me in the long run, as long as I pay off those d-amned debts! Maybe I should apply to Miss Caroline for some payout as well, as this could help her cause? Maybe I should even pile on the charm to her... after all she does have quite a dowry, and it would help to clear up some of those other pesky problems that have been plaguing me lately.

He gave a shudder at the thought of spending the rest of his days with such a woman. For in his set she was known as 'Pining Caroline' and she was only after wealthy gentlemen, preferably someone with a title. In fact, she had been after Darcy for several years, but then, James always knew that Aunt Catherine had planned for his cousin to marry Anne, uniting Pemberley with Rosings Park.

Pity that really, all that money tied up in one place! D-mned Darcy for having all the luck. Most unfortunate it was not me to get all that money, but there is no way I could tolerate that little sickly mouse for a wife. Too bad she does not look like those Bennets, then it might actually be enticing enough for me to join the fray there.

With that last thought there, he stepped outside his rooms only to come face to face with his brother, Richard. He froze where he stood.

Chapter 31

Richard turned upon seeing James exit his rooms and stood silently contemplating whether or not to turn away, or confront him with his treachery. He chose the latter. "Well, I am certainly surprised that you are even allowed out of your rooms, after all that has happened!"

James looked uncomfortable and seemed to lighten up once he found that he was not about to be beaten to a pulp... at least not at this particular moment. "Richard, it seems that I owe you some sort of explanation..."

"That is an understatement, James! Do you have any idea what hell I have gone through? I dare say that you are not likely to even care, but what really makes me angry is that you treated Harriet in such a way and then tried to saddle *me* with the guilt!" Richard sneered.

James crossed his arms in an easy manner. "Richard, I already knew you would go to Darcy for assistance, and I was hardly in any position to do anything for her. I knew that Darcy would help you, and he would hardly give me the time of day, let alone cover for *that*!" He looked condescendingly at his brother as if he were explaining the rules of billiards or some other game.

Richard was incredulous at his brother's nonchalant dismissal of his actions, "*You* are a *thoughtless cad*, James!"

"You always have been, but now even you have overstepped the boundaries! And to pass it off, as just an excuse that our cousin would help *me* and not *you*? G-D, you are a piece of work! We are not talking about a simple affair that has ended... *no*! You made a child with someone, and cast it, along with your *lover*, aside! To top it off, you conspired to have her claim it as *mine*! You should feel lucky that I have not pummeled you! Then on top of everything else, you accrued such gaming debits with such a reprobate as *Blake*!" he watched as his brother looked off to the side and shrugged.

Richard continued, I should be thankful that now it is not me in such low graces with our parents. Hell, you have made me look like a saint compared to you!" He spat.

James looked at him calmly and said, "Then I guess you should thank me for then."

Richard was incensed; he could not trust himself any further in James' presence. He shook his head again in furry then stormed away, then vowed to ensure that James did not get away with this. *He will learn to behave in a human manner even if it kills him. He shall pay for what he has done to... to everyone!*

~*~*~*~

Elizabeth was close to the point of nail biting, as she paced in the front sitting room that faced the street at the Gardiners house. Mrs. Bennet was being... well Mrs. Bennet. Her effusions over meeting the Countess for tea were all that Elizabeth feared, and all of her confidence nearly left her. That was until Darcy arrived with Georgiana, then she was sure it would be gone entirely. This would be the first time that Georgiana had met Mrs. Bennet and the rest of Elizabeth's sisters, other than Jane. That alone was enough to send Elizabeth into a fit of nerves. She dearly wanted to make a good impression upon Darcy's family.

When Darcy arrived in his coach with his sister, he very gracefully led her through the front foyer and was face to face with his intended; she was anxious to greet him. He smiled one of his rare ear to ear smiles, and she immediately blushed at his expression, wanting nothing more than to fling herself into his arms. But of course, due to the presence of Georgiana and Jane, she did not. She did, however returned his smile with one of her own, and raised an eyebrow—an action she knew would cause him to flush, which he promptly did.

Before the couple managed to embarrass themselves in front of their family, they both stepped back and gave proper greetings to each other, and Georgiana and Jane respectively.

"Welcome Mr. Darcy, Miss Darcy, we have been anxiously awaiting you."

"And we have been anxiously making our way here, Miss Elizabeth, Miss Bennet." Darcy nodded to Jane.

Georgiana smiled shyly at them, and barely managed to say above a whisper, as she looked from Elizabeth to her brother, "Good morning, Miss Elizabeth, Miss Bennet."

Neither Elizabeth nor Darcy noted the amused expressions upon their sisters' faces. As they began their pleasantries, the other ladies of the house slowly began arriving in the sitting room, in order to be introduced to Miss Darcy and, unfortunately, Mrs. Bennet was the first. The lady began her doting over Darcy, "Oh Mr. Darcy, it is so good of you to come and escort us to your distinguished family, and to bring your lovely sister as well. You know I cannot impress upon Elizabeth what an honor is being bestowed, by all of this attention by you, and your family…"

As she rambled, Elizabeth could feel her face burn with mortification as her mother's words and behavior evolved into all she had feared. She saw Darcy's embarrassed flush as well, and wished at that moment, that her mother had been left in Hertfordshire. She was sure that Mrs. Gardiner and Jane and she could do quite well without her.

Elizabeth saw Georgiana's eyes widen, and could only surmise that she was just as mortified by Mrs. Bennet's speech as well. That young lady, however, handled it with uncommon grace. "Mrs. Bennet, it is an honor to know Miss Elizabeth, as well, and of course Miss Bennet. They are lovely, and I am quite looking forward to getting to know them even more…"

This was all the encouragement that Mrs. Bennet needed.

"Oh, that is so good of you to say. I am sure then, that you will absolutely *love* to meet Lizzy's other sisters. They are about your age, and so lively. Yes, Yes, I am quite sure you will be quite pleased to get to know them."

Maybe I should feign a headache in order to keep mother from gong to tea? If Lady Catherine should happen to arrive while we are still there, she would definitely voice her disapproval and Darcy would be forced to admit that some of my family would be less than a good connection. Almost as soon as she thought that, she looked at Darcy with concern, only to see one of his burning looks that nearly melted her. *He is so passionate and yet such an angel, to be putting up with us all, and my mother especially! He must truly love me to be so steadfast!*

Now I need to intercept mama, and get her to stop her effusions, perhaps I should change the subject. "Mr. Darcy sir, have you had a chance to view the church, Saint John's? I understand that it is the very same one as your aunt and uncle were married at?"

He smiled and replied, "Yes, it was, and I can say that I am looking forward to having the distinction of sharing that same honor with them when we are married there. It is quite lovely this time of year with the light coming through the stained glass windows."

Mrs. Bennet was all effusions again, but at least she did not bring up the younger Bennet sisters, "Oh yes," she purred as her eyes lit up, I am sure that it must be one of the very best in town, as an earl was married there. Oh Lizzy, is it not most fortunate that your fiancé is so well connected to be able to bestow this honor upon you?"

"Yes mama, it is an honor that he has bestowed upon me."

Darcy quickly rejoined her statement, I should say that the honor is mine, madam. And I cannot tell you how happy she has made me in accepting my hand." He gave her an affectionate look.

Her warm feelings at his words were replaced by distress mortification as her younger sisters joined the group in their usual loud noisy manner.

This is going to be a very long day! Elizabeth now dreaded, not only the meeting with the Countess, but also Caroline Bingley later. She could only imagine what kind of glee Caroline would get observing her mother and younger sisters being themselves.

The introductions to the younger sisters were made, and Elizabeth noted Georgiana slightly withdrawing as they talked in their usual loud and unreserved manner. *Oh dear, poor Georgiana must be mortified at my sisters loudness, and unreserved manners!* Mrs. Gardiner arrived last, and tried her best to curb their exuberance as best she could, while distracting her sister-in-law as much as possible.

"Fannie, I was wondering if you might like to help me later on with the evening's menu, it seems that the cook could not find the proper cuts of meat, and I know you are quite efficient with those things."

"Why yes, of course Madeline, you should have said something sooner! You know I can deal with those sorts of things in no time at all!"

After some small talk, the group was on their way to Matlock House to meet more of Darcy's family.

Elizabeth went in the coach with Darcy, Georgiana, Jane and Mrs. Gardiner, and the others went in the second Darcy coach. *At least we can have some peace and quiet for now, but goodness what if mama and the other girls embarrass us as they are wont to do?* Thus she sat in this distracted mood until they arrived at Matlock House.

~*~*~*~

Darcy contemplated the goings on at Matlock House as well, but for very different reasons. He knew that Fitzwilliam had gone to stay there yesterday and wondered how the reunion of the two brothers was unfolding. After what James had done, he felt nearly certain there would be hell to pay for his treachery… *and against his brother of all people! Is there no end to his misdeeds?* Darcy fervently hoped that at least one of his cousins would be absent from the house, as he definitely did not want James there when his fiancée arrived. He also requested that the Countess ensure that Lady Catherine would be gone from the house for the day.

When they arrived, he was partially relieved that Lady Catherine was indeed gone, but unfortunately the Viscount was there to greet the party, and Darcy noted that his cousin almost seemed eager to meet them. He also saw that James was surprise when he came along as well.

"I say, Darcy, I had not thought that you would be here as well… what a pleasant surprise."

Darcy looked at him momentarily before responding, "Of course I would be here when my fiancée meets any of our family for the first time, James. After all, it would be rude not to do so and I wish to ensure that there are no... um... odd moments."

"My Darcy, are you already afraid that your new family will be cause for alarm?" James smiled smugly and teased.

Darcy gave him a cold stare. "Not likely, *James*, and it was not the Bennet family to which I was referring."

The cousins stared at each other as the Viscount narrowed his eyes and raised his eyebrow challengingly. Finally, James replied, "Well then, I shall try to be on my very best behavior." He turned on his heels and walked in front of Darcy to meet the ladies who were turning in expectation towards his cousin.

Darcy introduced Mrs. Bennet first, who by now was awe struck at the elegant interior, and barely able to speak above a whisper. To Darcy's relief she was nearly silent... for now.

"Mrs. Bennet, Mrs. Gardiner, Miss Bennet, Miss... Elizabeth." He smiled at his beloved and continued, "Miss Mary, Miss Katherine, and Miss Lydia, may I introduce you to my cousin, the Viscount James Fitzwilliam, and my aunt, the Countess Margaret Fitzwilliam?"

The Countess acknowledged each of them and James followed suit. He seemed to linger over Elizabeth and Jane's hands too closely for Darcy's taste, and he wanted nothing more than to inject himself between Elizabeth and his cousin. They took their seats and were offered tea by the Countess.

"Miss Elizabeth, I understand that you met our Darcy here, in Hertfordshire?"

"Yes ma'am, we were actually the first ones to meet there, when Mr. Bingley was surveying Netherfield Park."

"Ah yes, I had heard that, and I have also heard that you," the Countess looked to Jane, "Miss Bennet are engaged to Mr. Bingley?"

Jane smiled. "Yes ma'am, that is correct. We... that is Mr. Bingley and I are to be married at the same ceremony as Mr. Darcy and my sister."

"I had heard that, and you are to be married so soon as well? I believe that Darcy sent 'round invitations for less than two weeks hence. It must be very hectic over at your aunt and uncle's, what with all the goings on required of a double wedding?"

Darcy was grateful of his aunt's gentle manner, and sat back to quietly observe the interactions between Lady Matlock and Elizabeth and her family. He also noted how James was still staring at his Elizabeth, and at times, at Jane as well. Disconcerted with that, he shifted in his seat, subconsciously moving slightly closer to Elizabeth.

Mrs. Gardiner joined the conversation, "It has been busier than it has been at our house for... well I think I can honestly say, forever." She laughed slightly. "We are having quite a good time with all the preparations, and I must say that it is exciting to have such goings on during the holidays."

"Well Mrs. Gardiner... and Mrs. Bennet, I offer my assistance if you have need of anything to prepare for this great event. It would be my pleasure to help in any way that I may. I do so like to make myself useful, and it is no trouble at all, I assure you."

"That is most kind of you ma'am. I do not know that we are overwhelmed, yet. However I can imagine that it may... and likely will soon occur, and your assurances are of great comfort. I must be honest it is... and has been a flurry of activity ever since we set the date." Elizabeth responded in her natural way to the offer.

"Well if you would like, you could share some of your plans with me, and perhaps I may be able to assist in that endeavor to ensure that nothing is missed." The Countess smiled at Elizabeth, and the rest of their party.

"That is most kind of..." Jane started to say but was stopped by a loud commotion outside the door.

Darcy and the Countess sat up straight in their chairs as they heard the voice of none other than Lady Catherine who burst through the sitting room door like a storm. Her expression was one of fury. The lady stood as straight as possible glaring at Elizabeth. Everyone sat with a stunned expression at her loud and presumptuous entrance... all that is, except James, Darcy noted. It seemed as though his cousin was not all that surprised at the sudden appearance of the imperious lady.

"*What* is going on here, Margaret? I came as soon as I heard that you were receiving *these* people!"

Darcy could feel his temper rising rapidly, but before he could say anything the Countess began, "*Catherine*! How dare you barge into *my* sitting room, in *my* house, and insult *my* guests? I *must* insist that you remove yourself from here this instant!"

"I most certainly will *not*! This *gathering* is an abomination to this noble and ancient family, and I will not sit idly by and allow it!" She turned to glare at the Gracechurch party and continued, I *insist* that you... people, vacate this premise."

"*Lady Catherine! You will desist in behaving in such an abominable manner right this instant!*" Darcy boomed, his face as red and angry as anyone had ever seen him. "You will not speak to the Bennets in this way ever again! *Do I make myself clear?* Now... I shall speak to you *outside*..." at her incredulous look he demanded, "*Right now, madam!*"

Lady Catherine looked at him defiantly, but glanced again at the rest of the group with a glare before she obliged him, nearly running down the footman who had tried to prevent her from entering the room. Darcy and Lady Catherine were soon followed by the Countess who wanted to 'have a word' with her unruly guest. While they took the infuriated Lady Catherine to the study, they left the room with only the Viscount to entertain the rest of the ladies. The visibly stunned audience did not dare to say a word lest the lady be tempted to start her vitriol again.

Once safely ensconced in the study, Darcy and the Countess stood in front of the door staring angrily at Lady Catherine. It was a few minutes before anything was said. Finally, Darcy broke the deadly silence. I have *never* been so *humiliated* in all of my life! *What* on *earth* did you think you would accomplish by such an exhibition Lady Catherine?"

She glared with narrowed eyes. I was *trying* to make you *realize* what a *mistake* it would be to connect yourself with such people, Darcy! Heaven and earth they are kin to...what... common solicitors? And... what... *tradesmen*? *Those* people are below you! They are below *us*, and should not even think to aspire to such a station in life!"

"*Catherine*! *You* are the one that is out of line here! The Bennets are from a gentleman's family, and Darcy is a gentleman, so far they are *equals*! And, now you have brought shame and humiliation upon *us*! I am mortified by your behavior, and I must insist that you leave immediately if you will not cease this nonsense!" The Countess demanded.

Darcy stood firm, glowering in anger, wanting nothing more than to chuck his aunt out right then and there. He contemplated the reaction of Elizabeth and her family to his aunt's antics, and silently prayed that Elizabeth would not reconsider their engagement and break it off. That thought made him even angrier, and it took most of his self control not to throttle the pompous harridan, before he recalled the reason they were to marry so soon. "Madam, in light of your behavior I must insist that you apologize immediately to my fiancée and her family for your *foolish* and *thoughtless* words and behavior!"

The lady looked at him incredulously and voiced most vehemently, I shall under *no* circumstance do any such thing! I am the offended party! *Me*! You know that you and Anne were for…"

"*Enough! That* is the *last* time that I will hear this, Lady Catherine! You should have realized that at eight and twenty if I had an inclination to wed, I would have done so. *But* I had none, and most especially none to my cousin Anne. Do not even begin *that* argument with me now! And as for my association with Miss Bennet… Aunt Matlock is correct as well. The Bennet family is almost as long a line of gentlemen as the Darcy or Fitzwilliam lines… perhaps even further! I am the one who is being honored here, not her! As for your behavior I shall warn you that if today's incident has in anyway compromised my happiness in that regard I will *never* speak to you again. I may never speak to you again after this… this episode anyway!

With that he turned on his heel and stormed out of the room, but it was some time before he was able to regain his composure enough to rejoin the group. He went to the parlor and paced in furry for about ten minutes before he heard the familiar sound of Elizabeth's laughter.

When he entered the room everyone's eyes were upon him and he looked searching Elizabeth's expression before he acknowledged anyone else. He noted that his cousin James was sitting directly at the side of Elizabeth, and apparently tried to amuse her with some of his antics which grated even more on Darcy's nerves. At this time, he felt especially territorial and glared at his cousin for sitting in such close proximity to his beloved Elizabeth.

James looked at him in a silent challenge and said lightly, "Darcy, I have been *trying* to entertain you *lovely* fiancée here. She is such a gem, my dear cousin. I do hope that Lady Catherine has… calmed down?"

Darcy narrowed his eyes and issued a silent command to his cousin to vacate his present perch. He looked apologetically at Elizabeth, "My dearest, Miss Elizabeth, I must apologize for Lady Catherine, *again*. I cannot tell you how mortified…"

"Sir…" Elizabeth interrupted, and glanced to her family who were in quiet conversation with Georgiana and each other, trying to give them some privacy. I understand well that sometimes it is impossible to control our families' behavior, and do not hold it against you, as I hope others would not hold some of my family members behavior against me."

"I do not deserve you." Darcy stated with sincerity.

He felt some relief, but was still concerned over James' apparent ease in demeanor in light of the commotion created by Lady Catherine. He vowed to discover what his cousin was about. *How did Lady Catherine come to know of our plans to meet this morning?*

Chapter 32

Darcy was suspicious of James' appearance, and then the subsequent hostile appearance of Lady Catherine. He vowed to stay with Elizabeth for the rest of her time away from Gracechurch Street.

James is definitely up to something, going so far as to suggest that he would go with them to spend time at Caroline Bingley? What is that all about? Three months ago, he could not so much as stand to be in the same vicinity as Charles' sister. When Darcy had a moment of privacy to speak to James, he challenged him. "What is this all about, James? Did you have something to do with Lady Catherine being here today?"

James looked at him calmly. "Now, what makes you think that I would have anything to do with that, Darcy?"

"It is a *very* odd *coincidence* that Lady Catherine, whom I might add was *supposed* to be visiting a friend this very morning, and was not going to be around, suddenly appears in all her fury, and embarrasses herself, and *us* while she attacks Elizabeth… that is to say the Bennets." Darcy retorted.

His cousin raised his eyebrows, "And *why* would I be a party to such things? Why would I wish for *our* aunt to embarrass *us* in such a way? I mean really, your lady *does* seem quite lovely, Darcy. In fact, her entire family has such charming ladies." He glanced licentiously at Elizabeth and Jane.

Darcy frowned but said no more, as the Countess entered and brought the Earl with her. Darcy knew she wanted to introduce Elizabeth to him, and he was anxious for them to meet as well. After the group was introduced to the Earl, the Countess addressed the Bennets. "You must allow me and my husband the Earl to apologize for the unjust outburst by Lady Catherine. We are truly mortified by her unkind and misguided words. My husband and I hope that you do not hold her words against us, or especially against our nephew. It was most uncalled for, and we would feel most honoured if you would allow us to make this up to you by hosting the wedding breakfast."

This was just what would bring Mrs. Bennet out of her quietude, and she went into raptures upon this offer. "Oh my, dear, Lady Matlock that is most kind of you. We would be most honoured to accept your most kind and thoughtful offer. Oh, and do not worry about that earlier episode, for I am sure that the Lady was quite out of sorts with the suddenness of all of these developments and was overwhelmed. She will surely settle when she sees how happy Mr. Darcy and our Lizzy are."

Almost everyone looked at her in shock, but Mrs. Bennet did not seem to notice, and Darcy, for once, was thankful of his future mother-in-laws odd remark, as it detracted from his own family's misdeeds. The Earl and Countess stood looking at her with raised eyebrows and an apprehensive countenance.

Luckily Mrs. Gardiner proved that Elizabeth need not blush for every member of her family by offering, "That is most kind of you Lord and Lady Matlock. We thank you." She eyed Mrs. Bennet and suggested, I believe that we need to be going, as we are to meet with Miss Bingley."

Darcy was torn between being thankful for her intervention and irritation at the mention of joining Caroline. It was one of his least favourite activities—that, and having to assist with the breeding of the studs and mares at Pemberley. *At least with the breeding livestock, it served a purpose,* he thought wryly. *This outing would likely only serve to give me a headache and some aggravation.*

The Earl and Countess looked at Mrs. Gardiner oddly, but Darcy chose not to delve too deeply into that at the moment. He was determined to observe James, while they went with the ladies, and under *no* circumstances would he allow *him* to be alone with either Elizabeth or Jane. He had the footman call for his carriage and stood near the entrance as the ladies donned their outer garments in preparation for their shopping trip.

The Countess stood at one end of the entrance talking with Mrs. Gardiner and Mrs. Bennet, while his uncle came to him.

"Darcy..." he slightly hesitated, I was just curious as to how this arrangement came about with your Miss Bennet and her family meeting with Miss Bingley. I really am surprised as... well I must confess that it is quite baffling that that woman, of all people, would deign to spend time with your intended."

That speech drew some surprise from Darcy, "Why would that be so, Uncle? After all, Miss Jane Bennet is betrothed to Charles Bingley, and though she has been known to be a social climber, I cannot see her trying to alienate her future sister."

"That may be so, but... well I would not normally divulge this but... It was Caroline Bingley who had come here shortly after you came to town and spoke with your aunt... I mean about ... you know." He gave him a meaningful look.

Even though he suspected as much, Darcy paled at this piece of news; his uncle had been known to keep information of an inflammatory nature to himself, most likely he had thought that Darcy would be tempted to retaliate for Miss Bingley's interference. Though if truthful, that was not too far from the mark. This confirmation only gave him more cause for concern as he knew Miss Bingley would not easily give up her quest to claim him, or any man with his position of wealth and status, as a husband. The other question in Darcy's mind *was; what was James doing with Caroline? His thoughts were disrupted by his and the Gardiner carriages arrival.*

He and James escorted the ladies into their conveyances, and as he was about to assist Elizabeth into his carriage, his cousin beat him to the duty. He was somewhat comforted by her look of disappointment, and he immediately assisted Georgiana in before he followed her. He had almost forgotten his silent sister until he glanced at her and saw a concerned look upon her face he could not discern the cause. He promised himself he would speak to her later about what he had missed of the happenings in the sitting room, while he and the Countess were in the study with Lady Catherine.

They rode in near silence all of the way with James occasionally commenting on people and shops whom they passed. *He would never be able to appreciate a woman of value... he will never be able to see past all of the material things and real duty to one's self. No he could never appreciate a woman such as Elizabeth.* They were upon Bingley's townhouse before Darcy realized it.

When they arrived at the house he was surprised that Bingley was not to join them. Jane was invited and usually that was enticement enough for the man to join any gathering. "Is Bingley not to join us this morning, Miss Bingley? I would have thought that he would be anxious to join us." Darcy tried to bait their hostess.

She opened her mouth at first and said, "Ah… no, he… actually had some business to attend, and well… as I am at present his household's mistress I have decided to stand in his stead." She looked at him curiously, and glanced back and forth from James to Darcy before deciding to acknowledge the ladies. They had decided to go to some stores that had furniture and tapestries, under the pretense of decorating their new homes. They were close enough to walk but decided to have a carriage meet them later for the trip home.

As Elizabeth was within the party, Darcy did not mind this outing and said to her when they were away from their group, I must say Elizabeth, I am disappointed not to be visiting the modiste." He looked down into her smiling face.

"Why sir, I have been led to believe that gentlemen abhor shopping let alone the tedious task of fittings for clothing." She teased.

"That may be so in general, however, my dearest, I must admit that I find it quite a tempting thought to imagine me undressing you in those very garments." He whispered into her ear.

He noted her pretty blush and felt himself warming at the very thought of causing her to blush in other ways as well. She regained her breath and replied, "Sir, I am sure I do not know your meaning." Her feigned innocence only ignited his passion further.

"My dearest, I *am* certain you comprehend my meaning quite well." He looked at her meaningfully. I have several other ideas as to what I would like to see upon you as well."

She met his challenge with a quirk of her eyebrow. "And what would that be, sir?"

He leaned closer and whispered, *"Me."*

She gasped and her blush spread to her chest, he noted with satisfaction. But before she could respond, their tete a tete was interrupted by Miss Bingley.

"Miss Eliza, have you considered what you are going to do as far as design to your new homes?"

Elizabeth looked at the intruder. "No, actually I had not thought of that Miss Bingley…"

"Well, it is no wonder. I am sure that you had not had the guidance that *we*, of Mr. Darcy's society have had in relation to décor and entertaining that is typical of *our* set."

Before Darcy could make any comment Elizabeth replied, "That may be so, Miss Bingley, however, the truth of the matter is that I had not really thought of his home as needing any further 'improvements'."

She could not have known how this pleased Darcy and very much displeased Caroline. The Viscount smirked at her response, but managed to hide that from Miss Bingley. Darcy observed that his cousin had been walking and talking with Caroline, occasionally touching her near her waist, and leaning in to whisper to her, rather closer than propriety allowed. Darcy thought that if Bingley would see such a display, he would be hard pressed not to call out James for such an infraction. Darcy decided that that he would have a word with James about such public displays. *It would not do for him to behave in such a way to another lady, especially after having brought his mistress with child.*

The more he thought about the pair, the more suspicious he became. He was still no closer to resolving the mystery behind their sudden friendliness. By the time they returned to Bingley House, they were greeted by Charles who was noticeably disappointed to not have been included in the gathering, I say, Caroline, you might have considered inviting me along with you and Miss Bennets'… party, after all, you did invite Darcy."

Caroline shrugged. "No Charles, we were not intending on inviting…" Suddenly remembering Darcy being there, "Ahh, I mean it was not… Mr. Darcy was… unexpectedly able to join us this morning, otherwise we *would* have invited you, Charles."

"Ah, I see. I would have been most delighted have you done so." Bingley said with his typical easy going smile.

Though his friend seemed to be appeased by that explanation, Darcy was even more disgruntled. He began to realize that the outing might have been preplanned by Caroline and James. Alarmed now, and he intended to be on guard for any disruptions to their wedding plans. *Yes I shall have to be most cautious the next several days.*

~*~*~*~

When Darcy unexpectedly appeared with the Bennets and Lord Fitzwilliam, Caroline was disappointed. She wanted to take the morning's opportunity to show up that country upstart and her family, and most importantly, show the Viscount what she was made of. But instead, all she heard from *him* was how *lovely* the Miss Bennets were, especially Jane and Elizabeth. It was enough to make her ill.

The very last thing that she wanted to hear was how

'charming' and 'witty' Miss Eliza was. *She certainly has used her arts and allurements to charm the men! Why, that little strumpet! Who does she think she is?* Then suddenly it hit her; *that tart... why yes, if only I could get Darcy to see that his lady with the 'fine eyes' is such a harlot then he would likely disentangle himself away from her!* After musing for a few minutes, as to what she could do to make Darcy see how much of a mistake he was making in marrying Eliza. Caroline came upon a plan to arrange such an occurrence.

I wonder how it was she was able to entrap him? No matter, I can come up with arts and allurements as well! What could she have to offer such a man, that I do not have in great abundance? Certainly. I have more grace and beauty than her! I can play at the pianoforte much better than she ever could, and I also speak German, Italian, and French! So what if she is such a great reader? I know how to read! I am sure she does not read anything more interesting than tripe!

Caroline pondered what assets she lacked that made such a man as Darcy chose a simply country bred girl over her. She could not come up with any meaningful answers.

~*~*~*~

When Darcy arrived home, he was alarmed at his sister's silent. Though it was not unusual for her to be so quiet, this degree of silence was out of the ordinary. He determined the need to talk to his sister about what had occurred at the Earl's house. He directed his attention in as easy manner as he could muster so as not to alarm his sister. "Umm... Georgiana, I meant to ask you about how Elizabeth and the Bennets were after Lady Catherine's tirade."

Georgiana took a few moments to respond. When she did, she was nearly inaudible, "Yes, I... had rather thought that you might."

Darcy found her statement slightly surprising, and concerning. He furthered, I do not suppose that you could enlighten me as to their reactions, and how others behaved?"

She looked at him suddenly. "You mean what James was doing... do you not?"

"He nodded. "Yes, that as well." He watched her closely.

She took a deep breath. "I... I am not sure how to describe it, William... the only thing that I can say is that..." She hesitated and at Darcy's nod of encouragement, began, "It was almost as if I was watching George Wickham – the way he used to talk to me..." At her brother's alarmed look she clarified, I mean to say that he was as...what is the word...?

Well I guess the best description would be that he was smooth and easy with his addresses to Miss Bennet and Miss Elizabeth. He seemed to... to sit too close to Miss Elizabeth. I could tell that she was uncomfortable with this but did not feel that she could or even should rebuff him what with..."

"You mean with Lady Catherine's tirade in the sitting room?"

Darcy finished and looked defeated. He sat there for a little while before asking, "How did the rest of the family behave? I mean did they say anything about what our aunt said?"

Georgiana thought for a moment then replied, "Well, Mrs. Gardiner had approached Miss Elizabeth, as she looked devastated but then James went to sit by her. He tried to excuse Lady Catherine's behaviour by explaining her hopes of you and Anne. She seemed upset by our Aunt's behaviour, and I felt so awful for her. I wished I could have said or done something..."

"No dearest, you have done enough by just observing for me, for you know I want you to help me watch out for her… that is the best thing you can do for her, but I must ask you to promise me something."

She looked at him eagerly. "Yes, of course, you know I will do anything for you and Elizabeth."

He felt his heart warm. "If you see or hear of anything that may even remotely challenge her happiness that you will come to me… immediately."

"Of course, you know I would."

He smiled and thanked her, releasing her to her music master while he sat and contemplated his next move. He paced nearly the entire afternoon in contemplation, finally resolving he would head to Gracechurch Street… to Elizabeth.

Chapter 33

The one thing Elizabeth wished for when Darcy rode back to Gracechurch Street with her and her family was for peace of mind. She could not help but dwell upon the events of the day from the time she entered the coach to go back to the Gardiners. The entire outing with Caroline and the Viscount of Matlock was disconcerting, and Darcy seemed as tense in their quaint group as he would in a ball room. Darcy hardly glanced at her and spoke even less in the coach; a slight scowl on his face as he kept looking out the carriage window.

Lady Catherine has made quite a fuss over things and it seems as though she will be quite obstinate in her objections to our marriage. Elizabeth realized that Darcy's society may look down upon such a union as theirs, but she felt that there would also be many who were more sensible than to openly slight or accost them.

It was beyond rude when his aunt barged into our party, and leveled such venomous words at me, and my family. The nerve of that woman! Will she never give up on the fact that Darcy never wanted to marry his cousin? How did she think her nephew would react to her haranguing? He is not one to be trifled with, but now... She could not understand his unwillingness to meet her eyes now. She wondered if he was now rethinking their engagement after Lady Catherine's rampage, and his cousin's overly familiar behaviour.

The Viscount insinuated some intimacy between us after we left. Surely William does not believe that I encouraged him to take license the way he did. That man is obviously an amoral lecher to behave in such a way in his family's sitting room with a room full of young women... and with his cousins betrothed! The audacity of the man! I would no more find his repulsive behaviour to my liking than that of any common rake! She would not admit it, but since they were left alone in the sitting room at Matlock House while Darcy and the

Countess dealt with Lady Catherine, she felt like running away and never looking back.

She knew that she loved Darcy and wanted to marry him, but the strain that was being put upon them by their families made her wish that they would elope and be done with it, and tell the world to go to the devil. *I will not be so selfish, if nothing more than for poor Georgiana, who looked a fright with her doe eyes wide open as her cousin leered at me. She will be coming out soon, and we shall not taint her with that.*

Caroline Bingley is another puzzle. Why is she acting her usual false self, and yet bothering to invite us out? Perhaps she is just looking for opportunities to demonstrate how her fashion sense is so much more superior to ours? Elizabeth stifled a laugh. The carriage slowed as they approached the Gardiner's, and Darcy was the first one out, wasting no time assisting Elizabeth down. He looked at her with a smile that did not reach his eyes, which only served to deepen her apprehension. She looked up at him questioningly before taking his arm to be escorted in the house.

"Sir, is there something amiss?"

Darcy started and looked down into her eyes. "No dearest, not that I can tell at the moment, but I must beg your leave soon. I need to look into some matters." He sounded reassuring. I promise to return later, Elizabeth,. he said reluctantly. I own that I would much rather spend time with you."

Nodding her head, she wanted to extract another promise. "You will not be going back to Lady Catherine, will you?"

The ends of his lips curled up, "If you mean, 'will I go back to Matlock House and give my aunt the dressing down that she deserves', then, no, but I will not tolerate such behaviour. It is unbecoming, especially to someone of her station." He cringed almost as soon as the words were spoken.

Elizabeth bowed her head and went through the front foyer. *I can easily understand his mortification for his aunt's outburst, after all, I have become accustomed to such occurrences most of my life. I wish you would let me know what it is that you are planning to do, Fitzwilliam.* She voiced aloud, I will await your arrival this afternoon then." She could feel the stinging in her eyes, but fought her tears.

Darcy appeared to notice her demeanour change as escorted her to a private corner of the entry way. He took her hand in his. "Elizabeth, I am so sorry for what my family has put you through today. Had I known that Lady Catherine was planning to interrupt our morning, I would have postponed it until I was sure she was gone. I do not know what devil possessed her to think her display would change anything. I cannot tell you how angry it makes me. I am also none too pleased with my cousin, James."

The rest of the party noticed the couple hovering in the corner, and Mrs. Gardiner subtly cleared her throat indicating the need to observe some measure of propriety, with the presence of two servants in the entry way. They separated and Darcy looked apologetically to Elizabeth with a small smile.

"I shall be counting down the minutes until I can see you again." Darcy bowed over her hand as he kissed the back of it lingeringly. He backed up and nodded to the rest of her party, making his excuses.

Elizabeth watched him leave and enter his carriage. Just before he left, she saw him look out the carriage window and smile as he mouthed, I love you."

She could only conjecture what it was he needed to do, but felt reassured at his continuing assurances of his love and devotion.

~*~*~*~

Later that afternoon Darcy arrived at Gracechurch Street sooner than promised. Elizabeth was glad to see him, but as soon as she saw the frown on his face, she knew he did not bring good news. Once he made his greeting to the rest of the household, he applied to Mr. Bennet for permission to walk out with Elizabeth. Though her father knew about their reasons for marrying sooner, she could tell he was hesitant to grant them that liberty, but he eventually relented at her pleas, and they were finally out of doors and heading towards the park.

Elizabeth looked up at him; .I do not suppose that you will tell me what has brought you back earlier than expected, sir, not that I am complaining."

He walked a few paces in front of her, almost as if he had not heard her. He stopped suddenly and looked at her. I do not mean to be so mysterious, dearest. I have just been pondering the events of earlier today… at Matlock House. I am just concerned about my cousin and Aunt Catherine. I think that perhaps it was no coincidence that both there this morning."

"I do not take your meaning, sir. Surely you do not believe that the Countess…"

"Oh, no, *no*, I do not think that it was she that would try to cause difficulties between us. She has been our staunchest supporter in our marriage. What I believe happened was that Caroline Bingley told the Viscount that I was to bring you to tea there, and he sent Lady Catherine there this morning to cause trouble."

As Elizabeth thought about that, she grew quiet and became concerned. Darcy quickly added, "Please dearest, I do not want you to be uneasy about this. It is an issue I must deal with, or rather, we should deal with *together*. Actually what I wanted to ask of you is, if you would consider marrying sooner yet, than we have already planned? I must confess that today would not be soon enough for me." He smiled his beautiful dimpled smile which lightened her mood.

Elizabeth thought that an excellent idea, but other thoughts intruded and she frowned.

Darcy asked anxiously, "What? What is it my love? Do you think it too rushed? If you would prefer, we shall wait. But, I must add that I am now of the opinion that we should marry earlier due to the potential for problems to arise."

"Problems?"

"I should say issues, but yes, I think that we must consider it as an option. I *believe* some of my family has the potential to cause more problems for us. I thought that we could marry secretly. We could then have a public wedding with Jane and Bingley later, if you would wish to do so." He sounded hopeful.

"Do you mean to say that you believe your cousin would cause problems that could prevent us from marrying? Do you think that your aunt would also present those same problems, should we give them an opportunity to do so?"

Turning to face her. He grasped her hands, "*That* is exactly what I would not put past either one of them, if for nothing else but to spite me for doing something that displeases them."

"While I would prefer to marry with Jane and Mr. Bingley, I would also *prefer* to be married with as few complications as possible." Elizabeth answered as she felt her tears welling up, and Darcy looked at her concerned.

"Elizabeth, would you consider it if I could convince Bingley to marry with us in our own quiet ceremony? We could still have some 'public wedding', for our families. At least then I could protect you, and they could do nothing about it as it would be fait accompli. What do you say to that?"

Pondering the idea, Elizabeth replied, I think... yes, yes, Fitzwilliam, I will marry you anytime you so wish."

Darcy smiled almost as widely as when she accepted his hand, and disregarded propriety by grabbing her and embracing her tightly, kissing her full upon the mouth. She could see the happiness diffuse about his face. They returned to the house, and Darcy would discuss plans with Bingley when Charles arrived at Gracechurch Street.

They did not have to wait long for Mr. Bingley to arrive, as he was anxious to see his 'angel'. Darcy approached Mr. Bingley shortly after he made his greetings, and after informing their hosts of their need, they left for Mr. Gardiner's study for private conversation.

Jane puzzled over her beloveds need for a private word, "What is going on Lizzy? Is there a problem? Or is it about earlier today?"

Elizabeth wanted to avoid discussing the incident at Matlock House, as it still upset her. She understood that Jane felt the impact as well, as it was their family, after all, that Lady Catherine insulted. Now Elizabeth wanted to garner support for their plan to marry earlier, and with her closest sister, "Jane, it appears that we may have more opposition to our plans than we initially thought. Fitz... Mr. Darcy believes his Aunt Lady Catherine, and perhaps even his cousins are trying to prevent us from marrying. He took Mr. Bingley away to talk privately, in order to persuade him to marry as soon as may be with us."

Jane's eyes widened. "Lizzy, do you think it is really as necessary as that? I mean, I did see this morning that his aunt seemed upset, but do you think she or the Viscount would really do something to prevent you and Mr. Darcy from marrying? I had not thought that Lord Fitzwilliam is so very bad. In fact, he seemed rather friendly."

"I think that I am convinced of it now more than ever Jane. The Viscount was too friendly. With me being engaged to his cousin, he acted overly friendly for a man in his position. After what Mr. Darcy told me, I am no longer certain that they would not try to do something to compromise our reputations, and since you are also to marry soon, it may affect you and Mr. Bingley as well. By compromising one of us, it would ruin us all. Do you not see that?"

Jane looked apprehensive, but Elizabeth knew she had enough sense to see the truth of the matter, "Yes... I guess you are right, but it is so terrible to think that people would be willing to do something so... so... despicable."

"Well? Will you say that you would be willing to marry Mr. Bingley as soon as possible to avoid any such scandal?" Elizabeth was hopeful.

Jane did not answer immediately and after a moment said, "Yes, I would do anything to be married to him as soon as possible."

"Thank you, dearest Jane."

"Do not thank me, Lizzy. We would have done it sooner if we thought it proper."

~*~*~*~

The gentlemen rejoined Jane and Elizabeth after twenty minutes. Elizabeth now wanted more than ever to become Mrs. Fitzwilliam Darcy. She reminded herself what she had to look forward to, and shivered at where her intimate thoughts took her. Darcy came to her side immediately.

"Did you have a meeting of the minds, dearest?"

"I should think so my loveliest Elizabeth. Bingley wants to discuss our plans with Jane, and depending upon what she decides, we will marry in the same ceremony, or we will marry alone."

"I do believe that I have convinced Jane, as she said that they would have married sooner if they thought it proper."

"Funny that. That is exactly what Bingley said to me, so it sounds as if we will be wedded very soon, pending your father's final word." He looked worried, and added,

"Pray forgive me Elizabeth, but I need to discuss something else. I think it best for now that as few people as possible know about our plans, and... I think that if Mrs. Bennet knew, it might not be as secret as it needs to be."

Elizabeth knew the sad truth and acknowledged the truth of it, "Yes... as much as I hate to admit it, my mother hardly has a discreet bone in her body. I will not tell her, at least not until this is accomplished." She gave him a weak smile.

"Shall I go to your father then?"

"Yes, you shall!"

The couples waited until after dinner before they could even approach Mr. Bennet. Elizabeth felt knots in her stomach, worrying over weather her father would allow them to marry even sooner than planned or if he would throw up his hands and refuse to deal with this as he had been known to do before in difficult situations.

She could hardly eat anything due to her nerves. *I never thought that I would turn into my mother, and here I am now, all full of nerves, and anxiety. I am sure that things will work themselves out, if papa will just listen to Fitzwilliam, and not disregard his advice.* Though she loved and admired her father, she gained more and more respect for her fiancé as she became more familiar with him. She saw that Darcy was a man of action who would anticipate trouble, and act to ensure that issues did not affect those he cared, or was responsible for. It was another reason for her to look forward to spending the rest of her life with such a man. *He is the very best man I know.*

After dinner Mr. Gardiner suggested that the men separate from the ladies. Elizabeth knew enough to tell that her uncle noticed the close gatherings between the engaged couples, and she was fairly certain that her Aunt Gardiner would have mentioned the episode with Lady Catherine and likely the overly familiar behaviour of the Viscount. She could not help but feel as if she should be involved in their discussion; however, she knew her mother would become suspicious if she were allowed within the men's group.

For her it seemed like torture listening to her mother talk incessantly about wedding details. Luckily for her, the gentlemen joined the ladies within a few more minutes, and she was spared going bald, by adding more intelligent, quiet conversation to the gathering.

She noted her father with a defeated and withdrawn look, and was concerned. Wanting to know more of the details, she searched the faces of those that had joined them. Mr. Bingley seemed happy, quiet and content, her uncle was his usual reserved self, but she thought she detected a hint of worry upon his countenance. Darcy was wearing his mask, but she could not detect any change in his demeanour from earlier, and took it as a good sign.

He came over to sit next to her at the window seat, and leaned in to whisper. "All shall be well, Elizabeth. We shall be married by this time tomorrow, but your father wishes to speak to you after we leave."

She stared at him and nodded in understanding. *Of course papa will want to talk about this. Even he would take the trouble to discuss such important matters before they are to take place.* "Am I to presume, sir, that you have received his approval for carrying out your plan?"

He smiled into her eyes, "Indeed I have, Elizabeth. Bingley and I are to marry you and Jane in the morning, but he needs to impart some important information to both you and your sister. I would tell you myself, but I do not want to risk being overheard."

She smiled weakly, nodding her head. Though she always enjoyed Darcy's company, she being naturally curious, was burning to know more of the details. She understood though, why Mr. Bingley and Darcy made their excuses to leave earlier than usual. They had much to accomplish before the morning, and apparently so did she and Jane.

Darcy, of course, made his usual elegant bow and lingered over her hand caressing the back of it with his lips, while Bingley seemed like a child on Christmas Day. She and Darcy smiled knowingly at each other before he ascended into his carriage. She watched him ride away towards his town home with Mr. Bingley in tote.

I am sure not to get any sleep this night, and I do believe Jane is in for the same fate! The only thing she had left to do now was discover Darcy's encrypted message about 'important information' that her father would impart to her.

Chapter 34

Elizabeth was apprehensive as she approached the door to her uncles' study. She was her father's favourite child, and now her situation pained him. At that moment, she felt as though she were twelve years old and being called to her father's study for taking Kitty's favourite doll after placing it high upon a tree branch. She relaxed when Darcy came to her with a smile after he left her father. He said little about their discussion before he and Mr. Bingley left the Gardiners home. She understood that they were to make arrangements for tomorrow, but she still wished for more information about what they discussed.

In her heart she knew that her father could do little to protect her should something happen, and the best way to allow Darcy and Mr. Bingley precedence was to marry. *It would lend some credence to us, if Lady Catherine or the Viscount managed to place us in a compromising situation, and father has almost no influence here in town,* she told herself as she went to the study.

She squared up her shoulders, stuck out her chin, and knocked on the door. Hearing a muffled, "Enter," she opened the door and approached her father.

"You wished to see me, papa?"

"Yes, Lizzy, please sit down." He gestured to a chair across from where he sat.

Elizabeth looked at him apologetically. I understand, from Mr. Darcy, that you have agreed to allow us to marry tomorrow?"

She knew by the look on his face that he was pained, and it pained her to witness it. "Yes, I do not believe that I have to tell you how I wish there were some other way to manage this situation. I have learned though, that in delaying your nuptials much longer, both you and Jane would be at risk of being compromised by the Viscount Matlock in some way, and I cannot allow that to happen."

His brows furrowed.

Elizabeth felt for her father's frustration, and it caused her some anxiety, but she also wanted to ensure that her father would fully support her... their decision. She knew that she loved Darcy, and had known that for some time, but now, with their happiness being threatened, she realized how precious Darcy had become to her. "Papa, please understand that in allowing this, you are helping to ensure Jane and my happiness. I know that it seems too soon, however, I am not upset by this new development. Truly, Fitz... Mr. Darcy and I are quite compatible, and I have come to love him very much. He is the very best of men." She pleaded as tears ran down her face, and her father looked sympathetic.

"Lizzy..., I cannot tell you how much relief that is to me. My concern is for all what has come about as of late. You knew about that letter from Miss Bingley, and all of her accusations against Mr. Darcy, but did you also know about some of his relatives... ah... tendencies towards rakish behavior?"

Elizabeth hesitated before nodding her head, "Yes, papa, Mr. Darcy has already informed me about his families' involvement with some gamming, and... other *things*."

"Oh?" Mr. Bennet voice hinted of surprise.

"Yes, you see, Fitz... uh... Mr. Darcy, does not keep secrets from me. He knows that I would not discuss such private things with anyone. He trusts me with his heart, and I will not disappoint him." Elizabeth grew frustrated, blurting out, "If you have such serious reservations upon your part, sir, I feel it incumbent upon me to inform you that I would be fully prepared to elope with Mr. Darcy, should that become necessary."

Mr. Bennet sat stunned for a moment before he recalled himself, and laughed. I would not doubt that you would, however, I do not think that that will be necessary. As I have already told the gentlemen, 'I do not care about material wealth, but I do care about my daughters' happiness'. My concern for you was that you may not be aware of all that has been said in regards to Mr. Darcy's family while I have come to stay here. My lack of faith, though, demonstrates how little I know of your attachment to that gentleman, and how little I understand your devotion, but I am willing to trust your judgment, my dear."

Elizabeth's eyes lit up, "Does that mean that...?"

"That I am willing to go along with this charade? Yes, it is the best possible solution under the circumstances. I should mention, however, that we have decided... for the time being, both you and Jane shall still reside here, at least until the *planned* ceremony takes place."

He held up his hand at her look of surprise. "We thought it best not to add anymore scandal with a precipitous wedding. Besides that, if Mr. Darcy and Mr. Bingley's families were to learn of you and Jane's *earlier than expected marriages*, there is no telling what the fallout might be. We did not wish to put either of you through such turmoil."

Elizabeth nodded in agreement. "So... tomorrow, what will...?"

"Your Aunt and Uncle Gardiner, along with myself, shall arrange to take you and Jane out with some excuses that he and I are going to meet with some businessmen, and along the way your aunt and the both of you will be deposited to meet with a friend of hers." He had a twinkle in his eyes, "Really we are not saying anything untruthful, we shall just 'forget' to disclose that you and Jane are to be married along the way. Your aunt will request that your mother stay here in order to see to some urgent tasks things while she is out, thus giving your mother no reason to join you."

Elizabeth laughed at her father's cunning appreciating him all the more. *How I shall miss you dear papa.* "Is there anything else then, papa?"

"No, that is all. Now off with you now, I should think that you may want to plan for tomorrow, and I myself, have a few things to tend to." His voice regained some of its earlier sadness, but Elizabeth chose to dwell on that later as she had much to do before morning. She kissed her father on the top of his head and wished him a good night, and then went upstairs to her room where she could reflect on today's events. *Tomorrow shall be a new beginning*, she thought as she started to sort through her wardrobe for her best frock.

~*~*~*~

He wanted to ensure nothing interfered with his plans, and needed to work on a plan to 'catch' James and Caroline in their own web. He thought to send notes to both of them with the pretense that it was from the other, but he abhorred deceit so the next best thing was to assign someone to discretely watch them. So, he hired a couple of street urchins to keep an eye on Matlock House and Bingley's home, at least until he could determine if they were meeting clandestinely.

He knew that it would not be considered prudent to call out one's own relatives, but he was sorely tempted in this case. He was also anxious to have Caroline Bingley removed from town so she could not cause any more problems, but for that, they needed to wait upon Bingley's relatives up north. At present he was not complaining about his upcoming hasty marriage, though it was going to be difficult being married to Elizabeth and not being able to take her to his bed.

He continued to dwell on these more intimate thoughts until he could hardly keep his eyes open, finally falling asleep at two o'clock in the morning. *Just seven more hours and Elizabeth will be mine in the eyes of the church and the law, as well as in flesh.* He wished that he had not agreed to allow Elizabeth and Jane to stay at Gracechurch Street. He felt certain that was the part about this arrangement that Bingley disliked as well, but perhaps they could arrange some 'meetings' with their wives in private. With that thought, he finally settled into a decent slumber, his dreams were vivid and colorful.

Elizabeth came to him in the night with a very light gown of sheer material, decorated with lace and thin silky material, leaving nothing to his imagination. Darcy could feel his heart race and his trousers becoming very uncomfortable. He beckoned to her and she stepped forward in to his embrace. They began their kiss, lightly at first, growing more demanding until they were breathless. He felt even more aroused, and lightly caressed her shoulders, gently pushing aside the sleeves until her cleavage was joined by the full view of her breast.

Darcy bent down to kiss her, starting at her lips then moving over every area between there and her full, firm breast. He began to suckle at the hard tips of her nipples causing her to run her fingers through his curls and down his shoulders and arms.

Becoming even more excited, he picked her up in one swoop and carried her to the bed, laid her down and proceeded to draw off his shirt. When he looked back at her in the bed she was already joined by James, who began pushing her gown to her waist and was caressing her legs slowly, moving his hand up her legs towards her inner core. She did not seem to be objecting to his attentions, as she seemed to be calling, *"Darcy, Darcy... ooooooohh this is so wonderful... pleeeease do not stop."* She was mistaking his cousin for him. Darcy could feel the rage growing. He started to grab his cousin to remove him from Elizabeth, but he only seemed to be getting further back as he struggled to reach her. He tried to call out, but nothing came out of his mouth.

James looked in Darcy's direction, and smiled before he took Elizabeth in his arms. Darcy felt his heart racing in anguish and rage. He ran towards the bed with Elizabeth, and saw her nude and curled up in a ball, grasping her knees saying *"Oh, what have I done? What have I done?"* Tears were running down her cheek. Darcy wanted to run James through as he heard his cousin say to him laughingly, *"Now, you cannot have her, cousin. She will be mine! My mistress and lover!"*

Darcy found that he had a sword in his hand, but as he charged towards his cousin, the sword was gone, and his cousin had pierced his heart. He felt the burning ache, as he lay dying, and Elizabeth was reaching out towards him, only to be held back by James.

Darcy woke up practically bolting out of his bed, his covers thrown off, violently. His bedclothes were wet from perspiring in his sleep. Sitting up to the side of the bed, he contemplated the hidden meaning behind his nocturnal vision, thankful that today he would be able to protect Elizabeth from his family. *I am to be wed today and there is absolutely nothing that is going to get in the way of my happiness! They cannot separate us, no matter what now!* With that thought, he walked to his dressing room where his valet, Baxter, awaited his master already with prepared bath, and razor. Darcy was eager for this morning and was now rushing to get dressed then go down to breakfast. The minister would arrive at twenty till nine to go over the necessary paperwork with him before the ceremony. He also needed to get his mother's wedding ring out of the safe.

Bingley would be arriving about half an hour before the ceremony. Once Darcy retrieved his mother's ring he was able to sit and contemplate his next maneuver, regarding James. The more he thought it over, the more his dream put him in a foul mood. He was now certain that James had some nefarious purpose in mind when he came to the Countess' tea party. Though nothing was likely to happen while under his uncle's roof, he could not be so certain about James's appearance at the Bingley's home later.

He thought to keep a close watch upon Elizabeth as well, and wanted to warn Bingley to keep Caroline close at hand to ensure that she did not start any trouble either. If he knew James as well as he thought he did, then his plan would likely include somehow compromising Elizabeth in a public enough manner to cause scandal, though little did they know that she had already been compromised and it was due to *him*. That would not stop Darcy from doing it again with Elizabeth, but still it would be an embarrassment should *that* get out.

He had not forgotten about James' obligation to Mrs. Heatherton either. *Perhaps if there were a way to make him go take care of his other responsibilities, then he could not cause any more problems for us here. The only way that that would happen though was if the Earl and Countess somehow made him go… but it would take a scandal for them to do that. They would never want to acknowledge that they had failed their duties with Richard and James, unless they absolutely had no other choice!* Darcy continued to ponder this until Bingley arrived at Darcy House.

Bingley greeted his friend in a slightly more agitated mood than was his norm, I say Darcy… I do not know how to say this but… well I came upon Caroline this morning in the park. She did not see me however, and she was meeting with…" He sounded disgusted, "With the Viscount Fitzwilliam!"

Darcy tried to school his face to reflect calmness when he responded. I see, and what were they doing?" *Probably at this moment planning to tear up our peace!*

"They were walking along and talking, but it was not just that has concerned me… well it was the proximity that they were doing so, and the Viscount had the audacity to place his hand on the small of her back in a most indecent manner! I mean really if he were not your cousin Darcy, I would call him out!" Bingley started to sound somewhat irate, which for him was uncharacteristic.

Darcy suddenly had a thought along those lines, "Bingley, I do not expect you to give the Viscount any special consideration due to his relation to me. I would certainly want my relative to be accountable for his behavior, and if necessary he should be called upon to act responsibly." Darcy finished smoothly. *This may be easier that I thought!*

Bingley looked up at him in near astonishment, then said, "Well then, when we have claimed our brides, then perhaps you as my new *brother*, can go over to *our* relatives house and have a chat with him!"

"That, I will do, most readily, sir. After all we cannot have a scandal upon our hands as it will involve both our families."

"Indeed!" Bingley replied.

They would have continued on in this vain, if it had not been for the butler, Humphreys, announcing that the minister had arrived. They were on schedule and the three of them went over the necessary paperwork. After everything was seen to be in order, they had but a minute or two before the Bennet's arrival, along with Mr. and Mrs. Gardiner. Both gentlemen were noted to have a happy glow when Jane and Elizabeth arrived in the room. Darcy felt guilty that he had not included Georgiana in these plans, but felt it best not to delve into the suspicions he had about their own cousin with her. She was with the Countess frequently, and it would be difficult for her to maintain an easy presence if she knew of the sundry goings on.

Both couples were eager to begin, though Mr. Bennet noticeably tried to slow things down with conversation between himself and the minister, and Mr. Gardiner. Darcy called the room to order. I am sure we all know what has brought us here today, and if it is agreeable to everyone, shall we start the proceedings?" He said, not really asking, but trying to be as polite as possible.

"Yes, I believe that we are ready to proceed." The minister directed towards the couples.

Darcy's mind had been so busy thinking about his conversation with Bingley, he could not find the words to convey how beautiful Elizabeth was when he caught his first glimpse of her.

They stood side by side in his parlor, along with Bingley and Jane. The minister began, "Dearly beloved we are gathered here..." As the minister droned on, all Darcy could think of was his exhilaration of *finally* being married to Elizabeth, and when he heard, "Do you Fitzwilliam Alexander Darcy take Elizabeth Rose Bennet to be...?" he addressed Darcy.

"I do," he said in his most serious baritone while looking into Elizabeth bright and sparkling eyes.

"Do you Elizabeth Rose Bennet take the Fitzwilliam Alexander Darcy for your lawfully wedded husband, to have and to hold from this day forward, in sickness and in health for richer or for poorer, so long as ye both shall live?" The minister directed to her.

"I do." She said in her melodic and soft voice.

Darcy felt his heart swell as they said the rest of their vows, and at last they were pronounced man and wife. *She is mine! No more need for worry, or for impropriety*. He thought until he remembered that she would still be living with her father at Gracechurch for another week and a day. He hoped that he would remember to act with propriety around her until their marriage could be publicly acknowledged.

Bingley looked to be in raptures, but Darcy knew that soon he would have to pull him away. They still had to confront James. *At least there is nothing else that can happen to delay our vows, scandal or no!*

Darcy took this opportunity to thank the minister and Mr. Bennet and finally Mr. and Mrs. Gardiner for their assistance, I must tell you how grateful we are," He nodded his head towards Elizabeth who was smiling up to him with those lovely eyes, "and I want to take this opportunity to invite you all to Pemberley at anytime, as we are now family."

Elizabeth glowed even more with this invitation, "Yes, I do hope to see you all join us when you have the opportunity, and I have especially heard that the library is most excellent there. In fact," She teased, I have heard that it is one of the best in the country." He flushed, knowing that she referred to their time at Netherfield.

While his new bride chatted with her family, he joined

Charles and Jane who stood in a corner talking quietly, I hope, Mrs. Bingley, that you are able to join us soon at Pemberley… Mrs. Darcy, I am sure would be delighted to have her sister come, and I think that you will agree that the landscape is simply gorgeous, especially in the winter."

Jane smiled serenely, I thank you Mr. Darcy, and I hope that now we are brother and sister that you will call me 'Jane'."

"I will, if you will call me 'William'", he smiled appreciatively.

"I thank you, sir... William."

Elizabeth joined them then, "Yes, I will miss you... all of you actually, and I hope that you and Mr. Bingley will soon join us."

"Of course, Lizzy, you know that we will."

Darcy thought of something else. They had yet to decide their plans to leave once they celebrated the holidays with the Gardiners and the Bennets. This would be the first year that Darcy could remember looking forward to Christmas in a long time. "You, and Bingley will likely be joining us as has been our usual habit. We visit at Pemberley several times a year, you see. We have gone there to hunt during the season for as long as we have known each other, as a matter of fact." He wanted to reassure Elizabeth as much as anyone about the changes that would soon be coming to her life.

Jane looked gratefully to her new brother. "Mr.... I mean, William, I must thank you as well for doing this for us. I do hope things work themselves out as to the reasons we had to do this in secrecy, but I am grateful none-the-less that you and Charles are looking out for our best interests."

Darcy felt a swell of pride at her words of praise. I would not have it any other way, Jane. I would move heaven and earth for Elizabeth, and her family."

"And we have been looking forward to this morning as well. It is so sad that we shall have to part and not start our new lives together." Elizabeth joined.

Darcy looked at Elizabeth tenderly. "Soon my love, very soon this pretense will be done with, and we *will* be able to start our lives together, possibly sooner than later."

Darcy had the staff plan a tea and biscuits that was slightly more than what would customarily be served, but as there were few servants that were aware of what they were all doing, he did not want to create any suspicions.

It was a difficult departure when Bingley and Darcy had to relinquish their wives to Mr. Bennet and the Gardiners, but they managed to extract a promise that they would be allowed some private time within a day or so, and with that promise, the two gentlemen would have to sustain themselves. They would, of course, be joining them as was their usual habit, for dinner, as absolutely nothing in their habits were to change until they were publically recognized as husband and wife.

Darcy and Bingley took their newfound prerogative to kiss their wives goodbye, and also had some privacy to express some affection before their departure. Darcy took Elizabeth aside to his study under the pretense of giving her a wedding present. "This, my love, is for you." He gave her a velvet covered box that contained a beautiful pearl necklace with a large sapphire in the center surrounded by diamonds.

Elizabeth was speechless as she looked at the gift, "Oh William, this is so beautiful, but you should not have gotten anything for me, for you are the best present I could ever receive... and I had not the time to get you anything." She looked at him bashfully through her lashes.

He stepped forward to caress her neck and moved his hands to her shoulders. .Elizabeth," he said softly, "It was no great effort, as it was my mothers, and it is meant to be my wife's... and now you are my wife! So you see, as soon as you said 'I do' it was yours."

Tears welled up in her eyes at his tender words, and she stood on her tip toes to kiss him full upon his mouth. He greedily accepted her offer, and quickly deepened their kiss, moving his hands to caress her form and cup her bottom, causing a slight moan from Elizabeth. It was in this position that they were interrupted by Mr. Bennet who simply cleared his throat... several times before they realized they had company.

"I hate to interrupt this *private* moment between two newlyweds. However, if we are to keep up our pretenses as to a wedding in a few days, then we really *must* be going. As Mrs. Bennet, I believe, has other duties for us to attend." Mr. Bennet said dryly. Even Darcy knew Mr. Bennet well enough by now to know that he would not be amused by such a display, married or not.

Both Darcy and Elizabeth were flushed, more with passion than embarrassment though, and regretfully relinquished each other. "Sir, if I may thank you for allowing us this day. As I said before, I only suggested that we do so for their protection, and I *hope* that we can resolve those precipitating issues sooner rather than later." Darcy said meaningfully to his new father-in-law.

"Indeed?" Mr. Bennet sounded curious.

"Well it has come to our attention that there has been some activity that would be incriminating to certain parties should they not act... appropriately." Darcy finished.

Mr. Bennet indicated his interest but realized that this was not exactly the time to divulge all and simply said, "Then I hope that you can join your wife and new family this evening, and we may have some time to discuss this then, sir?"

Darcy replied, "Of course I will be *very* happy to join you all," More looking to Elizabeth than her father, "And perhaps, then we can discuss how to reunite with our brides, once this is resolved."

"Of course, of course... well then, until tonight, sir." Mr. Bennet said to Darcy. I wish to have a private audience with you, if you can spare a moment, sir?"

"Yes, yes of course. Elizabeth, I shall join you in a moment, if you do not mind?"

Elizabeth bit her lower lip, and nodded her head. She glanced back at Darcy with a fretful look before she closed the door.

"Mr. Darcy, I realize that you are a newly married man, and my Lizzy..." he paused to clear his throat, "is of a passionate nature, however, I need not remind you of our agreement from earlier, do I...? That you and Elizabeth shall appear as still engaged until the proper timing to announce this rather... expedient ceremony."

"Of course not, sir... Mr. Bennet. I had a momentary lapse there, but I might add, we tried to act discretely, after all we came into my study, and the doors were closed."

"*That* is precisely how an engaged couple would *not* act, sir. If this ruse is to work, you would do well to remember that!"

Darcy had to admit that his new father-in-law made an excellent point, and he had to concede that it would look scandalous even for an engaged couple to behave in such a way. *This is going to be a very long week or two*, thought Darcy wryly. "Yes, you are correct, sir. We will endeavor to remember propriety for appearance sake. At least until these issues are resolved."

Mr. Bennet raised his eyebrow, and appeared as though he might say something else, only to shake his head.

Darcy and Bingley watched as the carriage took their wives away, and once they could no longer see the conveyance, Bingley said to Darcy with a determined look, "Well, *brother*, shall we make our way to Matlock House and tend to our *other* business?"

Darcy raised his eyebrow and said, "Yes, we shall."

Chapter 35

The carriage ride to Matlock House was tense as Darcy and Bingley sat face to face. Bingley was still distressed over having to leave Jane with his new father-in-law. He wanted nothing more than to take her home and officially make her his wife in every way. But with this new situation, it was impossible to expose them to what the Viscount Fitzwilliam and Caroline were planning, not to mention Lady Catherine de Bourgh could or would do. *No, Darcy is right about needing to protect them. My G-d, after what the viscount has done to his own brother, there is no telling what the man is capable of!*

He did not want to believe that his own sister would betray him in such a way and all because of her obsession for Darcy. *No Caroline, I will no longer stand idly by and allow you to continue your social climbing antics. You will be made to heel, and you are going to soon learn what that entails! You can no longer do anything about Darcy, and your behavior towards that rakish viscount will earn you your first, very hard lesson!*

It could not be said that he was too disappointed about the outcome of the whole business, as he had his 'angel' much sooner than he anticipated and now his best friend was also his brother. Though, the part about having to live as if it had not occurred until the whole mess was cleaned up galled him. It was that, more than anything else that drove him from Darcy's house after he watched Jane's carriage take her away. He resolved to force the issue with the viscount, and then Caroline. He also hoped that it would not call for a duel, as those were nasty business and he was not as proficient as Darcy was with a weapon.

When he saw his sister and the viscount this morning, his first inclination was to march over, tear them apart, and confront the viscount; however, this was no ordinary morning, as he was getting married later this day. The moment he spotted them, his first instinct was to do precisely that, but he knew if he did, then he would alert Caroline and possibly the viscount, something was afoot. So, he controlled himself until after his wedding.

They arrived at Matlock House and were shown to a back parlor by the butler, as they wished to meet with the viscount alone. That gentleman had arrived to the house when the visitors were announced and seemed surprised when Bingley arrived with Darcy. "To what do I owe the honor of this visit by you and Bingley, Darcy?"

Darcy glared at him. "Believe me, James, if I had any other choice I would not be here at all."

"I am guessing then, that I shall have to apply to Bingley here for an answer."

Bingley had been listening to the viscount's banter and could feel his ire rising, "*Sir,* it has come to my attention that you have been seen in various *public places* with my *sister,* Caroline, and behaving most abominably. The latest episode was this very morning. I observed you to be very close in proximity to her... person, and touching her in an intimate manner. *That,* viscount, is why we are here!"

The viscount merely raised his eyebrow and shrugged his shoulders. "So we had a walk in the park, and were closer than you are 'comfortable' with." He had the audacity to roll his eyes upward, I must say that it was not my idea to meet there. Miss Bingley seemed rather... eager to come into my pathway. I assure you that had I had my way, that would not have happened."

"If that is the case, then why did you agree to do so, James? Why not *act* the part of gentleman and beg those excuses to Miss Bingley you are so quick to give us now?" Darcy retorted angrily.

"*That* would be abominably rude of me, would it not? After all, I am a gentleman."

Bingley snorted and said, "*That* remains to be seen! If you were a true gentleman, then you would not encourage such behavior! *Look,"* Bingley became more impatient with how things were progressing, "as the head of *my* household I must insist that you redeem Caroline's reputation with marriage!" Bingley blurted out.

The other two gentlemen stared at him for a few moments before the viscount laughed, "*What?* Marry Miss Bingley? You must be *joking!*

That is a ridiculous idea! Why, there is absolutely no *reason* for me to do such a thing! I must say, if this is why you have come, then I *am* highly amused, but if you truly believe I would entertain such an idea, then you are *both* sorely mistaken."

Darcy glared icily at his cousin, as did Bingley; both of them were so angry that it would not have been surprising to hear one of them issue a challenge at that moment.

Unfortunately now that they were married into the same families, that was no longer an option, and Bingley did not want to risk death before he could enjoy his marriage.

Darcy responded, I do not think that the earl or the countess would appreciate learning that you have not only behaved in such a way as to conceive a child with your mistress, but then trifle with a gentleman's sister. There are other issues to take into account, James. I should mention that I am aware of certain, shall we say 'problems' you have with another peer, which may be solved with the right 'strategies' so that you may be able to solve some of your 'issues'."

James turned pale at the threat inherent in his cousin's voice. "You would not dare!"

"Yes, frankly I would, James. Especially after what you have done! I have been keeping an eye on you, cousin, and I am aware of your movements… I think we both know the reasons behind that! Is it not enough to have put Richard through what you did, but now to treat a lady in such an infamous manner? Tell me, did you do this of your own accord for seduction, or were you commissioned to do this?"

"I… I am sure I do not know what you are talking about, Darcy! I have done nothing wrong!"

Darcy rounded on him, and stood a few inches from James' face, "Nothing wrong? Nothing wrong? How can you say such a thing, when I know that you have a known history of debauchery, gaming, and even plotting against your own family? You have been seen with our aunt, Lady Catherine, no doubt cavorting with her in order to disrupt my plans! I will not allow you to interfere with my life, James. I will see to it that the earl and countess know all. If you do not behave as a true gentleman, then you can figure out how to deal with your 'friends' yourself without any help from the family!"

"What are you talking about, 'behaving as a true gentleman'? I always…"

"No! No, you do not always behave as one! What we mean is for you to make your own decision within, say, a week, else we shall act accordingly!"

The thought of Darcy being Caroline's advocate was a sight Bingley never thought he would behold. Darcy usually held his sister in contempt, however, now that certain intelligence has come to light, Darcy seemed to be helping Caroline to make a match. *But, why does Darcy care at this point?*

It was not unusual for people in their set to behave as the Viscount did. That is to say, it was not too shocking before, but now… well this was personal. He now understood how the brothers and fathers of other families could feel so offended. That all had changed when he became aware of Viscount Matlock's machinations towards Mrs. Darcy, Caroline, and possibly even his Jane.

Suddenly he realized that his whole set of priorities had shifted. He now had to act as defender of those who were under his protection and that did not just include Jane, but Caroline as well. He spoke up with more authority, "Viscount Fitzwilliam, I will give you one week to act honorably or I will go to the earl and countess. Then I will call you out! I have had enough of your behavior towards Caroline."

"Judging by your behavior and hers, you are both likely to enjoy the others company to the same degree! As it is, I am not proud of her behavior, but I am disgusted with yours! You sit there ignoring all the rules set for decent society, acting as if you are exempt from these same rules, to treat people in such an abominable manner! All in all, I rather think the both of you deserve one another. Now with that said, I will not *allow* you to drag *our* family through a scandal. I *insist* you act honorably… *sir*!"

Such a speech from Charles Andrew Bingley was so shocking, that both Darcy and the viscount stared silently at him. In fact Bingley himself was amazed he had that in him. If the truth were known, he was rather proud of his recently acquired self esteem. He actually felt liberated.

Darcy spoke, I do not believe we will be dueling… or calling anyone out, but I agree that there must be a resolution, and the one proposed is certainly within rights, James. You should consider your next move *very* carefully before making any hasty decisions. In the meantime, I believe that you have some arrangements to make, as I have some outstanding issues with a certain tenant in Lancashire."

The viscount frowned at his cousin fiercely for a moment, finally saying to no one in particular, "Fine, I will *consider* my options, and for the time being I will stay away from Miss Bingley… that is, if she will stay away from me."

Without anymore pleasantries of conversation Darcy and Bingley stood up and stiffly took their leave. They would have to keep a close eye on the Viscount. *Oh, what an unhappy beginning to my wedding day, first I must send my bride back to her father, and then I need to practically call out my new cousin for trifling with my errant sister!* With those thoughts, Bingley left Matlock House to Darcy House. From there, he would go and confront Caroline about her part in the little rendezvous in the park, but first he wanted to ask Darcy about his revelations to the Viscount.

"Darcy, I thought we were going to keep some of the issues surrounding your cousin to ourselves. What happened back there?"

"Bingley, part of that came from frustration, and I am sorry to reveal what I did. I had thought I might be able to spare your sister the embarrassment of having a philandering gamester for a husband, but then again, there is nothing we can do to convince your sister that James is not being sincere in his attentions. I would not like to be saddled with someone who only values me for my material assets. Besides, you have time to gauge any public scandal. You do not need to force the issue, at least not immediately. As to the other issue, well… let us say that I have my reasons for such revelations."

Bingley thought about Darcy's explanation which, now, seemed to make more sense. He nodded his understanding. *No, Darcy, I would not want my sister saddled in a marriage without affection either.* He still needed to think about what to say to Caroline. He would insure that she could do nothing to disrupt his peace.

~*~*~*~

When the Gardiners and Mr. Bennet arrived back to Gracechurch Street with Jane and Elizabeth, Mrs. Bennet was in an uproar. The Gardiner children and the two youngest Bennet daughters were as noisy as could be. The nanny for some reason had been given the morning off, leaving Mrs. Bennet in charge of the household.

The returning party heard from that lady about her poor nerves as soon as they came through the door. They all tried to sooth her, reminding her that she not only had a wedding to plan, but needed to get the other girls ready for the Shetler's Ball. Suddenly, her poor nerves were forgotten in an instant as Mrs. Bennet effused enthusiastically about her certainty that by capturing Mr. Darcy and Mr. Bingley, Jane and Elizabeth would surely put the other three girls in the way of other rich men.

"Oh my, yes, we must be going to the finest warehouses for Lydia's, Kitty's and Mary's new ball gowns as well. We also need to go to the modiste and finish the fittings for your and Jane's gowns, Lizzy."

"Ma'am, we do have some little more time before we need to worry about that…"

"Oh, do not be silly, child! You have no idea what a time it is going to take to get you ready for your wedding day! You will need to look your very best, and since you are not nearly as pretty as our dear Jane, it should be especially important to you. But then again, you never have been one to consider your looks when it comes to men…" Suddenly it was as if Mrs. Bennet was struck with another thought entirely.

If Elizabeth dreaded having a discussion with Mrs. Bennet about how she should look to attract a man, then she dreaded the discussion about what happens after she has actually attracted one even more. *This is not going to be pleasant!*

Mrs. Bennet leaned towards Jane and Elizabeth and said, I suppose it is about time we had a little discussion about what your husbands will expect from you on your wedding night. Now, girls…" She was ushering them towards an unoccupied room in the back of the house. When Elizabeth cast a pleading look towards Mrs. Gardiner, she followed the group towards the small parlor as well.

They were all flushed with the thought of what was about to assail their senses. As Mrs. Bennet spoke to a mortified Jane and Elizabeth, she looked in any direction but towards them.

"Oh, good Madeline, this is so good of you to help me to explain to the girls what will be expected of them when Mr. Bingley and Mr. Darcy... umm... take them... to... well on their wedding night."

Elizabeth caught the sympathetic look from their aunt as Mrs. Bennet began, "Now girls, when you are wed, your husbands will join you in your bedchambers and lie down with you..."

By this time Elizabeth felt her entire body was going to burn up. As she already learned what would happen when Mr. Darcy joined her in bed, she had little to no desire to hear her mother's rendition of her 'marital duties'. She tried to tune out as she heard her mother say, "When you lie with him for the first time, it may be painful at first, and if he is skillful, he may touch you... down... there which will ease things for... you. Then he will lie on top of you and... and place his... hi... himself inside you... and you will feel some pain, as he begins to move in and out of you."

If Elizabeth could find a way to make herself invisible, she would take this opportunity to do so as she could not imagine her mother causing so much mortification to her in her entire life... not even with the dance at Meryton or the Ball at Netherfield... and possibly not even the one time at Johnson's general store when Mrs. Bennet all but announced that Jane was essentially going to be engaged to some suitor from town who 'wrote her some very pretty verses', and was expected to come to Longbourne any day to requests her hand in marriage... *but that had been many years ago. No this has got to be one of the most embarrassing moments of my entire life.*

She snapped out of her reverie in time to catch her mother say, "And if you are fortunate your husband will finish his activities and leave you to your peace until he desires you again in that way, but then of course after he has brought you with child he will likely not wish to repeat such activities again until after you have been delivered. Then, if you are fortunate you will only have to endure that again one more time, unless of course your first child is a girl and... well pray that you have a son first, then you will not have to endure that experience more than twice."

Elizabeth could not help herself from thinking that not only was she desirous of repeating said activities with Mr. Darcy; she could scarcely wait until they could repeat them. *So what if I am brought with child? He would not be likely to withdraw himself from me due to that circumstance.* Suddenly Elizabeth could feel herself becoming warm at the thought of engaging in 'marital duties', and now that they were actually married she could feel all of the frustration of their circumstances.

There was nothing more than she desired than to be alone with William in their bedchamber, and especially in his bed. She did not realize how much she was going to miss him for the next eight days... well she would see him of course but could they actually... manage to be together long enough for them to enjoy those carnal pleasures? She vowed to try and find a way to do so, for after all Mr. Bennet did promise to allow their husbands some moments of privacy now that they were actually married. Mrs. Bennet finally looked at Jane and Elizabeth's embarrased blushed and asked, "Now... do you have any questions, girls?"

Neither one of them seemed to want to ask any questions, nor could Elizabeth look at anyone for mortification at her mother's views of the marriage bed. Somehow she managed to look at her aunt whose look seemed to say, "We shall discuss these things later." *At least she has some sense when it comes to such things.* Elizabeth thought of the near mute Jane who seemed to be frozen to the spot where she sat, and was staring down at the floor still with a bright red flush. *Perhaps it is time we had a discussion as well.*

Elizabeth and Jane were left sitting in the parlor while Mrs. Bennet made her quick exit having dispatched her motherly duties. Mrs. Gardiner said in her gentle easy voice, "Do not worry girls it really is not as bad as all of that."

As soon as Jane had regained her bearings they to left the parlor to ready for another round of shopping for gowns. *It will not be soon enough for me to join William at our own home*, Elizabeth thought as her mother clucked on about all the lace and gown and jewels. She smiled when she remembered William presenting her with his mother's necklace. *Soon my love... very soon we shall be together and no one can ever separate us ever again!*

Chapter 36

After Elizabeth and Jane retired for the evening, Mrs. Gardiner joined them when the rest of the house settled down. She knocked on the door and they bid her to enter, she stepped in the room with a concerned look upon her face.

"I came here tonight to check upon you both as I feared you may have become alarmed at what you heard earlier from your mother," Mrs. Gardiner began. I also wanted to clear up any misconceptions that you may have formed about... well about what you may expect when you are with your husbands."

They both looked at her with a dark flush, though Elizabeth did more so due to speaking about the topic openly than the thought of the unknown. Mrs. Gardiner joined them on the bed and took both their hands in hers.

"Now I know that what Mrs. Bennet said was more due to her perception of how she views marital relations, however, not everyone has such an experience and... well in fact it can be rather pleasant if your husband's take the time to prepare you for... that activity."

Elizabeth could not help but smile as she tended to agree with Aunt Madeline in that respect. She felt that her first experience with Darcy was quite pleasurable, and the next time was even more so, but then he took his time with her and made sure she had her pleasure before he found his. She, in fact, looked forward to further conjugal activities with him as soon as may be, but certainly would not confess this to anyone, except perhaps to Darcy.

Mrs. Gardiner noted Elizabeth's smile and directed her next words towards her, "If you have not anticipated your vows, then you will be pleasantly surprised to find that your husbands will be able to provide you with much enjoyment in the activity as well… but it does take some patience."

Elizabeth felt as if she would burn up at that comment, but thankfully Mrs. Gardiner persevered. I do not wish for you to be unaware, however, your mother was correct when she said that when your husband first… penetrates you, you will feel pain and if you encourage him, until you become accustomed to him then, it will not be so uncomfortable the first time. After that, it becomes more pleasant all the more so as you become accustom to that activity."

Jane stared at the wall in front of her, still blushing. *At least this is not as frightening as ma'ma's speech! Jane would be scared out of her wits and would likely never consummate her marriage if she listened to her!*

"Now, do you have any questions dears?" Mrs. Gardiner asked.

Surprisingly to Elizabeth, the question Jane asked had more to do with after the act of consummation than before or during.

"Aunt Gardiner, what about… well… mama said, that when our husbands… or when we are with child, can one do this if you are?"

Mrs. Gardiner smiled, and answered, "Truthfully it is still possible to enjoy these activities when you are with child as well, and you should not allow that to determine whether or not you participate in such activities when you are with child."

Jane sat there and nodded her head without looking at anything else. Then she suddenly asked, .Aunt, how will we know when we are… you know, with… with child?"

Mrs. Gardiner took a breath, and then began, "Well, usually the first signs are fatigue and the absence of your courses, but that is a very vague sign. Later you will notice you are becoming ill at times, usually first thing in the morning, and you start to notice your breasts becoming more tender and feel fuller. But it is not considered definite until you feel the child quicken… that is when the babe's first movements are felt." She gave Jane an odd look at such questions, but did not ask further about it.

Elizabeth thought it a rather strange line of questioning for Jane to ask, but did not bother to think too much on it assuming that of all of the sisters, Jane would be least likely to act as she had with Darcy, well Jane and Mary anyway. She was still disturbed about what Jane saw when she and Darcy were observed in the library several days ago. She had always wanted Jane to respect her, and never have cause to question her actions or behaviours, and she felt as if she had seriously let her down in regards to *that* episode.

~*~*~*~

As promised, Elizabeth was delivered to Darcy House under the pretense of visiting with Georgiana. Of course, Darcy saw fit to ensure that Georgiana would not join them until a bit later. Darcy had some ideas as to what he wanted to do with his wife, and they did not include company. He sent one of his coaches to retrieve Elizabeth and Jane from the Gardiner's home, as Jane was to join Bingley.

By the time both gentlemen's wives arrived, they were nearly mad with desire, and getting somewhat irritable.

Neither of them had officially consummated their marriage vows... well in at least a publically acknowledged way anyway, and Darcy was anxious to exercise his carnal rights with Elizabeth as soon as may be. When Elizabeth and Jane stepped out of the carriage the men arrived eager to greet them and almost gave themselves away by kissing them upon their faces. Though Elizabeth was, by now, less embarrassed by such displays, both she and Jane colored at this affectionate demonstration in front of a servant. Since they wanted some time with their spouses alone, it was arranged at Darcy House due to the continued presence of Caroline at the Bingley residence.

"How are you ladies? Was the ride over here pleasant?" Bingley asked nervously as he looked at Jane.

Jane smiled and blushed, "Yes it was quite pleasant."

Darcy was staring at Elizabeth, momentarily speechless, "Well I suppose that we should go inside before we freeze out here. We would not like to have our bri...; lovely ladies take ill before we begin our lives together." He held out his arm for Elizabeth and placed a protective hand over hers when she accepted it.

"I am very happy to be here today, sir." Elizabeth commented as they walked up the stairs to the house.

"Well then, my dearest, you are in good company as I am very happy that you are here today as well." He smiled as he looked down into her face and felt a warm feeling coming from within himself as he saw her flush.

Darcy knew that it would be impossible to have any privacy at the Gardiners as there were too many people milling about, and he could hardly think with all of the commotion when he visited, besides that, he would not have the chance to take certain liberties anywhere else but his home.

The Bingley's went into the small parlor on the second floor while Darcy took Elizabeth to the library, though he was sorely tempted to take her to his bedroom and claim his rights upstairs.

This arrangement had to be, as neither gentleman wanted to rouse the suspicion of the servants, and it was possible for other family members to arrive which would necessitate an explanation that no one wanted to give at present. Richard would bring Georgiana with him in about two hours. He wanted to discuss some issues with Darcy, and that left precious little time for him to spend alone with Elizabeth.

For the time being, they sat in the library discussing travel plans to Pemberley, and Elizabeth's preferences for her sitting room and bedroom décor, which took all of ten minutes. Darcy noted long ago, that it was difficult to be in a room with Elizabeth for any amount of time before he became aroused, and today was no exception. They discussed plans for the Shetler's Ball, and certain attire that was required, when Darcy could not resist the temptation to start kissing Elizabeth along her jaw line, and down her neck. He pulled her onto his lap as he addressed her.

My dear you do not know how difficult it is listening to you talk of attire, when all I wish to do is remove yours from your person," he said, as he slowly moved his hand from behind her back to the top of her breast.

She smiled in understanding, "Surely sir, you are not having licentious thoughts while here in a library discussing such mundane topics?" She leaned forward and claimed his lips.

"Surely madam," he kneaded her breasts, starting with her nipple, "you speak in jest," He began to roll said nipple between his thumb and forefinger to her obvious delight. "As you know how very much

I would like to tear away every last stitch of clothing from you." He slid his hand under the neckline of her dress, "and instruct you in," he pushed the bodice of her gown off her shoulders, "the art of lovemaking and," he exposed first one breast then the other, "what better place to do said instruction," he lowered his mouth to her breasts to kiss the delicate skin, "than in the library?" He then began to suckle her hardened and pert breast to her delight.

Her response was to let out a low moan of pleasure as she could barely get out, "Indeed!"

Words were scarcely spoken for the moment as more grunts, groans, and moans emerged as they caressed and explored each other's bodies. Darcy managed to remove her bodice and had her exposed to nearly her waist as she helped him out of his jacket and vest, managing to pull his shirt tail from his trousers, then she massaged his back as her return for the favor to her lovely bosom. By this time most of their sense left them and they began to be bolder.

Darcy relinquished a breast, moving to her thigh, slowly drawing up the hem of her dress. Once that was found he slid his hand up her ankle and calf to her knee and finally to her thigh and beyond. He found her core, and she in return started to feel his firm arousal beneath her and rather hesitantly moved a hand over that spot causing Darcy to gasp.

He encouraged her to explore his body, as he wished to explore hers, "Yes my love, feel me. Feel my love for you." He took his other hand and placed it over hers encouraging her to massage his shaft.

She began to do his bidding, and her rhythm became more insistent. He unbuttoned his trousers at that point as his hardness became uncomfortable under the constraints of the garment. Darcy allowed Elizabeth to take more initiative as he began to massage her core with his other hand, finding the nub that caused her to gasp when he touched her.

"Oooooohhh …yeeeeeesss …Williammm…that feels …ssoooo goooooood." She moaned loudly. As his pace became more rapid, she began to massage his erect manhood with the same velocity. Suddenly he slipped two fingers into her wet folds and redoubled his efforts. She spread her thighs more to allow him to continue his attentions, and he obliged her by quickening his pace yet more until he felt her stiffen upon his lap and he could feel her womanhood contracting in rapid succession around his fingers.

She kissed him breathlessly, and began her attentions to his pleasure, stroking him with more effort until he felt his head would explode. He reached his climax and spilled his seed within her hands. For a few moments they sat, neither moving unless to ‚kiss each other breathlessly, until he realized that she needed to wash the evidence of his ardor from her hands. He felt for his coat which by now was upon the floor and dug through the material until he found his handkerchief, offering it to her.

After she wiped the milky substance from her hands, she said, I did not realize what it was that your body did when you… when you take your pleasure.. She flushed at that statement.

"Yes that is what happens when a man… releases his seed. Only usually it is within… inside a woman." He flushed with that admission as he was not accustomed to discussing such things, even if it was with his wife.

As he contemplated this, he began to feel the stirrings of passion building again and he leaned forward to kiss her, deepening their kiss with each passing minute, again moving his hand up to her breasts. Darcy could feel himself hardening yet again, and found it amazing that he could recover so quickly, but then again he was not one to complain about that either.

Both of then became so engrossed in their passion that they did not hear the doorbell nor the footsteps outside the library door until it open to a very shocked Georgiana, who was followed closely by Richard who grabbed the girl by the shoulders and removed her from the doorway immediately. Glaring at Darcy he then closed the door hard.

The couple looked at each other with a mortified expression upon their faces and Darcy wondered how he would explain this to his sister and cousin.

~*~*~*~

Caroline Bingley was furious. The night before Charles banned her from leaving the town house, practically accusing her of carrying on a public affair with the Viscount Fitzwilliam. To make matters worse, he did not even invite her to Darcy's townhome when he went there this morning. *This is intolerable! He cannot treat me in such a way! And I shall wager anything that he has gone over to Darcy's to carry on with that Jane Bennet while her sister offers herself up to Darcy! In fact I would wager my whole fortune that that is how she entrapped him and got him to agree to marry her! Well, we shall see what happens in a few months time when she ends up with a swollen belly and no husband! Ha! Then we shall see some justice!*

She became more desperate as time went on, worried that she would either be sent off to the Dugan's Estate, or she would need to find some alternative living arrangements. Marriage was much more palatable to her than being sent away from all fine society, but she was still secretly holding out hope that she could manage to entrap Darcy, and thus end this ridiculous business of his engagement to that chit from a small country shire.

She was busy pondering her own thoughts of how this could still be accomplished. Never one to forget a contingency plan, just in case another plan of hers did not work out, she still would keep the option open of an association with the viscount. *It would be nearly as exquisite to be the wife of a peer as one of the wealthiest men in the country*. The only way that she could achieve that, would be to allow him to compromise her in a public manner, and the Shetler's Ball would be the perfect opportunity.

Just as she finished her thoughts, the housekeeper announced a visitor. "Viscount Fitzwilliam to see you, ma'am."

Chapter 37

Once Darcy and Elizabeth righted their appearance, Darcy was the first to exit the library in search of Richard and Georgiana. He heard sounds coming from his study, and entered to find Richard pacing back and forth. Darcy was not sure what he wanted to say to his cousin, but he knew that he had plenty of explaining to do.

"Um... Richard..." He saw a glare of fierce proportions that he had never seen on the man, and stopped cold. I know what you are thinking..."

"*Oh? Do you? Do you really?* I think *not!*" Richard clenched and unclenched his fists as he glared at Darcy.

Darcy shook his head in frustration, I *can* explain this to you, and it is not what it appears..."

"*Oh*, I *beg* your *pardon* Darcy, I *thought* I saw you with Eliza... Miss Elizabeth, in a *very* compromising situation! You were undressing her, but I must be *mistaken*! You were *obviously* trying to help her with some malady, and her buttons suddenly came undone as well as her stays coming loose!"

Darcy was silent for a moment realizing Richard had gotten a *very* good look at what Darcy was doing to Elizabeth, "Ah, Richard, if you could just calm down I..."

"*Calm down? Calm down! Why* would I *calm down*? I *saw* you Darcy, and you cannot tell me that you were doing *anything* honorable with Miss Bennet! For G-d's sake Darcy, she is a *gentleman's* daughter, and you rounded on me for having a mistress! Who, by the way was nothing honorable, and was *not* a maiden!"

"Richard, if you could just give me a moment to defend myself..."

"*Why? Why* should I stand here and listen to your hypocritical tripe? *How could you Darcy?* What on Earth has gotten into you? I would never have treated Elizabeth like that!"

Darcy was surprised at his cousin's familiar use of his wife name, but chose to tackle that subject later. Besides, he was losing his temper at Richard's continuous interruptions.

"*Richard! Listen to me!* You do not know what you are talking about! Elizabeth was not being defiled by me because you cannot defile your *wife!*"

His cousin started, "*Wife?* What are you *talking* about Darcy? How could she be your *wife?*"

Darcy took a deep breath and looked up to the ceiling, pinching the bridge of his nose, before addressing his cousin, "A special license, that is how."

Richard paled momentarily while the truth of the matter struck him. He dropped into the nearest chair and kept staring at Darcy as his thousands of questions ran across his face.

Darcy contemplated whether or not to tell Richard about his and Elizabeth's hasty marriage, but due to the damming evidence, he felt it was warranted and he began, "Please understand, we did not wish to reveal this to anyone yet as, I am sure you know, that James has apparently been in collusion with Lady Catherine, to disrupt our plans to marry. Though, why he is taking so much interest in this, I have no idea. We… that is I felt I needed to protect Elizabeth from any scandal, and the best way to do so was to marry earlier than planned. I had already obtained a special license, and planned to marry in little more than a week, as you know. So it was not that much of a change. However, I need to find out how they were planning to interrupt *our* plans. Even though we are married, they could still try to harm the Bennet's name, and make Elizabeth's sisters' prospects more tenuous. I would not allow anyone to prevent our marriage in any event. Now, since we are actually married,"

He looked pointedly at Fitzwilliam who was starting to look uncomfortable, and explained further, "they can do nothing about it. Furthermore, if James tried to do something untoward to Elizabeth, I would be the one to demand satisfaction from him, not Mr. Bennet. I am sure you know how well a challenge from *him* would succeed.

James is so arrogant he would laugh at any challenge from Elizabeth's father, and then walk away."

He heard a snort from his cousin, "Yes, he *may* back down from you, and instead of dueling; you could demand he leave town. But, do you really think that this hasty secret marriage will protect... Mrs. Darcy after all he has done?"

"No, not in and of itself, but he is more likely to try seducing a woman who has one hundred times the consequence as... well, as *my wife*, if for no other reason than to try and extort money in order to buy his silence. As it was apparent to me, that he was already willing to compromise Elizabeth for whatever reason, I felt this to be the best solution to our dilemma."

At Richard's alarmed look, Darcy hastened to reply, I will not allow any harm to come to Elizabeth. I love my wife more than life itself. Unfortunately, I cannot announce that we are married until I stop James. After what he has done to you, and to Harriet Heartherton, not to mention the many other women he has seduced and debauched. He is not likely to stop unless he is *forced*. I need also not remind you that this could affect not just us, but Georgiana and Anne, as well. Our family's reputation could be in tatters, and he may continue in his ways unless we address this *now*."

"I see your point, and I agree. I shall also pledge my help in this endeavor to rein him in. I must confess though, it baffles me how you can be married to such a woman, and not want to exert your husbandly rights, Darcy."

"Believe me when I say that I would wish for Elizabeth and I to live together as man and wife without all of the sneaking around."

"Well, at least no one can say that you have not attempted to consummate it anyway."

Darcy looked sharply at Richard, I shall thank you not to speak of this *ever again*, Richard, and I must *insist* that you tell no other."

"*That*, I would not object to Darcy. However, I do think that you have some explaining to do to Georgiana. You do realize that she is bound to be shocked by her 'perfect' older brother groping a woman she believes to only be his fiancée in his library. It is bound to be quite shocking for her."

Darcy nodded in acknowledgement. "Yes, I know. I wish I knew what to say."

"Just *tell* her. She will understand, though, I think the next time you engage in such… activity, you should consider locking the doors, or go to a different room." Richard advised.

Darcy chose to ignore his cousin's jest at his expense, and left his study to find Georgiana. He searched everywhere until he found her in the solarium with a reddened tear stained face, Elizabeth sitting beside her. He slowly approached the pair and looked askance to Elizabeth.

Elizabeth immediately understood his wordless communication and she said, "It is alright now, William, I have told Georgiana of our news. She knows."

He hesitantly approached his sister, "Dearest, please do not cry. I was going to tell you. In fact, I would have had you present with us, but it was impossible to arrange as I… we did not want our aunt and uncle, and *especially* Lady Catherine to know."

The girl nodded her acknowledgement, barely able to look at him. I know," she said softly. "Elizabeth told me what was going on to cause you to marry earlier than planned, but surely you knew that you could trust me?"

"Oh dearest, it had nothing to do with that."

"Oh… I … thought that perhaps…"

"What?" He became more concerned with her reaction. "What did you think?"

He saw tears run down her cheeks as she began to cry again, and looked at Elizabeth.

Elizabeth softly began to explain, "William, Georgiana and I have had a conversation about what occurred earlier, and our desire to wed earlier, but she feared… that is she thought that you had not told her because of… due to Ramsgate."

Darcy felt as if someone drove a knife through his midsection. "No, no! Georgiana, that is not the reason at all, sweet pea. I would trust you with my life," He took out his handkerchief and started to dry her tears, I would never hold that against you. You were completely innocent of the whole affair."

She slowly looked up at him as if in assurance of his words.

"I… I heard Elizabeth say the same thing as well but… well, I still felt as if you did not feel I could be trusted with that information. I mean I know now that *some* people are like that and…"

Darcy felt all the more guilty at his young sister's witnessing him and Elizabeth in such a compromising situation and felt absolutely awful for having exposed her to his weaknesses. It was even worse to have her momentarily think that he could be anything like Wickham as well. "My sweet girl, please look at me." He brought her chin up to look him in the eye. I am so *very* sorry for even giving you a reason to think that I did not trust you to know about Elizabeth and my marrying earlier than planned. It had nothing to do with you or my trusting you, do you hear? Nothing whatever to do with my trust of *you*."

He sighed deeply. "You know of Aunt Catherine, and her designs on Anne and me marrying." He asked her as more a statement.

Georgiana nodded, and he continued, "Well, I hate to even have you know this much, but I fear if you do not hear it then you will not trust what I say about my faith in you. It appears that our cousin James has had some agreement with Lady Catherine to disrupt our plans to marry and," Georgiana had widened eyes at his proclamation, "They were trying to separate us, I know not how exactly, likely through a scandal. And the only way to protect Elizabeth was to marry sooner than planned."

Elizabeth joined the conversation at this point, "The only reason that we did not want to make it public was because William," she looked up and smiled at her husband, "wanted to find out their plan and expose them, not publically of course, but enough to chasten them enough not to interfere in the affairs of others… well, namely us. *We* did not feel that it would be fair to you to be put into the middle of this, and we felt that the less you knew about it, the better off you would be, but obviously we were wrong not to be able to trust you with that."

Elizabeth smiled at her new sister. "We were only trying to protect you."

Georgiana looked between both of them and asked, "Truly?"

They both nodded their heads, and said, "Truly."

Darcy saw the relief running over the girl's face, and gave her a quick hug. "Sweet pea, please know that we would never want you to be put in such a difficult position, and I am *very* sorry that you saw what you did. We never thought that you and Fitzwilliam would be coming so early and we... lost our heads for a moment."

The girl looked almost shocked again. I would never think that you were like that and especially with someone that you cared about, though, when I think of it I *was* quite surprised to find you and Elizabeth..." She flushed nearly scarlet, and her brother and new sister did as well.

They agreed that in the future if there were concerns that affected them, that they would discuss it rather than assume secrecy, as they found that it could be very awkward if they did not.

Soon they were joined by Bingley and Jane, who were blissfully unaware of the goings on earlier. Bingley spoke up, I say Darcy this is quite a room here, even in the winter. I do not suppose that you will be putting the flowers to good use for our wedding?"

By now the Darcy's forgot that they were still expected to 'marry' later, and they would not be able to publically acknowledge their union until afterwards. It was a sad reminder to them that they could not really be joined as a family until then.

Georgiana had looked surprised for a moment though. "We are still to have the 'big' wedding then?"

Darcy and Elizabeth acknowledged the need to continue with the plans, as there would be little else to do to discover what Lady Catherine and Cousin James were planning.

Bingley and Jane looked relieved at the news that someone outside of the couples, and the few essential family members necessary, knew about their marriages. I say, I will be glad when we can go out in public as man and wife, and not have to worry about what others are planning to do to interfere." Bingley stated.

Darcy agreed, "Yes, and our hope now is that we may be able to find out sooner than later. Then we can dispense with all the pretenses." He said with a bitter look.

"Yes but how can we accomplish that?" Elizabeth asked.

"The best way to find out is to go to the Shetler's Ball. The likelihood that they will try something there is probably greater, as it will be *very* public. We must keep a close eye on them though to ensure nothing happens to either Elizabeth or Jane. If I know anything, they will likely try to cause them to be discredited and try to disrupt our plans. If we are careful then we can catch them at their game, and all pretenses may be done away with."

The group was deep in thought when Humphrey's announced the Bennet's carriage had arrived to retrieve Elizabeth and Jane. After many heartfelt goodbyes, and a promise to call upon the ladies later that night, they regretfully parted.

After the ladies left the gentlemen, which included Richard, they discussed the plans for the ball. After hours of deliberation, they devised a plan and Bingley called for his carriage to depart.

~*~*~*~

Caroline Bingley stood up to greet her guest somewhat unsteadily, with a more pleasant manner than she felt earlier that morning. She imbibed on Charles' wine, consumed more than her usual, and earlier than she normally did. "Viscount Fitzwilliam, you are most welcome here, and such a wonderful surprise to have you in our home." Caroline nearly purred.

"Why, thank you Miss Bingley. It is good to see you." He looked around momentarily then began again, "I... actually wondered if... if your brother were at home?"

Caroline frowned, "Um... no, no he went out to..." She was rolling her eyes, "Darcy House, likely in hopes of catching a glimpse of his... ahem, fiancée."

"Ah," The viscount smiled slowly, "So you are," He raised an eyebrow, "All alone here?"

Caroline smiled slowly as well. "Yes... yes, I do believe so sir. Is there anything that I can do to help you?" She was eyeing him carefully.

"Well this is a most pleasant circumstance, madam. I actually hoped to have some time to talk with you, privately."

Caroline felt herself warm with the viscount's words. "Oh? Well then this is a most pleasant circumstance." Ignoring propriety she ensured that the door to the sitting room was secure, and invited him to sit on a chair next to her. "Now, sir, what may I do for you?" She batted her eyelashes.

He smiled at her eagerness to accommodate him, and he leaned forward slightly. I am sure that you know by now, that your brother has approached me to... what were his words? Oh yes, 'do the right thing by you', when he apparently discovered us walking in the park." He was watching her closely and unsteadily from what Caroline could see.

Looking at her companion closely, she realized he had alcohol on his breath. She quickly formulated a plan to ensure her escape from exile. "Viscount, I have had a discussion with Charles, and it does seem he has become quite implacable on this subject. He feels I have been compromised, and I assure you I told him that you are an honorable man, and you will do what you feel is right." She looked at him as if caressing his form.

Her gestures were noticed by the viscount as he, in what she would later conclude, was a loss of inhibition related to drink, got up and sat next to her on the couch. He swept a glance down at her body with a look that made her lower regions feel as if they were aching. "Miss Bingley..."

"Caroline." She purred.

"Caroline, what feels right for me is to..." He started to brush back some loose strands of hair and brought his hand down her jaw to her dresses neckline. "Kiss you." He leaned forward and did so, "And feel you within my arms." He began to caress her shoulders, his fingers just under the fabric of her neckline.

Caroline felt very warm in her feminine recesses, and enjoyed this novel sensation very much, "Oh viscount, you have no idea what you do to me sir."

He smiled, and continued to push the sleeves down her shoulders, kissing down her sparse breast line. "Caroline, if you would only allow me, I could do even more."

By this point Caroline had lost all her inhibitions as well, and said, "What sir, would that be?"

He glanced up from his task and smiled, "Allow me to demonstrate to you."

At her nod of agreement, he did indeed demonstrate how a woman could be pleased beyond measure, at least in Caroline Bingley's mind. After the viscount had sufficiently found his pleasure as well, they began to right their appearance. Neither one of them heard the approaching carriage coming up to the house. To their horror Charles Bingley arrived home, and burst through the sitting room doors.

Chapter 38

Colonel Richard Fitzwilliam stayed in Darcy's study while Darcy and Georgiana, along with Bingley, saw Elizabeth and Jane to their carriage. He felt rather displaced and restless, and not a little aroused at what he witnessed. Richard tried to convince himself that he was over his attraction to

Elizabeth, and now that she was his cousin's wife, she was irretrievably unattainable. *Oh, what a woman though! Such passion... D-mn Darcy anyway for being so bloody lucky!* There was no point in denying to himself that he was jealous of Darcy.

On some level, he always knew what it was to envy his wealthier and more handsome cousin, which is probably why he teased him mercilessly most of his life. Usually, Darcy was good natured about it. They had always gotten along well, almost as brothers, and normally Richard did not begrudge his cousin his privileges because he knew the price Darcy had paid for it. Darcy was always sought after for his wealth and connections… not that most of those were not shared with him, but as a second son he was only sought after as a relative of Darcy, or because he belonged to the noble family of Fitzwilliam.

Whenever a woman expressed an interest in Richard, he either felt as if she were trying to get to Darcy through him, or she wanted the family connection, but not now. Not with Elizabeth. When Bingley's party ventured into Hertfordshire in August, never did Richard know then that his peace of mind would forever be altered. Here was this country miss who had absolutely no regard for Darcy, and could not care less for who he was or what he did. In fact, Elizabeth almost seemed hostile towards Darcy at one point, but at the same time, she was warm and friendly to himself, and seemed to take an interest in *him*, Richard Fitzwilliam.

He knew it would be imprudent to entertain any ideas of wooing a woman of no fortune or connections as a mere colonel in His Majesty's Army, but he could not deny that she held certain charms that he had never before seen in a woman. With her lively manner and those eyes, and her lovely womanly figure... there would barely be a man alive that would not be able to appreciate her. But she was so much more than that. As he sipped his port, he sat heavily on the sofa, staring into the fire, remembering how entertaining she could be with her quick wit and parry's with Darcy and Caroline Bingley.

Suddenly his countenance grew cold. *Caroline Bingley, Lady Catherine, and James... the banes of my life! Oh how they do not deserve their wealth and privileges! To think that had it not been for their undue influence things, may have been different!* He got up to pace furiously. *What to do to repay them for their cruelty? For surely they should be punished! First Lady Catherine almost cheating me out of my inheritance, then my brother nearly cuckolds me with Harriet, and finally Caroline Bingley slandering me to Elizabeth! They deserve to pay for my agony!*

He tried to reason out what should be done to prevent them from irrevocably ruining Elizabeth's reputation, because she was the innocent in the whole of the group, and did not deserve to be treated so infamously. In times past, Richard would have defended his family to the death, but recent events had shown that they were the offenders, and this was the last draw for him. *Though I will never win your hand, Elizabeth, I hope to win your trust, and in time your friendship, for I vow to not let anything happen to you.*

He began thinking as a soldier... strategically. What he did know was, that Lady Catherine had always wanted Darcy to marry Anne, and she had always held to that belief steadfastly. *I would not put it past her to bribe someone to do her bidding, and soil an innocent woman's reputation just to get what she wants. Knowing James, he would be more than happy to do that soiling to! Perhaps that is what that blackguard and Lady Catherine were discussing last week when I met him in the hall at Matlock House?* That thought made Richard shudder, for he had a difficult enough time dealing with Darcy's handling of Elizabeth's luscious curves, and thinking about James touching her almost sent him into a fit.

James has the morals of a common alley cat, and probably a few diseases of one as well. There is absolutely no way that I will allow her out of my sight during the ball... none what-so-ever. If he were truthful, he would have to admit that that would have been the case anyway, as he always seemed to be seeking her out whenever they were at the same place. *For some reason, I just cannot resist her, and Lord help me if Darcy ever finds that out!*

If he knew his brother as he thought he did, then he knew James would do just about anything to compromise Elizabeth, so his plans must include some sort of distractions. *Perhaps some lovely but loose woman? Possibly some gaming, as James can hardly pass that up! But I need to keep Elizabeth away from him as much as possible too... well it would not be impolitic for me to pay my attentions to a woman who is to be my... cousin now, is it?*

He kept pacing back and forth, thinking about Caroline Bingley. *Now there is a social climbing woman if ever I saw one! She would be a good penance for James... umm... perhaps if I could get them paired up at the ball? She always seemed to like the powerful Fitzwilliam connections, and he is titled which seems to be something she covets. Not such a bad idea really.*

Lady Catherine would absolutely have a fit at that as well with him connecting himself to a tradesman's *daughter! What a lark!* As for his aunt, he tried to think of the best punishment for her, though not wanting to air their differences in public. He wanted to be assured she would not be tempted again to treat Elizabeth so badly. *Ah, but I know of one thing that will drive the old bat mad... no, that will have to wait until later, when everything is cleared up with this mess with James.*

Lady Catherine shall be made to suffer. His thoughts drifted back towards the object of his affections easily enough though. *Poor Elizabeth, she has already suffered such a rushed wedding I am sure devoid of all of the fineries... not that she would miss them, yet she so deserves to be treated like the lady that she is.*

Richard did not notice that Darcy had come back to the study to join him again. "Heavens Richard! Whatever are you doing pacing like that? You look as if you are about to embark upon a battle! For goodness sakes would you *please* stop that!"

Richard stopped at hearing Darcy's entreaty. "*What?*" he asked blankly.

Richard saw a hint of amusement in Darcy's eyes as his cousin addressed him again. "You have been pacing like that for at least the last five minutes. I know, as I have watched you."

Flushing at having been observed thinking about Elizabeth, of all people, he tried to cover himself. I was merely contemplating a strategy to ensure that nothing happens to… Elizabeth… oh and Miss… sus Bingley of course at the ball." He attempted to cover his embarrassment with a frown.

Darcy immediately dropped his amused mien and asked, "And? You were going to *share* those ideas with me, Fitzwilliam?"

"Well I had thought that perhaps we could keep James separate from Eli… Mrs. Darcy," Richard frowned momentarily, "And the only way to do that would be to ensure that they had others… *lots* of others to keep them company." He caught Darcy's glare. "What?"

"Yes, if you want to distract him. However, you forget, if Lady Catherine has commissioned him to do something to compromise Elizabeth, there is likely nothing shy of a pistol to stop him. He has the Fitzwilliam propensity to chase after women!" Darcy looked at Richard meaningfully. "Besides, I cannot bear to think of Elizabeth placed in a situation that may give him any opportunity. We need to keep an eye on him- *a very close eye!*"

"Yes, well I rather thought that we could enlist some help from Bingley. I even tend to believe Caroline Bingley may have her cap set to James, seeing how you are… soon to be known as out of the market."

"Well, that may work, after all. I almost forgot to tell you; Bingley and I confronted James about his going out in the park alone without an escort with Miss Bingley. Apparently he has been inappropriately close to her at certain times, and I myself have witnessed this as well. Bingley wanted to force the issue of marriage, I, however, felt it too hasty. James will not be forced into anything unless he believes there is something in it for him. I simply hinted that Miss Bingley has a sufficient dowry, and now he can sit and stew about that."

"So in other words, you gave him another focus, huh?"

Richard was impressed by Darcy's cunning.

"Precisely. Now he may be able to think about someone else other than Elizabeth, and hopefully, we can distract him enough for us to make our appearances, then leave, though you know how much of a sacrifice that will be for me." Darcy said dryly as he glanced at him sideways for a moment, and then they both burst out laughing.

Soon they separated and Richard parted company to join his friend from Brighton.

~*~*~*~

After a few deathly silent moments Charles Bingley finally found his voice at the shocking scene in front of him. He flushed scarlet at seeing the viscount with his trousers still slightly a kilter and Caroline most assuredly not in her best form, with her skirts up near her knees. When he found his voice it was nothing, if not furious,

"What in the hell is going on here? *Caroline*? *Viscount Matlock*! What do you think you are doing most *indecently*?" His glare could bore a hole through the both of them, more so to the viscount than to his sister.

Neither of them could say a word until they had made themselves more decent. Caroline began, "Oh, Charles! Do not be so... so... stodgy! The viscount and I were sealing our... our engagement."

Finally the viscount found his voice, "Hold up there just a moment, we are most assuredly *not* engaged!"

Both the siblings looked incredulous at him with their mouths agape. Caroline and Charles started protesting at the same time.

"*What*? You bloody blackguard! How dare you come into my home and violate my sister like that?" Charles roared.

"You... you ...You must marry me now! What if...?" Caroline said indignantly.

The errant viscount looked at them as if they had just escaped from Bedlam, "Look, just because your sister demonstrated her *charms* to me, very eagerly I might add, and I obliged her, does not constitute an engagement."

He did not see that there were now two extremely agitated people contemplating doing him great bodily harm, until Bingley's fist landed squarely across his jaw. He went backwards and landed on the edge of the sofa sliding to the floor with Bingley in quick pursuit of him only to be halted by Caroline, who begged him, "Charles! Do not kill him, *please*!" She was now standing between the two men with her arms out.

"If you do something so rash then we will all be *ruined*! He... he... simply needs time to think about this..." She looked behind her to see her lover rubbing his jaw, looking up at Bingley with a glare. I am sure you just surprised him is all. Is that not right, dear James?" Caroline turned and gave the viscount a tremulous smile. She was still a little unsteady on her feet from the spirits she consumed, but was now finding a sudden rude sobriety.

The viscount looked between the two of them and said, "I... I may need some time to think about this... I mean it is all so *sudden*."

Bingley could feel his ire rising, "Like bloody hell you will! You *will* marry her in haste you... you... *blackguard*!" For a moment they were at a standstill, until Bingley began again, pointing his finger at the viscount, "You cannot sit there and *tell* me that you need time to think about it. You sir, are a debaucher, you are! You took absolutely no time to think about seducing Caroline, and wasted absolutely no time in renouncing her, once your *pleasure* was had! *That*, sir, is not what I call gentlemanly behaviour! I had told you before, viscount, that I would give you a week to do the right thing.

And now the only right thing is to marry Caroline! You, sir, have that time to ready yourself!"

He looked at the couple in disgust and said, I suggest that you procure yourself a special license, for if you do not then you will have more to worry about than *me*!"

Still being furious at the man's blatant dismissal after catching him in his act of debauchery, he reached to grab him by his coat lapels, nearly dragging him to the foyer with Caroline screeching behind them, "Charles! Charles! Do not hurt him!"

Bingley grabbed the viscount's coat and top hat and nearly shoved him out the door with the man's own walking stick. As soon as the door was closed, he turned a cold hard glare at Caroline as she looked at him in defiant indignation.

"In my study, *now*, Caroline!" He said in a low threatening voice.

Caroline must have felt his ire as she followed, very apprehensively, to his study and once he ensured that the doors were closed firmly he said, "*Sit!*" Indicating a chair in front of his desk.

He did not join her, however, as he was pacing furiously back and forth trying to calm himself down after nearly killing a man for defiling his sister under his very own roof. He stopped pacing only after he noticed silent tears running down her face, he thought he could detect a hint of alcohol on her breath, and he immediately softened a little.

"Caroline... what on earth were you thinking to let that man in here without so much as a servant to chaperone you? Are you out of your senses, or was it the drink that took all intelligent thought away from you?" He studied her for a moment. "That is the only thing that could explain what I just came into!"

"I am sure I do not know what you are talking about, Charles! He is a good man, he was probably just... frightened at your bursting in the room like you did!" She glared at him then looked away.

"Do you really have *no* idea what he is about?" He said as he shook his head, and she sat silently looking down at the floor, he continued, "That... *man*, Caroline... he is not what any man would like to surrender his sister to! Shall I tell you what I know about the viscount?" He thought he could detect her color turning greener.

"Caroline..." He shook his head and began, "Against my better judgment I should reveal to you that you are not the first woman he has treated in such an infamous way." He got up and paced again, hands behind his back. "He has a... mistress... you remember the letter... Colonel Fitzwilliam's... while he was at Netherfield?"

Caroline looked up at him in interest, he continued, "That... *woman* was also the Viscount's mistress!" She looked as if she were beginning to understand her brother, and she stared at him momentarily before she looked away.

"Caroline... *he* is the baby's father *not* the colonel. What's more is that he *knew* it, and he tried to blame his own brother! I know the shock that you must be feeling but truly... he is not a man to be trusted and... well I almost hate to force the issue of marriage between you but... Caroline there are consequences to your behavior." He shook his head again.

"If something happens as a consequence of your behavior today, then you *will* be *ruined* if you do not marry him. As much as it pains me to say, I shall have to insist upon it. My honor... our honor depends upon it!"

Bingley, being unused to being so harsh to his sister, put his hand upon her shoulder and said, "You will have to reconcile yourself to this fate... I am sorry that it has turned out this way but you *must*." With that he patted her shoulder and left her to her thoughts.

As he left his study he turned to look back at her. She looked almost defeated, and he felt nearly sorry for her until he remembered what the viscount had said, 'your sister demonstrated her charms to me very eagerly'. The very thought that she would try to entrap such a man was disturbing, but to do so in such a way. *She is utterly compromised. If they do not marry then she shall have to spend the rest of her days in the north, for we could not bear the degradation.* He stopped himself then... *they shall marry... they shall!* With that determination he left the town house to see his solicitor and then Darcy.

~*~*~*~

The next six days passed more smoothly than that last day with the Gardiners and their guests. Mrs. Bennet was in fits with the wedding ceremony to take place so soon, and to top it all off, they were to attend the very exclusive Shetlers Ball.

As with any occasion such as this, Fanny Bennet was in her element. The only exception was the insistence of many of the senior family members that Kitty or at least Lydia, be excluded from attending due to her inappropriate behavior, sending their mother into fits.

"Why *should* we exclude them from this occasion? It is the *perfect* opportunity for them to find a rich husband, and we already have some lovely gowns for them to wear for the occasion!" The woman was nearly indignant.

"Mrs. Bennet, you must realize that this is not some small country dance, and we will be made a laughing stock should their restraint prove too much to bear, and they exhibit in front of the whole of London's society. For *then* your other daughters would be considered such a degradation and," Mr. Bennet was having his fun with his wife, "Mr. Bingley and Mr. Darcy may reconsider and call off the wedding."

That alone was enough to give his wife pause, though he knew that she would still try to wheedle her way out of him. In this instance, he was encouraged, not only by Elizabeth and Jane, but by Mr. Darcy as well. Eventually he did allow for Kitty to attend, but only if she were chaperoned the entire time by her older sisters, and only because Lydia would *not* be allowed to attend, lessening the chances for her to act silly without her usual catalyst.

He realized that Mary would likely be the dour young lady that she was wont to be, but she would ensure that Kitty's exuberance was kept in check. As for his other two daughters… well they were already married, and he never had cause to fear them exposing themselves to derision. At the prospect that there would be another wedding soon after his eldest two 'married' he smiled. Mary and Mr. Collins seemed to be perfect for each other with her sermonizing and his obsequious behavior. He was sure to enjoy at least a few years of amusement before death claimed him.

Mr. Bennet had been almost as pleased as his wife with that development as Longbourn was entailed to the odious man, and his wife was delighted that she would not have to leave when Mr. Bennet did succumb to his maker. With that happy thought, he went about his business of avoiding the furor of the ball and wedding planning until an express arrived. It was from Mr. Collins himself. After reading the letter, he requested a private audience with Mr. Gardiner, and with a grim look, he told his brother-in-law, "It seems as if Lady Catherine is still planning to disrupt our lives, and now she has another servant to do her bidding."

Chapter 39

To say that Mary Bennet was extremely disappointed would be an understatement. It seemed that Lady Catherine de Bourgh managed to lord some control over her toadying parson. William Collins halted his engagement to Mary due to certain claims of her family's impropriety. He wrote a letter to Mr. Bennet stating that, due to his noble patroness' strong objections, he was obliged to halt his plans to marry Mary due to the 'gross improprieties committed by his cousin Elizabeth against Lady Catherine', in accepting Darcy's hand in marriage.

It would be utterly amusing had it not been for the fact that now, poor Mary had to endure all of Mrs. Bennet's flutterings and spasms. To make matters worse, she refused to attend the ball, not that she would have put herself out to enjoy it in the first place, but still Mrs. Bennet was all nerves. "Oh, what shall become of us now, Mr. Bennet? You must make him marry our Mary! You *must*! He has already asked for her hand, and the date has been set! It is not done!" Mrs. Bennet went on and on in this vein until the other 'engaged' gentlemen arrived for dinner that evening.

Upon completing the evening meal, the gentlemen separated from the ladies, retiring to Mr. Gardiner's study. Once the port had been poured, Mr. Bennet gave the newcomers an account of the afternoon to the utter shock of Darcy and Bingley. Mr. Bennet even went so far as to show them the letter from the odious man.

Hunsford Parsonage, Kent

14th December, 1811

My Dear Cousin,

I regret to inform you of some very distressing news that I must admit is quite upsetting to me. It has been brought to my attention that my cousin, Miss Elizabeth, has recently become engaged to Mr. Fitzwilliam Darcy, the nephew of my most esteemed and noble patroness. She has entered this engagement without dully considering that he has already been promised to another. This news I feel that you are already aware of as, if you will recall, we had discussed that information some weeks ago at breakfast.

I must say that I was quite shocked that a relation of mine would do such a thing, considering that I am, after all, the most honorable lady's parson and she has condescended to receive my family once I was married to your other fine daughter, Mary. I must admit that it was alarming that your daughter Elizabeth could behave so abominably, aspiring to marry into the sphere outside of that which she had been raised, and my most noble patroness has impressed upon me all of the impropriety of doing such a thing.

It is due to this consideration that I must say that unless these issues are rectified, I must postpone, if not entirely withdraw, my offer of marriage to your most wonderful daughter Mary. My conscience and my patroness demand that certain dictates be followed. To align myself with such a family, and to such connections that deign to defy such honorable intentions, would be a travesty. I am therefore, now hereto informing you that I must take back our proposed alliances unless these dictates are followed, and then I will reconsider whether it would be prudent for this engagement to commence again.

Sincerely,

William R. Collins

Several different emotions passed over Darcy's face, and his father-in-law observed that the one that stood out foremost was outrage. I cannot believe that a man could be so weak as to call off his announced engagement just to satisfy *Lady Catherine*!"

"Well believe it, sir, because that is exactly what he did," Mr. Bennet responded.

"This is... he should be called to account for his mistaken assumptions! How dare he *assume* that because my aunt says certain things, then it must be so?" boomed Darcy.

"I believe that you have quite forgotten what kind of a man we are talking about, Mr. Darcy. He has little, if any, sense and even less courage to stand up to the lady." Mr. Bennet shot back.

Shaking his head, Darcy replied, "Mr. Bennet, sir, you must allow me to say how very sorry I am that she has brought this upon Mary and your family." Darcy tried to apologize again for his family's misdeeds.

"Sir, I cannot accept that as you are, after all, now a part of *our* family, and he is, after all, a part of *my* family." Replied Mr. Bennet rather of matter of factly.

Bingley read the letter over and over again in silence and finally joined the conversation. I think we should discuss some things in relation to the Shetler's Ball, in light of all that has happened here, gentlemen. It seems that there are several parties that would just as soon see things turn out badly for us all. And we should have a little planning in case things get... well, shall we say, out of hand?"

Mr. Bennet was now very relieved that Darcy had insisted that they marry sooner rather than wait for the ceremony Mrs. Bennet had planned. In fact, now he was even thinking that he wished that that ceremony was made public, in order to restore some peace in this household.

"Aye, I agree with you Mr. Bingley. I wish that we could forgo that event entirely. But I do understand how important it is to have Jane and Lizzy attend as they, as your wives, will be expected to perform under such scrutiny at such functions. And besides, what could happen if you are both there with them? You are already married and that shall not be altered," replied Mr. Bennet.

"Yes that is true, but there are many things that can happen to disrupt the evening, and I, for one, would feel better if we made a pact to ensure that they never leave our sight, not for one instant," Mr. Bingley stated.

Darcy agreed, "That seems most prudent under the circumstances. I have even enlisted the services of Colonel Fitzwilliam to help us keep an eye on Lady Catherine and James… the Viscount." He explained to Mr. Bennet and Mr. Gardiner. "They will be under the scrutiny of a man who was trained in military reconnaissance; nothing will get past him."

Mr. Bennet noted a look of determination in his son-in-law, and his esteem of the man who had 'stolen' his Lizzy's heart was rising every moment as he realized that Darcy would do anything to protect her from harm. His only other problem was what he was to do with poor Mary. He was really looking forward to the amusements her marriage to Mr. Collins would have provided him. He did, however, console himself with the fact that he had at least two fine sons-in-law that were respectable, honorable and decent—even if one was related to that despicable woman.

As the conversation turned to other, more mundane topics and the younger gentlemen became restless to join their wives, they decided to discuss this topic again if other problems arose. They were able to go to their objects of affection with a plan to ensure their security.

~*~*~*~

The day of the Shetler's Ball was fast approaching and

Elizabeth and Jane's nearly daily trips were becoming more of a source of comfort to each of the couples. They would meet at Darcy's town home and discretely separate for some private time, then rejoin each other later. The day before the ball was no exception for Elizabeth and Darcy, as she looked forward to enjoying carnal pleasures with her husband.

Once they were in what was to be her private chambers, she informed him, "My darling husband, do you know how much I look forward to seeing you each day?"

To this he responded, "Most assuredly not nearly as much as me, my lovely wife." He said as he kissed her down her neck all the while working loose the buttons to her bodice.

"Ummm...you sir, are a most masterful lover." She was stopped from saying anything else when he captured her mouth with his in a most delicious kiss.

"And you, madam, are wearing entirely too much clothing." Darcy pushed the sleeves off of her shoulders, beginning to caress her breasts, taking her nipples in between his thumb and index fingers. He moved slowly down to suckle her, all the while unpinning her hair that she had so assiduously put up that morning.

"And you sir, are going to make my hard work a mess with that... oooooohhh... yeeeeeeeessss." She moaned out in ecstasy when Darcy flicked his tongue over one nipple then the other.

"Do not worry, dearest, I shall have your maid help you after I am finished helping myself to you." He managed to remove her dress entirely, and it had slid to the floor along with her petticoats that he had managed to remove without her being aware, and he was now working on her stays.

She suddenly realized what he had said. "What do you mean by my maid, husband?" She looked at him with curiosity as she had not been aware of anyone being assigned to her as yet.

Darcy was undeterred from his mission, however. He began to shove her stays down her body as she was making quick work of his coat, vest, and shirt, and she had nearly gotten that item off of him before he replied,

"Oh, yeeeeeeeeesss Lizzy," As she suckled at his nipple he plunged his hands into her hair. I... mmmmmmmmm... have a... hired you a

mmmmmmmmaid." She unbuttoned his trousers and worked at his unmentionables with much diligence, as he was trying to reply to her question, "She is... oooohhh my... that girl from Netherfieeeeeeeeeeld." Elizabeth found his throbbing manhood and massaged him to his great delight, when he forgot all else and carried her to their bed.

"Well my husband, you are full of surprises are you not?" She smiled at him with her most mischievous look and pulled him down towards her.

He thrust one leg and then the other between her thighs, and began to massage her, from her breasts to her core with much diligence until he could hear her pleas for him to join her.

"Will… iam… oohhhhh… please." Her eyes were hooded in passion.

"Tell me what you want, Lizzy," Darcy demanded.

"You," she said in a near whisper.

With her declaration, he briskly entered her with a quick thrust which he followed with another and another. Soon she joined with her own thrusts in this sweet dance, until she felt her own pinnacle of ecstasy. Darcy feeling her edge closer slowed his rhythm, wanting to savor the delights of Elizabeth's lush warm tight core. He felt his body edging closer to his oblivion and slowed yet more.

"Ooooooooohhh… Liiiiizzzzzzyy… mmmmmmmm… you… are so… tight."

Elizabeth raised up her head enough to capture Darcy's lips, and their lips met with great hunger. Their tongues seeking each others. They did not break their kiss until they each thought they would faint from lack of air. Darcy's pace slowed considerably. As he moved within her, they held each other's eyes, each drinking in the other's inner self. It was worshiping and communion for the lost souls that they were before they found each other. Both felt peace within one another's arms.

Elizabeth could feel the heat rising within her, where they joined, and felt her release building, until she fell over the edge of ecstasy. Darcy was not far behind in reaching his, and soon they lay in perfect harmony, breathless and satiated.

They lay there spooning, in what would be her bed, asleep until a subtle knock was heard at her dressing room door.

Elizabeth awoke first in surprise and concern and tapped at Darcy's shoulder, "Darling! Husband! There is someone at the door!"

Darcy was barely awake and still in a post coital haze, "Yes love, it is probably Gertrude. Let her be for now and we shall…" He immediately shot up in bed and looked over at the clock on the mantle.

"Blast!" He said nearly under his breath, as if suddenly remembering something that he had to do.

"Lizzy, I am sorry about that. Please forgive me, I had made arrangements with your new maid that if you had not called for her by a certain time, she was to come and call upon you." He looked almost apologetically at his wife. I only wish that I had the time and energy for an encore, but alas that will have to wait until later, my love." He kissed her then quickly grabbed his clothes, and exited her room to go to the master's chambers.

Elizabeth waited until Darcy had left before she bid the maid to enter.

When the girl did come in, she kept her eyes averted and said tentatively, "Ma'am, I mean, Mrs. Darcy, I'm Gertrude... Mr. Darcy 'ired me ta be yer new maid thas if'n es agreeable to ya."

Elizabeth recognized the mouse of a girl from Netherfield, and said in a friendly manner, "That is fine, Gertrude. I remember you from Hertfordshire. How do you find town?"

The girl smiled tentatively at her new mistress. "Yes Ma'am, I member you's an Mr. Darcy, bean a kindes there, an the folks ere 'ave been very good ta me." She looked at Elizabeth, and gained more courage, "Mr. Darcy's made good n'shur's I been tak'n care of 'er."

Elizabeth felt less insecure now at the girl having seen her right after Darcy left her arms, and she began to accept the young maids help with righting her appearance before her father's carriage came to retrieve her and Jane again. She remembered Gertrude as one of the quietest servants she had ever known. *T'is too bad papa did not hire a maid such as Gertrude, then perhaps half of the things that have come out of Longbourn would never have been heard of!* Elizabeth mused.

Darcy came back after a quarter of an hour looking impeccable as always. He came up behind Elizabeth just as the maid had finished putting her hair up again. As soon as the maid noticed the master in her mistress's chamber, she bobbed a curtsy and excused herself to leave them alone.

"You..." He kissed the nape of her neck. "Look absolutely delightful."

Elizabeth saw his reflection in the mirror as he was caressing her shoulders, "And you sir, are absolutely irresistible, but unfortunately I need to go soon…"

He began to move his hands down towards the front of her shoulders, and was heading towards the objects of his desire. I cannot express how very much I wish you did not have to."

Elizabeth could see his desire and yearning, and she felt it too, but she realized that if they were to be free from the mechanizations of some of his family members they must continue this pretense of simply being betrothed. She tried to reassure him. "Dearest," she took his hands and held them in hers as she sat at her stool, "soon we will be able to give up this pretense and actually live as we should, but..."

He expressed his acknowledgement of the truth, but with some slight frustration. I am well aware of that, love, and I promise to make it up to you after this… *pretense* is done away with." He wiggled his eyebrows at her in a suggestive manner.

"And I will make it up to you as well, Husband."

Soon they joined Mr. Bingley and Jane who had the same expression of marital bliss upon their countenances as Elizabeth and Darcy. Both couples were having an increasingly difficult time saying their goodbyes after their 'visits', and spent an inordinate amount of time saying them each time they left Darcy House. The next time that they would see their spouses would be at the Shetler's Ball, and they wanted to work off some of the building tension. It would seem that it worked wonders, and the ladies soon headed back to Gracechurch Street.

~*~*~*~

Every one of the higher tiers of London society was looking forward to the Shetler's Ball. As it had been for the last fifteen years, it was a masquerade ball, and it seemed that everyone was trying to outdo the others in their dress and fineries. They also wanted to see the much talked of the Misses Bennets who had captured the hearts of two of society's most eligible gentlemen.

The ladies at Gracechurch Street were having almost as many nerves as Mrs. Bennet, who wanted her daughters seen in as advantageous a light as possible, which caused her daughters to suffer as much as her. She fretted over Jane's dress when she assisted her putting on her finest ball gown. "Oh dear Jane, it seems that either you have put on weight, or the modiste has not cut this dress to its proper proportions."

The dress just barely fit Jane's full bosom which was definitely displayed to advantage, but to or for whose advantage would likely be debated later. When Mrs. Bennet went to assist Elizabeth she found the same issue though not nearly as pronounced as with Jane's. She had to be shimmied into her dress as well, causing Mrs. Bennet to forswear that shop again even though Mary and Kitty's dresses fit just fine.

"They obviously are not able to cut their dresses according to measurement!" Huffed Mrs. Bennet as she surveyed her girls.

"But I really must say Jane and Lizzy you two look remarkably well... yes very well indeed!"

As they finished up the last touches, Darcy and Bingley arrived at the Gardiner's and were greeted by Mr. Gardiner and Mr. Bennet. The gentlemen retired to the study to finalize their plans for the evening. Darcy was quick to reassure his father-in-law about the arrangements made with various acquaintances to keep an eye on both Lady Catherine and the viscount.

"I have left nothing to chance, Mr. Bennet. I will not allow anything to happen to either Jane or Elizabeth, and Bingley here has bragged about Jane's beauty enough to leave many in anticipation of dancing with her, and paying her much attention." He teased Bingley openly to the shock of Mr. Bennet.

Bingley retorted, "Ah, but Darcy you forget that in doing so they will also be quite anxious to dance with, and pay much attention to her sister as well." He laughed as Darcy's face turned to his serious, almost haughty appearance, and he flushed scarlet.

Mr. Bennet joined the fray," Well gentlemen I do hope that that will not make it even more difficult for us, for I would certainly hate to have to call out more than one gentleman tonight for conduct unbecoming." The older man replied good humouredly.

Little does he know how close to the mark he is. Darcy was not looking forward to the night's events for as many reasons as Bingley, and this would hopefully end his Aunt Catherine's misguided entertaining the idea of him ever marrying his cousin, Anne. He had been concerned as well about some shocking information that Bingley imparted to him.

The viscount, Darcy knew was a rake, but he had always thought of him as perusing his pleasures with either courtesans, matrons, or the occasional servant. When he heard that James had utterly compromised Bingley's maiden sister, he became enraged at first then alarmed in quick succession. *If he would do that to Caroline Bingley, then there was no telling what he would do to Jane, or Elizabeth who are easily two of the most handsome women of my acquaintance.*

What was worse was the news of the confrontation that ensued after they were discovered. Bingley had given James one week to make his plans, and the arrangements for Caroline's settlement known, but he had not so much as contacted Bingley as of yet, and for Darcy this did not bode well. He knew well what honor and duty held under such circumstances, and if certain reparations were not made, then regardless of law, honor held that a duel would be the means to settle such an offense and this was not one till the first wound… it was one till death.

Chapter 40

When Elizabeth came down the stairs, Darcy immediately took notice. She was wearing a pale rose satin gown covered with a sheer material and the waist was fashioned to just below her breast line, only serving to accentuate her ample cleavage. If anyone were to ask about the embroidered flowers upon the sheer material Darcy would have been hard pressed to remember, as her beauty was overwhelming his senses. Bingley greeted Jane just after Darcy claimed Elizabeth, and the couples donned their outerwear to go to their respective carriages.

Luckily for Darcy and Elizabeth they were joined by the ever quiet Kitty and Mr. and Mrs. Gardiner, while Bingley had to content himself with Mrs. Bennet. They were also joined by the increasingly sober Mary who it would seem appeared resentful at her mother's insistence that she attend the ball.

The Darcy's coach had some light conversation, mostly between Mrs. Gardiner and Elizabeth. Darcy could easily discern that Elizabeth was both excited and nervous about her first official outing as his 'fiancée'. He knew that she would need some comfort, and he discreetly reached down to squeeze her hand then hesitantly let it go.

The Darcy and Bingley coaches arrived at the Shetler House just as the ball was beginning. Darcy eschewed the footman's assistance in helping the ladies down, offering his arm to Elizabeth. When their party was announced it seemed as if the whole assembly craned their necks to get a glimpse of the Bennets. Public spectacles had always made Darcy uncomfortable and currently being the center of attention was even less pleasing to such a private man. He could tell almost instantly the looks of appreciation for Elizabeth's person from the men in the room, and felt ever more protective of his wife, holding her arm closer and placing his hand over hers.

Almost instantly he was flanked by several of his acquaintances, among them being Richard and James, but a few other gentlemen from Cambridge as well. He felt a sense of resentment at having to put on such a display as an engaged couple, when they were already married, and felt his temper shorten considerably. There was nothing he could do to stave off the requests for Elizabeth's hand for a dance and within the first fifteen minutes her card was already filled, and to his great displeasure he had only managed to secure the first and last dances with her. What was worse was that the super dance had unwittingly been promised to James.

Darcy noted that Bingley was having the same dilemma with Jane as he was much easier to read than Darcy. Jane's dance card was filled just as quickly as Elizabeth's and her husband could not have been less pleased, but at least her dinner dance was promised to Bingley, much to Richard's disappointment. Bingley and Jane joined Darcy and Elizabeth, and Bingley commented, I say Darcy I almost wished we had forgone this dance for a quiet dinner and a visit with close friends."

Seeing the humor in that, Darcy responded, "Now Bingley, you are starting to sound like me, perhaps I am rubbing off on you."

The group chuckled over that, and Elizabeth said, I must confess sir, that I too now wish that we had forgone the ball to enjoy other pursuits." Elizabeth looked at Darcy with mischief in her eyes.

Darcy could feel the heat rise, and suddenly wished to find a secluded place to enjoy those 'other pursuits', but his thoughts were quickly interrupted by Mrs. Bennet's approach.

The lady discussed the elegance of the room and all of the fineries that decorated the hall, as well as the other guests. At the seemingly endless line of prattle, Darcy began to pity Bingley. When he and Jane left town, they would be back in Hertfordshire, where Mrs. Bennet was likely to join them much too frequently, for even their comfort. For that, he was at least thankful that Pemberley was far to the north, and at least two and a half days ride from his mother-in-law. Suddenly he wished that they were leaving for Pemberley rather than remaining in town, as he would be openly married to Elizabeth, and they would be done with this charade.

He would watch Elizabeth the whole of the night. Richard had promised to keep an eye on her as well, but still, he could not lose his feeling of foreboding. He scanned the room to see where his cousins were and noticed a plume of orange feather's coming toward them. Caroline Bingley had dared to weather the arguments from Bingley and came to the ball, knowing that

James would likely be present. Though Darcy did not particularly care for her, he did feel sympathy for her situation, as he knew all too well how things could have turned out for Georgiana.

Again he was brought out of his reverie. "Mr. Darcy, how are you this evening?" She smiled her predatory smile, then turned briefly to Elizabeth, "And you, Miss Eliza?" She asked insincerely and swept a condescending glance down Elizabeth's gown.

Darcy's sympathy for her left immediately, but he did manage to reply, "We... I am fine, *Miss* Bingley."

Elizabeth glanced up at him quickly, and covered her smile, I am fine as well, Miss Bingley." Elizabeth suddenly added, "And have you already had your dance card filled Miss Bingley?"

Caroline immediately looked at Elizabeth with narrowed eyes, "Why no... that is not yet but... well I have hardly been here this last quarter hour. I think it is a sign of good breading to ensure that those who are in ones social realm are given first priority to request one's company... in the dance of course, and there are plenty here whom I have not yet been able to be made aware of my attendance."

The couple hid their smirks well at her thinly veiled insult to Elizabeth and hints for Darcy to ask her for a dance. Elizabeth handled her with good grace. I see, well, since I have not had the opportunity to discern who is who among this crowd, I guess I will have to try and guess which of my promised dance partners are which then."

Darcy glanced at her with slight alarm and Caroline had a blank look about her as she stared at Elizabeth. Caroline did not stay with them much longer after that, and was soon joining Louisa Hurst and a friend of Reginald Hurst's. Once Darcy was sure they would not be heard, he said to Elizabeth, "Darling, I wish that you did not have to dance with anyone other than me tonight… it is this pretense! Now I wish that I had just insisted on an immediate wedding and we would have been done with it!"

Elizabeth replied, "Then we would have to deal with their scheming later on… no love it is best to be done with it tonight. Besides, I was much looking forward to the Viscount's attempt at seduction," she said cheekily.

Suddenly Darcy's eyes grew dark and he turned to her to whisper hotly into her ear. "Well, my lovely wife, *this* Fitzwilliam will be quite happy to seduce you."

Darcy thoroughly enjoyed watching the flush spread from her bosom up to the roots of her hair, and just as soon as he saw that, he took her in silence to the ballroom as the first set was about to begin. They started their set avoiding everyone's eye including each other's in order to maintain their composure, but once they locked eyes they could not keep their attention on anything or anyone else but each other, even when they were separated in the dance. Darcy felt as if this were an extended form of their lovemaking and hardly knew when the dance had finished.

~*~*~*~

It was Richard's turn to dance with Elizabeth, and she already felt bereft of Darcy's presence. Darcy wore a look of apprehension when Richard came to claim her hand for the next set. She vowed to enjoy the dance with her new cousin, as she did tend to like his friendly manner.

"It has been quite a while since I have seen you dance, sir. I do believe that you and… William, have quite the talent when it comes to that activity." Elizabeth teased.

"Well, we should be equal to that activity, as we were instructed at the same time." Elizabeth looked questioningly to him, and he explained, "While Darcy and I were growing up, we spent a great deal of time together, and though we were not in the same years at Eton, we did engage in the same activities from time to time. That included being forced to learn how to dance. In fact, I believe that is one of the reasons he had an aversion to dancing before." Richard laughed.

"Why then, do you think that he does not seem to mind dancing tonight, sir?"

"Because he has a lovely inducement to do so." He blurted out, and blushed immediately.

Elizabeth blushed as well, and they weaved through the movement, in silence. When they rejoined, she glanced towards Darcy and could see her husband following them through the dance, watching her intently. Richard's eyes followed hers, and he commented, I see that Darcy has already started his guard duty this evening Mrs.... Miss Elizabeth."

She smiled as she turned towards him in the dance, as the set required, "You know Colonel... Mr. Fitzwilliam, we are now related, and you may call me 'Elizabeth'." She smiled at his new title, or lack thereof.

He finished weaving through his steps, and smiled at her use of his recently relinquished title. Turning towards her, he replied, "Then you must call me 'Richard', or at the very least 'Fitzwilliam'."

"I think that 'Fitzwilliam' may be a bit too confusing for everyone, however, 'Richard' may do very well."

Richard's eyes widened, and his face softened. He looked as if he may have said something; however, he looked over to where Darcy was standing and shook his head.

Elizabeth thought it was an odd thing for him to not respond to her teasing, but she noticed him glance toward Darcy, and saw her husband with a menacing glower directed at them. *He looks as if he is quite displeased to see us dancing. What could he expect? It is a ball after all and he cannot expect to have me for every single dance under these pretenses of not being married already!* She felt her ire rise at him, thinking he disapproved of her actions on the dance floor.

"I think that Mr. Darcy is unhappy with me for not saving every dance with him, sir... er, Richard. He looks as though he is displeased about something."

Richard gave a wry smile. I do not think it has anything to do with you madam. After all, it was his idea to keep your earlier marriage a secret, and he cannot expect to have you all to himself tonight." Richard whispered as he looked down into her bright flushed face, "Besides, it will do him good to learn to share sometimes."

Elizabeth thought that that was an unfair comment by Richard, considering what she knew Darcy to have done for him. She felt the need to defend her husband and lover. I believe he has been known to be very generous with those who are under his care, and he takes good care to ensure that they want for almost nothing."

"That is true… Elizabeth, he does take good care of those he cares about. That is not what I intended to allude to." He said sadly.

"I am afraid, then, that I do not take your meaning. What is it that he has not shared with you?"

"It is nothing that could or should be divided, really. I have seen that Darcy has always had the advantage of being his own man, and answers to no one. Until recently, I have not had such an advantage. Unfortunately for me it has come too late to do me any good."

Elizabeth could sense that there was something else that was bothering Richard other than his relatives plotting to disrupt her and Darcy's happiness. *He has such a sad unhappiness about him lately. What has caused him to turn so melancholy, I wonder?*

"Is there nothing that we may be able to assist you with, Richard? Surely it cannot be as bad as that?" Elizabeth felt a concern for Richard's happiness and well being.

"No, my dear… Elizabeth, it is too late for anything to be done. I only wish that some of my family were much less selfish. For the record, Darcy is one of the best men I have ever known, and I am amazed that with all of us misfits he has turned out so well."

"Yes, he is the best man I have ever known as well. I do feel badly that our 'engagement' has caused so much turmoil within your family though. Discord is never a good thing for families."

"Yes, well, their discord is of their own doing, and I for one will not stand by and watch as they attempt to disparage, or discredit you at their hands."

"I thank you for your support of us. I hope that this does not tear the family apart. It was not our design to do so."

"Of course not, it is up to them as to whether they accept it or not. You must make up your mind to be happy with whatever decisions you make, because in the end it is you who must live with the consequences."

"True." Elizabeth knew what he said made sense, but could still detect a hint of sadness in his address.

They finished the rest of the dance in silence. Richard addressed Elizabeth before he took her back to Darcy, I thank you for the dance. I can honestly say that I have rarely had such a fine partner."

The looked that Richard directed to her was a familiar gaze, she had seen it before, but until she came back to Darcy she could not place it. When she caught her husband's eye she saw it in his eyes as well. It was the look of passion. Feeling disconcerted with that knowledge, Elizabeth unconsciously moved closer than propriety allowed towards Darcy. He looked at her questioningly, "Are you well, Elizabeth? Is there something the matter?"

"No, nothing is the matter dearest. I am simply happy to be back near you." Elizabeth watched as Richard addressed Darcy.

"Here now, Darcy, I would not allow anything to happen to Elizabeth, you have my word. By the way, Elizabeth would you care for something to drink?"

"Yes, that would be wonderful, Richard. Thank you."

"It would be my pleasure," Richard glanced at the two and frowned then made his exit from their grouping.

Elizabeth watched as he crossed the room to the refreshment table, and Darcy asked, "What is the matter, Elizabeth? You look as though you have seen a ghost."

"No, it was not a ghost... not exactly."

Before they could discuss it any further, they were approached by none other than Lord Blake, who had somehow managed to claim her next dance from the Baronet of _____ who needed to absent himself momentarily. He joined Elizabeth and Darcy when Lord Blake approached to claim her hand for that man's dance.

"I do beg your pardon, Miss Bennet, but I have been obliged by the Baron to claim this dance, as he was momentarily called out, so

I should say that it is my *gain* and his *loss*." The man smiled almost lecherously at her. He stood momentarily in expectation of an introduction, and Richard, who came back with the drinks, and made the introductions reluctantly. "Lord Blake, may I introduce to you Mrs. ... uh... Miss Elizabeth Bennet, Miss Bennet, Lord Blake."

A faint grimace graced Darcy and Richard's features momentarily, and Darcy glared at her new dance partner.

Elizabeth was wise enough to know that there was something about this man that her husband did not approve of, however she decided to put her best foot forward, and act as though it was nothing... at least to the man's face.

"I thank you for 'rescuing' me, sir, from having a vacant dance tonight. I am sure that Barron _____ will be forgiven, after all business must be taken care of, must it not?"

Blake smiled widely. "Indeed." And then he escorted her out to the dance floor, on his arm.

The music started, and Elizabeth was content to stay quiet while they made their first steps of the set, however, the earl had different ideas.

"Miss Bennet, I cannot tell you how delighted I am to have the honor for your hand..." He looked at her pointedly, while they turned in the dance, "... in this dance... it was most fortunate for me." He looked her up and down, which caused Elizabeth to miss a step, but she recovered quickly.

"I thank you for that compliment, sir." Elizabeth had no wish to continue with this conversation, as the man seemed slightly in his cups already, and became more assertive with his manner.

"Tell me Miss Bennet, how did you and Darcy meet? I mean... I do not believe that I have ever heard your name in town, and I would certainly have remembered such loveliness."

Elizabeth paused before answering, as she tried to regain her composure in light of such blatant flirtation.

"Well, sir, I am not from town, so it would be very unlikely for you to have ever heard of us, and as far as my... fiancé and I, we met in Hertfordshire."

They separated following the dance, and he watched her as she tried to ignore him. When they rejoined he leaned in a little closer than was absolutely appropriate for the dance, at which point Elizabeth noted Darcy watching them, looking more flushed than usual. Elizabeth also noted his clenched jaw and she knew that if Lord Blake did not cease his blatant addresses, he would be in danger of being called out by a very livid Darcy.

She did the best she could think of to put the man off.

"What think you, sir, about the current situation with the war financing?" She hoped he would be very put off by a woman who actually could carry on an intelligent conversation.

Momentarily stunned at such a question, Blake remained silent for a few minutes, only looking at her sideways. I see Darcy has found himself a most remarkable woman, with not only beauty but some intelligence as well. I should have expected as much from a man like him," the Earl said dryly.

Elizabeth was relieved that he stopped his objectionable words in favor of some more sensible conversation, but she was curious as to how her husband was viewed by others in his circle. "And what sort of man would that be, sir?"

Blake laughed at her question, breaking into a very wide smile. "A very shrewd, upright, and if you ask me personally, dry man... nothing entertaining to him at all, and very business minded."

Elizabeth smiled in spite of herself. "Well, sir, to me that seems to be very good solid sort of man, but I would have to disagree with you as far as him being dry and unentertaining... for I assure you that I have not found him so."

Blake's interest showed, and he did not resist asking. "Well now, Miss Bennet, I am sure you have seen another side of Darcy that we shall never have the opportunity to witness." He looked her up and down again as if examining a prize mare, and fortunately for Elizabeth, it was the end of her dance with the man. Darcy came to her side in an instant, staring Blake down. Blake smiled challengingly at Darcy and bowed over Elizabeth's hand. Before he left them, he took her hand and kissed it lingeringly.

"It was a great pleasure, Miss Bennet."

Darcy glared at the man as he walked away, his jaw still clenched. When they could no longer see him, he then turned to Elizabeth. "Dearest, I am so sorry about that. I should never have allowed that to happen. I should have stopped Richard before he made the introductions, but I was too slow…" He looked at her with concern.

"It is all right, William. He could not very well do anything to me while in a crowded ballroom, but I do have to admit he was…" She could not quite put her finger on it, but she had a feeling of unease about him that she could not quite define.

"He was what, Elizabeth?" Darcy asked in concern.

She took a deep breath, "Well, he smelled of spirits, and said some things… oh, but I am sure that he would be mortified if he were in his right mind."

Darcy looked at her with more concern than before, I wish that that were true, dearest, but unfortunately that is the way that man is. I saw the way he looked at you."

She placed her hand on his arm to stop him from berating himself, or going over to outright call the man out. "Sir, we must remember to act as we are simply an engaged couple. It would not do to have the world find that we married secretly because you called a man out." Elizabeth tried to reassure him, even though she felt less at ease than before. She still had the ordeal of dancing with the infamous Viscount Matlock, whom she had only just met within the last fortnight and had already formed a very ill opinion of.

When the viscount did come, Darcy and Richard were by her side, and promised not to let her out of their sight, especially after Lord Blake's behavior. To Elizabeth, he seemed friendly enough, almost charming, and if she did not know the man under this layer of charm, she could easily understand how any woman could be seduced by his sort.

He began their conversation easily. "So Miss Bennet, how long have you been in town?"

"About two and a half weeks, sir." She easily replied before stepping to the side allowing another couple through the line.

"And how do you find London?" He asked easily taking a turn around her.

"I find it very pleasant, sir." She turned around to him.

"I have seen you leaving Darcy House often, Miss Bennet. It seems as though we were not destined to meet again until this evening, and I must say that I was quite happy to make your acquaintance, at Matlock House."

"I thank you, sir," He held her hand as they made their way down the ballroom.

"I must say, I was quite surprised that my cousin wished to marry so soon. He is usually the sort of man who must contemplate everything from various angles, then agonize over the good and the bad points, until he settles upon a decision. It seems as though he made quite an expedient choice with you, Miss Bennet. It must be quite a shock to find yourself engaged, and then married in less than a month's time."

Elizabeth was not sure what his insinuation was, but thought better of confronting Darcy's cousin on the dance floor. "We have been acquainted for many months, sir, and he felt that with winter's approach, and it being difficult to travel during the coming months, followed by spring planting, it would be very difficult to wed later, and we did not wish to wait so long." Elizabeth let those last words slip, before thinking how the viscount may interpret them.

It was all that she feared. He looked at her sharply then lifted an eyebrow, with the corners of his lips turned up, "Indeed?"

They were silent for a while before he asked, "How do you find the prospect of marrying? I am told that too many young women it is quite overwhelming. I cannot imagine that it would be any less so as the wife of Fitzwilliam Darcy."

Elizabeth took a moment to compose her next words, and was thankful he did not pursue her earlier words, as he could very well have done. I think, sir, that as a lady has patience and a very good staff, as well as some solid basic knowledge of how to run a household, then she would do very well, especially as the wife of Mr. Darcy."

"I see. It would seem that my cousin has chosen himself a wife of uncommon sense, and such devotion. Why Miss Bennet I must say he must be quite anxious to have you learn your duties, as it has been told that you have been to Darcy House daily. Ah, but he is quite… diligent is he not?"

Fortunately for Elizabeth they were separated with other partners, and when they returned opposite each other again, she said, I am sorry, sir. I have quite forgotten what it was that we were discussing."

The viscount smiled, and said, "Do not worry, Miss Bennet, I am sure that we will have plenty of time to talk, later." He turned to face forward as the dance required, but Elizabeth was almost certain she could detect a small smirk upon his face.

Elizabeth became flustered with the man, trying to riddle out what he was getting at until he turned to her and said, I see that your fiancé and my brother are quite diligent in not allowing you out of their sight, Miss Bennet. Tell me, is that for your benefit, or theirs?"

She was speechless for a moment before replying. I am quite sure I do not know of what you speak of, sir, have they been watching me?"

"Well it is either that or they are try to ensure that one or the other does not have too much of your time this evening." The viscount replied matter of factly.

Elizabeth was surprised at his insinuation. She knew that the colonel, now Mr. Fitzwilliam, had had some slight preference for her in Hertfordshire, but did not think he could ever have had any serious designs on her, as he did not have the resources to take a wife of little dowry let alone her other barriers to matrimony.

The viscount had been staring at her and said, "It seems to me, that my brother would be just as happy to be engaged as Darcy… quite happy to be so, Miss Bennet."

"Sir, I am not sure that I follow you. What exactly is it that you are trying to imply?" Elizabeth asked slightly more breathless, as she could feel her throat constricting.

He paused momentarily and said outright, "Miss Bennet, it would take a blind person not to notice how Richard watches you," At her look of surprise he smiled and continued, "Have you not noticed that my brother looks at you the same way that Darcy does... he is in love with you."

Elizabeth paled, and tried to take a deep breath. The viscount took note of her pallor, and said, "Are you quite all right, Miss Bennet? You look rather ill."

Elizabeth stated, "I... I am rather... sir, I think that I need to sit out for the rest of our dance."

James looked around and saw Darcy starting towards them, but James was too quick, escorting Elizabeth through the crowd. They weaved through a great many guests heading towards the library at Shetler House. Elizabeth could feel her head spin at this revelation. The look of passion she knew well by now, as she saw it in Darcy, and she had seen it tonight in Richard's eyes, but it did not cross her mind that there was passion, or even lust behind it. She did not want to think of herself being the cause of pain or disappointment to Richard, but she had fallen quite irretrievably in love with Darcy, and did not know how she should act with him at this point, as she did not wish to further the rift that had been left when the whole mistress scandal erupted.

James managed to help her to sit down, handing her some water. Then he ever so slowly sat next to her on the sofa. She took several small sips, breathing deeply trying to regain her equilibrium. When she finally realized he was moving ever closer to her as if to embrace her, she suddenly found her bearings enough to jump up off of the sofa, and run towards the French doors leading outside. Almost immediately, she heard a commotion in the room she had just vacated and saw none other than Caroline Bingley.

~*~*~*~

Caroline Bingley saw the viscount exit the ballroom with a very pale Elizabeth on his arm. She knew that she had to act before he was found with Elizabeth Bennet, and then that little trollop would have her husband *and* her title that she most definitely did not deserve. Besides, if he had to marry, it should be her. She quickly followed them to the library finding him heading towards the balcony, but before he got very far she cornered him.

"Viscount! What are you doing in here while the entire ton is outside? And why have you not asked me for the first dance? It is customary for one who is soon to be wed to dance the first with their intended!" Caroline said, incensed.

The viscount stared at her momentarily then laughed, "You do not really believe that I would lower myself to marry a tradesman's daughter, do you now, Miss Bingley?"

Caroline's fury increased. "You, sir, are a cad of the worst sort! You do not even deserve the title that you have after what you have done! Do tell, do you normally go around seducing all sorts of innocents and try to compromise them in the worst sort of way?"

"Miss Bingley, in case you do not remember, which as I recall may not be too surprising considering your lack of sobriety, but none the less, you madam were the one to start your pretty little speeches, practically *begging* me to take you." He laughed again, "Now, Miss Bingley, I am only a man, and when a woman offers herself up to me in such a way, then one cannot blame me for... how shall I say this? Taking what is freely offered?"

Caroline was hysterical and furious, "Why you...!"

Suddenly they were interrupted by the Earl of Matlock,

"James! What in heaven's name have you done now?" The earl was outraged, and was joined by a rather smug looking Richard after hearing most of their conversation from the doorway.

Both Caroline and James flew around to view their audience, their mouths open wide in shock.

~*~*~*~

In the mean time, Lady Catherine had been trying to coral Darcy in another part of the house. She kept a close eye on her nephews all night, and when James danced with Elizabeth Bennet, she slowly neared to Darcy until James started to escort her away from the dance floor. It seems that she had needed to discuss estate business at the most inopportune time. Darcy was almost across the ballroom, and was about to follow Fitzwilliam and his uncle the earl into the library, when Lady Catherine called out to him.

"Darcy! I say, Darcy! I wish to speak with you on a most urgent matter." The lady said in her most commanding voice.

Not wanting to arouse suspicion and now somewhat secure in the knowledge that his cousin and uncle would see to it that James could not try anything with Elizabeth, he turned to his aunt vowing to only allow enough time to have the briefest of conversations, "Lady Catherine." He bowed.

"Darcy! I say I have been following you these last few minutes! Did you not hear me?" Lady Catherine demanded.

"Madam, I was going to see to something in the library. There was a question among some acquaintances of mine, and I wanted to find a book about the subject to settle an argument." Darcy improvised smoothly.

Lady Catherine looked almost eager to help him with that project. "Then I will go with you and we can discuss this matter there. It is far too public out here, and we would have some privacy there."

He hesitantly agreed to her request dreading what he would find. When he came upon the door to the library, he found it slightly ajar and could hear some very angry voices, one of them belonging to his uncle. When Lady Catherine heard the earl, she pushed past Darcy and barged into the room. Suddenly the whole room looked in Darcy's direction, and he dreaded what he would find. When he finally found the courage to enter and look around closely, he was more than shocked to find the viscount red faced, and a very happy, smiling Caroline Bingley.

As he searched the room for Elizabeth, he became concerned and searched Richard's face for any indication of Elizabeth's whereabouts. His cousin slightly nodded his head to indicate the direction of the balcony. Darcy discreetly left the room through the doors, and once outside, he found Elizabeth. She was hugging herself and had tears running down her face. With the look upon her face he did not think that he could feel any worse about allowing her to be anywhere near James. He came up to her and embraced her tightly caressing her head and neck.

"I am so sorry, Elizabeth; I should never have brought you here to endure this fiasco of an evening. Will you ever forgive me?" He was nearly in tears at the sight of her extreme distress.

She slowly snaked her arms around his neck and embraced him back. She took several deep breaths finally managing to say, "My love, there is nothing to forgive. You have not done anything... anything at all to deserve censure. You were right beside me all evening and made sure that there was someone to keep me safe. Nothing happened." She said very softly.

Darcy released some tension at her words of reassurance, feeling relief that the viscount did not go as far as he was capable, he was thankful that Richard and his uncle arrived when they did. It was obvious that the earl had discovered those two in a compromising situation and from the sounds of things there was going to be a quickly arranged wedding. All Darcy wanted to do, though, was comfort his wife and he most definitely did not care who saw them.

"Elizabeth, shall we go home?" He asked her looking into her face as he caressed her cheeks with his thumbs.

She looked up at him and said, I would like very much to get away from here, my love, but then it would mean that you would have to leave me tonight."

Darcy pulled her back to his chest and kissed the top of her head. "No, darling, not tonight. Tonight you will come home. To your home, and you will be my wife, and I will be damned if I will allow you to leave my sight again... ever."

He felt her arms tighten around him as they stood outside on the balcony until the library cleared out of all of his relatives. Darcy sought out Mr. Bennet, whom he found in a sitting room with some other, quiet gentlemen. He actually seemed to be enjoying himself until Darcy called him away with a look of distress.

"What is it? What has happened Darcy?" Mr. Bennet looked anxious.

"Sir," he straightened up before speaking in a more formal voice that would brook no argument, "Elizabeth has had quite a distressing night, and now that I believe the most immediate problem to be resolved, I wish to take my wife home."

Mr. Bennet first nodded his head in agreement, then suddenly looked up to Darcy as if studying the man. "And which home might that be, sir?"

"Her home, sir. The one that she belongs to, and that belongs to her."

Mr. Bennet stared at him then looked down and sighed deeply. "Take good care of her, Darcy. Otherwise, you will have more distressing relatives to deal with." He reached his hand out to shake Darcy's hand which Darcy accepted with alacrity.

He turned then and went to find his wife. They were going home, and if he were lucky maybe… *just maybe, she would yet be seduced by a Fitzwilliam… Darcy, that is.*

Chapter 41

The Darcy's left the Shetler's Ball without causing too much undue attention. When Mr. Darcy informed Mrs. Bennet that he was taking his wife home, the woman was silent for the next quarter hour. If Darcy were being honest, it was one of the more gratifying moments of his acquaintance with Elizabeth's mother. He managed to find Bingley in the mass of people and informed him that their mother-in-law and sisters were aware of their marriages, and as far as Darcy was concerned he was taking his wife home with him tonight. He also informed Bingley of the developments of the evening.

"It appears that my cousin and Caroline have been found out by my uncle as well Bingley. He walked in on them arguing over the incident at your house, so I think I can safely say that you will not be obliged to call him out. As far as what happened, I still do not know. I will talk with Elizabeth about the particulars later, but I do not wish to distress her anymore tonight. Darcy felt quite tired with the lateness of the hour and the stress of the situation.

"So you think that they will marry then, Darcy?" Bingley asked somewhat anxiously.

"Yes, they will definitely marry now. My uncle heard about what happened, and is insistent that they marry, and as soon as possible. I must say though," Darcy looked sadly towards the even more stressed earl, "He was none too happy with the way that things have turned out. I never would have thought that our family could cause so much grief."

Bingley smiled slightly in relief, and asked, "So what is to be done now? I assume that we should discuss this with the earl and countess."

Darcy nodded, then replied, "Yes, the duty of arranging this 'marriage' needs to be discussed, and soon, or so I gather, as they will be going to Matlock in the near future, and will likely stay there for quite some time. As for gathering our families together I have offered the use of my home here in town as neutral territory, and the earl had asked if you could meet with him and James there at two o'clock tomorrow afternoon."

Bingley smiled and nodded his head. "Oh yes, of course. The sooner the better I should think." Bingley looked down for a moment and then almost sheepishly asked, "Darcy… you are taking Mrs. Darcy home tonight with you?"

Darcy smiled despite himself. "Yes, we are going to our home and staying there until we go briefly to Longbourn. After that we will leave for Pemberley, and there we shall stay until after planting is finished. As I have told our father-in-law, we have been very patient, but after tonight I am taking my wife home, and we will live as man and wife from here on out."

Bingley furthered, "But do you suppose that Jane and I… that we could…?"

"Start living as man and wife? Yes, Bingley, there is nothing to stop you, unless of course you prefer to wait until…"

"Oh no, no, no, *no*… I most definitely want to take my wife home with me tonight. I only feel terribly for Caroline. I mean to have things end up so…"

"I would not worry about that too much, Bingley. They are of age and should have known what they were doing. They made their own mess, and now they have to live with it."

"Yes, I suppose you are right on that account as well… and at least we did not have to call him out."

Darcy gave a humorless laugh. "No, in a way, the earl did that for us." Suddenly Darcy could feel all of the stress of the evening, and said to his new brother, "Well Bingley, I bid you a good night. I am off now to home, and I will let the earl know that you will meet with him tomorrow."

"Yes, thank you, good night, Darcy." Bingley turned towards Jane and quietly escorted her towards where Caroline was standing.

Darcy bowed slightly to Bingley and turned to collect Elizabeth from Mr. and Mrs. Bennet, who by now, had found her voice again and was, unfortunately, rhapsodizing over the sly things that Jane and Elizabeth were. Never in his life had he wanted to leave a ball or dance as much as right now. As quickly as he could manage, he escorted Elizabeth out to their carriage and they were soon on their way to Darcy House.

Darcy made arrangements for his carriage to return to Shetler House to transport the Bennet's and the Gardiner's back to Gracechurch Street. He had plans for later, but that would come once he sent the notice of their marriage to the Times and other papers in Derbyshire and Hertfordshire.

~*~*~*~

To say that the secret marriage sent shock waves throughout the Bingley, Darcy, and Bennet families was an understatement. It seemed everyone had such varying reactions. For Mr. Bennet, when it took place, it was sadness, which was nearly compensated by the overwhelming joy of Mrs. Bennet, who had all but forgotten that the wedding that she so diligently arranged was a mute point now, as the couples were already married. But she would have the bragging rights to the fact that her two eldest daughters had snagged two of the country's most eligible bachelors.

The Fitzwilliam's were shocked but mostly pleasantly. The earl and countess, and to some degree Richard, felt the sadness in the fact that the marriage was even more hasty, due to their eldest, James plotting. The Fitzwilliam's sadness could also be attributed to the viscount's profligacy and amoral behavior which was bringing him into a hasty marriage with a woman that the countess could barely stand.

The earl was only slightly less pleased due to the fact that not too long ago he had secretly entertained hopes that his eldest would marry a duchess, or possibly his cousin Anne, but alas that was not to be. He always knew on some level, that it was unlikely Darcy would marry Anne as they were too dissimilar. That did not, however, stop him now from entertaining thoughts of Richard being attached to his cousin, and that thought still delighted him. But he would not pursue *that* until he had James safely married away, and they were tucked firmly in Matlock.

Lady Catherine was just furious about the secret wedding, vowing that she would find a way to have the marriage annulled... that is until the earl reminded her that they had been married for a little over a week, and the likelihood of it not being consummated was next to nothing, and as that would be about the only grounds she would have to concede the point. It was not until he mentioned that Richard was still very much unattached that she brightened again. Her plotting went into full mode to plan their marriage.

Richard was saddened that he was not the one to pull off the coup de grace of carrying away the lovely Miss Elizabeth, but there were other fine young ladies, and tonight was still young as far as he was concerned. His reacquaintance with Miss Kitty Bennet was surprisingly more stimulating than when he first met the girl, and she did seem somewhat partial to him. *Perhaps when she grows out of that silliness she will be much like Elizabeth?* He heard his father hinting to Lady Catherine that all may not be lost as he, Richard, was not attached to anyone... yet. That alone was enough to make him want to pursue other avenues.

James was still in shock that his plan of seduction had taken such a dark turn. Never had he ever planned to marry Caroline Bingley, but somehow Richard had managed to orchestrate events in such a cunning way that his own father was the one to force the issue and not that gullible Charles Bingley. *If only I could have seduced Elizabeth. Then I could have extorted monies from her in exchange for my silence. Now I am saddled with that horse of a woman Caroline Bingley!* Soon, he would be living in exile up in Matlock with Caroline Bingley as his bride, and there they would be until the earl either passed away, or condescended to allow them back into polite society again. *Well at least I will be closer to Harriet, and once she has done with her confinement perhaps she will allow me into her bed once more.*

The events of this evening were enough to put even Caroline Bingley in an unusually good mood. She would be married, and to a viscount. One day she would be the Countess Matlock and hold court in her own circles, and she would be of equal, if not of greater circumstance, than that Eliza Bennet. It was still difficult to think about a woman such as that marrying Darcy, but as she, a tradesman's daughter, had managed to get a viscount she did not dwell on it for very long. She was also contemplating the grand affair that would be her wedding. *It will be so much better than that of Eliza and Darcy, or even Jane and Charles... why they will not even have a real public ceremony!* With that thought she smiled more genuinely than she had since she was a small child.

~*~*~*~

Darcy House was lit in only the essential places... just enough to guide one through the darkened corridors and up the stairs. Darcy and Elizabeth arrived just after midnight to a very surprised Humphrey, who was told that there would be no formal announcement of the master's marriage to the general public until after the announcements in the papers in just a few days time.

Elizabeth felt somewhat at a loss to know what she should do, but with one glowing look from William, she felt her courage rise to greet the sparse servants with poise and grace. She was tired after the events of the evening, and evidently her husband could read her looks.

"Elizabeth, shall we retire for the night? I shall take you up to your rooms if you would like." Darcy said softly.

She smiled back to him gratefully. I think that that would be wonderful, William, but what of Gertrude? She has surely retired by now and I really do not want to have to wake her."

"I shall assist you this evening, Elizabeth."

Suddenly she could feel the heat rise within her at his thinly veiled suggestion, and she was more awake than she had been in the last two hours. Darcy offered her his arm and they headed up the stairs where they were once again in the family wing. He took her straight past the mistress' suite right to the master's rooms. At her questioning look Darcy said, I thought that your first official night you could stay in the master's rooms, along with the master." He looked at her very intently.

She felt her passion rise, and said, I should hope that this is not the only night I should be welcome in the master's rooms."

"Most definitely not!" He said in mock offence, I shall insist that you stay with me in my rooms at all times... day or night." He waggled his eyebrow at her as he opened the doors abruptly, dragging Elizabeth in with him. After securing the locks, he slowly approached and reached for her hands, kissing them both as he slid his hands around her waist. He brought his face to hers and began a soft, slow, lingering kiss that turned into a hard, demanding battle. They did not break that kiss until they were both breathless.

She placed her arms around his neck and began to caress his back and shoulders, while he began caressing her back and bottom until their passions were equal to one another. Then they began a somewhat frenzied attack on each other's attire. He made quick work of her dress, adeptly unbuttoning her bodice and shoving the dress down her torso, past her hips. All the while she was removing his coat and attempting his vest. It would seem they could not get to the other's flesh fast enough, and soon were groping and kissing passionately while inching towards the giant sized bed.

By the time they hit the mattress, Darcy had managed to remove the last barriers, and she was trying very clumsily to undo the buttons to his trousers. Finally, when their last items of clothing were removed they began their re-exploration of each other's flesh, caressing the other with desperation. Elizabeth kissed the indentation of Darcy's neck while he attacked the flesh around her breasts.

Elizabeth found the sensation of his chest's manly hair against her flesh oddly stimulating, and could scarcely find the words to convey this to him. Somehow it seemed that he could sense her desire for more of him, and after he quickly caressed her womanhood enough to ensure her comfort and readiness for him, he plunged deep and hard into her womanly recesses, gradually quickening his pace.

Elizabeth felt the fullness created by William's attentions to her, and was lost to the heated sensation that it created in her depths. His flesh rubbing with hers was creating more heat as they joined in a ritual as old as mankind that brought her to such raptures. She arched her back to join him, causing them both to cry out in ecstasy, "Oh G-d, oooooooooooooooohhh... more..."

Each time she called out, he would quicken his pace a little more and meet her stroke for stroke, making it harder and harder for him to hold off his orgasm.

"Ooooooooooohhhh… do not stop… uuuuuummm…" She cried out and could feel her pleasure rising as he thrust almost desperately into her, as if he were trying to meld with her flesh.

"Yeeeeeeeeeeessssssssss… oooooooooooohhhhh…

Wiiiiiiiillllllllliaaammm…" She was sucking in her breath, and was finally brought to her release in a blinding wave of ecstasy along with her husband, as she could feel his release deep within her. He felt her body squeezing and drawing him deep inside of her.

They lay joined in one flesh for several moments until the coolness of the room roused them. Darcy drew back the covers and they lay within each other's arms, finally able to spend their nights as husband and wife. Darcy kissed Elizabeth lovingly on her already passion swollen lips, "Good night, my lovely wife. Welcome home."

With that they were fast asleep and would not be disturbed until late that next morning.

Darcy and Elizabeth managed to find more intimate time that first morning as husband and wife under one roof. In fact, they had enjoyed pleasures of the flesh another three times, as one would wake then inevitably the other would be awakened and their lovemaking would commence until they were spent until the next interlude. It was nearly afternoon when Darcy and Elizabeth arose reluctantly for the day.

Darcy arranged lunch for the Bennets and Gardiners, as well as Bingley and Jane, who would bring Caroline along with them. After they were done, he would have to deal with the headier issue of James and Caroline's betrothal. That was another reason for the meal with the Bennets. He wanted to get all of the unpleasantness done with for the time being, and move on with his life with Elizabeth.

By the time their first guests arrived, Mrs. Bennet was again in full raptures about her daughters secret marriages, though now she was less pleased that she would not have the opportunity to show off her talents in town. She continued on in this vein even after Jane, Bingley and Caroline arrived. It was rare that Darcy could tolerate her babble for long, but somehow he was finding some perverse pleasure in Caroline Bingley's reaction to his mother-in-law's prattle.

He found his father-in-law equally amused. I say Darcy, it seems that Miss Bingley will have to put up this a lot more prattle and senseless chatter now that Jane is Bingley's wife, and will be living at Netherfield." The old man chuckled.

Both Darcy and Bingley were smiling at this, but at the mention of Caroline coming to Netherfield they both tried to change the subject.

"Sir, did you stay much longer at the ball after we left?" Darcy asked skillfully.

Mr. Bennet's face fell into a slight frown, "Yes, unfortunately we did. It would seem that Mary had actually found someone with whom she could find some distraction... to some baronet nonetheless! And of course Mrs. Bennet would not hear of us leaving before the young man had asked to pay a visit in the next day or so."

Bingley happened to ask, "What is the gentleman's name sir?"

"Withers... he is apparently an only son... much to Mrs. Bennet's disappointment."

Both Darcy and Bingley knew the man. He was a bit younger than they, and very respectable. He also had a claim to two estates, as an uncle of his recently died childless, and he had been raised with a private education which unfortunately did him no favors. He had little social skill when it came to conversation, but it was said he did have a thorough understanding of religion, and especially Fordyce's Sermons.

As far as Catherine's or 'Kitty's entertainments for the evening, she found her card as full as her eldest sister's, and even had a few gentlemen ask to call upon her the next day. Most of them were men of the uniform, which of course thrilled her mother very much, but none so much as the request to call by the former Colonel Fitzwilliam.

That news alone was enough to concern Darcy, partially due to Richard's history with women and more so due to his continuing attraction to Elizabeth. He hoped that Richard would move on, but did not think that Kitty Bennet would be the best way for him to do so as she was still so young and he was... well a soldier, and even a retired soldier was not likely to change his womanizing habits. *I will talk to him after everyone has gone, making it clear that in no uncertain terms is he to trifle with her. She would be better off with some lowly solicitor's clerk than to endure infidelity with him.*

When the family sat to dine Darcy found himself infinitely pleased to at last see Elizabeth sitting in her rightful place as the mistress presiding over his table. He did not even mind that Mrs. Bennet had yet to cease talking about the aborted plans for their public wedding ceremony, though by now they all agreed to a public reception to celebrate their marriages. The family spent more time than Darcy anticipated, and before long the Earl Matlock and the viscount, along with Richard, had arrived.

The first meeting between families it would seem, was destined to occur sooner than later. Darcy made the introductions between all of the parties, while secretly hoping that Mr. Gardiner, or at least Mr. Bennet, would take their leave. At first it seemed as if they would, but then the earl in an unusual show of civility, struck up a conversation with those gentlemen, and was engrossed with them for some time. In the meanwhile, Richard found Kitty, and was cornering her in a section of the sitting room, with Georgiana sitting quietly at her side.

Lydia looked upon this scene with what Darcy could only guess as envy, as he knew she was inexplicably attracted to… well any man who was not attached, and even some who were. Darcy tried to catch Richard's attention, and finally succeeded when he cleared his throat rather loudly for the fourth time, annoyed and with a raised eyebrow.

Richard got up at Darcy's prompting and joined him then. "What is it that you would like to chastise me for now, Darcy?" He said good-humoredly.

Darcy paused momentarily, choosing his words before beginning carefully. "Fitzwilliam, I had hoped that Georgiana could get to know Elizabeth's sisters without certain distractions." He looked at his cousin pointedly.

"And I think that it would not be a good idea for you to excite any expectations in Miss Catherine that you will not fulfill."

Richard's face dropped at that statement. "You mean to say that you think that I am not good enough for her, is that it Darcy?." He said in a low controlled voice.

"I said no such thing Richard, and you know it! My concerns lie with the fact that she is just seventeen, and you are nearly thirty, and the fact that though she has the promise of improving in manners and understanding, she does not have the sensibilities to take on a man so much older and with such vast experiences in the world. In short, Richard, neither one of you are good for each other. I am sorry to say so, and believe me it pains me to say so, but I wish the best for both of you. That is why I had to speak up… before either one of you formed a serious attachment."

Richard stared at Darcy momentarily before walking towards the earl and viscount, who were talking with Mr.

Bennet and Mr. Gardiner. Darcy again felt the stress of the day upon him, and immediately his eyes sought out his beloved Elizabeth. It seemed that one endearing look from her was a balm to him, and he smiled at her momentarily, then strode towards the gentlemen and invited them to his study.

Mr. Gardiner and Mr. Bennet, sensing Darcy and Bingley's need to discuss their business in private, begged their excuses and were soon taking their leave much to Mrs. Bennet's displeasure. Apparently that lady had managed to offer her goods and services for Jane and Elizabeth's wedding to Caroline, who tried vehemently to decline the offer, until Bingley insisted that they take her up on it, as Mrs. Bennet had gone to so much trouble, and it would be such a waste to not use them.

Once the Gardiner's and Bennet's left, Darcy and Bingley led Richard, the earl and viscount to Darcy's study. For a few moments there was an uncomfortable silence and it would seem that Bingley had regained some of his animosity towards James. Darcy noticed, and felt that it would be prudent to begin their discussions in order to expedite the arrangements and be done with the meeting as soon as possible.

"I believe that we have some planning to do, and in a very short amount of time. I have over heard that Bingley has accepted our mother-in-law's services and planning of what was to be our wedding, for that of Miss Bingley and James' wedding. With that said, I believe it would be a reasonable next step to begin the application for a special license. I would think that you, James, would have already visited your solicitor and began to settle on the marriage articles. After that is all said and done, then all we have to do really is to enjoy the festivities."

Everyone sat there silently, looking at Darcy rather dumbfounded, until Bingley finally snapped out of his awe of Darcy's succinct summation of what needed to be done. "That would seem the sensible thing to do, although I must admit that this should have been resolved a few days ago!" He stood up abruptly, and glared at James.

The earl was the next to respond, "Yes, that would seem the likely thing to do, but I must say that I am quite disappointed that this was not addressed with me when the incident happened! Hell, I wish that it had not happened!" He turned on his heel to join Bingley in his glaring at James.

Richard was the only one to remain silent, and had an odd looking kind of smirk upon his face, but he said absolutely nothing while it would seem he was observing everything.

James sat in his chair for a long while looking straight ahead at the wall before finally addressing his father. "Yes, I am well aware of your great disappointment in me, sir, but what would you have me do? For the longest time you had ingrained it into me and Richard, and even Darcy, that when we married it should be to a woman of greater wealth and consequence than we ourselves have. Though I must admit, it did often puzzle me as to how on earth Darcy could ever achieve that, it would be slightly less questionable in mine, or Richard's case. But I also wondered what were we to do in the meantime, before we found them."

The earl grew red faced, and nearly exploded. "You were to *honour* yourselves, and not defile maidens! That is the most *despicable* thing that you could do, James! Not go out and impregnate widows, then blame your brother, or defile maidens, no matter what the consequence of their births! I have a mind to disown you this moment!"

Bingley bristled at that remark, but said nothing, and just continued to glare at the viscount.

Darcy interjected himself, "It matters not what was to happen and what paths we have chosen. For some of us are quite content in our choices, but no matter now... the thing that needs to be done is for James to realize that he is honor bound to marry Miss Bingley due to... umm... circumstances."

Bingley jumped in, again, "Your d-mn right he is honour bound! He will marry her, and that will be the end of it!" He was nearly in James face by that point, and Darcy and the earl were moving to protect them both from brawling.

The earl said, "You have my word, Mr. Bingley, that the wedding will certainly occur, and it will be done to everyone's satisfaction. I will ensure that James fulfills his responsibilities and makes a good husband to your sister even if it kills him." The man was looking at his son with great determination.

James sat still and looked between the two men, but shook his head and said nothing. There was not really much else for them to discuss afterwards, and as the earl and Darcy were not wanting to risk the groom and the bride's brother coming to blows, they felt that the shorter the meeting the better.

When the gentlemen joined the remaining ladies, Darcy could see the strained faces of Elizabeth and Jane, and could easily guess the source of such a sight. He was in no doubt that that lady was still bitterly disappointed that it was not him that came drunk to Bingley's home and was seduced by her.

Luckily, he had managed to seduce his Elizabeth, and she had managed to capture his heart, and for that he would be forever grateful. Once their home was vacated of their guests, he fully intended to show her how grateful he was.

Chapter 42

Though it could never be said that Viscount James Fitzwilliam followed the dictates of his father the Earl Fitzwilliam, he did marry Caroline Bingley within a week of the Shetler's Ball. Charles Bingley insisted they use the arrangements originally made for the joint Bingley and Darcy nuptials. Mrs. Bennet was ecstatic that she would be credited for making the wedding arrangements for a future Earl, and fortunately for the Bingley's and the Darcy's, that was enough to distract her lamenting the loss of planning their joint wedding.

On a cool day in Mid December 1811, Caroline Bingley would become the Viscountess Fitzwilliam, and all under the planning of Frances Bennet. Charles Bingley frowned when he saw that his sister intended to wear a white wedding gown, though he did not complain, as it was a decent change from her usual orange hues that she had a propensity to favour.

The day of the wedding started out a little bumpy, though, as Jane was feeling ill that morning. At one point, Bingley even considered postponing the ceremony, enquiring of his wife, "Jane dearest, do you really feel up to all of this? It is likely to be a rather long day, and I do not wish for you to become more ill."

"No Charles, I shall be fine after a while. I am already starting to feel better, and I am certain that by eleven o'clock, I shall be just fine."

Charles looked at her rather skeptically. "Are you *certain*, Jane? I do not think that anyone would think anything less of us if we were to postpone the ceremony, and after all the viscount has been able to obtain a special license, so it would be no bother at all."

"No, no, Charles, I think that I shall definitely be better… in fact I am sure of it." Jane was hesitant to mention some suspicions that she had been harboring for almost a full month, but her monthly courses were almost two months late, and she knew that this may cause some anxiety in her husband. "My dear, I… that is to say, we… we may be soon joined by another family member."

Charles looked at her in non-comprehension. "Why? Who else could be joining us…?" He stopped suddenly in understanding. "Do you mean that…?"

Jane nodded. "Yes, Charles, I believe that we are expecting a child."

"Ohhhh." He took a deep breath, realizing what she was alluding to. "Do you think it happened at…?"

"Netherfield, yes, I do believe it did. Are you angry, Charles?"

"No, no, I am not angry, I am just… surprised. But, my love, I cannot imagine a better beginning for us. Our first nights together at Netherfield were wonderful. Truly I am thankful that Elizabeth chose to rest in her own rooms while you both stayed there." He smiled ruefully.

They were both surprised at themselves for anticipating their vows. They had developed a deep sense of understanding of each other in that short time, and Charles Bingley, being the impetuous man that he was, proposed to Jane Bennet while she stayed at Netherfield. They did not want to announce their engagement so soon after she stayed at his home fearing the scandal that would surely arise, however they also could not contain their passions for each other, and managed to severely breach propriety on one or two occasions while she stayed at Netherfield. Neither one would repine though, as they were now happily married, and cared little for what society would say or do, and their sister Caroline would be married, which would eliminate the threat to her prospects of finding a husband. It would remain to be seen as to the happiness of *that* marriage.

~*~*~*~

Darcy and Richard were to escort James to the church to meet the Bingley's, Hurst's, and the Bennet's. Both gentlemen arose early the morning of the wedding to ensure that the groom fulfilled his responsibilities. It did not surprise Darcy that James had been drinking well into the night before his wedding. *If I were to be marrying Caroline Bingley, I would need strong spirits to carry me through with it, also.* Darcy did not feel too sorry for his cousin though, believing that he brought it all upon himself. He wished that everyone could be as happy in their marriage as he and Elizabeth, and wondered aloud at what kind of felicity could be had when two people who were so conniving and deceitful married.

"Tell me, Richard, how do you think this will all turn out?"

"What do you mean, Darcy? The wedding or what happens afterwards?"

"You know I do not concern myself with ceremonies. How will they get along?"

Richard shrugged his shoulders. "It is neither here nor there. They have made their bed, or whatever it was he took her on, and now they must lie in it. It does serve them both right, as they deserve each other!"

"You sound quite bitter. I should think that you would be relieved, Richard, after all you now know the truth about Harriet and her babe, and you did not become ensnared by Caroline's mechanisms. You now own your own estate and are on your way to becoming your own man!"

"Ah, but what has this cost me?" Richard turned away from Darcy, and paced in his fathers' study. I have lost some of the respect of my most valued family members, and I have lost…"

"Lost what, Richard?"

Richard turned to look at Darcy sideways, "It is of no consequence now, Darcy. I must learn to pick up from where I have landed."

Darcy studied Richard for a few moments, deciding it would be best to leave well enough alone. *I wonder if he still regrets the loss of Elizabeth?* Darcy did not wish to dwell on that thought, as he now knew where he stood in his beloved's heart. He felt compassion for his cousins feelings, realizing that if their positions were reversed, he would feel her loss keenly.

"I think, cousin, that we should look to the past only as it brings us happiness, and not dwell on the things that we cannot change. You have many things to look forward to, and perhaps, in time, you too will find a woman who will make you forget about anyone else."

"I hope you are right, Darcy, I hope you are right."

They faced each other fully, and Darcy said, "Shall we gather the rogue groom, and head over to the church?"

Richard nodded. "Indeed we should. I believe that Mrs. Darcy awaits you there, and I assume you are anxious to reunite with your bride as soon as may be?"

Darcy laughed. "Of course!"

They gathered the still slightly inebriated James, and escorted him to the carriage which was to take them to St.

Mary's Church, where the ceremony would take place. They had to make an urgent and unexpected stop when James felt the sudden urge to purge the contents of his stomach out. They managed to make it to the church without any further mishaps. Darcy was then able to reunite with Elizabeth, who greeted him with her beautiful smile, and mischievous gleam in her eyes.

"My love, if I did not know any better, I would say that you are harboring secret intelligence."

Elizabeth stifled a giggle, and replied, I shall tell you later, William, it may in fact, surprise you."

"Ah, I seriously doubt that I could be any more surprised than what I have these past few weeks."

"We shall see." She said in an enigmatic response.

Soon the wedding of James Matthew Fitzwilliam to Caroline Eunice Bingley was underway, and any unhappiness surrounding that occurrence was soon forgotten, as the reception Mrs. Bennet had painstakingly planned for Elizabeth and Jane was enjoyed by everyone who attended.

~*~*~*~

Shortly after the New Year, Darcy and Elizabeth along with Bingley and Jane celebrated their wedding with a reception inviting their many friends, and then they were off to Pemberley where they would remain for another year. As it turns out the summer of 1812 would be quite a productive one for many in the Bennet family. For not only did Mary and Lydia marry though under vastly different circumstances, Jane and Elizabeth were increasing much to their husbands' joy. Elizabeth, though, did not have nearly the easy pregnancy that

Jane did, for she was more exhausted than she had ever been in her life, and suffered with morning sickness well into her seventh month. Darcy was concerned enough to call upon a physician specializing in maternal healthcare by the third month, and arranged to have Elizabeth examined by the specialist.

By the seventh month, the physician voiced some concerns about the rapidity of Mrs. Darcy's increasing waist and her continued fatigue throughout her later months of confinement, especially in light of the fact that Mrs. Darcy was an avid walker and rarely suffered such maladies ever in her life. With the constant stress during the ordeal with Lydia and Wickham, he ordered her on constant bed rest which was almost impossible for her to abide, and yet another reason for Darcy to want to throttle George Wickham.

It was six weeks of the most anxious waiting that Elizabeth had ever done. She fretted about what this misstep would cause her family, easily forgetting what they had been through the past fall. Elizabeth tried to distract herself by knitting some baby sweaters and booties, and read as much as possible from the Pemberley library, however the only thing that kept her sane was the last letter she received from Darcy before he returned to Derbyshire.

20th August 1812,

Darcy House, London,

My Dearest Elizabeth,

I hope and pray that you are in good health, and that you shall continue to be so through this confinement. I have chastised myself many times since I have left your side, believing that you are so much more important to me than George Wickham, and even your sister, Lydia's reputation. They have made such foolish choices and they should have to live with them. Forgive me for saying so, but the only reason that I took up their concerns were for you. Dearest, you were so distraught when you received that letter from Jane, that I felt in our best interest for me to tend to Lydia's elopement, lest any harm come to you or our child. I cannot tell you how much I have rethought the wisdom of leaving your side.

I have news, though I am not too certain how good it is, Lydia and Wickham have been found in a paltry area of town, and your sister has been removed to stay with your Aunt and Uncle Gardiner. George has agreed to marry her, though you may not be surprised when you hear that he has demanded a small fortune to do so.

It appears that he has been living quit well since he has left Derbyshire, and came by his rank only through performing various unmentionable duties for certain ladies of town. He has even gone so far as to hint that he has been hired for these duties by none other than the former Caroline Bingley! I have no doubt that the reason he had singled out Lydia was her connection to me, as well. The nerve of him! Due to this alarming news, however, Bingley and I have contributed to Lydia's settlement. It pains me to tell you this, as I am quite certain that she will live the life of misery from here on out.

After I have seen to it that the scoundrel has married Lydia, I shall hasten back to your side immediately. Elizabeth, please do take care, and allow Mrs. Reynolds to do her job, which is of course, to look after you in my absence. You are the most valuable thing that I have, and I could not bear it if anything happened to you.

With Great Love,

Your Husband,

William

Luckily, Darcy made it back to Elizabeth's bedside before she went into labor.

At dawn on a mild late August day Elizabeth awakened to cramping in her lower back and abdomen but thought nothing of it as she had felt this for weeks now. She was finding herself growing increasingly uncomfortable throughout the next hour, but did not wish to awaken Darcy as she knew he had not had much rest the past several weeks. She arose from their bed and padded to their sitting room with a book that she had been reading. Her powers of concentration were not strong though, due to the cramping that was increasing gradually. She got up and rang for her maid, Gertrude, who came to her dressing room who looked upon her mistress with terror. Elizabeth was finding her patience in short supply and snapped at the girl, "Oh for heaven's sakes Gertrude, what is the matter?"

The girl started at her mistress' shortness and mumbled, "Beggin' pardon ma'am, 'is jus' at... well..."

Elizabeth could not help her irritation rising at present and snapped again while she looked at the girl with an irritated and raised eyebrow. "Yes, Gertrude, what is it? Is there a problem?"

Gertrude managed to say, "Well... ma'am, you don look as ye feeln' none too good."

With that Elizabeth said shortly but a bit more loudly than she intended, I am fine! Just a bit tired and my back... ooooooooooohhhhhhh!" She doubled over in pain and had such a fierce grimace upon her face.

By that time, Darcy had risen, and was in the process of both putting on his dressing gown, and coming to her when he heard her loud moan. When he saw her doubled over he ran to her and said in a panicked voice, "Lizzy, what is the matter? Are you in pain?"

He slid his arm around her back and helped her to sit on the bench in her dressing room then looked up at Gertrude quickly and ordered, "Get the physician, and call the midwife immediately, and get Mrs. Reynolds up here!" in a gruff voice.

The girl did as she was told, and he was left alone with Elizabeth who still grasped her abdomen and was breathing deeply. He had a nearly terrified look upon his face and Elizabeth saw it. I am well, there is some pain now and again William... ummmmmmmm." She moaned again and he reached to pick her up and carry her to her bed in the mistress chambers, as it was the closest. As he settled her on the bed he noted that there was some blood upon his arm and on her gown and became nearly frantic with worry.

By this time he felt terrified that he would lose her, and felt the stinging of tears down his face. He knelt over her, saying a prayer for her and their child. Elizabeth saw him and tried to reassure him. "William, dearest, this happens when women give birth..." She was sucking in a breath and grimacing at the pain. He grabbed her hand cursing the slowness of everyone in not coming quickly enough. Just when he was about to frantically pull the servants cord Mrs. Reynolds entered the room, followed by the physician, Mr. Brown, and Gertrude.

Immediately Mr. Brown said in an attempt to calm Darcy, "Mr. Darcy, sir, now that we are here you may leave, we will see to Mrs. Darcy..."

Darcy nearly boomed, I am not leaving her! She is bleeding! I am not going anywhere! I will stay right here!"

Everyone but Elizabeth stared at him, but the physician quickly looked towards Elizabeth and immediately began his examination of her. Noting the blood Darcy mentioned but seeing that it was darker than one might expect, the doctor said in a neutral voice, "It appears that it is not fresh blood but I will keep an eye on her... perhaps it is just some bloody show which is normal for labor..."

Darcy was anything but reassured, "*Perhaps? Perhaps?* Sir, I have hired you to ensure my wife's safety and..." He turned around abruptly and strode towards the window.

The physician stared at his back momentarily before turning his attention towards Mrs. Reynolds. "Ma'am, I think it best to remove as much tension from both Mr. and Mrs. Darcy as possible, and I do think it best..." He said softly to the housekeeper who just nodded then walked towards where Darcy stood.

She placed a gentle hand on his arm and when he looked at her, he had reddened eyes and face, "Sir, there is nothing you can do for

Mrs. Darcy like this. She needs you to remain calm so that she can concentrate on bringing your child into the world."

Darcy gave her a blank stare, then closed his eyes and nodded. Mrs. Reynolds stayed with him for a few more moments until he seemed calmer, then she returned to Elizabeth's side. Darcy stood there facing the window for a few more moments taking some deep breaths before returning to Elizabeth as well. She was clearly growing more uncomfortable, and it was difficult for Darcy to keep his composure while she was in so much pain and distress.

He spontaneously leaned forward and kissed her tenderly regardless of propriety, as it was one way for him to sooth himself. Elizabeth said to him, "William... you do not have to stay... it is not... ahhhhhhhh..." She took a deep breath. "Proper... and people will think that... ummmmmmm..."

He grabbed her hand. "Shhh, shhhh, dearest. I do not care what anyone thinks right now. I will not leave your side while you endure this. I am not leaving you alone." He kissed her hand.

She smiled at him and tried to rest a few moments between contractions. Darcy took a cool cloth from Gertrude, who stood to the side of the bed awaiting more orders. It would be a long day for everyone, and by afternoon the midwife had arrived after having just delivered another babe. Darcy had not eaten and Elizabeth even commented, "Love, you need to eat! You did not have breakfast and you must not miss lunch!"

He looked at her amused and said, "Nor have you eaten, dearest, and I suspect that your day has not been any easier than mine." As he caressed her face he tucked back a loose strand of hair.

She smiled at his tenderness. "You, sir, are entirely too good for your own sake."

He smiled back at her, and kissed her sweaty brow. She was grimacing and writhing in pain and the midwife became annoyed with his presence, occasionally glaring at him, which he duly ignored. As the day progressed, so did Elizabeth's pain and labor and just before six o'clock she went into the last stages of labour when the physician and midwife deemed it time to push. Darcy stood by her side as he assisted her to sit up in a crouching position. Elizabeth held on to his neck and shoulders as she pushed down rocking on her heels. They stayed in that position until the midwife checked her again and could see the babe's head crowning. Both she and Darcy assisted her to lie back as she pushed a few more times, expelling the infant.

At five forty-nine in the evening their first born son took his first breath, wailing loudly with a healthy set of lungs. Darcy was as stunned at the joy the sound brought to their hearts at that moment, and at that point, everything besides their little family was blocked from his consciousness. Mrs. Reynolds took the boy and wiped him off, wrapping him in swaddling blankets before handing him to his mother, who had all but forgotten about her earlier ordeal. As she and Darcy looked down into their child's face they smiled at each other, exchanging a tender kiss. No words would adequately speak of what they felt ta that moment.

After about ten minutes Elizabeth began to feel more discomfort, nearly as bad as before, and Darcy saw the look of panic upon her face. "Elizabeth... what is it? What is the matter?" He began to panic again, and called for the midwife and the physician, "Doctor, Mrs. Barnes... come now! Something is the matter with my wife!" Darcy felt as if his heart were being torn from his chest as he watched Elizabeth in agony yet again.

Quickly the midwife and physician dragged him aside and he took his son in his arms, cradling him against his chest as he watched them examine Elizabeth. They seemed to be taking forever in assessing her, and they finally turned to him and said, "Mr. Darcy, it appears that we are not done yet... there is another babe waiting to be born."

Darcy stared at them in incomprehension momentarily. "Twins?" He said blankly then looked at Mrs. Reynolds, who wore a worried look upon her face. He knew that this was a dangerous situation. Women in childbirth died all the time, but with multiple births the odds were even worse. He paled as the housekeeper came to his side to assist and encourage him to sit before he dropped the babe.

He did as he was told, but sat only so far from Elizabeth's bed, and in such a position as to be able to clearly see her, and her to see him at all times. It seemed like hours, but was only another thirty minutes before she was pushing again. He managed to tear himself away from his new son, handing him to Gertrude, in order to assist Elizabeth in birthing their second child. Almost immediately there was another head emerging from her body, and with one last push their daughter was brought into the world. Both Darcy and Elizabeth looked upon their daughter with awe, they both felt that their new children were the most precious gift they had ever been given.

When the room quieted, Elizabeth lay in her bed holding their daughter while he again held their son as he sat next to her. They looked upon their children, then at each other in silence until Darcy said, "Do you realize my love that it was exactly one year ago today that we met at the edge of Netherfield Park?"

Elizabeth had almost forgotten that fateful day that lead to so much joy. From that day on she would be forever grateful that she had taken a walk that morning, running into the source of so much of her happiness.

Epilogue

Soon after the Viscount Fitzwilliam and Caroline Bingley were wed, they were sent to Matlock. In February of 1812 his mistress of nearly four years, Harriet Heartherton, gave birth to a healthy baby boy. James managed to visit his mistress and son many times in Lancashire, though Harriet did not always stay on Darcy's estate; the earl had arranged to rent a small patch of property to sustain her and the child for their lifetime.

The viscount immediately went through the dowry money Caroline brought to their union, and they lived off the stipends given them by the earl and countess from there on out. His relationship was tenuous at best with his family members, and soon he was on the verge of disownment. Due to his propensities towards gaming, the Earl and Countess demanded that he go into the countryside, fearing further scandal due to his tendencies.

Lady Caroline Fitzwilliam, as she was now fashioned, did not return to town for another four years. She delivered a baby girl in mid August of 1812. That would be her and the viscount's only child together, though he would eventually bring his son to live with them in Matlock, and they would raise him as if he were born of their union when Harriet died from pneumonia after a bout of the influenza. Richard Fitzwilliam would inherit the earldom from his father, as his brother died in a duel of honor. James had been found compromising a woman by the name of Lady Beatrice, who happened to be the youngest sister of a Lord Blake. Incidentally, he did manage to rack up more gaming debit with that... ahem... 'gentleman' before the duel was called, so he also left a hefty debit of just under ten thousand pounds to his heirs as well.

Caroline never succeeded to the title of Countess Fitzwilliam, as that title was reserved for Richard's wife, who after many studious years of following the dictates of the Earl and Countess, kept himself out of gaming dens and away from loose women. He followed the lessons of the church very closely as well.

After seven and twenty years, Albert Heartherton- Fitzwilliam married one Catherine Stone who was the daughter to close friends of the Darcy's. He became a curate in Matlock when the position came available, eventually moving up the ranks through the church, becoming an archbishop.

The retired Colonel Richard Fitzwilliam did become the master of Cantrell Hill in Wales, and the eventual Earl Matlock. Even through much bullying by his Aunt Lady Catherine, Richard married Anne de Bourgh, more for prudence sake than anything else. Richard wanted to rescue his cousin from her mother who was gradually becoming more difficult to manage after the Earl and Countess found out about her plotting with James to entrap Darcy and ruin Elizabeth.

The Fitzwilliam's refused to see Lady Catherine for almost two years. That lady refused to accept defeat or admit wrong doing on her part, and eventually went mad. She had to be kept carefully at Rosings, as she slipped further and further into her own world.

Richard had become a good financial manger, but his reputation for being a 'ladies man' preceded him, and impeded his ability to find a suitable wife. Their marriage surprised many in their circles, as he had at one time been thought to be quite opposed to the match.

Surprisingly enough, they managed to get along well enough to have four children; three boys and one girl, who could all share in their parents' fortune in equal shares, and there were plenty of shares to go around. Even his sister-in-law, Caroline, was pushing for their eldest son, Richard, to marry his cousin Victoria, but alas that did not occur. He, did, however, manage to snag the ever lovely Jane Elizabeth Darcy, eldest daughter to one Fitzwilliam and Elizabeth Darcy, much to his Aunt Caroline's displeasure.

Richard and Anne lived the first part of their marriage in Wales much to the displeasure of Lady Catherine, *and* the Earl and Countess Matlock. Anne de Bourgh barely spoke to her mother after her marriage to Richard, refusing to listen to the lady's endless excuses as to why she did what she did to try to entrap Darcy into marrying her, and ruin Elizabeth's reputation. She had never felt anything other than a cousin's fondness for Darcy, and had come to know Elizabeth as a friend after the Darcy's marriage was announced. Anne was barely able to arrange to meet with Elizabeth much, as Lady Catherine could scarcely tolerate hearing *that woman's* name.

The Fitzwilliam's did eventually remove from Cantrell Hill when the Earl passed away, thus Richard became the next Earl Matlock.

Their youngest son, Lewis Fitzwilliam eventually inherited Cantrell Hill, as his wife was from Wales, and they could not bear to leave her beloved country. Their second son, David, received Rosings Park, and restored the estate back to its natural beauty, without any of the topiaries, or other fripperies his grandmother de Bourgh was want to erect.

In April 1812, Marry Bennet became Baroness Mary Withers when she married Andrew Withers. They spent some companionable time visiting at both his home in town and the Gardiner's, and the Bingley's home. In fact, Mary did not return to town until just before her wedding was set to take place, so besotted she was with Andrew.

Interestingly enough Mrs. Bennet used the same modiste that she had for Jane and Elizabeth's ball gowns for the Shetler's Ball, and even more interestingly she noted the same problem with the cuts being wrong. Mary's gown was even tighter than that of Jane, but Mrs. Bennet did not think too much on that as now she had three daughters married to a great advantage who could throw the other two in the way of other rich men.

Mary and Andrew spent some time in London until the middle of June when they went to his estate in Burford, in sOxfordshire. There they stayed even through the next season as Mary was to deliver their first child in November of 1812. Luckily her first child was a son, as the next three were girls. The Baronet Jonathan Withers was quite the sought after bachelor in his day, as he had the handsome good looks of his mother's family, and the handsome bank account of his father's. He eventually married a lady of great wealth as well.

There were a few raised eyebrows in town as the Baronet Andrew Winters was known for his fastidious nature even more so than his brother-in-law Darcy, but then again, there were few women of his circle who could tolerate his occasional sermonizing. The fact that the Baroness did deliver before the normal length of confinement did not go unnoticed either, but few dared to comment upon it as the woman now had a very wealthy and powerful husband. There were rumors that he only married her because he compromised her, but nothing could be farther from the truth. For them it was love at first sight.

Lydia Bennet was allowed to go to Brighton in the summer of 1812 with the Colonel and Mrs. Forster, and, Lydia being Lydia, did of course continue her wild ways. She was in a fit of pique for months due to the fact that her three eldest sisters had married already, and was mopping and whining about her situation. Mr. Bennet allowed her to go as he would never find peace with Mrs. Bennet should the silly girl not be allowed to go. No matter what he tried he could not but be circumvented by his wife's continual quest to marry off every single last daughter.

In the middle of a warm July night in 1812 Longbourn received an express from Colonel Forester in Brighton. Lydia ran off with George Wickham to elope, or so the story would go. The next day Pemberley received an express from Charles and Jane Bingley beseeching Darcy's assistance to help find the errant couple. Though Darcy was *very* reluctant to leave Elizabeth behind at Pemberley there was nothing to be done but to go and help with the search in London. Though Elizabeth expressed a desperate wish to go with him, both Darcy and the physician forbide her from going anywhere as her time of confinement was so near.

For the ensuing six weeks that followed, with short notes and leads that they were following up on, Darcy managed to keep in touch with Elizabeth. Finally after five weeks they were found, and after a 'settlement' was reached, they were finally married. The Wickham's were sent to Newcastle to Major Wickham's new camp and Darcy went to Pemberley as soon as their vows were uttered. Within that next year Lydia would deliver a son and George Wickham would be sent to the continent never to be heard from again. Lydia remarried to a man with more sense and education; in fact she would marry a colonel in the encampment where she stayed last with her *dear* Wickham. They had three more children, two boys and one girl, who lived ordinary lives.

Kitty Bennet, or 'Catherine' as she would later be known, was the last to marry. She spent a great deal of time with her eldest three sisters after their marriages and became a quick wit, though not nearly so much as her sister Elizabeth. She developed the grace and beauty of the other Bennet ladies, which attracted many eligible gentlemen much to Mrs. Bennet's delight. But she was not so easy to accept just any proposal.

Like her elder sisters, she vowed to marry only for the deepest love, and she had to deal with Mrs. Bennet's constant harping about her not finding an eligible match 'just like your sister's' or becoming an old maid. She listened to that for three years until the summer of 1815, when she went to visit with her good friend Georgiana Darcy. By that time, Georgiana had recently entered a courtship with the son of a duke, and Kitty had unwittingly become the chaperone for them while they were not with Darcy or Elizabeth, or even Mrs. Annesley. While on one of their walks they met up with the new parson of the Kympton parish, a Mr. Henry Stillworth, who came to visit his patron, Mr. Darcy.

Kitty found that when she was around that man, she felt the stirrings of some odd, and new sensation, and she could hardly utter two sensible words when in his presence. They did end up spending a great deal more time together as the months drove on, and just before she was to return to Longbourn Mr. Henry Stillworth proposed marriage and Catherine Bennet accepted. It was with great joy and enthusiasm, that Mrs. Bennet saw her final daughter marry in the winter of 1815. They ended up having three sons who all became parsons much like their father. The oldest even having made the rank of bishop before his retirement from the ministry.

Georgiana Darcy was very pleased that she gained so many sisters when William married Elizabeth. She finally had someone with whom to confide in, and discuss matters that a girl of fifteen wanted to discuss. Their friendship would last their lifetime. She would even watch with pleasure when Elizabeth teased her brother though at first she was a bit alarmed, until she realized that he would tolerated certain things from a wife that he may not from anyone else. She was delighted when she was finally able to live with her brother and Elizabeth after they married without anyone questioning the propriety or her need for female guidance or companionship.

With the support of Elizabeth, she elected not to come out until she was eighteen, and by that time, she found the confidence in herself to judge a person's character much better than that of a shy girl. She knew what to watch for in a suitor, and avoided those who she perceived to court her only for her money. Eventually she met one Walter 'Alex' Scarbourough, the second son of a duke. Darcy felt confident enough in the man's reputation and income to consent to his courtship of Georgiana without reservations, as she had already told Elizabeth her feelings of the still shy Alex, as he preferred to be called, who would just as soon draw scenes in the country side or take long walks than attend balls or soirees.

It took Alex seven month's to get up enough courage to propose, and it took Georgiana almost less than a second to accept. So it was in the late summer of 1815 that Georgiana Darcy married Alexander Scarbourough, in what would be known as the wedding of the decade within the ton.

It seems that Mr. and Mrs. Darcy managed to plan and carry out some of the most fashionable celebrations that their society had ever seen. Some would even say they were trying to compensate for the total want of any sort of celebration for their nuptials but those who wished the family well knew better.

Georgiana and Alex moved to Marbury in Cheshire after his estate was renovated, which took longer than anticipated... much to the delight of her brother and sister, as she and Alex had to stay at Pemberley until those renovations were done. In the fall of 1816 Georgiana and Alex welcomed their first son, and he was joined by twin brothers a year later. Georgiana and Alex were finally blessed with a daughter, Elizabeth Anne Scarbourough, six years later. In another twist of fate Alex would become the six Duke Of_____ when his elder brother failed to produce a male heir, though Alex and Georgiana were very generous to his sister-in-law and nieces.

Jane and Charles Bingley would stay at Netherfiel slightly less than a year after they married. It seemed that Mrs. Bennet along with Mrs. Phillips and other town 'ladies' wanted to claim as much of the couples time as possible, and though the couple were known as one of the most patient and kind, the constant barrage of visitors and attentions nearly drove them to distraction. In the summer of 1813 Charles and Jane Bingley moved from Netherfield to and estate in the southern part of Yorkshire, much to the relief of the Bingley and much to the delight of the Darcy's.

Their estates were within a half day's travel of each other which made it easier to visit and made it more convenient for the Bingley and Darcy cousins to get to know each other well. Geoffrey David Bingley was the first of the Bingley children. Much to the dismay of both parents, his father was in London searching for Lydia and Wickham when Geoffrey chose to make his appearance in July of 1812.

Elizabeth and Darcy recovered from the birth of the twins, and they eventually had four more children, two more boys and two more girls, though it was only one at a time afterwards to their parents' relief. They all grew up receiving a good education and an excellent understanding of the world around them, making their families proud of their life's accomplishments. Darcy and Elizabeth were rewarded with a long and healthy life, and a loving marriage and they never spent a night apart since the hasty trip to rescue Lydia. With relations such as these, Darcy's' family had learned a great deal throughout their trials and tribulations. They knew that life was too precious to waste on regrets or misunderstandings and would carry that knowledge with them for the rest of their lives.

Finis

The main characters and occasional lines of dialogue and description are the original creations of Jane Austen.

4042955R00236

Printed in Great Britain
by Amazon.co.uk, Ltd.,
Marston Gate.